Praise for
THE WILD HIGH PLACES

"An intriguing protagonist, an exotic setting, and a clash of cultures combine to create a fascinating novel."
—*India Edghill*,
author of *Queenmaker* and *Game of Queens*

"A sweeping story of adventure, lushly written, intricately conceived, and meticulously imagined. Sure to appeal to Dorothy Dunnet fans and those who love tales of Victorian India."
—*James P. Mallory*,
author of *The Merlin Trilogy* and *Crown of Vengeance*

"I'm sure I've heard Zarabeth's name before, in some other context... perhaps I knew Jefferji in another life, or was also in a relationship with those sorts of spiritual energies. Regardless of when we met originally, I'm very glad to reacquaint myself with Tamisen's incredible story of birth, rebirth, and all that goes between!"
—*Janis Ian*

THE WILD HIGH PLACES

Zarabeth Abbey

Forest Path Books

Copyright Information

THE WILD HIGH PLACES
Published by
FOREST PATH BOOKS

To wonders, adventures, and
profound treasures waiting
forgotten in the dust.

THE WILD HIGH PLACES

Chapter One
Before the Rains

He'd been expecting the early morning call, half-awake even before the night-watchman patted the bottom of Jefferji's foot gently with the side of his worn stick. *Wake up, dancer before the god, Sri Krsna waits.*

Jefferji found his slippers tucked beneath his charpoy bed by exploratory touch, one foot hovering above the carpeted floor of the sleeping tent until he struck the curved upper portion of his waiting chappals. It was a large tent, full of sleeping men—brothers, cousins, household officers of Tengarpore. They didn't need to wake up.

It was Jefferji's job, and his alone, to pay the temple rent by dancing for the god and his divine Consort. This was the fourth year that Jefferji had danced at the Bharaj fair; it had never been so busy, more laughter, well-fed children, women dressing their long braids with coconut oil. A man could really believe that the long hunger was finally over—for this time, at least.

The face of the boy waiting for Jefferji outside the tent was strange in the shadowed light of the lantern he carried. The skies above were black and sparkling like mirrorwork, the sun on the far horizon just beginning to redden the scattered dust in the air. The Bharaj temple stood to the front of its high-walled compound, its great water-tank halfway along its south side.

Unfastening the shirt he wore over his thin sleep-crumpled trousers, Jefferji went down the cold white carved stone stairs and knelt to wash himself in the water flowing from the fountain, his face, his body, rinsing his mouth and spitting on the hard earth at the foot of the wall. He could feel beard when he rubbed his cheeks, splashing water into his face to help sharpen his senses.

His brothers didn't need to shave as often as he did. They told him that his animal nature was stronger than his human nature because his father had been a ferocious beef-eating English, and no kind of a Rajput at all. Jefferji didn't mind. He wore his hair long and his face clean-shaven because he liked himself better that way, and there were advantages to having a reputation as a man whose animal nature ran more strongly in his veins than in that of more sober, self-disciplined, abstemious sons of princes.

Dripping wet and purified by the living water of the fountain Jefferji hurried in to the long hall that ran from end to end across the back of the temple, where the storerooms were. The barber was waiting for him in an alcove just inside the doorway, with a pot of water steaming over a small fire; Jefferji rubbed his long-fingered hands over the welcome warmth gratefully as the barber sharpened his razor.

While the barber shaved him, one of the temple's women dried his body, anointing his skin with consecrated oil whose perfume would be pleasing to Sri Krsna. Jaisal Singh—in whose princely, if relatively impoverished, house Jefferji had been raised as an adopted son—had offered Jefferji's services to the temple; so it was Jefferji's duty, as well as his pleasure and his joy, to serve the temple and Sri Krsna with his dance. The Rajput prince Jaisal Singh was no devotee of Sri Krsna, but it was meritorious to offer respectful service to the god even so.

When the barber had finished, Jefferji hurried to get dressed, anxious to be ready in good time. Once he'd stepped into his linen trousers, the woman made ornate designs with sandal paste over the tops of Jefferji's bare feet, and when he sat down to paint his face she plaited his thick dark hair into a glossy braid that hung well down his back, dressing it with fragrant marigolds.

Sometimes his brothers or his teachers teased him, pretending that he didn't need to outline his eyes or powder his cheek to make himself both as pale and as dark-eyed as the most beautiful of cows. But paint was part of a dancer's preparation as much as the rows of bells—sewn in array on thick tapes of cotton—that he wrapped around his ankles.

He fastened the skirt, a fashion no longer worn except within the court of the Mughal emperor in Delhi, over his trousers. Shaking out the fine white wool scarf that Radha would use to cover herself, Jefferji went out into the courtyard, climbing the stairs onto the raised platform that stood before the sanctuary building in which the god rested. There were people in the courtyard already, waiting to greet the god. The compound gates through the cloistered walls were open; more people were arriving moment by moment.

Inside the sanctuary, the doors to the sacred place where the statues of Sri Krsna and his consort Radha stood were still closed: the god slept. In the dim-lit hall before the god's room Jefferji stretched, waking his body up, praying with his arms and legs and head and hands to the god. God was everywhere. Jefferji's mother had told him that.

She'd taught him about King David, too, who had "danced before the Lord" whether Saul's daughter—and certain of Jefferji's foster brothers and teachers, by implication—looked down on him for it or not. Her "Lord" had been Christ upon the cross; Jefferji knew very little else about him. Jefferji's mother had died when he'd been eight years old, and of the teachers that Jaisal Singh had for the young men of his household none had come to teach religion. There was no doubt in Jefferji's mind that Sri Krsna liked dancing, though, because Jefferji felt such joy in his heart whenever he performed.

The musicians had arrived. He could hear them outside the sanctuary on the platform behind him, tuning up, practicing a few phrases and passages, warming the drumheads over a charcoal fire, settling themselves together as he stretched and readied himself to perform. He could hear the temple servants unbolting the great wooden sanctuary doors and folding the heavy carved panels back to open the temple to the sun, so that when the divine Beloved had had his morning meal he could sit and contemplate the world. It was chilly inside the temple, but Jefferji didn't mind. He knew that he was going to warm up soon.

Walking with deliberate steps to shake the bells and awaken the music in his body, Jefferji started for the now-open doorway of the temple to cross the stone flags of the raised platform and take up his position facing east. Wrapping the shawl around his naked chest—it was Krsna who showed himself bare-chested, not Radha with flowers in her hair—Jefferji opened his mind and heart, muscle and instinct, to the cadence of the drums and the bells, finding his way into character as the beautiful consort of Sri Krsna making her way to the place of assignation.

Yes, she's beautiful, his teacher had said. *But that isn't what's important. What's important is that she longs for her lover with so pure and true a passion that he's drawn to her, he cannot resist her. When you dance the consort of the god, that is what you must communicate, Jefferji. Show me the soul of a lover longing for the divine Bridegroom with transcendent passion. Show me that pain, that joy, that desire, and the god will smile on you as he smiled upon his consort and smiles still.*

Jefferji began to dance. The sky above was getting lighter moment by moment; he could see the vague and indistinct faces of the people gathered there on either side, massed on all three sides of the courtyard, waiting for the appearance of the god. Watching Jefferji dance.

Radha fought her way with determined steps through the underbrush of the forest, stumbling from time to time but never losing sight of her ultimate goal—her wished-for union with the god, her lover. Alone in the forest clearing under the sky, Jefferji danced Radha's passion, her desire, her fear and her joyful expectation.

Then—as the priests unfolded the sandalwood screens in front of the sacred space, and carried the bejeweled and decorated statues of Krsna and his consort to the front of the temple to observe the dawn and the entertainment—the music softened into a dream. Radha-Jefferji lay down on her side on the cold stone to sleep, palms flat to the earth and fingers carefully arranged to show that she was overcome by the rigors of her journey and the turmoil in her heart.

The watching crowd greeted Sri Krsna in the statue, wishing him good morning, hoping that he had had a good night and that he and his consort had enjoyed each other as best suited a god and a god's lover. Their voices awakened Sri Krsna where he lay sleeping on the cold stone platform, between the courtyard and the temple's columned hall with its age-blackened pillars that were carved with legends of the divine couple.

Leaving the shawl behind—bare-chested as befit the virile god, his hair coming loose around his shoulders—Jefferji danced the awakening of Krsna, now, telling of his delight in the beautiful Radha, his tenderness and his desire. How he cherished her!

Moving through the forest, Krsna played his flute to draw all of its inhabitants into his song of joy until the voices of the instruments resonated with the cheerful and longing song: *Radha, Radha, Radha, I am coming to you, to embrace you with affection and express my love for you.* It was a sacred dance, but the people who had come to watch made their own music even so, calling out words of praise and encouragement.

In some portion of Jefferji's mind he knew that he heard the voices of some of his brothers, sons of Jaisal Singh. Some of his brothers liked watching him dance; others were embarrassed by the fact that he did.

Yet the part of his mind that heard his brothers' voices was one far removed from Jefferji and where he was. Who he was. He was Krsna, who sought Radha in the forest, alive with youthful ardor and passionate desire; but Radha slept the deep sleep of the exhausted, and did not stir.

Where was Radha? Krsna sought her to the east. Where was she? Krsna sought her in the south; retreating toward the temple Krsna sought her to the west, and all the while the people in the crowd were calling out to him. *She's there. She's asleep. You just passed her! She was right there! Radha, Radha, wake up, your lord has come to speak sweet words to you, don't make him seek for you in vain!*

But the human heart was deaf and blind in the embrace of the flesh, and hard to rouse to union, even when the god sought to be united with it with such soul-searing intensity. It was irrational, it was insane that the god had to woo the soul and not the other way around. And yet the god was determined, and would prevail. The people watching raised their voices in earnest supplication: *Wake up, Radha, arise, my soul, your lord searches for you, go to the embrace of the beautiful Beloved.*

Krsna was discouraged. Even a god may on occasion lose heart; he tried so hard to reach out to his devotees, and to what end? The soul that he desired to embrace slept on, captive in the fetters of material reality. Then finally—as Jefferji drew Radha back on with the shawl that served as her upper garment, and returned to the earth again as mortal—Radha seemed to hear the people urging her to rise and seek her lord.

Everybody knew how the dance was supposed to end, but dancers were unpredictable. The musicians sometimes made a mistake. Who could be sure whether it would come out right this time? The people knew that it was up to them to make sure. They had to call for the soul's awakening—their own souls' awakening—to go into the embrace of the smiling god who sat in his statue with his consort at his side, watching Jefferji dance in the thin morning light. *Radha, wake up.*

She was confused at first, wondering where she was and how she'd come to be there. The musicians played some hints from her earlier journey to remind her. And then the music said that Sri Krsna was near. The news electrified the poor girl, frightened as she was of the embrace of the god, but with a fierce and fearless longing in her heart that overwhelmed her timidity—sensible though it was—and impelled her to go forward.

She could hear the echo of his flute; it seemed to be coming from one particular direction, and she ran joyfully through the forest between the trees and over the rocks and through the shallow ford of the river to find where Krsna had been. She had forgotten all her fear, consumed by white-hot longing for his embrace.

When she finally fought her way through the last vines, when she turned around at last and came face to face with her lord and lover, the crowd held its breath. Radha, transfixed by his beauty, stood for a long moment as if arrested in mid-movement, gazing at her lord with adoration and sublime desire.

This is a woman who is loved by God, Guru-ji had told him. This is a soul that knows itself to be loved and in the presence of its divine Spouse. How do you show that, Jefferji? How do you make the dance speak? The dance is what it is, but it is nothing, even as perfect as you make it, without the passionate desire of the heart. Show me. Show me the longing of the soul to sit at the side of God and know what paradise is in the forest when Krsna is there.

Trembling, Radha put her feet down one after another and approached the god. The statue in which the god sat didn't move; it never did when there were English watching, so Jefferji knew that there were English watching. It didn't matter. The people could see the god reflected in Radha's reactions as he took her in his arms and kissed her on her perfect brow with fervent love, how he embraced her, how they began to dance together—hearts singing with joy to be united.

When finally Radha lay down in her lord's embrace to rest with her head on his shoulder, his arms around her, speaking in drowsy tones about their love, she fell asleep, and Krsna held her without stirring. And the priests came, then, to carry Krsna's beloved away into the temple, where she could be guarded as she slept.

Jefferji was only half-aware of the crowd's applause and the cheering. He always ended up more than half-drowned in the story, and it exhausted him. Of course he had to believe, or he couldn't dance the god and the divine Consort as they were to be danced. It was the first and most important thing that he had learned, the thing that had given him escape and anchor after his mother's death had orphaned him.

When he wasn't dancing he was just another young man with an uncertain future and no real notion of how he was to make his way in the world, and that was all right, because that was the Rajput way. But when Jefferji danced he knew the soul's desire for the sight of God, and saw God in the dance as he was making it, and knew for whole instants of time the joy of contemplation of the eternal Presence.

And yet he was neither Radha, nor Sri Krsna. He only danced them, and the spiritual exercise left him with longing, heart and soul, that could not be assuaged by time or common exercise. He was only a man, and—being of a gross and animal nature—desire expressed itself physically in his body.

The priests turned him over to the women. The women washed the sweat from his body with scented water and laid him to rest in a large and deeply-cushioned bed. There was a young woman waiting for him there who put her slender arms around his neck and whispered in his ear of her longing for his embrace as she stroked him with deliberate care, showing her desire to please the god.

Jefferji embraced her in the bed as carefully as he could, mindful of what was due the consort of a god, the Radha that was within her. But his nerves were wrought up to so tense a pitch that he was overwhelmed by his own body as he lost himself in hers; that she cried out in ecstasy was the grace of the god—nothing to his credit.

They fell asleep in one another's arms, spent and satisfied. When later the priest woke Jefferji with his breakfast, he was alone again. So he ate his meal and dressed himself, paid his respects to Sri Krsna in the temple, and went out to find his brothers and see how negotiations were going for a new stud horse for their father's stables.

▲

Almost every lake that Lieutenant Broderick Holyoke had seen in Rajputana had been a pathetic excuse for a body of water: six feet deep at the most and usually a mere quarter mile square; artificially excavated tanks in varying states of disrepair. All of them shabby, shoddy, pathetic kennels of more or less dirty water. The sacred lake of Bharaj was not much better for being as natural as they came in this distressed country.

It was better to go a day or two without a decent wash than to lave oneself in the muddy fluids of an open sewer, and as for drinking it, a man could poison himself. How these natives survived their own environment was more than he could readily understand. And how the Brahmins among them could look down on the British as dirty as well as unclean defied all sense and reason.

"It's the only town in all of India with a Brahma temple, or so I'm told," Captain Fontenoy said from the saddle of his own mount alongside—apparently misinterpreting Broderick's meditative gaze. "Not that there's any getting near the temple on horseback during the fair. Hard enough to go on foot. We're going to see Shree Kreshna ourselves."

Turning the head of his cavalry mount away from the unappetizing vision of the hordes of humanity crowding the hard-packed earth between the paved road and the lakeside booths, Broderick followed Fontenoy without speaking. They weren't going to see Shree Kreshna. They were going to see some people Fontenoy knew, preparatory to recruiting someone's bastard half-breed son into Company service.

The road took them away from the crowded lake into the less populated areas, toward the eastern districts of the town where the orchards stretched as far as the eye could see and where monumental temples beautified the land. The streets were almost clean, the trees were in fresh green leaf, the sun was to the east, the air was agreeably clear, and all in all it was not altogether unpleasant to be out for a ride on an April day.

Their route paralleled a long wall that ran without a break for blocks and blocks; a temple compound, clearly enough, because Broderick could see the upstart dome of the sanctuary rising above the trees that shaded the top portion of the wall. Tall walls, tall trees, tall temple, and the temple itself had been freshly whitewashed for the occasion—Broderick supposed—and shone bright and almost respectable under the morning sun.

He could hear music, sitar lute and tabla drum. There was apparently a junction in the road up ahead, toward which increasing crowds of people made their way. Although Broderick had steeled himself to the inevitability of it all he still found it annoying when the street into which Fontenoy turned led them into the thick of that deepening mass of locals.

Now that they were closer to the gate, Broderick could hear someone singing—that horrible, thin, nasal falsetto of the common opera. He had to press his horse to the extreme side of the street, all but walking in the gutter, to get around the press of people who were gathered there, and then he had to stop, because Fontenoy had.

The compound gates that broke the long wall of the temple compound had been pegged back, pinned open. As wide as was the court that interposed between the monument within and those great gates, the place was fully as crowded as the lakeshore. A temple, just as he had surmised. A columned hall open on all four sides, a tall building set well back with a low fore-chamber and a high dome at its rear, lingam and yoni, in effect. *Shree Kreshna*, Broderick told himself, struggling hard for a philosophic sense of resignation. *And they'd be going in.*

Captain Fontenoy dismounted, leading his horse into the crowd. Broderick followed. He didn't dare climb down. Captain Fontenoy was not a tall man; his profile and the color of his suntanned skin were by no means remarkable in the crowd—there were persistent rumors about a native grand-mother that Broderick had never heard Fontenoy deny—and Broderick couldn't risk becoming separated from him among these multitudes.

They made slow progress, even with the path that the horses opened up before them by virtue of sheer bulk. There were tents set up all along the inside of the temple walls: sweets-vendors; traffickers in fabric and perfumes; sellers of flowers and offerings for the temple; great sheaves of banners and of puppets made of gilded paper; brightly painted earthenware. A perfect riot of cheap and tawdry goods, but presenting a very cheerful appearance, if not too closely examined. Astrologers. Priests.

The courtyard between the columned hall and the temple steps was raised in the manner of a stage. The musicians were there, and the banshee-voiced singer. Broderick could hear bells. A dancer. An uncommonly tall woman, and not beautiful, but her every gesture unmistakably feminine. Her hair was garlanded with marigolds, with jasmine flowers, with what else Broderick couldn't tell.

For a freakishly tall woman her dancing was as seductive as the best nautch girls Broderick had ever seen. Too bad the girl had no figure; she was as flat-chested as a man and had no curve to her buttocks to speak of. Maybe it was *because* she was a dancer. A popular one, too, Broderick noted, to judge by the audience she had. While Broderick was trying to discern why it was that the long gauze sleeves of her bodice gave her arms and shoulders a distinctly unattractive masculinity, Captain Fontenoy spoke.

"Geoffrey Tamisen," he said. "He should have been sent to school in England, I suppose, but his mother wouldn't be parted from him. And then she died, but Jaisal Singh's lady had promised his mother that he'd be raised a son of Tengarpore, so there was that, as well. It wasn't something I was in any sort of a position to insist upon."

"What?" Broderick asked, bewildered, remembering in the next moment to be polite. Captain Fontenoy was respected, no matter what irregularities there might be in his lineage. Broderick needed to stay in his good graces until the scandals he'd left in Bombay were well and truly behind him. "I'm sorry, sir, you startled me. I was watching the dancer. Peculiarly fetching, her way of doing, though she must be the homeliest dancer I've ever seen, poor thing."

Captain Fontenoy had turned to one side and picked up a child, setting it on the saddle of his very patient and long-suffering horse—so that it could see the entertainment better, Broderick supposed. Up on the level of Broderick's own seat the child made an impudent namaste; Broderick ignored it.

Captain Fontenoy looked up at Broderick and met his eyes full-on. "The dancer." He said it slowly and carefully. Enjoying his joke at Broderick's expense, Broderick was bitterly sure, knowing that Broderick couldn't let a single sign of resentment escape him. "Jaisal Singh's foster-son, Geoffrey Tamisen. The family gets the campsite free, when Tamisen dances."

Of course. Broderick had heard the stories, hadn't he? Troupes of young boys dressed in women's clothing, trained to dance for the erotic amusement of Moslems otherwise deprived of female company.

"Again, my apologies, sir." It was the only thing Broderick could think of to say. "I had thought I heard you say Geoffrey Tamisen, and supposed the one of whom you spoke to be English."

Lieutenant *Ganders* Tamisen was spoken of from time to time in Bombay, after all. Yet another golden youth of promise and legendary heroism who had gone north for murky and mysterious reasons and failed to return, leaving a new and—as it happened—pregnant wife to bear a posthumous son who would logically have been repatriated with his mother. It was a natural mistake to make.

Captain Fontenoy nodded, but it wasn't to acknowledge the justice of Broderick's protest. "That is exactly what I need to discuss with him." Fontenoy reached to lift the urchin down from his saddle. "Down you come, my lad, there! Go and buy some sweets for your family."

And the child in its thoughtless arrogance suffered itself to be lifted down with the absolute confidence of someone who had never been the butt of a nasty practical joke in its life. Broderick didn't know why anyone should be allowed to grow up without a taste of what the real world would have in store for them.

Mounting, Captain Fontenoy cocked his head at Broderick by way of issuing an order. "Let's go. The dance is almost over, and Geoffrey will be wanting his lunch. I'd quite like mine."

And this was the man Fontenoy wished to take under his wing, and bring away to Peshawar where a comfortable, and well-feathered, place was to be made for him? This hideous travesty of a female dancer was to be preferred and promoted as a man with a fine future, whilst Broderick was to hold himself grateful for a second chance, hard duty on the frontier, far from the comforts of civilization?

It was unfair. They had no proof of any malfeasance—or even inadvertent oversight—on his part.

The native servant had embezzled the money from the mess fund. The native servant had disappeared at the same time that the funds were found to have gone missing. And if poor honest Broderick Holyoke had stolen all those rupees, where were they? His life was an open book. His private accounts were there for anyone to examine who pleased. Yes, he received presents from the mess-wallahs, tokens of personal friendship and appreciation and a natural desire that he continue the relationship in trade with one vendor and not another. What of that? The natives looked on him as a benefactor.

Eighteen months from now, no one would remember the

muddle with the mess accounts. No one who knew about the girl would dare to say a word about a marriage that had somehow never quite come off. If the baby was a boy and fair enough to pass for British, Broderick could easily adopt it as his ward and give it every advantage he had lacked, and why not?

Fontenoy's name was one to conjure with even among British regulars, which was a little hard to understand—but veterans of the Mahratta and Pindari wars stuck together like mess-mates. Eighteen months from now, with Fontenoy's protection, Broderick could return to his unit as if he'd never left, with a bit of field experience to talk up as well. He had to hang on to that.

It was in a mood frustrated and resentful that Broderick followed Captain Fontenoy around one side of the temple's promenade, toward a camp of brightly colored native tents pitched at the farthest extent of the temple grounds.

⛰

Captain Fontenoy could tell that young Lieutenant Holyoke was not in the least interested in his surroundings as a matter of principle. Holyoke was one of the new breed of Company officer, the kind to whom anything to do with India was beneath contempt except as a source of revenue. Raw salesmen in service, really, pulling strings, bringing chance acquaintance with retired nabobs to bear to get an appointment; no soldier at all, but a rank speculator in uniform.

He didn't like Holyoke much, and although Holyoke was unfailingly polite to him, he didn't think Holyoke liked him either. Fontenoy's family was no longer quite the thing, after all. His paternal grandfather had married a Moslem lady of rank from Hyderabad, making Captain Fontenoy himself "country-born," an increasingly devalued status in India as more and more British-born citizens of purely English or Scots heritage entered the ranks of soldiers and the East India Company's rank-and-file alike.

Geoffrey Tamisen was actually more respectable than Fontenoy was—all four of Tamisen's grandparents had been

British. Unfortunately. It meant complications, and at the worst possible time. But Fontenoy had the opportunity to answer the challenge, if only Tamisen would make the right choice.

All this time he'd thought Tamisen's maternal grandmother had been of mixed parentage, Indian and British alike. Evidence to the contrary—that she'd been as much an English-born captive of Tipu Sultan as Tamisen's grandfather, damaged as he was, answering only to his captivity-name—had come as a surprise to everybody. Fontenoy's superiors in Bombay had not been completely happy about their newly discovered responsibility for a young man hitherto left in happy anonymity at the court of a Rajput princeling. But the legacy of Ganders Tamisen could not be denied.

Now that Tamisen was certified beyond doubt as a white man through and through, with family in England to take an interest in his welfare—and inheritance—the government would accept him, howsoever reluctantly, into its generous embrace. Fontenoy was looking forward to opening Tamisen's future to him. Tamisen was going to be rich. And what Fontenoy had on offer for Tamisen could make them all richer yet.

Not for Tamisen the slightly irregular marriage to that young widow with her substantial holdings that Jaisal Begum—Jaisal Singh's wife, the hawk of Tengarpore, the mother of Jaisal Singh's inheriting son Madhu Singh—had been arranging for Tamisen's future, after all. Jaisal Begum had always treated Tamisen the same as any of her husband's foster sons. It had been just as well that it had been Ganders Tamisen that Jaisal Singh had loved, rather than Tamisen's mother.

They'd become friends, even, Jaisal Begum and Tamisen's mother, at least to Fontenoy's limited judgment. Tamisen's grandfather—Daoji, half-mad, a once-cabin-boy made prisoner of war, and a veteran of the court of Tipu Sultan—had been cherished in comfort and honor at Tengarpore until his dying day. Tamisen had been five years old when Daoji had died. Famine and fever had taken Tamisen's mother within three years after that.

Jaisal Begum had defended Tamisen against all comers as fiercely as if he'd been her own child. Fontenoy was in a position to know. He'd meant to take the boy Tamisen away from Tengarpore and raise him as a responsible young Englishman. He'd even tried, on one memorable occasion, the first and last such attempt he'd ever made.

Because Jaisal Begum would have nothing of it, and neither Fontenoy nor Jaisal Singh himself had been able to persuade Jaisal Begum to relinquish the boy. Tamisen's mother had left Tamisen in Tengarpore's care. Tamisen remained the ward of Tengarpore.

Now that Tamisen was of an age—nearly nineteen, a promising young man, well thought of in the community for his piety—Jaisal Begum had arranged a marriage for him, one that offered material benefit to the young widow, to Tamisen, and to Tengarpore itself. But there was no getting around the fact that proud Rajput widows did not usually remarry, and that Tamisen was only Rajput by adoption.

This particular widow, however, was a clear-eyed and practical woman intent on protecting her own interests. Her dead husband's family had made their expectations clear: she to go into monastic retirement, them to assume ownership of her dower lands as well as the increase she and her husband had made of field and flock. Fontenoy had yet to hear whether Tamisen himself had been consulted, or even apprised of the plan.

Tamisen had finished his morning's performance. There would be no more to see of his dancing until after sundown. The crowd was dispersing into the temporary bazaar west of the temple proper, where the snack vendors and the souvenir salesmen had set up shop.

Leading his good grey Farouk away from the precincts of the temple complex itself, Fontenoy found a boy to bring him to where the men of Tengarpore had their corner of the encampment, which proved to be a pleasantly tree-shaded enclosure in the Bharaj temple's park. There Fontenoy expected to find both Madhu Singh—Jaisal Singh's heir, Tengarpore's inheriting prince—and Tamisen himself. Madhu Singh had made time in his schedule to be here to meet with him, a concession to the long-standing friendship forged between Captain Fontenoy and Jaisal Singh in the saddle of war.

Madhu Singh was waiting for Captain Fontenoy now at a table that had been set European-style beneath the green-leafed trees. There was wine in crystal decanters, and a great dish of sweets for a centerpiece—sugared fruit and boiled milk confections—to keep the samovar company. Fontenoy had to smile at the samovar. It was an efficient way to keep tea or coffee at the ready for what guests might come. It was also an artifact that might well remind one of Tsar Nicholas in St. Petersburg whose suspected interest in India was of such concern to political officers.

"Welcome to our camp which rejoices in your presence, Captain Fontenoy!" Madhu Singh cried in very passable English, standing up from where he sat at the table to hurry forward and greet them. "Come, sit down, be comfortable. You bring the gift of another guest with you?"

Holyoke had held back respectfully, half a step to Fontenoy's left, and bent his head with carefully measured courtesy.

"This is Lieutenant Holyoke," Fontenoy explained. "He comes with me to Peshawar, so it is to be hail and farewell, of a sort." And just as well, really, but there was no need to go into any details.

"You honor us, Lieutenant Holyoke," Madhu Singh said, beckoning to one of his camp followers. "Let Kemal, here, consult your preferences, and arrange all for your comfort. Kemal, a tent for Lieutenant Holyoke, if you will escort him." Or, in other words, perhaps not really very subtle ones, *you may be excused for the time being whilst I see whether Captain Fontenoy has business for me.* Then Madhu sat down.

"You'll be wanting my brother Jefferji, I expect," Madhu said as Holyoke was led away. "He'll be with us shortly. It takes him a small space of sacred time to set himself to rights." There was a subtle undertone there of a shared joke—*Tamisen enjoys the attentions of admirers to recover his energies after he has danced.* "He looks forward to seeing you, Captain. Sit. Sit. Please."

Madhu Singh had made of Tamisen a special ward as well, the chivalric generosity of a Rajput gentleman toward an orphaned boy scant several years his junior. Fontenoy didn't know how much of what he'd discussed with Jaisal Singh had been shared with Madhu Singh; enough to know that Tamisen might be going off for some months at least, yes, but did Madhu know why?

Fontenoy settled himself at the table with grateful readiness. The camp chairs were somewhat Spartan in their design, but he'd been in the saddle since early morning. If decorative objects from China were chinoiserie, did that make furniture on a newly fashionable British model "angloiserie," perhaps?

Madhu Singh would be master of Tengarpore, and it was not to be disdained. That was all the more reason why Tamisen had to be away, now that he was to be placed officially under oversight of the Bombay Presidency. As far as the Bombay Presidency was concerned, at least.

Jaisal Singh was by no means rich as Rajputs went, but he had excellent connections, and many sons of very respectable caste lineage. There were Rajput noble houses that would not take one of Jaisal Singh's daughters, but plenty more that were eager for a wife of good family, and willing to pay well to acquire a connection with Tengarpore. All in all, it was a fort—an estate—a family whose traditional authority might well tempt the Bombay Presidency to exploit any opportunity to take it in charge unto itself.

"How is your father?" Fontenoy asked. This was a polite question, and Fontenoy trusted Madhu to respond to the social signal with confidence in the knowledge they shared between them: Jaisal Singh was dying of the accumulation of his years and the wounds of the wars he'd shared with Captain Fontenoy, and Ganders Tamisen. "I mean to relieve you of Tamisen's presence, for a while. If he is agreeable to my proposal."

Madhu Singh hesitated a bit before he answered. "Thank you, Captain Fontenoy. You—and Jefferji's father—remain the dearest friends of my father's warrior years, for which alone we will be always in your debt." Madhu waved a servant to come forward with the hubble-bubble pipe as he spoke. The servant offered the hookah to Fontenoy first, a guest-courtesy; Fontenoy breathed deeply of the fragrant tobacco smoke, innocent of opium or bhang in respect of the hour. "Even were we unaware of your continued thoughtfulness for our welfare."

So Jaisal Singh had shared the problem of Geoffrey—Jefferji—Tamisen, and why he had to go away. That simplified things. Fontenoy had asked to be the one to broach the subject with Tamisen himself; he'd been putting off deep contemplation on how, exactly, he was to approach it, and he was running out of time. He'd known Geoffrey Tamisen from almost the moment of his birth. Now, finally, after all these years, he would be able to be a true friend to the child of Ganders Tamisen.

Captain Fontenoy took a deep and grateful draw of the fragrant tobacco in the offered water pipe, and passed the mouthpiece to Madhu Singh with a polite bow. There was nothing like a little whiff of tobacco to hearten a man after a long ride.

"I don't mean to keep you, Madhu, please," he said. "It's very pleasant here. I'm looking forward to availing myself of this very generous table. Before Tamisen gets here."

At which point, it went without saying, the culinary depredations of a young man with the proverbial bottomless stomach would reduce the most generous of provisions to skeletal remains.

Smiling, Madhu stood up. "Of course. I can arrange to occupy your Lieutenant Holyoke, if it suits your purpose. I'll see if we can't persuade him to spend an hour or two looking over some horses we've bought, and provide an unbiased opinion as to their worth. By your leave, then, Captain Fontenoy?"

Practical man. An Englishman's taste in horseflesh was not the same as that of a Rajput, but there was no question that, of all the things on which a person could have an opinion, they were closest to one another when discussing horses. And Madhu was clearing the way for the conversation Fontenoy needed to have with Tamisen.

"Of course." Fontenoy leaned back in his chair, wishing for one moment for the cushions and bolster of a traditional Rajput camp rather than this less comfortable European model. "I have everything I could want, right here. Perhaps you could hunt out a Marwari for him, as a remount. Thank you." Madhu Singh would know quite well that this was a joke—a rather unkind one—but Holyoke wasn't here and Fontenoy was tired from travel, and a little irritable because of it.

Marwari horses were not sold to the British. Only a Rajput of noble birth could ride a Marwari. And yet Jaisal Singh had insisted that as his foster son Tamisen was to have one of that royal breed as his own. There had been controversies and discussions, and the perhaps inevitable speculation over whether Tamisen were not Jaisal Singh's son in fact. Tamisen's mother hadn't known for certain that she was even pregnant when Ganders Tamisen had brought her to Tengarpore.

The arguments had been resolved by making over to Tamisen a mare who was among Marwaris homely, and apparently infertile, surely almost fourteen years of age now. What was her name? Cilantro. Cassia. Cardamom. Something like that. No. Coriander.

The little breeze was pleasant, not yet too warm. The air was fragrant with the perfume of fried food, incense, and the smoke from cow-dung fires. Life was good. Fontenoy had a glass of wine and basked in the feeling of comfort and ease and physical happiness.

After the space of a little while, someone came trotting across the grassy lawn that separated the encampment from the sacred grounds. The servant's respectful cough stirred Fontenoy out of a not-quite-nap. Looking around him, Fontenoy saw the pilgrim who approached.

He might be losing focus at a distance—he was forty-five years old, after all—but there could be no mistaking Geoffrey Tamisen. Jefferji. There was no such tall and angular a green-eyed beast in all of Jaisal Singh's household, other than Jaisal Singh himself.

It was a good thing that the Bombay British had never actually seen young Geoffrey Tamisen, Fontenoy mused. They never would have believed him other than Jaisal Singh's get, especially since none of Jaisal Singh's own blood children had inherited quite so much altitude, and Ganders Tamisen had not been a tall man. That would have presented an entirely new set of challenges, and even more of a threat to Tengarpore's autonomy.

"I apologize," Tamisen said as he gained the table, not the least bit out of breath. His father, too, had been made of iron, with an endurance that had been almost savage—or demonic. "I did not wish to greet you with paint on my face. I find myself alarming at close quarters. There are streaks."

Tamisen's English was almost perfect. He had a trace of an accent—how could he not, having been raised in a Rajput court?—but in facility of speech and the ability to manage conversation, the care that his mother had taken to speak only English to him had born fruit. Jaisal Singh had had all of his cadets tutored, as well. Tamisen would have no difficulty holding his own, among British officials.

"That was—what piece were you dancing, earlier?" Fontenoy asked, presenting his cheek to be kissed. "I'm afraid the English lieutenant I carry with me to Peshawar didn't seem to know what a proper Englishman should think."

Tamisen laughed, tipping half a glass of wine into his open mouth as though he were drinking from the water stream of an ornamental fountain. "I endorse his reaction. I should have paid more attention to my feet during the forest path journey. I owe the memory of my teacher an extra hour of rehearsal, I'm afraid—right after lunch. I'm famished. Have you eaten?"

Men Tamisen's age were open gullets attached to appetite. Fontenoy grinned. "Perhaps there's a curry coming," he suggested, because there had certainly been curry aromas coming from the kitchen tent. But he had to turn to serious subjects. It could be difficult to be serious, in Tamisen's company. "I've news for you, Tamisen, some requiring consideration, some offering rich rewards."

"Curry is good news." Tamisen had his eyes on something behind Fontenoy as he spoke: luncheon, Fontenoy expected. "Yes, sir? I have heard rumors about weddings. One in particular at which I would dance only in the strictest privacy, but no additional details, as yet."

His wedding night, in other words. Fontenoy had a brief thought for the widow. Tamisen had entertained admirers, male and female, from rather an early age—scarce sixteen, Fontenoy thought. If practice made perfect, wouldn't he be an accomplished lover?

The dancing would have to stop now, of course. There was no way in which a servant of the Crown could dance in heathen temples for pagan gods. Let alone at Tamisen's level of expertise—female roles as well as manly ones. Which would be the worst blow to young Tamisen—having to put his dancing gear away, or having to leave his childhood home behind? Why hadn't he thought that through? *Because I am a thoughtless old maid of a man*, he told himself, savagely.

The arrival of the curry, the flatbread and the chutney, the pickles and the garnish dishes and the yoghurt, made a convenient break. "I see that there's my lunch, here," Fontenoy said. "What are you going to eat?"

The expression of anxiety that came and went in Tamisen's face was too careful and precise to be genuine. A dancer was an actor as well as an athlete. Tamisen was sharing fun. There was enough food to feed four men, laid down on the table. English serving-ware, but the plates were lined with an all-covering piece of freshly washed leaf.

"Only the merest morsel from your dish, by your leave," Tamisen said, halfway through one large flatbread deep-dipped in lamb curry already. "Where do you go from here, sir? Have you been to see Jaisal Singh?"

Almost Tamisen said "my father." Fontenoy heard it, but—he thought—only because he'd seen Tamisen learning his several languages as a boy, halting and hesitating over the correct word. Tamisen knew that he was the legitimate son of Ganders Tamisen. He also knew how to respect the home Tengarpore had provided him. Jaisal Singh had been a good guardian. Ganders Tamisen had never come back to his wife and son. A man who danced in temples saw more of the unhappy stories of less lucky people than many others did.

"We've been in touch," Fontenoy said carefully. "I shared with him some information that may be of interest to you, Tamisen. I mean to take a strictly personal excursion. And I want you with me." Fontenoy had taken six months' leave. If things went well for him, he'd pension off his servants and retire to Hyderabad, or perhaps Madras.

It was a red curry, and the yoghurt smoothed the fire out wonderfully. Yoghurt suffered during hungry years. There was nothing like a good thick rich creamy yoghurt to give a man good hope for the future.

Pickles and bread dredged deep in relish as well as in lamb curry were disappearing down Tamisen's throat at a truly remarkable rate. Dancing was clearly very challenging to the delicate mechanism of young men's stomachs. Tamisen was doing a creditable imitation of someone paying close attention to important conversation, even devouring curry all the while.

Fontenoy kept going. "When my uncle Zafar died last year I found some unfinished business amongst his papers. His life's interest, Hindu mythology, Mahabharata."

Not, strictly speaking, mythology, not if one was a Hindu. The exact parameters of Tamisen's personal relationship with his divine Beloved was Tamisen's business, however, so Fontenoy merely continued without further disclaimer.

"All these years I half-suspected him of involvement with some occult society, actually. Mysterious visitors in the dead of night. Arcane manuscripts bundled out of sight and never seen again. Some government's secret service, perhaps."

It wasn't outside the realm of possibility. The government in Delhi was a fragment of its former self, its dignity propped up by the diligent care of the Bengal British—who could hardly deploy the Emperor's prestige to their advantage if the Emperor hadn't any left. And yet Delhi still commanded a centuries-old intelligence service that the British East India Company found very useful in its diplomatic relationships with Mysore, Kabul, and the Lion of Lahore, the one-eyed Ranjit Singh who'd made himself an empire amongst the Sikhs of the Punjab.

"'Zafar'?" Tamisen asked; the curiosity seemed genuine, though the question remained polite. "It seems an odd name for a student of the Mahabharata." Tamisen knew perfectly well that Fontenoy's family were either Mohammedan or Christian, and unlikely students of the Hindu epics accordingly. "A romantic, then, perhaps, hoping to give no offense, Captain Fontenoy."

The waiters had come with sherbet and milk-sweets for

dessert. Fontenoy waited until they'd gone. "Yet it seems that he was just a harmless old crank after all. No offense to cherished memory, of course. Elements of his interest seem to have led him down some very intriguing avenues, though, well worth investigation. Antiquities. They're all the rage in London, whether or not the Lucknow market's lost its cachet. I'd quite like your help in running something to earth."

The situation was complex: Scindia would pay for a map of Badakhshan; Mysore would pay more; the British in Calcutta most of all. Englishmen traveling in the waste places of the world were universally suspected of being spies, and none of the adjacent polities—Kabul, Bokhara, China—cared to set boundaries on their spheres of influence. Uncle Zafar's antiquarian interests gave Fontenoy a cover story, and more.

Tamisen was clearly digesting this information; ingesting, as well, copious amounts of sherbet. Fontenoy could understand. There were pistachio nuts, and rose water, as well as sugar in abundance. Not something Madhu Singh would wantonly bestow on anybody, not even Fontenoy, so a present from some outside admirer, perhaps? For Tamisen, for "Hari-prasad," the dancer before God?

"I wouldn't be asking much from you by way of stealth and dissimulation. But I'd like your company. You're good with languages. I'm not." Tamisen had learnt English and Urdu as milk-tongues, Persian and French during his schooling, the southern language spoken by his Guru-ji. And then there was music. "I go as a dealer in antiquities. If we do well there'll be a positive notice in official circles. And, of course, I hope to see a little bit of money out of it."

"'Meat must be seasoned ere it be called a meal,' Jaisal Singh says," Tamisen quoted, thoughtfully. How much did Tamisen understand? His range of experience had been broader, deeper, richer than many a young man of his age already. A boy could become a man without obstacles to overcome, but seldom as completely and never in as short a span of time. An adventure could be the making of Tamisen, in many ways. "But I may be needed here at home, Captain Fontenoy. We may need ready cash. I can help with that."

Fontenoy sent up grateful thanks to the curiously melded God of Christian faith and syncretic elements of his own upbringing. An opening, as good as if it had been scripted for him. It was all the more welcome for the awkwardness of what he had to say—

"There is something else, though, Tamisen. It isn't your fault, but your presence at Tengarpore in the next few months could be a problem. You should be away from there. You've done nothing wrong. But your continued residence could be exploited in such a way as to present a risk to Madhu Singh. Shall I explain?"

Now he had all of Tamisen's attention, but it was in an unhappy way that Fontenoy regretted. "What is it, sir?" Coffee was laid on the table, and nougat. Fontenoy could smell the coffee, bitter, spicy, rich. He took a thimbleful.

"Your maternal grandmother's people, Tamisen. Bombay has had a letter of inquiry from her nearest relations, what's left, after all these years. The Bombay Presidency has been asked to verify your location, and to send word on how you're situated. The family line runs out with you, it seems, and you're the sole remaining heir. There'll be a little money. But."

Tamisen was listening carefully, without interrupting. He had a cup of coffee in front of him as well, but he was staring at its nutmeg-flecked surface with little apparent interest in drinking it.

"Here's the thing, Tamisen." *Jefferji, my boy*, Fontenoy wanted to say. But he'd never stood *in loco parentis* with Tamisen. That had been for Jaisal Singh, and Jaisal Singh was no longer up to the task. Jaisal Singh was dying. "There will be a bit of uncertainty in Tengarpore when Jaisal Singh has gone to rest. The Bombay people have shown a willingness to help out during transition periods by sending people to take temporary custody of household affairs."

Strictly in order to be of use to the family trying to juggle inheritance and the orderly conduct of legacies and so on and so forth. Motives of disinterested benevolence only. But more and more there were people amongst the officers of the British East India Company willing to take advantage, to lift the burden of administration of a princely house by taking the governance of such principalities to themselves.

"And you, Tamisen, are too good an excuse for a party to be placed at Tengarpore to assume custody of a young

Englishman raised outside of his own community and, clearly—you'll forgive me, Tamisen—clearly in need of his own people. Remove you? Possibly they will try. Move in and make themselves at home, in the name of custodial guardianship? Too easy. Tamisen, we must get you away from Tengarpore, until things are well settled."

Now, finally, Tamisen spoke. "I can—" Fontenoy heard the trace of that stammer again, something Tamisen had long since grown out of and put away. "I can hear words, Captain Fontenoy, but they carry no meaning. I have to get into a quiet place, to think."

This, this was why he was unfit to be a father, Fontenoy told himself, half-wild with self-reproach. He'd taken the wrong road into his argument. He'd said too much all at once. He should have taken much more time to feed the information to Tamisen slowly and carefully. He'd botched it.

And yet Geoffrey Tamisen was his own man. His pursuit of dancing in the service of Shree Kreshna had been of his own choosing, and could not but have given him avenues of development that Fontenoy could only imagine. Fontenoy and his friend Ganders Tamisen and Jaisal Singh hadn't been all that very much older when they'd started off to war against the Maratha and the Pindaris. It was possible—Fontenoy told himself—that Fontenoy's courtesy-nephew, young Tamisen, was more of a man than Fontenoy had realized.

"Your presence at Tengarpore puts the house in jeopardy of interference," Fontenoy said gently. "You must stay away. It has been decided. Your things have been sent to the Hirpa temple, and your Myamah is waiting for you there as well. With letters." She'd been Jefferji's nurse when he'd been a baby, and had stayed to look after him ever since. "You will on some future day return to Tengarpore and be welcome, but not until the danger is past. As to between now and then—come with me into Badakhshan, Tamisen. Be my partner in an adventure that could be the making of us both."

It didn't matter if Tamisen couldn't grasp what Fontenoy said now, not in detail. All Fontenoy had to do was make sure Tamisen heard three critical elements: Hirpa, letters, Badakhshan. Had he?

Fontenoy could honestly say he'd done his best, howsoever

clumsily. So long as Tamisen found his way to the Hirpa temple—scant hours from Tengarpore, but not a place the Bombay British would think to look, not immediately, anyway—Tamisen would find the information he would need to make up his mind: whether to go north with Fontenoy, or to betake himself into Bombay to make himself over as an Englishman. So long as he was away from Tengarpore. That above all was critical.

"Hirpa," Tamisen repeated, standing up, then standing there as though he was fixed in place for a long moment. "Thank you, sir. If I may be excused, please?"

Fontenoy nodded, painfully aware of the emotional turmoil Tamisen was in, of how badly Fontenoy had managed this from start to finish. "Of course, Tamisen. I'm sorry, but it must be done. I hope to have you with me when I go north into Badakhshan."

There was more to it than artifact hunting and the secret maps waiting for their introduction. More than testing an unproven but potentially valuable intriguer and possibly contributing to the store of knowledge so avidly pursued by the spiritual heirs of Oriental Jones and his fellow enthusiasts in Sanskrit studies. There was Deravass Khan, whom Fontenoy hadn't seen for more than fifteen years, and who had finally found what he'd been searching for: any trace of Ganders Tamisen. Thanks to Deravass Khan, a treasure waited for Geoffrey Tamisen in the north that had nothing to do with any of the many reasons to which Fontenoy would admit for taking him on an expedition to Badakhshan.

Of the sad fact that Ganders Tamisen was dead there was no reasonable doubt. What Deravass Khan held for the son of their old friend was as close as Tamisen was ever going to get to meeting his father.

He was being sent away from his home, away from the people who had been his family, brothers and uncles and teachers. He was being sent away from Jaisal Singh. Captain Fontenoy said he was a threat to Tengarpore. He didn't understand what he could have done to deserve it.

What he'd done to keep himself occupied since his meal with Captain Fontenoy, Jefferji couldn't say. Had the servant not come to find him in his tent, he wouldn't have known that it was time for him to step into costume, and to dance—him, who'd never come late to his music in his life. He didn't know how he was going to do it.

Staring at his face in the mirror, Jefferji dipped the two mid-most fingers of his right hand into his paint pot. This evening's dance was all about the longing of the soul for the Beloved. There was no need to alternate roles. He only needed to paint the part of the divine Consort, moon-faced Radha, fair one, beloved of Sri Krsna. Jefferji put her on like an embroidered skirt.

Always and ever before, he had felt the approval of Sri Krsna in his heart when he put on Radha. A gentle smile of affection, a breath of the divine within him that relaxed him from the inside out. Not now. The face that stared back at him from the mirror was not that of a dancer wearing the beloved Radha. It was only Jefferji Tamisen, with white paint smeared across one side of his face.

He considered himself for a moment, then rubbed the paint to better smooth it out against his cheek. It stung a little, because the barber had shaved him close this morning. He would paint dead white across his mouth and be Radha without lips, Radha without a smile, Radha unable to speak. The silence in his heart was terrible. How could he endure it?

A bargain had been made. Whether he could dance full of joy or not, he'd dance. That'd been the agreement. Sri Krsna's people were waiting for him. With a deliberate and careful hand, Jefferji drew the crimson mouth of Radha across the tense unhappy contours of his lips, while two of the temple women dressed his hair: marigolds, jasmine, roses, so that Radha could go covered in flowers to seek her lord.

The bodice was of filmy gauze spangled with flowers stamped out of gold foil. The skirt reached only just below his knees. He wrapped his anklets carefully over the fabric of the white cotton trousers he wore beneath the many-layered skirt, tight from ankle to knee, and loose above. There wasn't enough paint in all of Rajputana to transform his long bony shins into the white gazelle-like grace of Radha's adorable limbs, and he needed the fabric to protect his bare skin from the bells.

Once he had danced bare-legged with bells and found himself bloodied when he took them off. There was no shame in offering such tribute to Sri Krsna, who could make suffering over into ecstasy, but blood defiled a temple.

He could hear the musicians warming up. He knew there were people out there waiting for him. He had to do this. He had to do this well. Smoothing out the frown lining his forehead Jefferji went out from behind the screens that marked off his dressing space and onto the stage, to bow to the images of Radha and Krsna who were there to enjoy the entertainment.

It was not Sri Krsna anymore. It was not the divine Consort. It was only two little dolls, dirty and shabby and old, dressed in soiled silk brocades and cloth-of-gold that had gotten frayed around the edges during the lean years so recently gone past. Sri Krsna was chipped in the face and needed to be repainted. Jefferji's Beloved had turned his face away, and would not meet his eyes.

Jefferji tried to open the doors of his heart, but there was no greeting there from the god, no warm glow of the welcome and beloved Presence. His heart was cold and silent within him. For the first time in his life he would have to dance on technique alone.

The tabla struck the tempo, held its breath. Jefferji could almost taste the crowd holding its breath in turn. Standing as silent as a statue carved of stone and rain admixed Jefferji schooled his muscles to obedience. Not one bell, not one single silver-throated chime could be allowed to sound, not one out of all the dozens upon dozens that were wound around his ankles. It was one of the benchmarks against which to measure the quality of a dancer, male or female. The bells a dancer wore spoke with one voice, or not at all.

Selecting a melodic line, casting a net for the song he would dance to, he sounded the bells on one ankle, and then those on the other. He had to get something started. *Look at all those people waiting for you to dance*, Jefferji told himself sternly. All of Sri Krsna's beloved devotees come to celebrate their love for the god and his of them. Jefferji shuddered, shook the involuntary tremor into one of the wilder of the bhakti's songs, and howled out loud in anguish in his heart.

Where are you, my lord, my beloved, where are you, my soul? Can't you hear the sound of my heart breaking? I seek you far and wide. I find you not.

Jaisal Singh called him "son." But he called them all "son," foster children, nephews, the two brace of hawks his lady Jaisal Begum had given him. Madhu Singh, the oldest of Jaisal Begum's sons, Madhu Singh who was to inherit. Would he close the gates of Tengarpore against Jefferji now, heartlessly, implacably?

Yet Madhu Singh was a good man who had taken Jefferji under his wing when he'd been newly bereft of his mother, who'd made himself Jefferji's champion to silence childish taunts against an orphan boy besotted with Sri Krsna. Madhu would be a good lord, the protector of the defenseless and their shield. He would not turn his back on Jefferji without good reason.

One of the women was singing. Jefferji could hear her voice in his heart as he danced. *You are beautiful beyond princes. Have you forgotten me? Oh, come back, dark one, and let me again delight in you. Alas. He will not come. I am forlorn and forgotten, I am discarded, I who have no treasure but his name. And even so, my heart, my soul, I cherish the pain I feel in his absence, because I have known the ecstasy of his embrace and have heard him call me his Beloved.*

There'd been other boys in the house. He'd been housed and clothed and fed along with the sons of princes. He'd been taught by the same teachers, trained by the same armsmasters as the sons of Jaisal Singh, and no distinctions drawn—until now. There'd only ever been two differences between him and the other boys: he had an English mother. And he danced for Sri Krsna. Jaisal Singh had never rebuked him for it. Jaisal Singh had loved him like a father.

I'll go down into the forest where it shares secrets with the river, deep and warm and thick with fertile earth. I'll go down to the place where washerwomen beat the cotton against the rock. Have you seen him? I'll ask. Has the lord of the flute not come this way?

Yes, he was a cadet of Tengarpore, the son of a prince by definition thereby, and it is destiny—the destiny of all Rajputs—to go forth to win a kingdom, a fortune, a bride. But none of his brothers were being sent away.

And he was unique within the walls of Jaisal Singh's house; he was "Hari-Prasad," a dancer before God, a good one. These days teaching sons and daughters of noble houses to dance as one of the accomplishments of an aristocrat had gone out of fashion, but it was still an ancient and honest part of the Rajput tradition. He'd believed that Jaisal Singh didn't mind. Was the truth of it that Jaisal Singh simply didn't care? Had Jefferji been an embarrassment to Tengarpore all along?

I see the maid coming from milking; her pot is full of milk, and yet she staggers as she comes, and has spilt half of it. She's drunk with the Dark One. I'll hurry on the path by which she came. If you are there you will not scorn me for my love.

He knew the song, and yet it brought no comfort to him, no matter how yearningly—passionately—the musicians played the melody. *If only I could once more see you, my eyes would not regret if they went blind. There's nothing more beautiful to my soul than you who have gone away from me. I don't hate her, she who keeps you from me. We're sisters, she and I. She will suffer as I do when you are gone, and I will pity her.*

Jefferji kept the beat with a fierce concentration of his body, but his heart was not in it. He couldn't sense the god within him. He couldn't find the voice, he couldn't see the image, he couldn't surrender himself to the dance in the service of Sri Krsna. He'd never danced blind and cold and alone in his whole life, not since the day that a dark man from the South had come and led him away to the temple to be comforted by the presence of Sri Krsna and learn to dance. Never.

Pressing his lips together firmly in the hopeful arch of a gopi's smile, Jefferji danced. It wasn't the fault of the people who had come here to watch. It wasn't Captain Fontenoy's fault. He'd go and ask his father outright, he'd ask Jaisal Singh if he was to be Tengarpore's Jefferji or the orphan son of some dead Englishman. After this final dance he would be free to go.

It's better to be in the place that he has left than in a place where he has never been, and he's been in my heart for lifetime upon lifetime. Why does he forget me, oh, when I long for him above all things?

Yes. He'd go home and demand to know from Jaisal Singh himself whether Fontenoy was telling the truth, or whether Tengarpore simply wanted to be rid of him. Could it be that Sri Krsna had no further use for him, even though he'd loved the beautiful lord from his childhood? Could it be?

Now as never before, Jefferji felt the great heart-cry that ended the dance, resonating through every fiber of his being and shared—amplified—intensified by the singer, the musicians, even the audience, who wept in desolate grief as the spirit moved them. *Oh, how can you be so cruel? Please, please, my lord. My soul is starving for one drop of you.* With one final and ferocious leap of despair Jefferji gained the corner of the stage and dropped down into the darkness.

This was the last night of the religious portion of the festival. The fair itself was winding down. His part was over. The rest of Tengarpore's contingent would be held up here for several days yet finishing up business, and then they'd be bringing the new livestock—horses, camels—along home at a gentle pace. But Jefferji had paid the temple for Tengarpore's camping space. He had to get away, even if it was to be to Hirpa, not to home. He couldn't bear to wait a moment longer to escape this place and the sharp surprises it had held for him today.

Coriander stood waiting in the paddock for him, her white spots ghostly in the night. Her fine crescent-shaped ears—the mark of the Marwari breed—were pricked forward, as if she wondered what was going on. He couldn't stop to explain. He didn't know what he could possibly say to her. He saddled her, he fastened his things behind the saddle, and was out past the startled night watchman and through the fairground gate into the night before the sweat he'd raised in dancing had dried on his face.

Chapter Two
Parting of Ways

It was fresh new dawn on the cold sweet waters of Lake Shahiva, the sun silver-bright in the sky. The caravan had camped where the river fed the lake, several days out of Fayzabad, one of Badakhshan's busiest market towns. Boy squatted down along the stony shore to rinse her mouth, spitting, and rubbed her hands dry to warm them up, looking to the east where the sun sparkled off the still-snowy peaks.

The river ran grey-white and turbulent with the spring melt off. It would be difficult to ford, but their several routes took them north to Khorog where there were bridges, and south to Ishkashem where there were bridges also for safe passage. They'd had a cold journey through the Hindu Kush mountains of Badakhshan, but the world was well on its way to its spring warming, more welcome in this place full of mountains for the fact that it would not last long.

Boy knew that her name was Peri because it was what the lord called her. But to everybody else she was Boy. Only he ever said her name. Only he knew. Everybody else who knew she'd ever had another name was dead, and she neither remembered nor cared what that name might have been.

And from the moment he had found her hiding amongst the dead of her ruined village and held out a piece of bread to lure her out into the daylight, she had not ceased to see to his affairs and pursue his business with the savage thoroughness of a girl who had murdered the Cossacks that had bespoiled her village and everybody in it, and slashed their eyes when they were dead so that they would never find their way out of Hell.

They were far from their Adyghe homelands on the shores of the great black sea, a long journey through Persia and into the mountains beyond the mountains to find a sanctuary in the high Pamir on the way to China. The lord had found a safe hiding place for what few of his people remained to him. It didn't matter to Boy. Where the lord was, was home.

Now she would follow him down the Arakht road toward Ishkashem, with the caravan that had hired him to protect them on the way from Fayzabad to rendezvous in Zebak on the road south to Chitral and Kabul. The lord had his New Wife with him, and his new child. He'd traveled to Murghab west of Tashkurgan by way of the Wakhan Valley before; this time he judged it an easier journey for mother and child.

So the lord—with four and twenty of his sepahi cavalry, his Hell-riders, and sufficient beasts and men to carry shelter and supplies for the divided party—would be taking a less direct route home, traveling south with the caravan that had hired him, money to pay for supplies. People misjudged the effectiveness of the sepahis, because they were women. And people were always finding themselves sorry they'd taken the Hell-riders lightly.

The rest of their caravan—seasoned in escort and protection in their own right, comprised of most of the men and most of the goods and cattle for the lord's sanctuary valley—would take the more direct route, north to Khorog and then east. They would be home and reunited with their loved ones while the lord was still on the road. And yet all of the lord's people had been away from Sanctuary for more than a year. The additional delay had not been welcomed by anybody. But he was lord.

Her lord had slept last night with Ismara-New-Wife in a place set off and a little space removed, because he was a practical and prudent man. There were times and places at which, in which, his word had to be absolute and final and fiercely enforced, but the better part of leadership lay in judicious application of discretion and making of allowances.

Arakht was not much more than a village, but it was both their stopping place and their separation place. There was alcohol. Caravan law forbade the consumption of alcohol for all but carefully defined medicinal uses, so no one had tasted a drop for weeks—not since they'd crossed the Persian border east into Herat.

With the unwelcome announcement of the lord's decision to split the caravan, a moderate degree of relaxation in camp discipline was not inappropriate, to give people their chance to work their way toward acceptance. Even so, the lord couldn't be seen to countenance disregard of his own rules directly. Therefore he'd spent the night with New Wife in her enclosure, guarded by his sepahi Hell-riders. Therefore Boy had sat up in his tent, making repairs of incidentals, taking reports.

Now it was the early dawning hour. Men who'd danced late into the night washed their faces and poured water over their heads and put their minds to the tasks at hand. It was time for her lord to appear as the giver of orders once again, and there was—as they'd both known there would be—trouble.

New Wife's women let Boy in to New Wife's yurta. On one knee beside the screen that shielded New Wife's bed from the common interior Boy spoke, quietly. There was no need to cough or raise her voice. She knew that her lord had been awake almost as long as she had been, listening to be sure that nothing in his camp required his immediate presence and intervention.

"A good time to walk the camp, lord," Boy said. "One of the camel drivers saw the sun rise through the bottom of the flask." Or, in other words, had still been drinking when the sun came up, and was still drunk rather than sobered by the aftermath of drinking. Camel drivers frequently grew to share the temper of their beasts, or were called to become handlers of camels by a natural sympathy of temperament, so a drunk camel driver was a problem.

"Wait for me outside." His voice, which was the voice of an avenging angel, held no sleep. "I will be with you shortly." That was so nobody need know he was already dressed.

New Wife didn't care for men, not intimately, and had a baby of less than a year besides. Boy's lord did not embrace

New Wife, out of respect for both of these facts. And yet to save New Wife's face and give her respect, it was necessary to pretend their lord lay with her from time to time, child or no child, or risk unspoken aspersions on her ability to serve him.

One of the women brought bread and tea to Boy as she stood waiting outside the door flap. She could hear the sounds of a camp preparing to move, and there were voices raised in more than ordinary ill-temper from the place where beasts of burden were to be dressed for the day's work.

After a short period of time her lord came out with rose water fragrant on the shoulders of his coat and a piece of bread in hand. "Where do we walk?"

Captain Katische had set four sepahis on guard at New Wife's tent, two at a time, because the lord was there. Although Boy stood behind them—between them and the tent—she could sense their relaxation. Their lord was there. Now all they had to do was follow his lead. She knew how it felt. Three parts of victory was faith in the vision of the man who led them to war, and their lord had never failed them.

"Music, my lord," she answered, because she had been asked. It was not an answer in the words of men, perhaps, but he was an angel, and drew inferences like lines of glittering diamonds from "where do we walk" past "you can hear the sound of men's defiance, lord, you know what it means" to "and so I will be following you in that direction." He'd heard that rebellious music for himself. He already knew. She could tell.

He rubbed at his beard as if it annoyed him—he liked to keep clean-shaven, but a beard was part of any man's traveling dress—and started off toward the sounds of trouble in the camp. Captain Katische had already sent four more of the sepahis as escort; they followed at a respectful distance.

A distinct space had been left in their campground between two parties, and one was in more disorder than the other.

Her lord didn't hurry; he strolled at a leisurely pace eating his breakfast—*Here I am. I'm coming to ask you about the progress of your preparations. You might want to be mindful of what you're doing.* He was noticed. Boy could hear the raised voices calling warning, but there was still shouting.

The lord's lieutenant was Mahad Musadi, and he came to meet her lord on the border of the main party's camp. "Rustam declares rebellion," Mahad said. "Indeed you had some doubts about him, lord."

Her lord nodded, but casually, as if about some unimportant matter, and didn't speak. It was already embarrassing to Mahad, Boy knew, because Mahad had been sure Rustam was a steady man. And he might be, too; just not one who should drink.

As her lord ambled through the camp, the men left their tasks to follow him, because trouble in camp was unsettling and they relied on him to sort it out. Mahad was perfectly capable; the lord wouldn't have entrusted him with the responsibility otherwise. But while the lord was here, his authority would reinforce Mahad's delegated authority. These were the politics of a caravan. Nobody knew that better than the lord. So Boy followed him without fear or trepidation, to see what he would do.

Halfway across the main party's camp amongst the loads lying ready for the pack ponies, Shashka—Shikander Beg, refugee Circassian warlord, protector of caravans for hire—found a cluster of men in an uproar, and waded into the melee, pushing people to one side and another as he went. Someone was shouting.

"I'm not going to Zebak! I'm going home! And no one can stop me, I don't care."

There were obscenities, but the man's meaning was clear enough. Shashka barreled through. Someone else said "Stop your filthy mouth," and "You stick up for yourself, Rustam, be a man," and "That's the way to show him," though who was showing whom the way to what was not yet clear.

There was a certain degree of satisfaction in the simple physical act of pushing people out of the way. Shashka didn't usually get to do that, it was usually "yes lord" this and "just as you say, lord" that, and a man could have more than enough of deference and submission from time to time.

"Yah, yah, Rustam!"

Shashka was sending twenty-five men ahead over their usual route, north and east to Sanctuary, carrying only ten more with him down to Ishkashem and east along the Wakhan River. There were twenty men in total here, most of them camel drivers. Shashka got through the crowd to find Rustam grappling with Walli, and Gulam cheering Rustam on. Gulam didn't see him.

Shashka raised his voice to make himself heard. "What's going on?"

As soon as he spoke, there was a rush from either side to pull the two men apart. Gulam's first instinct was apparently to push away the men who tried to restrain Rustam.

Shashka noted it well. "You. Walli. You know the rules about brawling in camp." He had an idea of who was responsible, but he wanted to know if Rustam would step up to the blame to save Walli unearned punishment. "Explain yourself. Or take eight strokes for disturbing the peace."

Listening as much for any muttering in the crowd of men around him as for the responses of the principal combatants, Shashka waited while Walli and Rustam found their footing.

Rustam raised his head. "Well, I'm not going to Ishkashem," Rustam said. "That's all."

There was dust on his face but no damage that Shashka could see. Rustam was a big man, and wore a quilted coat. Walli hadn't finished dressing, by the looks of it. The contest had been unequal. Shashka filed the fact away for reference when the penalty was decided.

Rustam was not, it seemed, too drunk to hear the weakness in his argument, the insufficiency of *that's all* as an explanation. "Why should *we* have to work someone else's stinking caravan for a few stinking pieces of money while the others get to go straight home, by your stinking leave, by your leave I mean, lord?"

Shashka raised his hand. Rustam shut up, which was a point in his favor, but as Peri had suggested, Rustam was still drunk. There was no way to overlook it, and right now Shashka didn't even want to. He already knew that people were unhappy, whether or not they were all agreed that they needed money where they could find it. That didn't mean he meant to stand there and listen to abuse.

"Because I stinking said you stinking would." *That's right*, he heard someone say, behind him. Not loudly, but the sentiment was there, which meant Shashka was on the right track. "It's six to ten for brawling, Rustam, but I'll save your back. You'll need it. Eight. Take off your shirt."

Peri had his quirt there, passing it quietly into his hand. Under other circumstances physical discipline was something he would delegate, but he'd been defied to his face and that meant a signal demonstration was in order. Eight cuts would be quite enough. He was annoyed enough to make them really count.

Walli hadn't spoken. Now, looking resentful but resigned, he started to undress; "Not you," Mahad said to him, and the two men closest to Walli drew him back into the crowd.

Shashka agreed. He didn't want Walli. A man wasn't disciplined for brawling when his opponent was drunk and he'd defended himself. Walli wasn't Shashka's problem. Rustam was.

Rustam saw that he was singled out for blame and got stubborn as only a man who'd been drunk for hours could be. "I'm not taking any stinking licks from your stinking quirt, lord"—at least it wasn't "stinking lord," Shashka noted—"like a stinking animal. It isn't right. You want my shirt, well, come and get it."

Shashka thought about it, but not for long. "You're stinking drunk. You *are* an animal. You deserve to be beaten like one. Take off your shirt or I'll do it for you, and you're going to want it. You know how cold the nights get."

Rustam was bigger, but Rustam was drunk. That meant he wouldn't feel a blow like a sober man, which meant getting him down was going to be all the harder. On the other hand, Shashka was awake, Mahad would profit from the fresh provision of an object lesson in camp discipline, and there was nothing like a good fight to cheer a man. So Shashka was just as glad when Rustam spat on the ground, contemptuously, without speaking.

Hearing a patient, half-stifled sigh behind him, Shashka handed his quirt back to Peri and took off his coat, then his long vest and his shawl sash. No sense in dirtying his garments. The crowd of men drew back to give them room.

Rustam looked a little startled, but still defiant. Stepping up to him, Shashka put his right hand on Rustam's shoulder; Rustam did the same. Shashka nodded.

"Now," Shashka said.

Rustam closed his left fist and struck Shashka in the gut as hard as he could, which was sufficiently hard enough to break Shashka's breath. But since Rustam was stupid with drink, Shashka had seen Rustam's fist coming far enough ahead to dodge most of its impact by turning to his side and driving his elbow into Rustam's stomach in turn.

He had the advantage of the difference in height. He could get to the soft part of Rustam's belly more easily than Rustam could get to his. But the blow didn't have the impact Shashka had hoped for, its force dulled by the padding of Rustam's coat. It was a good warm coat. It was a shame to have to tear it. With luck it needn't be damaged beyond repair.

Shashka's momentum had carried him to one side of Rustam. Rustam's reflexes were duller than normal, so he wasn't turning to face Shashka as quickly as he otherwise might. Shashka got a kick in, and it was a good one. A good, solid, satisfying kick that almost toppled Rustam. Almost. Rustam had been turning; his body blocked Shashka's leg, and Shashka staggered backwards, his balance in serious question for a moment or two.

In that moment Rustam lunged, his hands outstretched for Shashka's throat. Rustam was sobering up fast. Shashka didn't care. The angle of Rustam's attack was wrong for Shashka to plant a foot in Rustam's chest and push, so he ducked under Rustam's reaching arms to smash a fist up under Rustam's jaw. This time Rustam went down.

Shashka got the front of Rustam's coat, pulling it out and away as Rustam fell. The tearing of the fabric was audible, but the resistance it offered brought Shashka along with it. He fell over Rustam, who made the obvious choice to wrestle.

Rustam had weight and reach on Shashka. Shashka had savagery and instinct on his side, and tutoring in the art of fighting with whatever weapons he could find at hand; and that received from Cossack comrades tussling good-naturedly with him by the fires at night on their way from St. Petersburg to his home in Kabardia, where they were to execute the Tsar's war against his family. Shashka hadn't known about that last part at the time. Rustam didn't know what he'd gotten himself into.

Dirt in the eyes was for children. These were rocks, sharp bits of gravel, and while Rustam roared with angry frustration—clawing at his face—Shashka pushed him over on the ground and tore his quilted coat back, hand gripping the collar. He'd started the tear earlier, at the shoulder; it was at the shoulder that it came away, now, the sleeve half separating from the body of the coat in such a way that it pinned Rustam's left arm to his side. That gave Shashka a clear shot at Rustam's ribs, and he took it.

He had the momentum of the fight on his side, now, but it didn't save him from being tripped up and brought down heavily in the dust. The impact knocked the breath out of him in a pained grunt. Rustam tried to catch him a blow at the back of his head. Luckily for Shashka he could roll and gasp at the same time, so Rustam's blow caught him on the side of the face, where it could daze but not bewilder him, and as Shashka rolled away he got hold of the coat again. That finished the coat.

Without the protection of the quilted padding Shashka's punch had a much more satisfying impact on Rustam's stomach. The effect stopped Rustam long enough for Shashka to get another in, and a sharp hit at the base of Rustam's skull to boot. Two hands at the back of Rustam's shirt collar, Shashka pulled against the fabric, Rustam's own weight an ally in the task.

It was a loose shirt of the common pattern, so there was a lot of slack to it, making tearing more difficult. Twisting around in Shashka's grasp, Rustam came up with his head against Shashka's chest, a terrific force that flattened Shashka on the cold hard ground. But Shashka got his boot into Rustam's ribs this time, heel angled just so, catching the exact right place.

Rustam was white-faced and fish-eyed, and looked like he was going to vomit. Shashka got out of the way. Rustam didn't vomit, he just couldn't speak, so Shashka grabbed Rustam's shirt at the waist and pulled it up over Rustam's head to tangle him up and trammel him while Rustam struggled for breath.

Rustam raised himself up, kneeling on the ground. Shashka leaned over him from behind and took him by the throat.

"Who is lord here?" Shashka shouted, hoarsely. He knew the answer and so did everybody else, but the point needed its ritual confirmation. There was no will to fight left in Rustam. Shashka pulled him over onto his back and leaned down over him, fist braced on bent knee.

He was open and vulnerable, and he'd deliberately chosen to be. If Rustam had been able, he could have hit Shashka full in the face, punched him in the stomach, kicked him in the groin. Rustam wouldn't. He was beaten.

"Where do you go?" *You miserable stinking piece of shit.* Shashka didn't say it. It was enough for now that Rustam was defeated.

Rustam was struggling to sit up. Shashka stood up and stepped back. Rustam rolled over, hands to the ground, then straightened himself, gathering his shirt together in his hands. Shashka hadn't torn the shirt away; it was loosened, but intact. With the deliberation that spoke of aching muscles Rustam pulled it off, baring his back.

Coming to Shashka's side Peri gave him the quirt.

"You are lord here," Rustam said. "I go south with you, to Ishkashem. Mine was the fault, lord. Walli had no part in the offense."

"Because you say it, I excuse one cut."

Rustam was sober now. He'd feel seven as he would have felt eight, earlier.

Shashka himself wasn't angry any longer, and he was depleted physically by the exertion. "One."

Rustam took all seven without breaking from his place, and when seven had been told off cut by cut, Walli came with another man to help Rustam to a seat on a pack saddle. Gulam picked up the torn pieces of Rustam's coat. Shashka watched him. He didn't feel he had to say anything to Gulam. He made his point by watching. Gulam had incited. That had been noted and marked down against him, but a cooperative and respectful attitude going forward would answer for a multitude of errors.

Peri was back with a basin of water, and dusted Shashka off, back, shoulders, thighs, with rough efficiency as he washed his face. She was none too gentle about it, but she meant to be sure she knew if he was injured. A hurt wouldn't always answer to a tender touch, but a brisk salute would raise an echo without fail.

The water stung his face where it was cut, but he didn't mind. He was in for his own share of aches and pains, but on balance it had been well worth it. He'd reinforced his authority and Mahad's with it. He'd beaten a bigger man. Rustam had escaped a worse beating for drunkenness, and Mahad hadn't lost a seasoned worker, one of their family. They were all orphaned in the wars, to a greater or lesser degree. They needed each other to find the courage to keep on.

Slowly, Shashka got himself dressed. He had a long day ahead of him, business to transact, debts to settle in Arakht, rendezvous to arrange with the master of the caravan that had hired him. But there was nothing like the occasional fistfight to relieve worry and frustration, and let a man breathe in peace with himself again.

Here was Mahad Musadi again, now, Shashka's lieutenant for the main party going up by way of Khorog, coming up from behind the scrim of camel drivers to stand at Shashka's side. "I'll send word for you on the river road, when we've arrived," Mahad said. "Safe journey, lord."

Shashka nodded. "And to you."

His camels would be starting, their heads turned south. He needed to tie off his loose ends. Peri had saddled the Cherkess stallion and brought him, sitting at the ready on her Birkit. Mounting, Shashka stroked the reins lightly against the side of Cherkess's good strong neck, and rode ahead for the Ishkashem road, so that the caravan-masters would be left alone to start their laden beasts for their long journey.

The moon was full and the road was one that he and Coriander had learned well over the years, one by which they'd just come up to Bharaj not eight days ago. Jefferji gave Coriander her head and left her to it. She was much smarter than he was, in the dark. He believed in her understanding of how quickly she could safely go, and he had enough on his mind to absorb his troubled thoughts to abstraction.

By the time they reached the well at Jetra and stopped for a drink of water and a short rest, it was in the early predawn hour, with the moon still lighting the western sky even as the sun started to brighten the eastern horizon. Jefferji fed Coriander a turnip he'd been saving for her all night and tried to make up his mind. The road up to the hill on which the Hirpa temple stood branched off of the Udaipore road hours north of Tengarpore. What was he going to do?

He could go straight to Tengarpore. He'd left early. Surely he'd be able to get to Tengarpore and confront Jaisal Singh in time to get back to the Hirpa temple, and be there when Captain Fontenoy came to fetch him.

Yes, Captain Fontenoy had told him he was not to go to Tengarpore for fear there were British there to take custody of him for his own good, to serve as a pretext for establishing themselves there while Jaisal Singh ailed and died and Madhu Singh assumed the princely musnud.

Jefferji knew well enough how to slip out of Tengarpore and back in again without being detected, didn't he? Hadn't he done that again and again over the years, cutting across the fields, running to the Hirpa temple to see his teacher—his Guru-ji—before Jaisal Singh had made up his mind to allow him to come and go as he pleased? Couldn't he come and go with no one the wiser?

Maybe he hadn't been undetected. Maybe the night watch had simply turned a blind eye, out of sympathy for the desperation of an orphaned boy seeking the comfort that he had in dancing for the Beloved. Would they not turn as blind an eye to him, now, and let him in?

It was possible. But there was something else he had to consider, no matter his misery, no matter his desperation. Captain Fontenoy had warned him away from Tengarpore, and he wouldn't have done that without coordination with Jaisal Singh. Jefferji was a cadet of Tengarpore. Such men knew how to keep faith and to honor the instruction of their war leaders, and if he—Jefferji—broke faith and dishonored instruction, he was no Rajput-by-adoption at all.

Maybe Captain Fontenoy was right and maybe he wasn't, but Jefferji was in no position to second-guess him, and nobody who drew breath could question Captain Fontenoy's motives. How could Jefferji jeopardize Tengarpore's independence under such circumstances as Captain Fontenoy had laid before him?

How could he shame Tengarpore, Jaisal Singh, Fontenoy, everybody who had tried to teach him how to be a man and the son of a Rajput prince, by running to Tengarpore to cry to his adoptive father? How could he shame his mother, his father, his grandfather who had survived captivity in the courts of Tipu Sultan, by putting his own selfishness over everything and everyone he had known and loved since the day that he'd been born?

It was too simple a decision by half. Jefferji wished he could find some complexities, some ambiguities, some grey areas, but there were none. Either he accepted instruction that came from his courtesy-uncle, Captain Fontenoy, as good a deputy as Jaisal Singh had available, or he could crumple into self-pity and confusion in the face of the first real challenge he had confronted since his mother had died.

It didn't even really matter whether he was crumpled into self-pity or not, only whether he went to the Hirpa temple, or on to Tengarpore.

So when he and Coriander reached the place where the way to Hirpa led east from the Udaipore road, they turned east.

The morning was early yet, and a pearly mist teased the eye around the trunks of the old trees, the brightly striped holiday tents, the temple walls away to the south of the compound. Broderick Holyoke hurried across the bare, packed earth toward the little table that had been set under the tree next to Fontenoy's tent, where Fontenoy stood bareheaded and freshly shaved, drinking a cup of tea.

"I'm told he saddled and left just after the dance last night, sir," Broderick said, nodding at Madhu Singh to show the respect that would probably be considered appropriate. "Took the Udaipur road at a fair clip."

The humidity was unpleasant to a significant degree. The sun would burn away the fog but not dry the air, and then they'd have unreasonable heat as well as the humidity. There were moments on end when the weather in Rajputana was tolerable, but to Broderick's estimation they were few and far in between.

"He said nothing to anybody?" Fontenoy asked Madhu Singh. Broderick thought that Madhu was respectful of Fontenoy's concern, but not particularly worried about Tamisen. "I hoped to have a second talk with him."

Madhu Singh almost shrugged his shoulders. In early morning undress there was a certain dignity about Madhu Singh—born of the privilege and power, Broderick could easily guess, for which Madhu Singh had been destined from the moment of his birth—that made one understand he was his father's heir.

"His nature is mercurial, and his habit has always been to hurry. When we were boys, he'd run all the way to the Krsna temple on Hirpa just to greet the god at sunrise, and it's easily five of your English miles on the straight through the fields."

Wholesome exercise, running. Encouraged decency by channeling the energies into physical hygiene—which had gone awry with Tamisen, apparently, because Tamisen's dancing was indecent, on top of idolatrous.

Fontenoy sipped his tea. "Awkward. I had meant to discuss things a little further with him. I told him there'd be letters for him at the Hirpa temple, I'm sure he's gone for them, and here's word just come by courier this morning. I can't meet Tamisen at the Hirpa temple. Plans adjusted on the fly."

"News that perhaps my father and my mother have also in hand?" Madhu asked, as if of some unimportant matter, but Broderick smelled a secret. He was good at that, smelling secrets. He'd never have become Lieutenant Broderick Holyoke if he hadn't known where to find secrets and how to use them to his advantage. "Surely you can send a fast courier, Captain Fontenoy, turn Jefferji from the road. Any of our people would be glad to ride ahead with a message, to be of service to you."

Fontenoy shook his head. "I must make rendezvous. And I would hate to think of Tamisen missing his chance." There was an unusual depth of passion in Fontenoy's voice that seemed disproportionate to the stakes as Broderick knew them—although Fontenoy had resolutely ignored any hints from Broderick to share information. "I need him with me, Madhu. He has the breeding of a Rajput and an unusually good ear for languages. All he needs is a chance to show what he's made of."

Fontenoy's tent was struck, and its appurtenances gathered ready for packing up. All that remained was for Fontenoy to finish his breakfast. Fontenoy's orderly brought two teas; a refill for Fontenoy, a cup for Broderick. It was hot and strong, well sweetened, rich with cream. A little surprising, really, because Broderick knew Parker didn't like him.

Maybe it was Parker's way of saying "good riddance." Fontenoy was going to Peshawar, within reach of the kingdom of Kabul where fame and fortune were to be won, Broderick perforce with him. Parker would be going back to Kari Patna to tell what tales he liked.

"They say now that Kabul rests with Shah Shuja, the British will advance on Herat," Madhu Singh said. His tone was casual, but Broderick could tell he was by no means reluctant to fish a little for inside information. "That Dost Mohammed Khan has fled with his treasury to Bokhara in the north."

With a twitching of his lips like that of a man chewing over a stray bit of escaped tea leaf between his front teeth Fontenoy looked out toward the temple walls, contemplatively. "Treasury. Twenty years ago I left something very valuable north of the Hindu Kush, but not in Bokhara. East of Badakshan. Somewhere in the mountains of the high Pamir."

And now Fontenoy sought Tamisen's company to go retrieve it? In Bombay people had known only that Fontenoy had apparently been ordered to Peshawar rather urgently on some pretext unidentified. Nobody knew why, and Fontenoy had completely ignored Broderick's best efforts to press for details on their way here.

Tribal knowledge in Broderick's unit told of times when Fontenoy had been a much younger man, with vague but intriguing experience of the savages in the wild high places where Captain Wood had gone in search of the source of the Oxus. The British government wouldn't send for Fontenoy in such a hurry for any trivial errand. There had to be something more to it than that.

Could it be the treasury?

If it wasn't, why would Fontenoy be so coy about his errand? There was no one here but Madhu Singh and one extraneous officer, Holyoke by name, sent north for living burial at some thankless diplomatic post. It was undeserved punishment for largely undefined offenses—of which he was innocent—and Broderick resented it.

Conviction dawned in Broderick's mind as clear and as bright as the sun on a morning in the cold season. Of course it was the treasury. Shah Shuja had spoken many times of the wealth he'd have once he regained his place: money to repay to the English for their investment and fund his government. All he'd ever asked for was the initial investment to raise some troops, and British armies from Calcutta and Bombay by way of a demonstration of sponsorship.

And yet when his enemy had fled from Kabul and its treasury was opened for inventory, there'd been nothing like the riches Shah Shuja had promised. He'd expressed his surprise and his frustration so persuasively that the Political Envoy had been confident of his sincerity, by report—*Where are my pearls, my gems, my gold?* he'd cried. *My enemy has despoiled me of my ancestral property.*

Captain Fontenoy had been sent for because somebody had information on the location of the looted wealth of Kabul, somebody who needed Fontenoy to bring it back. No doubt some choice jewels would find their way into his saddle roll before a proper inventory was made, and who could blame Fontenoy for that? Where was Dost Mohammed Khan, to say that Fontenoy had stolen thus-and-such a gem? Who would miss a handful of diamonds out of a bucketful?

"Then let my brother Jefferji assist you in your quest to bring your long-lost treasure back from Badakshan." Madhu Singh held out his hand to shake that of Captain Fontenoy. *In the manly British fashion,* Broderick thought to himself, sarcastically. "Good fortune to you both, and the reward of valor. I'll remember you to my father. Good speed on your journey, Captain Fontenoy."

The treasury of Kabul, the vast fortune of Dost Mohammed Khan. How could it be right that the credit for such an accomplishment should be shared with a native-raised boy, a dancer of obscenities, a man who displayed himself before the world in women's clothing, playing the part of the willing concubine of one of their everlasting heathen gods?

Captain Fontenoy shook Madhu Singh's hand and stood, watching, as his host made for the far end of the encampment, on about his business. Then Fontenoy sighed with a sort of deep determination, as though having had been forced reluctantly to the distasteful expedient of approaching Broderick for a favor.

"Hire a boy to show you the way, Holyoke, and get to the Hirpa temple," Fontenoy said. "As quickly as you can. Bring Tamisen with you to the Residency in Peshawar. I'll wait for you there, the both of you, only hurry."

Of course Fontenoy would wish to take an ignorant youth as his interpreter. Tamisen would not blink at the pilferage that would make Fontenoy's retirement an oh-so-comfortable one. In fact, Broderick realized, Fontenoy could buy Tamisen's silence easily enough with a portion of the loot he meant to steal. But why should he, Broderick Holyoke, sell his cooperation on the cheap? Why shouldn't he have some of that treasure for himself?

He needed a moment to decide exactly how he was to put that question to Fontenoy, based on speculation as it was. In that moment Fontenoy tightened his mouth—Broderick saw it in the muscles at Fontenoy's jaw, outside the camouflage of Fontenoy's moustache—and sweetened his proposal, putting his hands to his hips, glancing at Holyoke out of the corner of his eye.

"Come as quickly as you can, and I shall be very much obliged to you, Holyoke." It was a transparently obvious offer. Fontenoy had the details of the misdemeanors that were laid at Broderick's door. Fontenoy had the power to deliver the details of Broderick's disgrace to the people in Peshawar. Or to withhold them. But Broderick was halfway in on the secret, now, and knew how to interpret Fontenoy's offer: supporting evidence of something Fontenoy wasn't telling him.

If he was right, there were riches to be had for the taking. Fontenoy meant to share them with Tamisen and none other, but with Tamisen in his actual care Broderick would find a way around that easily enough when the time came. For now—

For now he had to take care not to get ahead of himself. "I understand, sir," he said, with a crisp respectful nod. "Leaving directly. To be meeting you in Peshawar at the very earliest opportunity."

Let Fontenoy believe that a bargain had been struck: Broderick's cooperation, in return for Fontenoy's casual neglect to turn over the details of Bombay's shakily substantiated and supposed derelictions of duty, with miscellaneous conduct unbecoming an officer and a gentleman.

When Broderick arrived in Peshawar with Tamisen in tow, Fontenoy might discover that Broderick wanted much more than to bury those reports. With the implicit *quid pro quo*—would Fontenoy have the stones to deny it?—to hold over Fontenoy's head, well, the sun shone bright on Holyoke's future. It was time he set off to chase any remaining clouds away and get Tamisen started for Peshawar.

It was not as long from Bharaj to the Hirpa temple as it would have been to Tengarpore, but it was long enough, and the sun overhead made travel the more wearying for man and beast alike. Jefferji wasn't sure what time it was, but by the sun it was at least half past any hope of a mid-day meal, and every time they stopped under the trees at a well to water themselves, it was harder to get going once again.

He had to get to the Hirpa temple. He'd rushed away from Bharaj without telling anybody where he was going; he was in the wrong for that. His best hope of lessening his fault was to get to where he'd been supposed to go as quickly as possible.

He bought bread and ripe melon from a boy on the road going up toward the hill of the Hirpa temple, and shared it with Coriander as they went. He was walking beside her, now, to lighten the burden as much as possible. He'd mount and go again when the sun had fallen in the west, to cast its long beams through the hazy atmosphere and shine brightly on the whitewashed dome of the temple, still miles away.

There were people on the road in a hurry, coming toward him, so Jefferji moved to the side of the road to give them room to pass. They slowed, instead, and three men came hurrying forward, men Jefferji recognized. From the temple. Charbit, Sooven, Parnie. And a horse, the aged and long-since retired messenger's mount affectionally called the Farting One, dressed in saddle and riding gear.

"You are in good time," Sooven called, when still some lengths removed. "You must hurry on to Hirpa. We will bring Coriander. Take Farter and go."

Jefferji hesitated. He and Coriander were partners. She didn't like to be left out of the action. But who knew what was happening? These people had come from the Hirpa temple to fetch him, tipped off by the boy who'd sold him food, perhaps. Coriander wasn't saying anything, standing in the road with her head down.

Then the Farting One demonstrated his special skill, and Coriander threw her head up and away, flaring her nostrils as if to say *Take that thing away from here*. She didn't mean it. She and Farter were cordial acquaintances, though they'd never been friends. It was as good as an omen for Jefferji, though. Nodding gratefully to Sooven, Jefferji climbed into the saddle and turned Farter's head back up the road to the Hirpa temple.

"And don't let him tell you he's been working all day!" Sooven called. "He's got a good trot in him, and it's all for you!"

And *well, we might as well get started*, Farter grumbled, deep in his manufactory of hideous stinks. Jefferji patted Farter's flanks with the flats of his feet by way of a strong suggestion that a trot would be appreciated, and they were away.

With the help of a fresh horse, it was full daylight still when Jefferji rode through the familiar gateway, then into the familiar compound and around one side toward where people were waiting for Farter in order to wash and groom and feed him.

The Hirpa temple. Jefferji had spent more time there than in any place other than the fort of Tengarpore itself. It was his second home, his second school, the place where the Beloved was indwelling for festivals and for people who came with passionate prayers to ask for reassurance, aid, or even just a word of greeting for the god and the divine Consort.

Would Hirpa be empty for him now as well?

More waited than just Farter's custodians; there was one of the laundrywomen with an armload of toweling, and the boy who was responsible for bringing the hot water for a man to shave, carrying his own towel-wrapped cakes of new-cut soap. And—and Myamah, tiny and frail now, who had been so strong and tall when he had been a child; Myamah who'd suckled Madhu Singh and had been given to Jefferji's mother to be Jefferji's wet-nurse after he'd been born. That long ago.

That long he'd been the focus of Myamah's life. She'd walked barefoot from Tengarpore to Lackberly to fetch Jaisal Singh home, so that he could bring Jefferji back to Tengarpore when Jefferji had run away to the Hirpa temple after his mother had died. How was he to part with Myamah?

"Come along, then, Jefferji," Myamah said. "The boy was right. You disgrace decent company, in your state."

There were too many towels there for one Jefferji to need, and they were headed to the back of the temple where the water tanks were, and the boilers. The sun did much of the work of heating water during the summer months, but there was always a need to boil water for laundry, and a man wanted hotter water to clean what remained of the paint from his face.

Jefferji hadn't stopped to wash before he'd run away from the Bharaj fair. He'd rinsed his face, yes, but he could too easily imagine that he still looked a fright, like a sadhu with his face streaked with the dust of a cow's leavings.

The barber was waiting in the laundry to shave him, and there were five tall heavy cans of steaming water from the boilers, ready and waiting for his bath. The bath-attendant boy set a timeworn open-slatted stool down over the gutters in the floor, and waited while Jefferji stripped off his stained and smelly clothing and sat down.

It was a surprise to recognize the temple's senior barber: it was Denalji himself. Denalji shaved the priests, so how—

Jefferji wondered—did he himself rate such a privilege? It was to be a thorough wash, too, one that started from his shoulders down, then from his feet up, and the actual shaving to be done last. Jefferji waited until Denalji was shampooing his aching legs to ask the question that was uppermost in his mind, howsoever obliquely. "I don't understand what's going on, Denalji. I've been told I have to go away."

Denalji took a moment on his way up from Jefferji's left shin before he answered, and by the time he did Jefferji had almost forgotten the question—the soapy massage felt so good. The bath-attendant boy had brought what Jefferji could only guess was the temple's best soap, thick tan suds with the sweet fragrance of sandalwood, as though there was going to be a festival. If Jaisal Singh was too close to death there would be austerities at Tengarpore, and no such soap as this.

"There was a letter from your Uncle Fontenoy," Denalji said, iron-hard fingers working the cramped muscles of Jefferji's thighs. "To Tengarpore." Raising his head Denalji gestured to the bath-attendant boy to give Jefferji a cake of a different soap for a different purpose, then returned to his own work in process as he kept talking.

"There—wash the paint out of your hair, Jefferji, make yourself useful. Your uncle warned us that Bombay might take advantage of your father's death to send an English agent here, to be a sort of resident. Remember that you're English by birth, Jefferji, and that Jaisal Singh has never asked for endorsement of Madhu as his heir. Not from Calcutta. Not from Mumbai. Not from any European of any description."

Your father, Denalji said. Jaisal Singh *was* his father, in a sense that had nothing to do with whether Jefferji's mother had been faithful. Jaisal Singh would never acknowledge the right of any English to grant or deny their stamp of approval for Madhu to inherit. It wasn't like those northerly states in which Colonel Todd had had so many difficulties with Ochterlony, and besides Auckland was Governor-General now.

"He's asked me to come to Badakhshan with him," Jefferji said, slowly, rubbing the rich lather into his scalp. "So that no such English will have an excuse. I suppose I must. Is Jaisal Singh—very—is it close?"

"There's no use talking about it," Denalji said, wiping his hands on a towel. "It comes when it comes. Let the boy rinse you, Jefferji, because you must be ready to leave earlier in the morning than I intend to get up to shave you, so it will have to be now. This isn't your fault. This is Prince Rama exiled from Ayodhya, isn't it? Get rinsed."

Rama had left home because his father told him to. He could have challenged it, resisted, rejected the injustice, but he'd bent his neck to his father's will and gone into exile simply because it was the will of the King as much as that of Rama's father. Jefferji had danced Prince Rama. He'd danced Rama's father. Even the demon-beguiled queen. When Denalji put it that way—

The boy poured can after can of warm water in a practiced stream over Jefferji's head, so that it cascaded from the crown of his head to his shoulders and divided to sluice across his back and chest, getting the most rinse out of a limited supply of water.

Jefferji willed as much of his confusion and distress as he could down the drain with it. And once Denalji had shaved him—once he was as washed, relaxed, and smooth-cheeked as even Myamah could wish him—Jefferji wrapped a towel around his waist, lay down on a low-slung charpoy bed against the wall to wait for clean clothing to get dressed again, and fell asleep.

He was so deeply asleep that Myamah had to shake him vigorously. "You, hsst, wake up, Jefferji, hurry, hurry, get dressed." She was thrusting a thin cotton tunic at him and pulling at his upper arm to get him to sit up, shaking out white cotton Rajput trousers at the same time. Jefferji sat up obediently, still mostly asleep, and pulled the tunic over his head as Myamah got his feet threaded through the legs of the trousers.

"Stand up, stand up. Don't you understand? You must be quick or you will miss her, and you must not miss her. It is she herself who has come and at such a time, Jefferji. For the love of the Dark One, get dressed!" She pushed his feet into his openwork sandals without much help from him. He stood up, fastening the trousers at his waist. They weren't his. Nor was the formal tunic she pushed at him impatiently. "Hurry up!"

Myamah dressed his hair with quick efficiency, taking no apparent notice of whether she pulled it or not. She wound his pagri turban for him as she had not done for years now, but Jefferji didn't mind, because she had a right to do as she pleased with him, after all those years.

Putting a three-tiered wreath of marigolds around his neck she pulled him by the hand until he was moving as quickly as she liked, then pushed him to hurry ahead of her, fastening the ties of the unfamiliar tunic as he went. Whose clothes were these?

They ran through the eastern arcade of the temple and down the cascade of white marble steps into the courtyard as Jefferji tried to puzzle things through. The clothing of dead persons wasn't shared, except in poorer families: it was an offense to the rank of the dead. But this clothing was unfamiliar in its fit, and of finer quality than he was accustomed to.

Only as Myamah pushed him to his knees on a small carpet spread over the stone of the temple courtyard did Jefferji realize—his back perfectly straight, his head perfectly still, his hands perfectly posed to express heartfelt reverence and awe—that he was wearing clothing that had been made for Jaisal Singh, who was perhaps not going to be needing replacements for his current wardrobe.

He'd slept for a few hours, no more; the light still lingered, and the full moon was rising fast. The night watchmen stood at the threshold of the temple precincts at the ready, waiting to close the gates into the sacred grounds beneath arches draped with night-blooming jasmine whose perfume breathed into the twilight like a benediction.

The torches were lit, if scarcely needed yet. There were horsemen coming, household warriors of Tengarpore, and in their midst, dressed in tunic and trousers of black and gold and a beaded headscarf bejeweled with mirrorwork, riding the Colimbrana stallion himself—Jaisal Begum.

He'd never seen a woman on a stone horse—a stallion—in his life, but she was Rajput. He knew that she could ride: astride like any man, like the warrior that a woman of a Rajput princely house was expected to be, and with the Colimbrana stallion beneath her as perfectly mannered as if it had been her husband who rode him rather than the Hawk of Tengarpore. As mild-mannered as a mare. Jaisal Begum. No wonder Myamah had been beside herself with anxiety.

One of the temple's senior administrators came forward, two men behind him carrying a stepped platform to set down beside the Colimbrana stallion. Jaisal Begum dismounted. When she turned around she seemed to see Jefferji. Though she could not have been said to hesitate, it seemed to Jefferji that she somehow regretted seeing him there. Because he was leaving, maybe? He bowed his head. He kept it bowed. He sensed her passing as she climbed the stairs into the temple. When she wanted him she'd send for him.

Two of her guard closed the temple gates while the night watchmen stood waiting, not getting in the way. Four of them followed Jaisal Begum up the stairs. Two would take up position to either side of the temple's great carved wooden doors, Jefferji knew, and two of them would mirror those posts just inside the temple. They'd be unarmed, because the Hirpa temple was sacred ground.

One of them gave Jefferji a light tap on the shoulder as he passed—"You'll be wanted, Jefferji," he said. "Follow me please."

It was Borindra, halfway in age between Jefferji and Madhu Singh. They hadn't always gotten along, but it had been Borindra who'd worked with Jefferji when he was learning stave fighting, and now he sounded affectionate and friendly. *Now that I'm going away*, Jefferji thought, bitterly, but he asked Borindra's pardon in his mind immediately. It wasn't like that. He had to work on his attitude.

Standing up, Jefferji followed Borindra with very little stiffness in his body—it was a wonder what a good shampoo and a nap could do—as Borindra went left through the temple doors, not straight through the antechamber into the great sanctuary, and down the east ambit. There were small audience chambers let into the inner walls the length of the ambit. Jefferji knew that. He was more familiar with the Hirpa temple than most of Tengarpore's young men. Borindra waved him in to one of those chambers with a gentle push that was almost a pat, and left him to wait.

Not for long. A carpet had been laid down against the innermost wall of the audience chamber within the god's ambit, and on it, cushions and bolsters, lamps, a tall flask of cooled wine, two glasses. But two people came through from the sanctuary, both familiar, so neither glass was for him. Jefferji was a little relieved. What would he do, if Jaisal Begum had asked him to take a drink with her? Die of embarrassment.

She'd never said a cruel word to him, but he'd always been wary in her presence. She was a hawk. He was her natural prey, no matter how much she'd loved his mother, or how much her husband had loved Jefferji's father.

She'd shifted her long head covering back, draping it down across her shoulders. She had Old Fanum with her, one of the senior priests, a man who had been at the Hirpa Temple for as long, it was said, as there had been a temple here at Hirpa. Jefferji had never made up his mind whether such a thing was even possible, but a wise man—even a shrewd boy—reserved judgment, because the Hirpa temple was only two hundred and fifty years old.

"Sit, Jefferji," Jaisal Begum said, settling herself into the cushions like a brooding eagle on its nest. "It's good to find you here. I was afraid time would run out. I have things to say and no time to say them, so you will be still, please, and let me speak, and if Old Fanum can't answer any questions you have later, then there are no answers to be had."

Old Fanum had poured her a glass of wine. She drank off half of it and held her glass out for a refill, nodding from Old Fanum to the decanter meaningfully as she did so—to communicate that he'd better pour for himself before she drank the lot of it, Jefferji guessed. He sat down with careful precision, making sure his hands were respectfully arranged and his feet well out of sight.

"There is a marriage arranged for you, Jefferji. She is young although you will think her old at twenty-six, and in her family the women have borne healthy children until the age of forty-five. She offers a good price for your body, caste-less though your blood is, because she needs our protection from her husband's family. Here is the present she has sent, or in the words of the British in Bombay—how is it said?" She was looking at Old Fanum; Jefferji kept shut. "Earnest money?"

Then she turned her attention back to Jefferji. "She is a kinswoman of mine —a distant relation, I grant you, but of respectable descent. You gain considerably by the relation, but she's a widow, so she comes with... humility."

Cheap, Jaisal Begum meant. In a sense. As a widow, Jaisal Begum's kinswoman could call on neither her husband's connections nor her own, and had limited choice of partners if circumstance forced her to marry again.

"There is a farm. Much honor will accrue to you if you become her protector. And you'll bring a good piece of land to Tengarpore." *Yet.* She had something more to say. Jefferji could hear it. "And yet you may not wish to take a Rajput wife, Jefferji, if you stay with the English. It's your choice. I will protect her and her farm as our own whether or not you claim her as your bride. In some ways that would be better all around, but you will have a place that is yours, either way."

Marrying into acreage was a time-honored way to increase an estate and add to the resources of a ruling house. Tengar-pore was giving Jefferji wife and land, because Jaisal Singh was his foster father. What if he didn't want to be a farmer? Jaisal Begum's widowed kinswoman would still have honor and protection; Tengarpore would still get the land. All he'd have to do was stay betrothed, and never come back.

The understanding was as overwhelming as it was abso-lute, though he knew better than to argue with Jaisal Begum. Her great-grandmother had once put her own infant children to the sword, and ridden out against an enemy to die in battle rather than submit to domination.

"Where is the farm of this woman, and has my trunk been sent there already?" That would be awkward. He'd be needing a few things, if he was going to Badakhshan with Captain Fontenoy.

But Jaisal Begum shook her head. She was taking some-thing off from around her neck—two somethings, apparently, pouches on cords, to set them down in front of her. That one of them was than the other was clear to see even by lamplight.

"No, Jefferji, here. They will store what you choose not to take with you." Opening the newer of the two pouches, Jaisal Begum poured its contents out into the cupped palm of her left hand. Green, blue, white gems, pearls. "I have brought here that which is offered, and that which is yours; it was to have been waiting for your arrival, but this is better. Now. This is offered. My kinswoman gives these jewels from her estate to show how she will maintain you in honor and comfort."

No such thing. These jewels were from Jaisal Begum, to hire a husband. Why didn't she just give them to her kinswoman and be done with it? Because her dead husband's family would claim the money, then. The widow would lose the leverage of having soon-to-be husband Jefferji Tamisen to protect her. And Tengarpore wouldn't get the farm. Of course.

Pouring the gems into a little heap by her left knee Jaisal Begum tossed the older packet to him, startling him so that he almost failed in his catch. "And this other, your inheritance. Some of these were given to us by your father to keep for your mother; the rest, by your grandfather, before he died. Now they're yours."

He knew by the weight of the packet, by the rough outline of stones against the soft old leather, that these were jewels as well. He opened up the pouch and looked inside. It was tricky; the knot had clearly been untouched for years. Even still, Jefferji could tell that these gems were as large as those Jaisal Begum had shown him, or even larger.

What was he to do? One by one he picked stones out of the pouch and laid them down. Their cut was exquisite. By the expression on Jaisal Begum's face she'd seen them before, and knew quite well how to value them.

When the pouch was emptied there were eleven jewels in a row in front of Jefferji, and some things left at the bottom of the pouch still. There was a turban jewel that Jefferji recognized as Daoji's, heavy and old, luminous with pearls that gleamed golden in the low light—a keepsake from the court of Tipu Sultan, wrapped in a bit of leather to protect the pearls. Something still more. A regimental badge, a military insignia of some sort.

His father had left these jewels with his wife, pregnant though neither of them had realized it yet, the son in her womb to be orphaned before he'd had so much as a chance to meet his father. Jaisal Begum had held them in sacred trust. Jefferji traced the outlines of the badge with his fingers, thinking. There was a lion, and flags. He didn't want to be married. "You know that Captain Fontenoy wants me to go north with him, Jaisal Begum. I don't know when I'll be back."

Of course she knew. She'd probably known before he did.

Picking through the jewels from the pouch Jefferji selected a ruby—a particularly handsome one, but he'd just met these jewels, he had no feeling for any of them, apart from the badge and Daoji's turban jewel—and stretched forward to set it down at Jaisal Begum's folded legs. He couldn't just leave here and not come back. Jaisal Begum had to keep something that was his; that way he'd never be completely gone. "Would you see that the noble lady has this for her expenses, while I'm away?"

When Jaisal Begum nodded and swept the first clutch of gems back into its pouch—the ruby among them—Jefferji knew that they had a compact.

"Your place with my kinswoman will be kept for you, Jefferji, whether you come back to us or not."

There was no dishonor in marriage to an absent husband. It was a fact of life for Rajputs, and Jefferji was assured of at least a roof, a bed, and a meal, when next he came to Tengarpore.

Jaisal Begum stood, so he stood as well. Old Fanum stepped back, draining his glass of wine hastily.

"Now I have to ride for home," she said. "I only came to bring the jewels, fortunate to find you here to speak to you. Come and kiss me goodbye, Jefferji. There may well be another widow at Tengarpore when you return. I'm sorry you have to go like this but it can't be helped. Jaisal Singh has always loved you very dearly, first for your father's sake, then for your own."

She gave him no more than a wingbeat's span of time to bend and kiss her cheek. Jefferji didn't mind. Up close her face was white with grief and sorrow, terrible with the wisdom of a woman who had seen three children buried and two not born. If the widow to whom she wished him to be married was her kinswoman it was better if he went away, because he would never be able to match that strength of character.

⛰

"Sit still," Myamah insisted, and tweaked Jefferji's ear. "I've never done this one. And it must be right. I need to practice."

Old Fanum had called a boy to bring Jefferji to Myamah's room once Jaisal Begum had left, because the priest apparently wanted to be alone. Possibly just to finish the wine. Possibly because he was troubled for Jaisal Begum's sake, though there was nothing to do about the fact that Jaisal Singh was dying.

Myamah had fed Jefferji his dinner, but then she'd made him sit down and brushed out his long hair and started to practice a pagri turban on him. Jaisal Singh's pagri. He had a fine suit of Jaisal Singh's clothing, though Jefferji hadn't filled out yet, as a man of more mature age might gain in gravitas across his chest and shoulders. All of it a modest bit of redirection, Myamah explained, as if to ease Jefferji's discomfort.

If a man as tall as Jaisal Singh; in what looked like Jaisal Singh's clothing because it was; wearing Jaisal Singh's distinctly tied pagri turban that no son or client of Jaisal Singh would ever dare to wear while Jaisal Singh yet lived; if such a man left the Hirpa temple when some Bombay British happened to be on the Udaipore road, none of them would mistake that man for a British orphan boy. Not even if he was riding a distinctly second-class Marwari rather than the Colimbrana stallion.

"There," Myamah said, and lifted the turban off Jefferji's head to shake it out and fold the fabric loosely across the bedstead, apparently satisfied at last. "I'll be even better next time. Do you want some tea?"

Jefferji stood up and stretched, shaking his head *no thank you*. He had to be careful about stretching, because the room that the temple had put at Myamah's disposal had a ceiling sized to her but not for him. He could only just barely stand up straight.

"Drink it anyway," Myamah said, handing him a cup. "You need some tea. Are you going to Badakhshan? Bring me back some rubies to pray on."

Well, of course Captain Fontenoy would make at least some mention of his plans in his letter to Jaisal Singh, that would be only natural. And of course there was no harm in sharing secrets with Myamah; she would knew how to keep them. Had she learned things he had yet to find out, though? How much did he really know?

"I'll do my best. But I'm not sure why I should go to Badakhshan. What's in Badakhshan? Besides rubies?"

Sitting down on the bed, now that he'd vacated it, Myamah smoothed the long tunic of her salwar-kemiss over her knees. "Rare treasures from the past to make your own. A princess bride, perhaps." She had weight to make up from the famine years, and not all of the pampering Jefferji sought to do had put the flesh back on her; so maybe it was never coming back, and she was just getting old. "A city, a citadel, a proud place in the king of Kabul's army. What may not await you in Badakhshan? You know what you have to do."

Yes. A Rajput rode out to make his fortune, and came back with riches and honor or not at all. That was what it meant to be a man, and the foster son of Jaisal Singh. Unless a man became a farmer instead. Or married the Divine consort and became the servant-spouse of a temple. Jefferji wasn't ready to be married to a farm *or* a temple.

"What do you know, Myamah?" He shouldn't have run away like a frightened antelope. He should have stayed at Bharaj and asked for more. But he wouldn't have seen Jaisal Begum, if he'd done that. Now he had a form of leave-taking, howsoever hurried and confused.

Myamah nudged him with her shoulder: *Listen, and I will tell you.* "Why should I know any more than you? There is a map. It may mean a trove of antiquities. Your Uncle Fontenoy does not grow any younger, and has no family to solace him in his old age. Therefore he goes to Badakhshan to seek old coins and statues, and bring them back to sell."

Myamah spoke the words sweetly, but Jefferji could tell that she shared his dismay at the proposed separation. Myamah put the best face on things, though, to reassure him. Myamah always did. Myamah always had.

"Then, when you return, he can make a good report of you at Holkar's court, and also to the British that he knows in Bombay and Madras and in Calcutta. A man with as many languages as you have is sure to be very valuable."

Positive notice in official circles, Fontenoy had said. "Myamah, what are you to do, if I go to Badakhshan?"

"How dare you speak to me about such trivial concerns?" But she patted his knee with gentle affection, comfortingly. "I may go visit my family village. I may take a pilgrimage. I've never been to bathe at Varanasi."

There was a ring of truth there that comforted Jefferji. She'd spoken with longing of pilgrimage places. He'd promised himself that he'd take her, once he had the where-withal. The money.

Fontenoy had talked about money. Jefferji thought there was good hope of finding some in Badakhshan, and that might be more lightly spent than an inheritance.

"Well, make me a program of your plans." It was going to be a wrench of no small proportions, leaving Myamah behind. There was no question of her following, though. It would be too cold. Jefferji had heard it said that snow lay on the ground from September to April in the north, and year-round in some of the mountain passes of the Hindu Kush. He'd never seen snow in its native habitat. He was curious about it. "I have to be able to find you, when I come back."

Myamah took his hand, and held it tightly. "See that you do." Do what? Come back. It was the first sign of emotion that had escaped her. "Now go to bed. One of the god's rooms is waiting for you, and I know that you have already washed. See if Sri Krsna will send a message in your dreams. It will be all right, Jefferji, truly, at least in time."

She didn't know that the god had fallen silent in his heart. Maybe the sleep-healing that the Hirpa temple had in store would mend the rift. Maybe it was to be of no use, but he had to try. Whatever happened, Captain Fontenoy would come, and Jefferji would leave. He'd go to Badakhshan, and by the

time he got back, maybe he'd be allowed to return to Tengarpore.

He kissed her on the cheek as he had every night for as long
as he could remember, but not as he had saluted Jaisal
Begum. There came a time when wondering what-ifs became
a pointless exercise because the only way to know what might
happen was to wait and see what did. Taking up the spare
butter-lamp from its shelf in Myamah's room, Jefferji closed
the door behind him, and made his way to where a bed
awaited him within the sanctuary of the Hirpa temple.

Chapter Three
The Wild High Places

A temple offered healing. That was part of what a temple meant. It was the residence of a god or goddess, it contained the resonance of the divine. Jefferji had confided in Old Fanum. Old Fanum knew as few others might the anguish in Jefferji's heart to find the Beloved gone from the statues—admittedly old, admittedly tawdry, if examined with unfriendly eyes—in which the god had dwelt with the divine Consort. Old Fanum had made special allowances.

So when Jefferji had changed into clean clothing for the second time today—out of respect for the presence of the god—it was to a cell-like room that shared a wall with the place in the sanctuary where the God himself reposed that Jefferji was brought, and shown to a plain bed, and left alone to meditate on his heart's loneliness.

There was a medicinal potion for prophetic dreams waiting for him in an old gold-washed cup, a potion compounded with honey and opium; Jefferji drank it down. Sitting for a while cross-legged on the bed, he opened up his heart as best he could and listened for the voice of his dear one. There was only the hush of the innermost sanctuary. Had he truly expected anything else, hope though he might? There was only desolation and loneliness. He lay down.

In the middle of the night he awoke, abruptly, with his heart pounding. Someone was here. Someone was in the room. Who was it? He strained his senses to the utmost, but he could hear nothing over the roaring of his own blood in his ears. There was nobody here. Clearly he'd been dreaming.

The little ghee lamp burned steady and true, and its nutty fragrance made him feel half-starved. When he'd been little, and it had been times of dearth and want, he could remember robbing the very lamps to drink their oily nectar, much to Myamah's outrage. He'd outgrown such gluttony and no longer cared to drink ghee from a lamp, but he was awake now, and he was cross about it. No dreams. No signs. No help.

There was a sovereign remedy for hunger pangs; he'd seen the older men resort to it when he'd been little and famine had laid over them. Opium armored the belly against the ache, opium could save the life of a man with the flux. He carried some with him wherever he went, done up in a cake and issued by the kitchens for the comfort of men and beast alike.

Perhaps that wasn't quite the way of it, Jefferji mused, hunting for a bit of opium cake on the bedside table, not finding any. Opium was for the comfort of men and *horses* alike. Pounded grain, raisins, ghee, and opium. He'd left his supplies with his saddlery. That was frustrating, but as his eyes grew more accustomed to the light he saw that hospitality had supplied the want after all. On the low table by the bed was water in a jug, a cup, and a little plate with raisins and almonds and sweet opium cake of the sort taken for dessert. Life was good.

Jefferji took the cake in one hand and the jug of water in the other, sitting up to lean his back against the wall and wonder what time of night it was. He could go out and see, but he felt foolish. The priests would fetch him out of here in the morning. The statues of Sri Krsna and his Consort had been closed reverently away. Sri Krsna slept.

The cake of opium fell into his lap and started him awake again. Checking for the water jug with a sudden horror of having spilled it in the bed Jefferji found to his relief that it was on the table, safe and sound. He must have put it down and fallen asleep for just the moment it had taken for the cake to drop out of his hand; he'd eaten very little of it, really.

So it was early in the night. He wasn't rested if he'd fallen asleep on such a small nibble of opium, but now he was awake and annoyed. How was he supposed to get himself to Peshawar? Well, with Captain Fontenoy, of course, but apart from that? All he really knew about Peshawar was that it lay on the Uttarapatha north of Lahore where Ranjit Singh made his capital. North of Amritsar. East of the Khyber Pass. South of Badakhshan. *Well, yes, north west north east, Jefferji*, he mocked himself impatiently. *No problem finding the place, then.*

Hadn't there been trouble through the Khyber Pass? Wasn't there always, unless the gatekeepers were paid off? Hadn't he heard that no man attempted the Khyber without the safe conduct of a small army? What had he been thinking? Was he out of his mind? He had no idea where he was going, why he was going, what he was going for. How he was meant to try out being English? What good would being English do him if he was to get himself lost in the high cold mountains, or killed by thieves on the road?

"You will go to Ferozepur like a sensible fellow," Guru-ji said, sounding a little cross. "If you can't find some British there, you can hire some Sikhs to accompany you to Amritsar, at least. You have money. Would Captain Fontenoy of fame suggest you meet him in Peshawar if there were any trick to it? And he doubtless knows all about the jewels. You must concentrate, Jefferji, concentrate."

It was so good to be scolded by his teacher that Jefferji almost didn't mind the scolding part. "Yes, Guru-ji," Jefferji said, sleepily. He tried to open his eyes, but he didn't seem to be able to, no matter how he wished to see Guru-ji.

It had been Guru-ji who had first taught him to dance, and to understand the terrible joy he felt when Sri Krsna touched his heart. Jaisal Singh had hired a replacement dancing-master for Hirpa, some years ago, because he'd seen the advantages that the education had given Jefferji in combat as well as in the service of the god. The suppleness of movement, the muscles of the body moving in harmony.

Why had Jaisal Singh hired a new teacher? Because Guru-ji was dead. That was right. A heaviness in his lungs had taken him three years, four years ago. "As if that made the least bit of difference," Guru-ji grumbled. "Now listen well. I have something very important to tell you."

Jefferji strained to open his eyes, and could not. He shook

himself awake with a ferocious effort, but Guru-ji had gone. There was a wide lake of green wheat blowing in a cold wind around his knees as far as the eye could see, and angry clouds black with thunder all around.

It didn't seem to matter. The rain would come, the grain would drink, and all would be well. Hearing a noise of some sort coming at him from behind Jefferji turned, but not quickly enough to avoid being knocked flat on his back on the wheat-cushioned earth. There was a beast, with its paw on his chest; he couldn't breathe. A lion. The lion on the regimental medal, perhaps? It shook its head above him where he lay, and roared; its breath smelled oddly of green herbs and tobacco.

Then it lowered its great head and looked into his eyes with an intelligence that seemed almost human, opened its massy jaws and plunged its teeth into his chest. He could feel the sharp cold stabbing of the beast's great fangs, slicing though tissue, shredding his lungs, striking straight toward his heart with inexorable deliberation. Jefferji closed his eyes, afraid, but it didn't seem to hurt. There was some power in the great beast's teeth that resonated with Jefferji in quite a different manner.

He held his breath, waiting, waiting for the beast to pierce him to the heart and let all of the pain there drain away, and not wanting the pain to leave him. When at last he felt the stabbing of those teeth into his heart his entire body convulsed in a spasm of grateful relief. He woke, to his chagrin, to find himself still sitting up in bed, wondering what time it was. Disgusting.

Guru-ji was here, now, really here, with his old red shawl around his shoulders, rocking back and forth as he sat on the floor of the little room. "You bleed," Guru-ji said. His eyes were wide and staring, the whites unnervingly bright in his dark face. "Oh, my dear Jefferji. The lion waits to cut you to your heart."

At a loss to understand what was going on Jefferji cleared his throat and bowed to his teacher, somehow eye-to-eye with him although Guru-ji sat on his worn red damask cushion and Jefferji on the bed. "Good-morning, Guru-ji," Jefferji said politely. "Have you slept well, my master?"

Guru-ji cried out in anguish, as though the sound of Jefferji's voice gave him physical pain. Cried out, and then was silent. Behind Jefferji, between him and the wall as though there were no bed there, slim luscious Parvati rose with a fragrance of sandalwood, commanding Jefferji's attention as she ever did with every movement of her body. Where had she been? Jefferji knew her perfume; there'd been no trace of it in the air of his cell.

"The teacher has not slept for three days," she said. "The god himself is occluded in the temple. This morning between midnight and dawn the doors to the god's house burst open, and the statue for worship toppled to the ground."

The monsoon season with its heat and its humidity could have unpredictable effects on wood and on the stone that balanced atop it accordingly. If Guru-ji had had a dream, if there had been a disturbance in the temple, if so small a thing should happen as the boys failing to obtain sufficient fuel to keep a drying fire burning in the sanctuary day and night, there could well have been more dankness in the sacred place than there should have been.

Jefferji had been well schooled by Parsi devotees of the physical sciences to see the miraculous hand of God working in the world through regular and discernable cause and effect of transcendent physical laws. Still this word of statues toppling in the middle of the night made his blood run cold in his veins.

"What has the teacher dreamt?" Jefferji asked Parvati, low-voiced and full of dread.

"I saw my chela," Guru-ji replied. Although Jefferji sat in front of him, he didn't look at Jefferji, but rather past him, as though he gazed into a leafless winter forest rather than at the stone wall of a small room. So persuasive was the image that Jefferji had to struggle not to look back over his shoulder, to make sure.

"As proud as a young stag he stood in the meadows of the high Pamir, the great plateau between the mountains and the cold vast plain that rolls away forever. And the lion came dressed in a woolen garment with boots upon his feet, walking upright like a man. But he had claws and great rending teeth, and when he took his prey the stag knelt down in the tall grass and offered up his throat to the lion, and at that moment I could hear a voice."

There were musical modes and preferred songs for every kind of music Jefferji had ever heard in temple, language without words through which a man could know the nature of the dance that was called for before he heard the title or the words. Guru-ji spoke little, but everything he said was in cadence, and he could burst into a song of praise for the Dark One within a phrase or two regardless of what he might have started out to say.

"'He goes into the mountains,' the voice said."

Jefferji knew the rhythm of Guru-ji's recitation. Guru-ji spoke as if of an upcoming wedding, rather than the nightmare he seemed to be experiencing.

"It was the voice of a god that I heard, a voice with the sound of a river at its flood. 'He goes and he returns, but he never will come back. The dancer goes to meet the holy music. Goodbye, Jefferji. You will always please me, when you dance.' That is what the god said, Jefferji. You rose up bleeding but in triumph from the grass, and there was a shining in the antlers of the stag that could not be looked upon."

Jefferji didn't know what he could possibly say in response to this fantastic recitation. "It is true that I go north to cross the mountains," Jefferji said, placing his words slowly and with care. "But not to seek the god in lion form, Guru-ji. I do not understand your dream."

He almost thought that he didn't want to understand it. There was no denying that it sounded ominous. Guru-ji shook his head slowly, as if to say *Nor do I*, then fixed his eyes on Jefferji's face, looking at him, now, and not the imaginary forest beyond.

"You'll know him by the hawk who stands beside him," Guru-ji said. "A red one, almost golden, but its eyes are as dark as blood, and she has wisdom of which she herself is innocent. The lion does not mean you any harm, of this I am convinced. But neither stag nor man can suffer the embrace of the divine and walk away."

Taking up a handful of dust from the bare earth Guru-ji sprinkled it over his old grey head in uttermost desolation. "You are going away, my chela," Guru-ji said. Where had he gotten the dust? The floor was covered with matting. "Sri Krsna mourns. Oh, Jefferji, my child, my child."

His teacher was clearly distraught, and as much as Jefferji wished to comfort him he couldn't help but feel that the old man was overreacting. It was perfectly clear about the lion and the biting. The lion was the English and everything they stood for, the teeth were his fear that he would not find a place either here or in Peshawar, the warm welcome release of his heart's-blood his secret fervent conviction that he would find a sanctuary and be welcomed there. Obvious.

Only his teacher would not leave off rocking back and forth on the floor and grieving, and Parvati had apparently gotten up and gone away.

"Sri Krsna cannot save you from this. Oh, my child, it is your fate, and he has loved you. Never again. Never again. Never again. You dance for fierce and more pagan gods, now, Jefferji. You will return from the wild high places but you will never come back—never again—never again."

"Never again will I trust even so simple a task to that idiot boy," a priest that Jefferji didn't recognize said, as if he were agreeing. Jefferji awoke with a brutal start, and lay on his back trying to collect his wits. What had his teacher said?

"This is quite unacceptable. My sincere apologies, young lord, I'll have the boy beaten in the morning if you like, but it will do no good."

Something about the lamp. Jefferji shivered, although the room was warm enough to raise the sweat on Jefferji's face. The priest nodded, as if he understood exactly what Jefferji was shivering about. The cooler air rushing in through the now-open door, perhaps. Clearing the atmosphere of dreams. Yes. No? Jefferji wished the priest would share his arcane knowledge, but the priest—Ramji, that was right— was no help.

"See, here, there is a crack in the lamp, and the ghee has run out of the bottom. I'll have it replaced in the morning, and I'm deeply sorry, young sir. Can I bring you a cup of water? Do you want for anything to help you sleep?"

There was neither carafe nor dish of opium cake on the table, only the empty cup of sacred wine with a leaf to cover it. Jefferji shook his head, not wanting to speak and break the spell. To his relief Ramji seemed satisfied. "Then I will leave you. Sleep and dream, young sir, may Sri Krsna grant you what you seek."

The room was dark now, without the lamp. Jefferji pulled the thin sheet up close to his chest and stared into the darkness, trying to catch it all in his mind, trying to snare the dream before it could slip away. A lion. The wild high places. Guru-ji. Never to dance for Sri Krsna again. *But I will always dance for you in my heart*, Jefferji thought, as fiercely as he could. *Always.*

There was a whispering, with a faint sound of a flute so beautiful that there was no arguing with it. *Goodbye, Jefferji, my beloved. Thank you for your dance. You are to hear a music that will exalt you, but not from me.*

The touch of the god, even to say goodbye, struck Jefferji down with love and tenderness. He closed his eyes and slept, and the next thing he knew it was morning.

Jefferji awoke, blinking sharply twice in the golden glow of the replaced ghee lamp, trying to understand what had brought him here up from the depths of his dreaming. There had been dreams. He knew there had been. Something about Guru-ji, and Ferozepur, and Peshawar, stags and lions. That made no sense. And the longed-for voice of Sri Krsna had brought him no comfort.

He couldn't lie in bed puzzling it out, though. He had places to go and things to do, and he had to go out into the jangal behind the compound walls to do them—that was where the latrine building was. He hoped he was in good time, before the sun rose.

On his way back, Jefferji stepped into the court that separated the temple dormitories from the kitchens to pump ice-cold water over the back of his neck, splashing it into his face, rinsing his mouth. The pump drew from a well that ran deep into the bosom of the hillside; the goddess of the spring it tapped was remembered on feast days as the protector of the Hirpa Temple and its people. Water that rose of her own will to the parched lips of an aged and impoverished temple was worth a tribute in silver in and of itself. He took another mouthful from the pump mouth, just to taste. Who knew when he would drink water that sweet again?

In the winter months, when he had come early or stayed late with Guru-ji, there was always a pan of water warmed over the fire waiting in the kitchen so that the son of Jaisal Singh could wash his face. He'd told them and told them that he was no such thing. They had simply shrugged.

He hadn't wanted to let them take him for something he was not, even though he was as tall as Jaisal Singh, and as green-eyed as a Pathan, and could sometimes be mistaken for the lord of Tengarpore in the twilight. That would have been an abuse of hospitality. So year after year he made his protest, even when it had become obvious that they weren't listening to him.

Year after year they only asked him, gently, whether or not he was the dancer-before-god Hari-Prasad who was also called Jefferji Tamisen, from the household of Jaisal Singh. That, he had been unable to deny.

And maybe it was just as well. The British could come, now that someone had claimed an interest after all these years, to accuse them of having conspired to smuggle a young British orphan out of their hands. But if that happened anyone here only need say that someone wearing a custom like that of Jaisal Singh, of a height and a habit of movement and riding a Marwari horse in the manner only permitted to princes, had left the Hirpa temple toward the Udaipore road, and that nothing more was known of him.

That would only work if Fontenoy came to claim him before any British did, so Jefferji would have to rely on Jaisal Begum to put as many obstacles in their way—in that event— as she could. Her husband was dying: nobody was to leave Tengarpore. Her husband was dead: the gates were closed, and could not be opened again within nine days' time, a Hindu custom in a Rajput house. It would be enough. Maybe no British would even come.

Myamah had risen before him—when had she ever not?— and was waiting for him in the doorway to one of the kitchen's side rooms. She had breakfast waiting. Through the open doorway into the kitchen, Jefferji could see the early shift of cooking staff at their tasks, while the spice grinder worked his magic for the good of all who came to partake of the Hirpa temple's bounty.

One of the men happened to catch Jefferji's eye, and blushed. Jefferji grinned at him cheerfully. Birlar loved Sri Krsna with as pure and heartfelt a passion as any gopi of Vrindavan. And based on Jefferji's direct experience as the surrogate recipient of that adoration, he was convinced that Birlar was headed straight to a cushion at the lotus feet of the beautiful god when the time came for him to transcend mortality.

With Birlar in the breakfast kitchen, Jefferji was happily not surprised that there were eggs with their intense golden-yellow yolks, and plenty of them. But there was also chicken stewed to delectable savor, with lentils and eggplant and cubes of fresh paneer cheese.

That was a more universal signal of fondness and affection, because Birlar was not in charge of who was offered chicken, and who not. Nor was he responsible for the steaming jug of hot black tea boiled with peppercorns and sweetened with sugar and milk, and a vegetable curry, and flatbread and rice and pickles both sweet and savory.

So they were feeding him up. That meant everybody knew that he was leaving and that he didn't want to. Jefferji didn't mind. The famine was passed away from the land. He had an adventure to face, once Captain Fontenoy arrived.

Myamah had cooked Jefferji's breakfast almost every morning of his life. When he was away from Tengarpore he would have to fend for himself. He knew how to cook, of course. Jaisal Singh sent his young men out into the field on their own with grooms and arms-masters with them, to teach them to find forage for their horses, tinder and fuel for the fire, as comfortable a place to sleep as could be made out of the stony ground. A warrior was expected to be responsible for his own needs.

A Rajput was not a Pindari, to steal from the poorest people, traveling with women as rapacious and cruel as themselves. A Rajput was an honorable man, drew steel only against other fighting men, paid for what he needed, and went without if he could not find his dinner for himself. That was what a Rajput was. What was an Englishman?

Under Myamah's watchful eye Jefferji ate as much as he could stomach and then a little more. She looked at him as though to store him up by staring, to fix an image in her mind's eye that would sustain her after he was gone.

She could have lived a life of idleness and comfort; she had nursed Madhu Singh. Instead she had nursed *him* from infancy while his mother lay at death's door, suffering the injuries that the child of a man could wreak on the body of a woman in its birthing. Myamah had nursed him ever since, made a place for him in bachelor's quarters when his mother had died, fought battles for him as fiercely as any bear. What kind of life did she face, without him?

"You should ask the priests to buy you a girl," he said. It was time to get dressed and get on with the physically and emotionally draining business of standing around waiting for Captain Fontenoy. "Someone to look after you. When I come back I will marry her, and you shall have babies to spoil to your heart's content."

He could see her lips twitch in a familiar gesture, *You are being clever and you are not as clever as you think, oh beloved child.* Before she could speak, though, someone called to him from the courtyard outside the kitchen.

"There is a British just now arrived, Jefferji. Alone." Whoever it was sounded dubious and cautious, so Jefferji knew there was a potential problem. "He is asking for you. He says that his name is Holyoke, that he has been sent by Captain Fontenoy."

Jefferji couldn't tell whether Holyoke—hadn't that been the man traveling with Fontenoy, the one he and his brothers had encountered in Bharaj?—was also actually outside in the courtyard. Myamah clearly knew what she thought about the whole thing, though; her mouth went through some tightening, her forehead creased in a fierce scowl.

"Jefferji is having his morning meal," she called back, clearly and firmly. "A man must not be disturbed. Where is this person called Holyoke now? Tell him to wait."

She was accustomed to having her way with him, but she wasn't in a position to speak for the Hirpa temple, and Jefferji was curious about why Fontenoy wasn't here with Holyoke. What would he do if Holyoke had been suborned by the British with designs on Tengarpore? Well, he'd run into sanctuary, he supposed, or refuse to answer, and make his way to Peshawar as best he could by himself. Not very well, then. But he'd find a way to manage. He hoped.

Wiping his mouth in good English fashion Jefferji stood up from the table, and made a namaste toward Birlar in the kitchen, and to the kitchen in general. "Thank you all," he called through to them. "I am truly a prince this morning."

If he looked at Myamah she would argue with him, so he didn't. Two could take advantage of their long acquaintance.

Ducking his head beneath the too-low lintel of the door into the courtyard, Jefferji was glad to see only the temple servant there. Not someone he recognized. The Hirpa temple prospered, and could afford to feed more acolytes and support staff month by month. It was good, if it made him a little melancholy, seeing so much that was unfamiliar in the place where he had learned to dance and love the Dark One. When the Dark One had loved him.

"I'll go greet the God," Jefferji said. "The English may want breakfast. I'll find him once I've paid my respects." He would have gone out of the courtyard to the freshly swept ambulatory, and turned toward the front of the temple, but the servant put his hand out to Jefferji's arm to make him wait.

"Just one thing, though, Jefferji," the servant said. It was a familiar term of address, perhaps, but they were all servants of the Hirpa temple and Jefferji didn't mind. "There is also a woman come to greet the god. Just so you aren't taken by surprise."

Making the face of a man receiving information and appreciating it—with the "but I'm not sure why I needed to know this" hidden away, since by definition the man was sure that Jefferji had needed to know it, or he wouldn't have said anything in the first place—Jefferji nodded thanks. This time the servant nodded with a relieved smile, and Jefferji was allowed to go his way.

He hurried up the steps into the temple, passing a few servants on his way. They greeted him politely as he went past. Washing his face and hands in the little trickle of ever-running water at the top of the stairs, Jefferji went through.

Two men stood to one side of the temple's main doorway where there had been men of Tengarpore last night, but there was only one worshipper within—a widow, dressed in white from hand to foot. The one of whose presence Jefferji had been warned. Nothing to do with him.

Jefferji bowed with formal precision just inside the temple's hall, focusing his energy on his hands palm-to-palm in front of his face. *I am here, Dark One, your servant Jefferji.* The familiar energy of the temple calmed and nourished him as he went forward. He was comforted just in being here, lonely though it had become for him.

Stepping up to the knee-high stone screen that stood between Sri Krsna and his people to keep the god's space sacred, Jefferji put his hands before him once again. He had many things to say to Sri Krsna. But as he tried to collect his thoughts—where was he to begin?—he found himself distracted by the widow, who had come up to stand beside him at an arm's length and pray out loud. What was she saying?

"You have answered my plea, oh my Beloved. You have brought me a husband who is honorable and good, and goes forth to raise an army."

People didn't actually do that, anymore. The British had dispersed the Pindaris and forced the Maratha Confederacy to terms, and now they had taken Kabul for Shah Shooja, and were widely understood to be moving on Herat. Perhaps Persia. And a husband? A widow talking out loud about remarrying? Jefferji frowned, to concentrate his mind by concentrating his muscles.

I have come to leave Myamah in your care, to whom I owe much for the love that she has shown me. Let her eat yoghurt and honey, my Beloved, let the cold not trouble her joints, let her have gossip and a warm place in the sun in winter, a cool place in the shade when the hot weather comes, a dry place always. And without ants. I will buy her a girl to do her wash.

The woman beside him spoke aloud again, and again it broke his concentration. "You have made him strong and tall, celebrated in name, a servant in your temple. He will bring honor to my house. By your benevolence he has been raised as a prince among us."

It was impossible not to listen, now. Jefferji turned his head to hear her better, almost despite himself. By the wisps of silver that only just barely showed at her temples she was surely nearly twenty-eight years old. Her head covering of white gossamer cloth sat far enough back from her face to reveal her hairline, and she had a perfectly bewitching hair-line, as softly curved above her brow as the dark sky against the curve of a waning moon. He couldn't help but notice that.

"He honors me with rich gifts, jewels of great age and renown. Truly it is a match worthy of my family, and my dead husband cannot complain that I have brought his name down in the world's estimation."

Oh, now Jefferji understood. He could stop this here and now—no. He could not stop this. People were watching, even if it was just her two attendants and a few priests. Jaisal Begum meant to place her kinswoman under Jefferji's protection. If he rejected her before the god and the divine Consort, what would become of Jaisal Begum's careful plan-ning?

Jefferji lifted palms now pressed together with new deter-mination, and spoke out loud. He had developed his peripheral vision. It was a requirement of art. It wasn't as good as looking directly at her, but it would do to grasp the outlines of her reaction. If he thought hard about it he could half-believe that he smelled her perfume.

"You provide for your servant far beyond my merit," Jefferji said. "You grant it to me to honor and protect a chaste and noble woman of wisdom as brave as she is beautiful, the jewel of her ancient lineage." Of course she was. Whoever she was. It was only polite to say so. "But how dare I ask such a woman to be wife to an empty bed? I am going away."

"I am betrothed," she told the god. "I am shielded by the honor of Tengarpore itself, that protects its own. I will not be forced to sell my body and my husband's farm in marriage to an unworthy husband to keep my people from starving. For this I bless forever the name of the man that you have sent me, whether he joins with me in body or not."

If only his senses weren't so beguiled by the teasing, float-ing alchemical intoxication of her perfume. "She is a Rajput and a warrior," Jefferji told the god. "Devout in heart and deed, the defender of what has been left to her in trust. I am honored to be admitted into her presence, through no merit but yours, Dark One. May all of the vexations of her life melt away like frost upon the grass. May she prosper in peace and plenty until my fate brings me back to gaze upon her face."

And may she take what husband she desires, as best pleases her own will and pleasure. That he couldn't say out loud. In the language of courtship, that was a harsh and unforgiving rejection, tearing up a figurative contract and throwing its pieces into the fire. That would ruin everything.

She was turning to face him, so he turned as well. She had dark eyes, and the sort of mouth that always seemed to smile. She was smiling now. Raising her hands in the position of prayer until the tips of her fingers touched her forehead, she closed her eyes, abruptly, and bowed, smiling all the while.

When she had straightened up and opened her eyes he bowed to her, returning her salute in full measure. When he came back, if he came back, it would be worth much to win the regard of such a woman—but by his own effort, and not as due to him out of mere dutiful gratitude.

Then she turned around and went away, holding one side of the fine shawl draped over her head up to the corner of her ear where lobe met throat, as if to beckon him and send him on his way with the same gesture. Jefferji watched her elegantly proportioned feet in their white shoes as she walked across the stone floor of the temple hall, fascinated. How had she known to come here, and so early in the morning? Where was her farm? Had some messenger been dispatched before Jaisal Begum had even left Hirpa?

It was quiet in the temple with the woman gone. He could hear people praying softly all around him as they came to pay their morning respects to the god. He could hear the beating of his heart, the breath in his nostrils, the click and tap of priests arranging the offerings—flowers, fruit, sweets, milk—to feast Krsna and his divine Consort. Nothing else. Sri Krsna was silent in Jefferji's heart, but the silence was quiet and melancholy. There was no hint of anger, disappointment, rebuke, disapproval. There was nothing at all.

Finally Jefferji gave up on praying and went out to find out what Lieutenant Holyoke had to say; to talk to Old Fanum about what he was to do with the gems Jaisal Begum had left with him last night; to see what Coriander had to say to him after leaving her on the road to Hirpa, and make arrangements for a girl to fetch and carry for Myamah, when Jefferji was gone.

Broderick had saddled and taken the Udaipore road for the Hirpa temple as soon as Captain Fontenoy had given him his assignment. Gunnery could bear the additional weight of the boy guide the Bharaj temple had recommended to him easily, but for himself Broderick could hardly wait to be rid of the distasteful proximity of a dirty beggar boy behind him on Gunnery's back. It reminded him too much of someone he'd known, the "Bung-Hole Boy" that had once been.

He'd ridden while there was light to see, and arisen unusually early on the following morning impelled by a combination of desires: to get to the Hirpa temple and thence to Peshawar as quickly as possible; and to be away from the room the boy guide had found for him in the caravanserai at Minarch, with its filth, and the vermin in the bedding, and the stink of native cooking coming in on all sides through the uncovered windows.

Fontenoy had all but promised silence on the matter of the rumors held against him with respect to the irregularities in the mess accounts, which was a significant consideration worthy of his utmost effort on the one hand, and actually rather funny on the other. In Bombay, they were apparently convinced that the hint of conduct unbecoming an officer and a gentleman was an unbearable burden to bear. If they knew some truths about him, irregularities in the mess accounts would be the least of his worries.

The day was clear, and the air warmed quickly. The boy had left Broderick at the fork in the Udaipore road, taking his bit of gold with a good enough grace, as well he might. Broderick had included more generous a tip than he might have done had he had more by way of spare change.

Now, as Gunnery trotted east toward the hill the boy had pointed out, Broderick stared out over the rocky ground, the meager vegetation, the lonely little trees twisted with hardship and yet still brave with green leaves. He felt a curious pang of tenderness. There was nothing of Madras or green Gujarat to this landscape. How could he feel kinship?

Was it simply that this wretched waste of land—the green leaves of its wild trees concealing their sharp thorns, the constant companionship of rocks and dust—was his own life reflected in landscape? He was a bare-twigged milkweed bush, miserable, stunted, standing by itself, neither seeking nor expecting any help. If not for the bitterness of its sap, it would be eaten by goats, even by camels. It was bitterness that saved its life. There was a lesson in that, Broderick felt, of sublime complexity.

Madhu Singh, who would inherit Tengarpore and its lands and people from his father—Geoffrey Tamisen's father as well, for all Broderick knew, though he had private doubts about the exact relationship between Tamisen and Captain Fontenoy— had been born acacia-thorn, not milkweed. He'd had armor given him from infancy. He knew nothing of the bitterness of surviving by becoming too unpleasant to bother with.

Broderick had never had the luxury of a father. Oh, he'd had a sire, there was no question of that, nor that his sire and his mother had been properly married by an ordained minister, and eleven months before he was born as well. The story got a little confused after that. Milkweed stood alone, fatherless, penniless. Milkweed neither hated nor wished to harm; milkweed simply wanted to be left alone to make its own way in the world as best it could. Nobody chose to be milkweed.

But when the moment came for the seed pod to burst, milkweed cracked open to free a fantastic flight of gossamer angels, fairies, seeds born on the silkiest of kites to catch the wind. Like the piss-a-beds of Broderick's childhood, the dandelion with its white cotton whirligigs, only a thousand times more soft and pure, gleaming and beautiful.

Gunnery had slowed his pace to climb the hill, finding his track carefully. It was more rutted where streams of rainwater had rushed downhill over the years than it had been on the flatter surface behind them. Up ahead, gleaming, with the sun breaking over its compound walls, Broderick could see the ornate dome and tower of a Hindu temple, whitewashed, all but glowing in the morning light.

The slope flattened out as the road neared the top of the hill. There were green trees, the scent of flowers gentle on a welcome little breeze. Broderick laid the loose ends of the reins briskly across Gunnery's shoulders left and right to get the stupid brute's attention. *A little faster, please. Remember who is your master.* It was nothing personal. Gunnery was a good brute and Broderick had no complaint to make of him, but Broderick was in a hurry.

The gates were open and there were the message runners seated there at their ease. Broderick considered riding up to the temple steps—because he'd found out early on that it was resented, which made it a good joke—but he had to be on his best behavior, because he meant to keep Tamisen in a cooperative mood on their way to Peshawar. A month, they'd told him. He was going to have to bring Tamisen along for that long.

People told him that a Marwari horse was made of iron and could wear out horseshoes in a single night's ride, too, but Broderick had begged leave from the uncaring universe to see for himself, of course. If it was going to take Broderick and Gunnery a month to make Peshawar, the less Tamisen and his ugly Marwari mare delayed him, the better.

One of the runners stood up as Broderick approached, coming forward to take Gunnery's cheek strap whilst Broderick dismounted for a good stretch. "And what name, Lieutenant, sahib?" the runner asked, his English heavily accented but intelligible. "Please. I will have the horse tended."

"I'm to meet Tamisen here," Broderick said. "Geoffrey Tamisen? Ah, Jefferji?" Unpleasant fellow, the temple servant. Clearly he knew who Tamisen was. "And some breakfast wouldn't go amiss, while I'm waiting." Gunnery would enjoy a rubdown, and might even get some nice bran mash out of the bargain.

Gunnery was going to need his strength. Broderick had no interest in spending the night here. The sooner he could get Tamisen away, isolate Tamisen from any outside points of contact—God forbid any British—the better he would be able to develop some influence over Tamisen that could prove useful when Broderick came to deal with Fontenoy again.

The runner said something to one of the others as one of them came forward to replace the first man at the gates. Guard post rotation; Broderick approved.

Someone had notified an official of some sort, who came hurrying over the wide paved courtyard to meet Broderick as the runner led Gunnery off to stables. "For Tamisen, they say, officer? And breakfast. By all means." Much better English. "Come with me, if you please."

Not quite. Close. It should be just "please," but that was a point of idiom. There was a world of difference between "please" and "if you please," if this jumped-up functionary but knew it. He followed the official toward a little park that stood east of the temple itself. A nice lawn, a bit of a watercourse even, servants running to place chairs and a table.

"Very nice," Broderick agreed. He could see more servants coming at the run; his breakfast, he hoped. He was almost certain he saw a teapot, a chocolate pot, and a coffee pot, each with its own carrier. They meant to treat him well. But the food?

Meager little eggs in a sauce spiced with one of those infernal mixtures that found their way into everything a native touched unless they were watched carefully enough. Half of an underfed chicken, probably tough, covered with a thick glutenous gravy peppered and sweetened with an over-generous hand; one of those mealy lentil dishes, altogether too much of that flavorless local cheese, dishes of the local pickle. Flatbread. Rice that looked as though it had seen better days.

Broderick sighed and set to. He'd be expected to leave a donation for his meal, after all. A man ate when he could, whether or not it was a decent dish of mutton and potatoes.

There was a cigar for afters, carried out to him as he sat in his chair drinking coffee gone cold and admiring the dappled light. And finally—after taking his own good time, Broderick thought—here was Tamisen, no, not in any particular hurry. There was a servant behind Tamisen with another beverage service, and another servant behind that servant with another side table to set the beverage service on.

"Lieutenant Holyoke," Tamisen called out to him. "A surprise, Lieutenant. Have you come to help me wait for Captain Fontenoy?"

A good question, an intelligent question, and a good opening. "In fact yes," Broderick called back, not so loudly, as Tamisen came closer. "In a manner of speaking. You've had your breakfast, have you? There's been a change of plan."

Not the best news Tamisen had heard, Broderick surmised, but a man had to learn to accept disappointment. It took the servants a minute or two to set up their second beverage service: Tamisen was having tea. Broderick decided to get right to the point.

"Captain Fontenoy, in fact, is in receipt of new orders, as I understand. Yesterday morning. You had taken off—you had left already, or we would have all gone together, but as it is he asked me to come and bring you to Peshawar with me."

Had Tamisen heard him? Had Tamisen understood? Tamisen took his tea in a Chinese bowl, blowing on it to cool it with his head bent. He was bareheaded. There'd be a delay while he finished dressing, then.

"I see," Tamisen said. "Well. You and I to Peshawar, then. I hope you know the route. Have you been to Peshawar before?"

There was a subtle note of uncertainty in Tamisen's voice, but Broderick judged it to be associated with the change of plan, rather than with the prospect of Broderick's company. Tamisen didn't know Broderick. He didn't know anything about Broderick. Did he? Had Fontenoy put a flea in Tamisen's ear? And, of possibly even more interest, had Fontenoy told Tamisen anything about the treasury of Dost Mohammed Khan?

"No, I have not." That would be an open, honest, persuasive admission. True. "I've some notes in my memorandum book, though, the best references. And we can get any help we need from one of our outposts—ah, excuse me, I meant to say British outposts—as we go." Contacts that Broderick would minimize, needless to say. Fontenoy might not have said anything to anybody, but it would be better not to presume that no rumors had followed Broderick from Bombay.

"We go right away, then, I would expect." Tamisen hadn't finished his bowl of tea, but he was right along Broderick's path even so. "Is that what you would recommend? I'll have to see to Coriander. And pack a few things."

No tiresome appeals for further explanations, or for a little reassurance. It made Broderick inclined to like the man more than he had earlier. He considered that favorable impression, and then put it in quarantine for future consideration. There was no sense in rushing to judgment.

"Good." Broderick made a point of examining his cigar, as if to judge how much longer it would take him to finish it. "Shall we meet in... where? The courtyard? Two hours? You'll be doing some leave-taking, I presume. I'll be waiting."

Tamisen pushed away from the table—carefully lifting his chair so as not to tear up the beautifully tended lawn—and turned away. Without comment. Not a man to waste words. That was going to be a good thing, Broderick decided, because they were going to be a month on the road with only each other for company.

It was a good start, all in all.

Broderick settled himself for a little bit of a nap while he waited for Tamisen to get his affairs in order and they could get on their way.

　　　　　　　　　▲

"I'm not happy about it, either, Myamah," Jefferji said. They were alone together in her room. She was confident, now, that she knew how to wrap the pagri turban he'd be wearing until they'd gotten a few days north, he and Broderick Holyoke. "But we'll both have to make the best of it, I'm afraid, and I'll be seeing Captain Fontenoy soon enough."

"I do not need looking after," she said. "And hold still." She was stitching the folds of Jaisal Singh's pagri turban, tiny little stitches at intervals. He needed to be able to take it off at night and put it back on again in the morning, and have it look as though he'd wrapped it himself with a confident hand.

But what did she mean, looking after? Oh. The girl. The one he'd suggested she would need to be her helping hands, when he was gone. Her voice was steady, and very firm indeed; he'd insulted her, then.

"Do not forget that a woman is a warrior too. You are to go out into the world, Jefferji, and find your kingdom. When you have won it you will send for me with elephants or I shall not come at all."

She'd had children of her own body, even if they had been taken from her by sickness or by want, each before its third year. He should have remembered. It was as she said: she was as Rajput as Jaisal Begum herself, and a veteran worthy of respect for the wounds her body had sustained and the scars she carried from childbearing and childbirth. "Five elephants," Jefferji said. "And a howdah of solid gold. And drums."

The pagri tied to her satisfaction, Myamah stepped away, handing him a light blue sleeveless coat suitable for the hot weather. He had one arm halfway into it when she reached out suddenly and caught him close to her; Jefferji returned the embrace with a full heart, knowing that it could be their last in the breathing world.

"Only make me proud," she said. "Prove your upbringing to the world, noble, brave, and true. I will come on a donkey. On an ass. Barefoot, if I have to, so see that you stay clear of the rains, if I'm not to have an elephant. Only keep yourself well, my child, I ask for nothing more."

He wouldn't promise what he wasn't sure he could fulfill. A Rajput redeemed a promise unfulfilled with his own blood, and that would rather defeat the purpose of promising to stay well.

Myamah helped Jefferji settle his coat across his shoulders, following him out of her room and into the temple courtyard. He could see Coriander waiting for him, Holyoke, Old Fanum. And he needed a word with Old Fanum that he hadn't managed, last night.

Myamah handed him the box in which she had always packed his noon meal when he went off to see his Guru-ji. It was heavy. There would be boiled sweets of milk and anise seed. She accepted a kiss on the cheek, but then—standing on her dignity, or perhaps not willing to trust herself to prolong this parting further—she turned away, as if to get out of the sun.

He didn't want to say goodbye. He didn't know whether he could find words. She'd taken that out of his hands, her back as straight as walls of red sandstone, her head held as high as that of any queen.

How could he do less?

He handed the lunch box off to one of the temple boys and went to greet Old Fanum, there in the courtyard trying in vain to engage the English Lieutenant Holyoke in conversation. Old Fanum didn't seem to be getting very far. As Jefferji got closer it became clear that while Holyoke could speak some usable Urdu, his command of the language was restricted to that required to make his own needs known and his instructions understood. Come. Go. Bring.

When he saw Jefferji, Holyoke nodded—with what Jefferji thought was exasperation, howsoever politely muted—and stepped away toward a tall grey gelding with fine thoroughbred lines; his own horse, clearly enough. Old Fanam turned toward Jefferji with a look of irritated frustration, one that he made no attempt to disguise—the privilege of the old, as he'd explained to Jefferji more than once.

"Truly an ox," Old Fanam said, and the Lieutenant betrayed no reaction whatever. "British officers these days have no education."

It was an old complaint, one Jefferji that knew from experience would require no response.

Jefferji made a respectful namaste. "I'm glad I found you again. I have a favor to ask. I need to put some money out to hire." Old Fanum would know why. "Can you help me?"

Glancing around them quickly—no one was nearby, it was just the three of them, and Holyoke wasn't looking—Jefferji pulled the leather pouch Jaisal Begum had given him last night out of his bosom, and opened its mouth to let spill its contents into his hand.

Blinking, Old Fanam took Jefferji's hand to raise it toward his face; where he could see the jewels better, presumably. "I wanted more time with these, last night," Old Fanum said. "Ah, yes. Your patrimony. And generously supplemented, at that. Did she tell you, Jefferji? This beautiful emerald comes to you from Tengarpore, and no widowed kinswoman about it."

Interesting. Old Fanam spoke with authority. He'd clearly seen these jewels before, possibly in his role as witness to contractual transactions.

"I don't care to carry these with me, revered father. Can you take them as collateral, and give me notes for spending money on the way? That way they would be staying at home. Where they'd be safe."

Still holding Jefferji's hand palm uppermost Old Fanam

turned the stones one way and another with his thumb, admiring the flash when a facet caught the light. "Oh, I'm sorry, Jefferji. Truly I am. I don't have the wherewithal to take this on pledge. We have no security, you know, and boys thirsty for God can run right up over the walls into the temple as easily as though there were no walls at all."

Old Fanam's barb was pointed. Jefferji blushed, and hoped Holyoke didn't notice from the little distance at which he stood.

"I'm sure they'd be safer here than around my neck. Look at them, they frighten me. I've never seen so much money in my life."

Tengarpore was not rich. During the worst of the famine years, Jaisal Singh had melted down his grandfather's chased armor for its gold to buy grain for starving farmers. And all that time Jaisal Begum had held these gems in trust for Jefferji from his dead mother and father. Rajput honor could be a fearful thing. If Jefferji had known—

"Put them away," Old Fanam said, folding Jefferji's fingers down around them. "You can get to Churu in ten, fourteen days. Ask for the Krsna priest in the street of jewelers. He may be able to hold them for you, but truly, Jefferji, I'm sorry. Hirpa couldn't cover the loss. And we dare not risk the British coming to hear of them, and taking your inheritance to themselves. In your best interest, to keep them safe for you, of course," Old Fanum added, a familiar note of cynicism creeping into his voice. He didn't trust the British.

Gazing at the now-closed fingers of his hand Jefferji struggled with his disappointment. He didn't want to have to carry them all the way to Churu, but it was true—the Hirpa temple was by no means wealthy. It made very good use of the money Jefferji's donated dancing brought in every year at the rains festival.

Would he be here to help, this time? There and back again, after the rains? All right. Churu, then.

"Thank you, revered father. I'll try again there."

"And keep them out of sight," Old Fanam warned, as the boy led Coriander up so that Jefferji could mount. "It's a lot of money."

Jefferji shook the gems back into the purse quickly.

Holyoke was turning his head towards where Jefferji stood with Old Fanum, and there was no reason Holyoke shouldn't know Jefferji had a trove with him, but it was also none of Holyoke's business.

Putting the pouch away quickly beneath his shirt, its stout strap firmly settled at the back of his neck, Jefferji stepped up into Coriander's saddle to get back to the Udai road and on his way to Peshawar and Captain Fontenoy.

That night was the traditional time for a surprise raid was a truth indisputable. This, Shashka—Shikander Beg, also called Kavkazki, from the mountains of his youth—knew. But there were problems. For one, when a caravan halted for the night as caravans would unless they were forced to travel in the dark because of desert heat, the pack animals were unloaded, fed, and watered.

So in order to rob a caravan at night a raider had either to have pre-knowledge of where the lightest and most valuable goods were to be found or would have to load the beasts of burden up again to carry booty away. And where was the bandit who could unfailingly guess which pack was meant for which animal?

There was no use trying to steal something you couldn't carry away.

Also at night it was dark. You couldn't see where you were going. Neither could your pursuers. But the consequences of confusion could be disastrous, and there again the animals would just all run away and leave the goods you were after sitting immobile on the ground, which did nobody any good whatever. No. Night-raiding was good for taking slaves, less so for any other sort of robbery.

Shashka smoked his cigar, a habit he'd acquired in St. Petersburg years ago. He rode Cherkess on slack reins, waiting for someone to try to steal his horse. He kept an eye on the road, the hills, and the trees by the river.

The front of the line could be stampeded up the road and away, the rearmost third turned back against itself in confusion while you drove off the fattest camels, the sleekest ponies. The middle of the caravan was where the most valuable goods were to be sought. That was where men entrusted their silk and medicine from China, jade, brocade. At the end, there were merely the stragglers. And the rear guard, of course. That and provisions, hardly worth the trouble of taking them away.

In seven days they'd be in Zebak. There weren't many really good places for an ambush on the road now that they'd cleared the Purta valley, but it didn't have to be a perfect place. One camel was prize enough for a few men who could seize an opportunity. The caravan-master knew what to do to guard his goods if they were attacked, but—unfamiliar with the people in this caravan—Shashka didn't know if they had the self-discipline or presence of mind to stop and sit down in the face of an assault by armed raiders screaming at them. It was human instinct to run.

The road followed the contour of the land up and down again in an unceasing series of hills and valleys coming up green along the Panj. The land of his birth and boyhood had been green, very green, and by these standards wet. *His* hills had been mountains so thick with trees, oak and beech and pine, that a man could hide in the forest forever. The rivers had been white and black, snow-fed and furious. The sky had been a deeper blue. The beautiful villages of his home, stone and timber, fields golden under the sun...

He heard a pistol shot, distinct and sharp, and then the war cries and the confusion of raised voices as the caravan realized that it was under attack. It caught him off guard. He'd been brooding. He couldn't see how many men there were. He didn't need to know that yet. First things first.

"Ground and cover!" he shouted, knowing that his soldiers would hear his voice among all other voices, because they shared their milk-tongue. Putting Cherkess to the gallop, Shashka hurried toward the concentration of the most confusion, pushing, swearing. *Get off the road. Get down, get down.* The raiders had guns. That was not good.

Three of his sepahis joined him from the rear of the caravan. The caravan was down, at least this portion. There was cover to be had for man and beast beside the road, and with the road cleared it was easier to tell friend from foe. The raiders were on agile ponies, at least six, maybe ten.

If they'd hit all along the line there were possibly as many as twenty or thirty of them. It didn't matter. Whether there were three men or thirty, the job was the same. The caravan was under attack. There was only one thing to do about it. Engage the enemy. Kill them.

Setting Cherkess at one mounted warrior, Shashka struck on his way past, aiming for the throat. The man wore no visible armor, but the scarf around his neck made it difficult to tell whether the saber cut had got the man's attention.

Cherkess was Kabardian, and Kabardis were the nimblest horses in the world; he'd wheeled around before the other man could more than turn his horse's head. Shashka knocked him off his horse with a pistol shot, and one of the lancers finished the job while Shashka went on for the next target.

The ability to coordinate his response was what gave him the advantage against even a numerically superior force. There might be fewer of his than theirs, but his had the discipline of soldiers, rather than the catch-as-catch-can bravado of a band of men set on plunder. There was another thing: these raiders had come for loot, not lives. Shashka's people had more clarity of purpose. They'd kill as many as they could.

The shouts of the sepahi cavalry were easy to distinguish in the shouting, because women had clearer and more carrying voices. He could place them, roughly. A man fired at him, and the bullet tore his clothing, but it seemed to be an older weapon, the powder apparently old or too loosely packed, and the bullet had enough force to stagger him in saddle but not to overset him.

He didn't feel that strange blunt impact preceding pain that would have indicated he'd been shot, but the horseman on whom Shashka rode unquestionably felt Shashka's saber, because it bit deep against the side of his head.

Someone rammed him. Cherkess fought the collision and kept his balance, but Shashka lost his seat. It was a long way to fall, but he'd done it before, so the experience had no novelty and he could think about things on his way down. The impact knocked his saber from his hand, which wasn't good. The man who came after him held a short sword, though, and had to lean well over in his saddle to strike—easy to pull over. Now they were both on the ground.

Shashka's knife was shorter than a sword, but it was as long as he needed it to be. He stabbed the man in the neck, blinded all at once by the blood shooting from the wound. Shashka wiped his eyes roughly to clear his vision. Cherkess had found him on the ground; Shashka pulled himself back up just in time to clear the field for the sepahi who ran Shashka's opponent to the ground at the point of a lance.

He had three pistols and he'd fired one already. He was reasonably sure he got his second shot but his aim failed him. Peri was at his side on her horse, though, always near him. She had his sword, and an extra from somewhere. No. From one of their attackers.

People were running away and he wasn't finished with them. They had attacked him. They owed him blood for their impertinence. He wasn't done killing them. He was only getting started.

Two more, then Peri leaned deep down to catch hold of Cherkess's reins and restrain him. The shooting had stopped. The sepahis were calling to one another, not shouting to coordinate their movements. Captain Katische appeared out of the dust at Shashka's right and touched her rakishly tilted Astrakhan hat in casual salute. It hadn't shifted a fraction from its usual place.

"Spirited but inefficient," she said. "Some may have escaped. No more than three, I think."

If they were gone there was no use trying to kill them. Shashka shook the reins free of Peri's restraining hand and let Cherkess walk to work off the edge of Cherkess's residual pent-up energy. Up the line to the head of the caravan he rode. He saw no dead camels, nor any wounded among the caravan's people crouched down at the side of the road.

Captain Katische collected the sepahis and formed them up for inspection. They were all there, and all upright on their horses. The raiding party's horses milled on the other side of the road. Some of them were riderless and confused. Some of them were down. Peri shot one of them in the head, and it stopped its frantic thrashing.

"Well done," Shashka said, and touched his forehead, saluting the sepahis. He'd lost his turban. Peri would find it, with its jewel spray. "My thanks to you all. See to what hurts you have, and let the caravan provide what bandaging or medicine you need."

He could see the caravan-master standing in the road collecting his own reports. After a few moments Shashka joined him. "Three ponies lost," the caravan-master said. "Five horses taken from them in return. Some injured, none badly. Those women that ride with you, they aren't soldiers, Kavkazki lord. They're demons."

He'd heard that said of the Hell-riders before. "My demons will go on with the caravan." The caravan-master would want to move away from the scene, if only because of the discomfort that came of proximity with the dead. And there was better water farther along, of course. "Leave some men behind to bury these."

He would examine the bodies. The dead had things to tell him about who they were and how dangerous any friends they had might be. He was sorry there weren't more of them, but it was past the time for killing rage. It would take a while to ebb away from his body, but already the dead were fading in his mind from surrogate Cossacks to merely men unfortunate enough to be dead. If there were any who weren't dead he'd—well, he'd do his best to remember that they weren't Cossacks but human beings, and let them go.

He and the sepahis had had good luck. But they'd earned their fee honestly, at the same time. It would mean more business if he wanted it when the time came, and less likelihood of trouble in the future.

Peri brought him his turban. Of his cigar there was unfortunately no trace, but they'd be in Zebak in four days, then on to Ishkashem.

He could buy more cigars when they got to Ishkashem.

In the darkness of the felt-curtained tent, its one light low, Boy couldn't see the scars that told the history she had with her lord. In the daylight he was older, bearded, harder. Here, in the dark, with his face softened in shadow, he seemed as young again as when she'd seen him for the first time—with a corona of light behind his head that almost blinded her. But ever and always he was beautiful. He'd never stopped being beautiful to her.

She took away his garments, one by one. His shirt was torn across the back. His coat was more deeply cut, one sleeve slashed, a ragged tear in his trousers. He'd stepped on something sharp and hard enough to gouge a channel out of the instep of his boot, but it was skin she cared about, not fabric. She could mend a boot, a shirt, a pair of trousers.

He didn't speak. He was always quiet after he'd killed. It took so much of his energy to still the rage, he didn't dare relax his self-vigilance. It had been so from the moment he'd first coaxed her out of her hiding-place with a piece of bread in his gloved hand: *Come out. No one will hurt you. I promise.* He was an angel, now, as then.

With a soft cloth dampened in a basin of hot water, Boy cleaned his face, his back, his breast, his shoulders, sorting out his hurts and cataloging them by reference to scars she could feel if she couldn't see them. Scrape of a lance, three fingers' width, one thumb toward the spine from the arrow's mark. Skin tender, bruised, not broken, over the muscle behind the shoulder, where a tree branch had pierced through his flesh upon a fall down the ravine at Viny Oaks.

He suffered it patiently, because they both knew she wouldn't quit until she was finished, and it was less trouble for them both if he let her get it over with. A man didn't always realize he'd been hurt.

Every time he met an enemy could be the last time. There was so much blood to be avenged. But once he finally had avenged it, what then? He'd disappear into the sun, from whence he'd come. She would go blind on that day from staring into the sun, looking for him.

Done. She put the soiled cloth into the basin, set the basin aside. There was a scratch, a scrape across his collarbone; she'd washed it, but it had bled into the air since then and the water was dirty now. She kissed it instead, feeling out the raw flesh with her tongue, tasting sweat and blood. His blood. She knew the smell of him. One day he'd go away where she couldn't follow. Nevertheless, she'd follow. There was no universe without him.

He took her head between the palms of his hands and

kissed her, tenderly, as though tasting his own blood in her mouth. She understood his need; didn't she know his body as well as he did? Better, because for him it was just his body, and for her it was the earthly form of an angel.

There were never enough people to kill. There was always something left that kept him from rest until he'd shaken himself free of memory for one more day. He hadn't killed his prisoners, today. He'd wanted to, but he'd remembered that they weren't Cossacks this time. Just ordinary bandits. Enough of them had been already dead.

Outside their tent it had been years ago, and he'd been a man no more savage than he had to be, careful and conservative of life. Here in the dark, he was naked in his history. She could clothe him. The rugs on which they slept were soft from years of use.

He drew her down to lie beside him, kissing her in the dark. The felted walls of their tent were quiet, and warm, as absolute as iron between them and the world. He was safe here and now with her, and she with him. The sepahis would keep watch. No harm would come to her lord. She forbade it.

He wouldn't go to New Wife, to Ismara, tonight, while the pollution of blood and killing rage was still on him. He'd stay with Boy instead. She knew every inch of him by heart, and wished that she could be his skin, to stand between him and the sword. In the dark it didn't matter if he'd been hurt. In the grip of passion he wouldn't notice any pulled muscles or strained joints. He would tomorrow. Tomorrow would come soon enough.

She held him, breathing slowly now, sleeping in her arms, and glared the darkness down with eyes that burned like embers in the spirit-dangerous night.

Chapter Four
Peshawar

A short ride out of the Melon Market Gate from Patiala found Captain Fontenoy among the necropolis with thieves and beggars, sadhus and saints, holy men and scoundrels of all descriptions. There was no danger here by day. The pious Mohammedans of Patiala sought their favorite saints alive and dead, and pleasure parties rode out for amusement to take the air on the wide verandah of some dead noble's empty tomb.

One dusty trail led off the main road and up onto a modest little hill having, as its sole point of recommendation, the fact that it was not overlooked by any higher prominence in the vicinity. There was a pleasant breeze rising off the river, and enough picnic parties to mask the passage of one casual rider among the tombs. Dismounting, Fontenoy led his horse, his good Turkish Farouk, among the ruins and the rubble of bushes that clustered against broken walls.

A man on foot in such a place went in and out of sight from all aspects of the surrounding environs, and such a wanderer would excite too little interest for anyone to wonder if he didn't reappear. There were always ways down off such a rise. It was easy to assume that a man had sought a moment's shelter to ease his bladder, and gone on.

Near the top of the little hill, but modestly to one side, were the remains of a pavilion, its roof long since fallen to the ground. The stairs down into its cool half-hidden floor were still there. Fontenoy brought Farouk down them carefully. Farouk didn't mind stairs so long as they were out of doors, but within walls he didn't know what to do with his own hoofs.

In the heat of battle Farouk would charge up even narrow stairs in pursuit of prey for his rider, and had consequent perplexity on the subject of how he was to get himself down the stairs and out again, once that end had been gained.

Someone had very considerately filled a tub of water in a sheltered spot where the wall had only mostly fallen down, and set a few handfuls of sweet hay down beside it. Fontenoy smiled. Sanders was in residence. Fontenoy unbridled Farouk so that Farouk could snack and sup at pleasure, and after some moments' wait in the shadows where a fountain had once been, he ducked his head and disappeared into the ruins of an empty water tank. He hoped that Sanders had brought beer.

Such places could be labyrinths, in the dark, but Fontenoy had accustomed his eyes to dim light before he entered this black passageway, and knew the way by touch as well. Some steps down, then to the right. So little light escaped from behind Sanders's concealing curtain that anyone coming in from bright sunlight might very easily miss it entirely, emerging from the other side somewhat dusty but completely innocent of all knowledge of its secrets. The entryway was low, and would not betray itself to a man feeling his way with hands held out, trailing along the walls on either side.

Fontenoy found the leather curtain, thick and heavy, and knelt to pull the stiff folds back so that he could duck into the sanctuary. Inside, the room was dimly lit by a single lamp such as children had in the nursery. The man that Fontenoy had come to see lifted the lamp for a moment—long enough for him and Fontenoy to verify their mutual identities—and then shaded it once more.

"It's about time," Sanders said, his mild irritation in no way muted by the low tone in which he spoke. The narrow aperture that drew the air into this place channeled the small sounds of wind and vermin down into this concealed room with startling clarity. Sanders stretched out his hand, and Fontenoy very gratefully received the brown ceramic flask of beer. Sanders had heard him coming. "I've been waiting for you for nearly two days."

Or longer. Fontenoy sat down on a convenient crate. Sanders had a buxom wife and many children. Money was not a problem—his wife's family was rich, and generous as regarded contributions to the upkeep of Sanders's several sons. But he did become a little overwhelmed, at intervals, by the ceaseless din of a happy household, and came away to this place for a few days' meditation. His wife firmly believed that Sanders would become a saint, some day, and was only more proud of him for his short pilgrimages.

"Had to make a detour to Bharaj, and speak to my young friend Tamisen." An apology was not required, but an explanation was only polite. "What have you got?"

Raising himself slightly from where he sat, Sanders drew a faded envelope of red oilcloth out from underneath him. Using it as a cushion, that was a good sign—enough documentation to make a pillow meant a meaty report.

"A harmless self-defense party of civic-minded fellows—in other words, opportunistic raiders—was ambushed northeast of Kabul not three weeks ago," Sanders said, passing the packet over. Fresh news, then. Someone had had hard riding of it. "Slaughtered almost to a man, left for dead. Only five survived. They say the leader was fair-haired, red beard, blue eyes, wore unfamiliar clothing. His name was something like Keroushi."

Sanders had a dish of biscuits on the crate that held the lamp. Picking one up, Fontenoy fixed it between his teeth to open the envelope, pulling its contents out so he could more properly deal with them one-handed.

"Kavkazski," Fontenoy said, just to make sure. Of course it was Kavkazski. "I thought he'd disappeared a year ago. Frozen to death, I'd hoped. The Russians have a habit, don't they? You'd think they would be better at winter." And maybe they were, at winter in flat places, where horses could pull their troikas across frozen wastes. But there wasn't much steppe-land in the Hindu Kush. Still less in the high Pamir.

Sanders shook his head. "He went to ground somewhere around Roshan, by report. We caught his scent in Damascus months ago, posing as a harmless merchant. But he's got cavalry. Lancers. And who knows? They may have smuggled some artillery through, north of Herat, while people were distracted by the excitement of the siege and all those Persians."

There'd been Russians as well as Persians in the army besieging Herat. There were copies of news writers' reports among the documents Sanders had given him, Fontenoy saw, fanning through the papers to get a quick look at the material. He saw familiar names—Pottinger, Conolly, Burnes—and smiled.

"Why not leave him to the locals? I imagine there are plenty of princes in those parts who would be eager to acquire a cannon."

The hard brown hills that clomb into the Hindu Kush north-northeast of Kabul could be unfriendly to people accustomed to fighting on open ground. The natives were good at border raiding, too, canny and cunning as any red-haired Scot. It was said that they were the descendants of Greek and Macedonian soldiers, left behind there by Alexander the Great on his way to conquer the world.

"He came in with at least a strong detachment, and seems to have left it somewhere between Badakhshan and China. He's moving on caravan routes. He's got gold, connections. We've never had one so deeply embedded before, almost one of them. Comes and goes as he likes, quite easily."

While their own people, Fontenoy knew, were frustrated at every turn by misdirection and outright deceit on the part of the local inhabitants. After a deep draw at his flask of beer Sanders continued. "Through Persia, where he can easily get anything he needs: provisions, reinforcements, gunpowder. The latest advances in small arms and rifles alike. And, no doubt, would like us to understand he owns the entire range of mountains."

Laying claim to the Hindu Kush by its classical Greek appellation, the Asian Caucasus. Maybe Kavkazski was just his name, but it was unquestionably a Russian one. The Punjab was increasingly unstable in the aftermath of the death of Ranjit Singh. There was hopeful talk of annexation, an expansion of British paramountcy. A Russian army, howsoever small, on what could easily become the newest British frontier, could not be allowed to dig in and make itself at home.

"I'll see this safely to Peshawar," Fontenoy promised. "If I hear anything about a man called Kavkazki up in the Pamir I'll give you a report. What has Peshawar said about Tamisen, by the way?" He was going to need equipment. He was going to need a guide. He was going to need young Geoffrey Tamisen, dexterous and adept in the Rajput arts of war, a man with a good grasp of several languages.

"Anything that will keep Ganders Tamisen's get away from their women is good enough for Kabul, at least," Sanders said, leaning back in his seat. "Is he much like his father?"

How much did Sanders know? Did he know about the dancing, about Tengarpore, about Shree Kreshna? Fontenoy hadn't felt the need to give too complete a picture of all of Tamisen's abilities.

"Yes and no." That was fair to say of any man's son. Fontenoy knew there were some who'd never seen more in Ganders Tamisen than an adventurer, but an adventurer was exactly what was needed, here and now. "I'm hoping Peshawar will consider this as a field test, with an eye toward future employment."

"There's a degree of concern about your judgment, old friend, blind eye in fond memory, and so forth. But yes. We particularly like his languages, and ability to pass for native. If he proves himself his father's son—well. I envy you. This will be one of the last splendid romances, Fontenoy."

With a friendly power firmly installed on his ancestral seat in Kabul, the Maratha settled, Pindaris dispersed, famine fading into memory—peace and plenty were all they had to look forward to.

Fontenoy shook his head. "There'll be nothing for it but to marry," he said. "And sit in the sun all day listening to my weary bones. I don't believe I'll ever see the day. Can I send you anything?"

The story was that the commissary was exceptionally well stocked at Peshawar. That was likely to be nothing more than a story, but it was only polite to ask.

"Some boxes of cigars," Sanders said, wistfully. "And

three hundred pairs of shoes for my at least three hundred children. Godspeed, Fontenoy."

Fontenoy nodded. Sanders hooded the lamp. Fontenoy crept out from underneath the protecting curtain into the still black corridor once again, and went out to see whether Farouk could be dragged away from his snacking to continue on to Nabha before dark.

The caravan-master had paid them off, and generously, in Zebak. Shashka had spent the money immediately in Ishkashem, for supplies and provisions. Now there was nothing between them and Sanctuary but the Wakhan valley and the westernmost boundary of Tashkurgan. And they were on the Wakhan road, following a tributary that paralleled the Panj until they were closer to the head of the valley. Sanctuary came nearer day by day.

It was the Cherkess stallion who smelled it first, turning his head back to catch Shashka's eye. *You. There. Rider, lord. Shikander Beg. Smell that? Blood and steel and gunpowder.*

Cherkess had reason to know about blood and gunpowder.

Shashka drew rein. Peri rode up beside him on her mare Birkit, as red as she was. Together they waited for one of the forward scouts to come back with information on what was happening on the road ahead. Shashka knew he wouldn't have long to wait.

Then in the path ahead, one of the sepahis—Babira— came out of the scrub and brush that grew up on the stony banks of the river Kokcha and halted, side-on. She'd an arrow in one fist, and signaled in a simple code: between fifteen and twenty men, to the northeast. A caravan. Dropping her arm, Babira waited for Shashka's nod, before she signaled her sisters to come in and form up.

Captain Katische came trotting sedately down the middle of the road, an unlit cigar between her teeth. The smell of tobacco smoke on the breeze might be masked by that of the gunpowder, or it might alert the prey. She'd light it later, from the heat that rose from the bloodied wounds of the corpses lying reeking on the ground.

"There is a small train with camels and mules," she said,

her deep voice thick with anticipation. She made French sound savage. "Ten men defend. Twenty attack. We should kill them before they are close enough for your lady to hear them scream."

Shashka's own caravan lagged four hours behind the advance scout, his new wife with her infant son among them. He trusted the men he had on escort duty, but he'd left back half of his Hell-riders to be sure of things. That meant he'd cut his forward scout to half his available force. There could be no profit in *this* trouble, only the risk of one of his people injured. But Shashka had feelings about suffering smaller parties to be ambushed by superior forces. As the women of his villages had been by Cossacks.

"Clear the road." Shifting in the saddle, he pulled out his pistols and checked the priming while Cherkess shifted his feet with restless impatience. When Shashka nodded at Cherkess's ears from behind, Cherkess started forward eagerly, as if he'd smelled his orders. Cherkess had never needed urging to the attack.

Babira led them all down through the uneven ground on the side of the road, their approach masked by the brush and scrub trees. Shashka heard shouting; a man screamed, or maybe it was a camel. The sepahis drew up in a long line, well dispersed, Babira watching Katische who was watching Shashka in turn.

In the broken ground between the trees along the river and the hard, brown hills that rose to the north, a small group of men and carts lay in desperate defense, assaulted all around by brigands who crouched behind the rocks and bushes, shooting. From the sound of it, the defenders had few weapons, and that smell of blood was coming from some-where. It was an unequal contest. Unequal contests made his blood boil. The only good unequal contest was the one in which he held the uppermost hand.

Wrapping the reins slack around the scabbard laced to his saddle, Shashka drew his sharp curved Circassian sword—the "shashka" of his people—pistol in the other hand. "Vengeance!"

It hadn't always been his war cry. He hadn't always led women to war. Now they answered him with their own call, eerily staggered in the air, their hard, cruel voices as savage as eagles. "Vengeance!"

Vengeance. Those were mere bandits, not Cossacks. That huddled band of men trying to defend their lives and property were ordinary merchants and traders, not women working in the fields with their babies on their backs. It didn't matter. All of those armed thieves had to die.

Shashka charged the backs of the attackers, scattering the horses they'd left in their rear, riding down the first man who turned and noticed them. Holding his pistol in reserve, he cut the next man with his saber where the neck joined the shoulder, and then there was a great deal more blood, which was good. It laid the dust.

He had the advantage of surprise, even outnumbered. Victory was not yet won: yet his, regardless.

Out of the corner of his eye Shashka saw movement, and turned Cherkess with the pressure of his knee. One of the bandits had found a horse, and sought to escape. It was not in Shashka's best interest to permit it. Dead bandits were dead, no more, no less, but live ones could raise friends and family to try for vengeance of their own.

Checking his pistol to be sure he hadn't already discharged its ball, Shashka said the words he knew Cherkess was waiting for. "Go fetch."

The brigand had a head start, and possibly some prior familiarity with the terrain. But Cherkess was a Kabardian mountain horse, who could chase a man downhill as easily as up it. And for all that a horse was a prey animal Cherkess had the instinct of a lion. The brigand's horse knew a lion was after it, and ran fleet as a gazelle, taking advantage of every hillock and hump to slow pursuit and gain some distance.

Cherkess didn't care. Cherkess went over hump and hillock, sure-footed as a satyr, and as the fleeing horse and rider neared the cover of the forested river banks Shashka took aim and fired. His body knew Cherkess's body; they'd been together for seven years. His aim was steady.

The bullet found its mark. The rider fell, and in so doing his weight unbalanced the horse so that it fell too. Shashka was glad to see it struggle free and rise. He had no quarrel with the horse. Dismounting, Shashka approached with caution—even a wounded man could take revenge on an incautious enemy—but the man was dead.

Shashka shouldered the body up and across the horse's back; who bore it with commendable self-discipline, considering. Patting its neck for encouragement, Shashka remounted and started back to join the sepahis.

Peri met him halfway. The legs of her red horse were black with more than sweat. Reaching for the reins of the horse that bore its dead rider, Peri fell into place beside him, saying nothing. That was all right with him. It meant there was nothing he needed to know in any very great hurry.

At the battle scene, the sepahis were piling bodies in a heap upslope well clear of the site of the affray, while seven men—defenders, Shashka presumed—dug a pit grave. He didn't care whether brigands were buried or not, but it was unhealthy to leave dead animals lying about, and someone might come looking for them.

He found Captain Katische sitting on a camel-pack frame, waiting for him and—yes—smoking her cigar. She was Hungarian, and eccentric in many ways. There was a wounded man half-reclining on the ground, leaning up against the same camel-pack frame. He seemed to be a little more richly dressed; the leader, Shashka guessed.

"We are on our way to our village of Old Fort, thirty miles away," Katische said in French. She had no Adyghe, Shashka no Hungarian, so they used a foreign language common to them both. "We got a runner away, but we were too hard-pressed. We're not sure help is coming. We're certain that it could not have come in time, and help from Old Fort could not have saved us in any case, because we are few, and only farmers."

For Katische to know these things meant that the wounded man spoke something enough like merchant-Persian to make himself understood. Nodding, Shashka crouched down on his heels beside the wounded man. "Where are you hurt?"

The wounded man was a fair man with blue eyes, his hair cut short beneath his flat Herati cap. It was a long way from Herat. "No place in particular." His sleeveless sheepskin coat was blossoming all down his right side, a cheerful color. Red. "Thank you. Who are you? How are these your people?"

The wounded man's Persian failed, or else Shashka's did. *How are these your people?* What did he mean?

"My name is Shikander Beg Kavkazki, traveling from Meshed to Tashkurgan." And then doubling back a bit, but that was his business. A moderate degree of misdirection did no harm, and strengthened Sanctuary from discovery. "Do you know who attacked you? I think two of you are killed, and two wounded, including you. Your other men appear mostly unharmed."

The wounded man shook his head, and coughed. Shashka took the water flask Captain Katische offered and held it so that the man could take a drink. He didn't look Herati, he looked Greek. There were men in these mountains who were as European as any Kabardian from the Caucasus.

"Not my men any longer, Shikander lord. You saved their lives. Now they fall to your responsibility, I'm sorry to say, because really we are of little use to anybody." Did the wounded man think he was dying? Perhaps he merely had a sensible turn of mind, planning for contingencies. "And those were ignorant savages from Fayzabad. No one raids on this road. We have nothing worth taking. They should be left to rot."

If he was dying, it wasn't in the very immediate future. His voice was strong, if a little unsteady. Shashka shook his head. "I can't leave them out on the road. I have people coming behind me." But he appreciated the man's point. "Tell me your name. Where are you going? Is it on this road?"

Katische had said thirty miles. The man beckoned for the flask. "A man could want a little charras for the pain," he observed hopefully. Shashka had none, but he did carry a lump of raw opium in one of his coat-pockets, a treat for Cherkess.

The man accepted it, nibbling at it with evident appreciation. "My name is Lamish, of the village of Old Fort. One of your men can guide you. I don't want to ride Kudrun. She-camel. The bandits drove them off when they attacked."

Which explained the saddle, perhaps. Riding in a cart wasn't going to be much more pleasant, but when a man lay in a cart he was obviously at less risk of falling off a camel. "What are your views?" Shashka asked Katische, who sat there solemn and silent, smoking her cigar.

"We have to clear the road. Which means to move these off it. You should go to Old Fort, Shikander lord. We may find a good foraging place."

A good point. Shashka had cattle to feed. It had been a weary journey already, all the way from Meshed, and not yet finished.

Ismara and her women had traveled in caravan before, because her father was a caravan-master—that was how they'd met. Being attacked en route, especially so close to the thriving slave market at Fayzabad? He'd wanted to make the journey easier for them. He was failing.

"Your headman is Mekmout, there," Lamish said. He was beginning to fade, but he'd lost blood and taken opium. "Yours to instruct. He's a sound man, but prone to singing."

Shashka didn't want another headman. He had several of his own already, perfectly adequate, and no taste for assuming any more responsibility. He had a young wife with his caravan, and an even younger son. But the duty of a lord was to accept headmen when they offered themselves, because there was a brotherhood of the spirit between men whose curse it was to have the lives of others in their care.

Standing up, Shashka all but knocked into a man standing close behind him. "I'm Mekmout," the man said. This was a much more local sort of person, dark-haired, dark-eyed, skullcap, scarf around his neck. "I'd like to get some distance before we camp, since we're a day out yet with the beasts in such disorder. 'Then you'd better get started, Mekmout,' you say, and 'yes, lord,' say I."

Headmen as a species knew what needed to be done and did it. This one was clearly feeling the strain, but an hour ago he'd been engaged in desperate battle. "Serve out a measure of brandy," Shashka said to Peri, who knew where he kept it because she'd put it there. "Say that it's medicine, and that it is my will that all partake."

Katische was right; they did need to be sure the road was clear. He'd send one of the sepahis back to let the caravan know that there was a change in plan.

Peri was at his elbow already with a dram. "Medicine," she said. "Drink it, as the lord wills." He took the dram and drained it, gave it back. Peri could be very literal-minded. One had to be careful what one said to her.

"Go and wash yourself, and Birkit's legs," Shashka said. "You both stink." She didn't mind the smell of blood; not even the smell of *his* blood. She was a connoisseur of sorts. But after the fight was over, he no longer enjoyed it.

"You as well, lord," she said. Calling Birkit to her with a click of her tongue she took Cherkess's reins, and went away down through the trees to the side of the river running deep and brisk between its banks to get cleaned up.

▲

Boy had smelled the caravan man Lamish, and he wasn't dying now though he'd been struck in three places yesterday. The lord had brought them all safely to Old Fort. There were green fields with thriving crops. It would be a worthy addition to the lord's holdings, should he stoop to accept it.

The lord sat in his saddle, looking up into the little valley, poised and proud. And as she looked at him she remembered the first time she'd seen him, reaching out to her in her hiding place with a bit of bread in his gloved hand to lure her out into the open with such resonance in his voice that she went. *You can come out now*, he'd said. *You're safe with me.* "Whose valley is this?" the lord asked Headman Mekmout.

Boy knew the answer. Sometimes he had to ask obvious questions, though, to disguise his nature. It was dangerous to be an angel in an evil world. Demons walked. There was great honor to be won for a demon who killed an angel, depriving him of his mortal form. He had to be protected.

She'd crept into his tent on that first night, and curled up at the foot of his bed with a knife held at the ready, all night long. And every night after that she'd crept back to watch, no matter how his people tried to stop her, until finally he'd had a pallet brought, and laid alongside the furs on the floor. It had been years before he'd admitted her into his bed, but he'd let her keep the knife.

"This valley is yours, lord," Headman Mekmout said, with surprise. It was as clear to Mekmout as it was to Boy, obviously; her estimation of his potential value to the lord increased by a measure. "You saved our lives. All we have is yours. Our master Lamish says so."

The lord looked down at the reins of the Cherkess stallion in his hand. "Well." The place was well situated; Boy could smell the fresh water of the little lake at the foot of the tall rocks on which the village rested, and see green forage on the slopes beyond the fields in crops. The beasts of the caravan they'd rescued were going forward at an increased pace, now that they had home in sight. "Show me this place, then."

Mekmout started for the fort, the lord followed, and Boy followed after him. It was the great blessing given to her by God, after she'd been orphaned of her entire village. Since the day they'd met, ever and always, she went with him, and when he went in to one of his wives she slept outside the door.

The road ran north from the river up a broad flat stream bed that had opened after a mile or so into a valley where the walled village stood on its rocky pedestal. The walls were badly neglected, ruined and caved in, the dust and dirt of thoughtlessness piled at their feet. Her village hadn't had so fine a stone wall for its protection, and certainly no once-proud wooden gate barred and cross-barred with thick beams bolted with great iron bosses, lying ashamed and impotent to either side.

But they'd had a well, and a good one too. This place also had a well. Wells were important. It had been wrong of the Cossacks to foul it with the bodies of dying women and children. She'd left the Cossacks lying where they'd fallen, and the lord had burned their bodies as he went away.

The village within the walls was too small for its enclosure, its houses clustered in the Hazari manner with their blind backs to the world. There was no arched entryway, just a broad gap in the inner walls on the side that faced away from the main gate. Inside, there was a common square—which was not Hazari manner—and another well, and the square-edged tower that she'd seen coming up from the road. That would be Lamish's place, surely. That would be the lord's place.

The lord dismounted, so she dismounted, and they went in to the tower. Boy looked around her with disgust: no, it wasn't fit for the lord. There was no light, beams had been allowed to sag, and there was an old, mean, notched-log ladder leaning up against what had once been a staircase to the next level.

He left the tower, going out into the sunlight again. Boy cast a last quick look all around her and followed behind. The square lay bright and open. There were not above thirty households here, to go by the number of dogs. It was no wonder that the farther valley fields did not lie under cultivation: there were not enough working hands.

Mekmout the headman was there. Lamish had been carried into one of the houses on the western face of the village, where it would catch the warm sun in the morning. He was a poor master to decline to live in the best house, in the tower; it showed a lack of will to be a proper lord.

Boy would have work to do, to make it fit to be the abode of an angel and his wife, her women and his son.

"I'd like to rest my people here for a few days," the lord said. They'd been long weeks on the road from Meshed; they were all tired. "You seem to have good grazing. We will wish to trade for your eggs and butter."

Boy was glad to hear it. New Wife was worried about her milk. The baby son had yet to lose weight, from Boy's secret reports, but there was no sense taking chances with the health of the lord's young wife Ismara, and the lord's young son.

"Use Old Fort as you wish, lord, and all that is in it, goods and men," Mekmout said. "We're yours. There's stabling here, both outside and within walls." He gestured. The first stories of the houses, he meant. Winter quarters for animals. "Now 'where is bread and salt to greet your master?' you ask, and 'coming directly, lord,' say we all."

A man came running out of one house with a chair—low, but proper, with arms and a back—to set down on top of the rug that had been unrolled hastily on the bare ground, so that the lord could sit. Another man who came with two boys brought a brazier and coals to heat tea, while someone's daughters were here with a basin and a jug for the lord to wash his hands, their whitest napkin to dry them.

A woman with a full red apron and a long white blouse hurried out of Lamish's house bearing a tray with bread and yoghurt, dried apricots, honey, and the all-important dish of salt. The best salt, white and gleaming in the sun. It was a very adequate welcome. Boy was satisfied.

She backed away into the tower again, leaving her ears near the door to hear if the lord had the beginnings of a thought about wanting something. The lord was solicitous of New Wife's comfort and dignity. He would wish as decent a habitation as could be devised, for her and her women. Boy was chief of devisement. It was up to her to assess what needed to be done to suit the place to the lord and New Wife before the rest of the caravan arrived tomorrow morning.

The market city of Churu was as of a much to-do as Holyoke had seen since he and Tamisen had put Sikar behind them, the day before yesterday. They'd come in past mile after mile of vendors' stalls, fabric, spangles, fruit, bread, sweets—all before they'd even arrived at the city. Market day, Holyoke had told himself, but then he'd realized there was no market day at Churu. Every day was market day.

Through the middle of the city ran a long avenue of trees, with broad roads to either side and shops along the outer margin. Beneath the shade of those trees not a single blade of anything green could possibly grow, not even watered as the earth clearly was by the nutrient-rich outpourings of the human body. There was simply too much traffic for the stoutest weed to stand a chance.

"Stay here, darling," Tamisen said to his mare, petting her nose. "Look, this man will give you a nice crunchy turnip to eat. Maybe a snack of oats. Lieutenant, what do you think? Does Gunnery like turnips?"

Whether or not Gunnery liked turnips Holyoke had no idea. The beast liked to eat, on that much the evidence was clear, and Gunnery knew Tamisen was talking about food. One could tell it by the pricking of the ears. "I'm not sure he's ever tried one. First time for everything."

The Marwari mare that Tamisen rode was a sturdy and able beast, no question. But Tamisen spoiled her, keeping up a running one-sided conversation day by day. It was annoying.

Since it was Tamisen's suggestion, Tamisen quite naturally paid the cost of Gunnery's turnip, which was right and proper. With his mare and Holyoke's gelding to laze in the shade of the trees in the care of a groom—from whom Tamisen had asked directions—Tamisen strode out across the road to the far side, and from thence into one of the side streets running back from the main road.

Broderick followed a few paces behind, giving himself as much space as possible to separate himself—British lieutenant, and all that—from the too-tall, awkward, ungainly, be-turbaned gone-native queer duck of a dancing boy who was Captain Fontenoy's choice on whom to bestow riches and privilege. Following the groom's directions, clearly enough.

The side street Tamisen had chosen was quiet and dark, cool, peaceful. There were no small boys shilling for customers around these sober doorways; grown men in small groups, yes, watching with casual interest, but when Broderick stared back hard at one or two or three they turned away.

"Tell me again what we're doing here," Broderick suggested. Hadn't there been some whispering between Tamisen and that priest at the Hirpa temple, some furtive communications and heads bent over something held in hand with backs turned to Broderick, something almost certainly about money? "What street is this?"

"I mean to visit Old Fanam's brother. Small financial transaction. And I'm short of cash."

Broderick ignored that last, in case it had been intended as a barb. Yes, Tamisen had paid their way so far, but something was due Broderick for his aegis as an officer, surely. And he couldn't be blamed if he didn't know the language. Tamisen had money to spare, obviously enough, or he'd have said something to Broderick about it. A traveling purse, courtesy of Captain Fontenoy? Nobody had ever casually handed so much as ten pice to Broderick Holyoke for a bite to eat, a modest snack, a bit of a treat.

Was it his fault he'd learned to pick even the meanest bit of money up off of the ground when he saw it, on the parade ground, in the mess tent, under a pair of boots set out to clean? Wasn't that fair finding? But nobody cared. They'd called him a nasty little sneak-thief. They'd put a rope around his neck and pretended that they were going to—

No, that had been the drummer boy. Not him. He'd never been dragged screaming and struggling to the gallows by a coarse hempen noose around his neck just to give some drunken apes in uniform a laugh. That had been the drummer boy. His mother had been a...

His mother had been a country parson's daughter, widowed a few years after following her husband to India. Her name was Florence Seraph Petrie. His father's name was William Smythe Willoughby. He was named Holyoke because his mother's family had taken him in and adopted him when his mother had died and his father remarried. Holyoke was the name of the small family holding that would have come to him had his father not remarried. He had—

Broderick gave himself a mental shake. It was all right. He had to be careful, that was all. It had been six years and no soul the wiser, but he knew how to survive. He would not relax his vigilance. He was Lieutenant Broderick Holyoke. And there were no souls on the sunset side of the Western Ghats who could challenge that truth, and be believed for it.

Broderick didn't quite care to be following Tamisen this deep into the market, because he'd lost track of how many turnings there'd been since they'd set out from the boulevard where they'd left the horses and he felt uncomfortably conspicuous. He was just as glad when Tamisen found the place he'd sought to make his small financial transaction and relieve his shortage of cash; it was apparently through one narrow awning-shadowed doorway, amongst a dozen almost identical others.

Tamisen greeted the boy who was on watch there with a nod and a friendly word, and was graciously allowed to enter. Broderick followed, stepping across the threshold into the pleasantly cool and faintly perfumed darkness. Broderick could hear Tamisen's voice. As his eyes adjusted to the dim, Broderick saw Tamisen duck his head beneath the low beam of a narrow doorway and step into the room beyond. By the time Broderick got there, Tamisen had sat down, and there was an old man with him. There was nothing to sit on. Just the rug, and cushions.

With a certain show of ill-tempered awkwardness, Broderick sat down cross-legged on the ground like any heathen

Hindoo. The boy who'd ushered Tamisen in poured rose-scented water over Broderick's fingers without so much as a by-your-leave, laying a linen napkin down over Broderick's bent knees for him to dry his hands.

Sunlight filtered through the wooden-slatted shutters that ran around the tops of the walls for ventilation. Two other men, probably related to the old man on the rug, came in to sit down beside him. The priest's brother, what name had Tamisen given, Old Fanum's brother? Broderick hadn't decided if "brother" meant co-religionist, blood kin, or both.

The boy brought a tray, placing it down on the rug so it caught a ray of the sun from the skylights. Tamisen took the bag Broderick had noticed hanging around his neck and poured a cascade of jewels onto the tray, where they glittered very fetchingly. Everybody sat still for a long moment, then the old man picked up the tray and turned it, angling it in the light.

"One of these comes from Mysore," the old man said. "I recognize the cut. There was a shop there that produced elegant faceting, until the master died—possibly thirty years ago?"

Tamisen shook his head in reply to the implied question. "I'm sorry, sir, I don't know the history. But my grandfather was in the service of Tipu Sultan, before he was cast out for marrying a Christian woman. It might have been a gift, I suppose. I've been told he was a favorite."

A catamite, more like. There'd been British soldiers among the unfortunate Colonel Bailey's imprisoned troops who'd betrayed their faith and their salt, voluntarily undergoing the agonizing mutilation that was common to Jews and Moslems alike, turning Mohammedan to gain privileges. This trove represented ill-gotten gains, then. Judas money.

The old man nodded. "Beautiful stones, sir. Do you wish to explore a sale? The boy said that my esteemed colleague and the wisest of priests from the Hirpa temple sent you."

Tamisen shook his head again, *no, not for sale.* "I asked Old Fanam—excuse me, your venerated brother and concealed saint—to take them in trust and hold them for me. I'm going to have an adventure in Badakhshan, and I'd rather not be carrying them around my neck. But he declined on the grounds of poverty."

Picking up stones one by one, the old man held them to the light, turning them in his fingers and admiring them as though they were plump grapes he meant to devour. "The boy also said you gave your name as Tamisen, from Tengarpore. What then is your relation to Jaisal Singh, if I might ask?"

An intriguing line of questioning. Did the old man think the gems might be stolen? Tamisen hadn't given a very satisfactory account of them. Stolen, yes, perhaps. There was something in that thought that seemed surprisingly attractive, suddenly.

"My foster father, sir. My father entrusted my mother and me to his care before I was born, and Jaisal Singh sheltered her—and my grandfather Daoji—all the rest of their days."

Nodding, the old man put the tray down and pushed it across the carpet to one of his sons while the boy handed coffee and sweets around. "Examine these," the old man said. "Identify the least of them, and give me your valuation. What do you have to say about it?"

The least valuable of them was apparently the largest, a great golden topaz as yellow as a ground corn. The old man's son put it down, shook his head, and spoke for the first time.

"The household of Jaisal Singh is known to be honest and honorable," he said. "We can't afford to hold them for you either, I'm afraid, if they're not for sale. Our associate in Peshawar handles financing for the Dograh rajas. Mohendra is your man. How much cash would you desire for the journey?"

The old man's son looked from Tamisen to Broderick and back again. Broderick felt a flush of resentment that prickled in his gut, but didn't reach his face. He straightened his spine, staring, affronted. It was one thing to let Tamisen pay—quite another for someone to suggest *he* was dependent, in any sense. Dependent, him, Broderick Holyoke, on a catamite's grandson.

"Isn't there some way I could leave them in your hands?" Tamisen asked, taking evident care to pass over the insult offered to Broderick in silence. "I'm uncomfortable with them on me. I have nightmares about the strap breaking."

The old man's son reached out, raising his eyebrows, and

nodded. Tamisen got the idea, and passed him the pouch. Son turned it over in his hands, tugging at the strap.

"You'll be fine between here and Peshawar. Things are quiet. Hire an escort if you're nervous, but we really can't afford to cover a catastrophe. It's a shame, if you don't mind me saying so, because we could get you a buyer on those two that would make us all a lot of money. Shall we say three thousand for traveling money, to cover any unforeseen events? Four?"

Holyoke blinked. Four thousand rupees—four hundred pounds—on trust alone. Suddenly Broderick hated Geoffrey Tamisen with all his heart, skinny uncouth bastard son of a faithless whore and a native nabob—unless he was expected to believe that romantic story about Tamisen's supposed father—raised like a spoiled puppy in a litter of doubtless filthy rich princes. Tamisen probably hadn't so much as gone hungry a single day in his entire life.

Up to four hundred pounds on unsecured loan just because he'd grown up under the roof of Jaisal Singh, and Tengarpore was respected and honored. It was more than Broderick could dream of raising on account, and him an officer in the British Army even if Bombay had curried him raw, albeit in private, over the mess accounts. What had Tamisen done to earn it? And it was just a fraction of the whole.

"Three thousand will be more than enough. I'm not sure I'd even know how to spend four thousand rupees." Tamisen looked a little pale in profile. Of course, if Broderick could see Tamisen in profile, Tamisen would be able to see him. He'd take Tamisen from behind, while Tamisen was talking to his mare. No. That might be taken as conduct unbecoming.

Son smiled and stood up.

"Have another cup," the old man suggested, gesturing at the tray with the coffee service. "These are very fine walnuts." He bowed his head to Holyoke, the first notice the old man had taken of him until now. "Will you take whiskey? Boy. Bring the officer a glass of whiskey."

Not from behind, then, Broderick thought, accepting the generous glass of whiskey that came his way just because he was with the pampered son of a provincial house weltering in ungrounded esteem. *Face-to-face.* Not for four hundred pounds; not for the treasure in the bag around Tamisen's neck. But for Tamisen's enjoyment of his privilege as his right.

They'd be alone on the road. Broderick would find his time. If Tamisen was sensible no harm need come to him. But sitting in a jeweler's shop, eating imported walnuts and drinking good malt whiskey, Broderick swore a solemn oath to himself that those jewels would never reach Peshawar in Tamisen's possession.

The road between the gated wall and the village had changed in the few days since Shashka had first come to Old Fort. It had been swept end to end, the debris piled up and cleared away. Standing in the open ground between village and outer wall Shashka gazed around him with satisfaction, then directed his attention to Lamish, lying at ease in a commodious willowwork chair.

"My people and cattle alike are the better for the rest you have provided," Shashka said. "Thank you. We should be out of here and clear of the valley by noon." The camels had already started, and the scouts of course had been away as soon as there'd been enough light for the horses to see where they were going.

Lamish waved his hand. "No, lord, we thank you. Look at this place. I can't believe it's only been five days." Lamish apparently felt unable to stand up, pleading weakness from his wounds. Some of his children had carried him out in a basket-litter. There was no reason why Lamish himself should not have seen to his own house long ere now. Old Fort could be made decent and defensible, if only a man set his mind to it. "If you cared to rest here a while longer, what could not be accomplished?"

Once Lamish had recovered his health, maybe he could be shamed into better stewardship. There was no reason he should not heal. His wounds were clean, and neither deep nor crippling.

"It's nothing any man couldn't do as easily, and better." Once he'd said it, Shashka suddenly felt he'd put too barbed a point to a possibly unfair criticism. They were few here. It wasn't up to him to say how Lamish deployed his limited resources. "We need to get home."

The supplies Shashka was bringing with him were wanted. His people had been on the road. His other wives hadn't met Ismara, though he'd put his First Lady on notice in one of his letters.

Lamish nodded, with a knowing smile. "Yes, I understand. But come back soon, or send us word. From this day forward I serve as your warden here. Send me your instructions and I will see it done."

All right, then, finish clearing away to either side of the gate. Rig some levers and set that gate to rights. Throw some ladders up your outside walls and re-cement the stone and all those places where the surfacing has broken away. And while you're at it, repair the top of your wall so that a man can walk its entire length. And devise a gate into the village itself. Any man with a dozen sepahis could come in here and make slaves of your women and children.

Unfair again. Shashka swallowed back his irritation. These people were farmers. But *his* people had been farmers. That was why they had lords for their protection. He was not lord of these people, and had ill protected the villages that had come to ruin while he'd been dancing at his wedding, so on balance they were better off without him.

There were Cossacks everywhere. He couldn't protect all the defenseless people in the world. It was enough of a job protecting what were left of his own.

"A man with so fair a village, so fortunate in fields, can want for no direction." Shashka did his best to keep reproach for Lamish's lack of enterprise out of his voice. Not every man was cut out for good lordship; maybe it was simply not in Lamish's nature. Farming was a fairly straightforward process: plow, manure, plant, water, weed, harvest. Repeat. What more did Old Fort need? Nothing. "You should rest, and not over-tire yourself. Your people depend on you."

And now that the required courtesies had been exchanged, Lamish should go away, and leave Shashka alone. Shashka had to leave too. Starting the caravan was the caravan-master's business. Shashka's own continued presence was neither required nor appropriate.

Lamish nodded cheerfully, though his head seemed a little unsteady on his neck. Maybe his latest dose was wearing off. Where did he find the money to buy opium? Old Fort could easily be made to generate surplus crops, but they didn't seem to be making much of an effort to do so.

And yet the caravan whose rescue had brought Shashka and Old Fort together had carried quite a bit of high-quality opium from the English manufactory at Patna. Shashka hadn't really thought about it. He'd been too busy seeing to things that Lamish should have been managing, had Lamish not been wounded and incapable.

Shashka watched Lamish off back toward the village, borne aloft on his litter by his children like some Turkish potentate. Any irritation with Lamish was unfair to Mekmout, who was a very competent man. Maybe, Shashka mused, he *should* play lord to Old Fort, and make Mekmout his lieutenant. So long as Lamish's supply of opium was uninterrupted, there'd be no trouble.

But Shashka had complications enough already in his life. And that reminded him. "How is my wife?" he asked the air, knowing that Peri would materialize out of nowhere to answer him.

"She is unwell," a voice near his shoulder said. Between "is" and the final "l" of "unwell" Peri appeared. "She is afraid to resume the journey. It's hard for her. You should have left her in Meshed."

As if he could have left the girl under the protection of a man who could make his own daughter kneel in the dust in the street with her face uncovered, as though the impertinence of her father's servant had been her fault. *Do not be insulted, take this object of mine, let her serve you and perhaps give you sons. She is no longer my daughter but your slave, to use as you wish. Take her, and restore my honor.*

Peri—who had received the insult, in the beginning—had covered Ismara with a length of silk to veil her and taken her into Shashka's tent. What else could they have done? And from that moment, Ismara had been his to protect and care for.

"I take only warrior women to be mine," Shashka told her. Peri knew perfectly well he couldn't have abandoned Ismara to her father's safekeeping. Had he done so Peri would have been the first to brood and scowl about it, and think loudly about whether he'd failed to display good lordship. "Such women as Ismara are heroes, not to be insulted by insinuations of unfitness for hardship. I will not be rebuked by my own Peri."

It took a brave woman to endure such a journey with an infant son, in the possession of a husband from a different tribe whose customs and language were alien to her, carried away far and far to the east where she was unlikely to see her friends or family ever again. And Ismara loved her friends with a peculiar passion, but Shashka didn't take it personally. God had not made every woman for a man, nor every man for a woman. Who was he to have opinions about divine providence?

"You could share her morning meals before you ride ahead. She would feel seen, and her women would praise you to her." There was something about Ismara that had touched Peri's heart, and made her jealous of New Wife's well-being.

It was true that their road was well scouted and secure and that neither Shashka nor his sepahis rode within the caravan-beside it, rather, forward scout, rearguard, column in line alongside. But for a few hours, from time to time? Why not? Did he trust the Hell-riders with everything that was dear to him, or didn't he?

"Very well. Today. I'll join you at the road south of the valley."

They wouldn't be loading the women for another hour. Riding with his wife's household meant camels, which would be a grievance with Cherkess. Cherkess didn't like camels, and Shashka couldn't blame him. Cherkess had been four years old before he'd ever seen a camel, and then it had spat at him. He cherished his resentment like a true Kabardi.

A concealed valley. Good grazing. Productive fields, sweet water and plenty of it. A wall widely enclosing a little village with plenty of room for expansion. Lamish's place was a good one. Maybe the Cossacks would pass it by.

And with that hopeful thought in mind Shashka stepped up into Cherkess's saddle to ride back to Ismara's open-air tent, temporary as it was; to take bread and coffee with his new bride, and get out of caravan-master Timkhin's way.

On the third day after Shashka's caravan had left Old Fort Valley, Shashka—riding in the forward scouting party—pulled the Cherkess stallion to a standstill, watching the riders coming on fast up the Wakhan road. Traders were seldom in a hurry.

Temare—one of the scouts with him—rode back with her lance loose across her crooked arm, point lowered: *No need to prepare for battle*. That was good, because stopping the caravan to take up a defensive position meant—stopping. That took time. More time to start again, and the late reconnaissance party he sent out every night hadn't found a good watering place short of their planned evening encampment.

"Two riders well mounted, Shikander lord," Temare said. "One carries pennant with your colors." Two shades of blue, the color of the sky, the color of the rivers of the land of Shashka's birth. He'd sent Kharif ahead when they'd left Old Fort to carry a report to Sanctuary, but it took longer than three days to get to Sanctuary and back to the caravan's current location. So Kharif hadn't gotten to Sanctuary before he'd turned back: and there was a problem.

With a frown Shashka nodded to Temare to follow him as he spurred forward down the road to meet the two approaching men halfway. Generally he found it helpful to catch trouble before it lighted, when surprise was on his side. These were his own men, though, Kharif and Tunis—whom he'd left at Sanctuary, surely? The horses were lathered; they slowed and stood in the middle of the road with their heads low while the men dismounted, hurrying towards him on foot.

Yes. Tunis had been home in Sanctuary Valley, with Shashka's wives and children, his people, flocks and farms. The valley was well defended by rock and water, but so had been the villages of his first home, far to the west. Shashka decided to dismount.

They were both out of breath. Looking at Shashka, Tunis took a deep breath, as if grimly aware that Shashka would not like his message. "No harm has come to any, lord," Tunis called out, several steps away.

Shashka was unconvinced. Folding his arms across his chest he waited as they got their wind back.

"I've only just come from Sanctuary, lord, to tell you, and found Kharif on the way. The road at Swell has slid off Tilted Slope. There was an earthquake. The road lies in the river. You can't get through from Murghab, lord. Not with camels. And as to carrying stores on our backs, only you can direct such a thing."

Shashka could see it happening as Tunis spoke, the earth shuddering, the slope above the road breaking apart, the road collapsing. To say *only you can direct such a thing* was as much as to say *we would be risking our lives and nobody is doing that without your direct orders.*

"Was anybody lost?" Yes, Shashka knew the place. They'd widened the footpath that wound along the pregnant curve of Tilted Slope well clear of the flood-line, but the ground was covered in loose rubble, and the road in frequent need of reinforcing and pair.

"The earthshake came at night. No one is hurt. First Lady has started the repairs." There was a certain degree of pride in Tunis's voice that Shashka could well understand. It was a very challenging steep. Detouring around such a piece of ground after an earthquake had not been an easy errand. "I am sent to bring you the news, and to say that we hear from your caravan that all is well and that they are on schedule."

Well, that was something, at least.

"You have letters?" Shashka asked. "Good. They're very welcome." Shashka turned to Temare, who waited for his word. "Take these men back, let them eat and drink. We'll discuss this later. Send Timkhin to me." When they'd settled in for the night.

The scout dismounted, walking with Kharif and Tunis back down the road to the caravan and the commissary camels. Shashka raised his voice. "Thank you, Tunis." This was bad news. "You've had a dangerous journey. And Kharif, thank you as well." A man who'd crossed Tilted Slope with the road out couldn't be dismissed without due acknowledgement of his effort just because Shashka was frustrated by this change of plan, nor should Kharif's effort be casually dismissed.

"Thank you, lord. Anander still walks beside a camel, doesn't she?" Tunis replied. As if he'd made the journey just to see the woman on whom his heart was set.

"Indeed she does," Shashka called back, smiling. Peri had taken custody of the bag Tunis had been carrying, the letters Tunis had promised, so the task of sorting and distribution was in process.

Captain Katische had ridden up to join him. "Homecoming to be delayed again, lord," she said. "What will you do?"

There wasn't enough at Murghab to keep his people for any length of time, as Katische knew quite well. He had no caravanserai there, and only women and old men with whom to build one, because he would have to send every able-bodied man he could possibly spare ahead to Swell to repair the road between Murghab and home.

"I think we'll make camp early." They were three days out of Old Fort to their rear. "And turn back tomorrow." He could hold his people there in relative comfort, relative security, until word came that the road past Murghab could be trusted with goods and men, young wives and infant sons.

Peri reached across the space between horses, holding a packet for Katische to take. Katische rode one of the short shaggy ponies of the Hindu Kush, and Peri her graceful Birkit. It wasn't a far stretch. "From Philippa," Peri said. "And Jans."

Friends of Katische's, left behind in Sanctuary to till fields and mend lodgings, to tend chickens and sheep and goats and camels, man the watchtowers, and work the will of First Wife in the absence of her lord.

Katische took the letter and turned it over. Shashka didn't see any obvious evidence of opening, but that apparently surprised Katische as little as it did Shashka. Tucking her letter away into an inside pocket of her riding coat Katische rode back into the caravan to find Timkhin with the news.

"And for you, lord," Peri added.

The packet of letters she offered—tied up with string, as thick as his hand was wide—would include a journal kept day by day and month by month, and a summary that his First Lady made for him. Sometimes First Lady sent notes to Peri as well, which Shashka would read to her.

He needed to talk with Timkhin. He should call on Ismara, to tell her that his plans had changed and why, so that she would hear it from him directly. And then, maybe, hours from now, he'd be at liberty to read his First Lady's letters to see her report, everything she felt he would need to know on his way home, and what she had to say about his children.

Chapter Five
Sowan River Basin

Nice juicy bunch of grass here, Coriander said to Gunnery. *No, here. No, wait, over here.* Leaving the reins slack against her neck, Jefferji let Coriander seek her pleasure, looking into the clear blue sky.

They'd crossed the Sutlej at Ferozepore, where the Bengal British had quartered in their attempts to cultivate first the acquaintance of Ranjit Singh, and then their relationship with his heir Kharak Singh. That had been several days ago. Jefferji had fallen into the habit of marking time: first day by day, then mornings and afternoons, as they slowly approached Peshawar where he'd be able to cry clear of Lieutenant Broderick Holyoke forever.

Just now Holyoke had dismounted and left the road four hours into the day's journey after a late start, murmuring vaguely about a hygienic task requiring his attention. Jefferji could only wait. It was yet another day before they would reach Rawal Pindi, that much closer to the Indus crossing at Taxila. Thence to Peshawar.

They might have made better speed if Holyoke had been willing to risk deviating from the notes he'd made in his memorandum book, apparently in Bombay, to take any actual travelers' accounts along the road into consideration.

Perhaps Holyoke was right to insist that the people they met along the way were part of a vast criminal conspiracy of people whose ancestral way of life was to murder travelers and steal their goods on the road, just as Sleeman had it. Jefferji had never met a soul who believed it. Robbers on the road; yes; bhang-crazed murderers, no.

Jefferji had given up the effort as wasted on the insecure person Holyoke seemed to be, with the degree of bluster that frequently characterized people who were defensive about their delusions. Holyoke had talked to Fontenoy. Holyoke claimed to know Fontenoy's schedule. If Holyoke—anxious as he seemed to be to rendezvous with Fontenoy in Peshawar—remained inflexible on the subject of the route he had mapped out, well, Jefferji wasn't going to waste his time trying to change Holyoke's mind.

Personal errand accomplished, Lieutenant Holyoke came back out of the scrub at the side of the road, smoothing down the front closure of his field uniform blouse. Jefferji turned his attention from the calm serene skies back to Holyoke's rather annoying company.

"Anything new up there?" Holyoke asked.

The question made Jefferji frown, and he didn't know why. It was an innocuous question, surely, but like much of what Holyoke said, it had a subtle edge of *you amusing bumpkin* to it that Jefferji was starting to find irritating.

"Three partial clouds and two crows."

He was glad of Holyoke's company all the same. He'd never been so far from Tengarpore in his life. Still, he was the one who handled the buying of dinner, as well as arranged lodging and provisioning for the road. It hadn't taken Jefferji so very long to realize that Holyoke didn't know the road to Peshawar any more than Jefferji did, so he could just as easily have found his own way to Peshawar, by himself. Holyoke needed *him*, not the other way around.

"Glad to hear it. Well. Off again, shall we?" Holyoke said, climbing into the saddle.

Gunnery was a cavalry mount, a tall chestnut gelding, very well trained. He'd stood as still as a post in the road where Holyoke had dropped his reins during Holyoke's absence, casting an envious eye at Coriander as she browsed in the grass at the side of the road.

Jefferji had contemplated pulling a clump of grass and

feeding it to Gunnery. He wished he had, whether or not Holyoke would have made a face if he'd caught Jefferji at it. Jefferji was still smarting over the face Holyoke had made at him four days ago, when he'd risen earlier than Jefferji had expected and caught Jefferji by surprise in the middle of a set of exercises. *Good God, Tamisen. What on earth is the meaning of these, these, these wavings of your arms and legs?*

In Jefferji's opinion, Holyoke had no cause to gawp at him. Surely Holyoke knew very well what a man practicing his figures in the morning looked like. Men danced all over India. If they weren't dancing they were warming up for wrestling, or performing their morning prayers.

Riding on in silence, Jefferji tried to think of some topic of conversation he might raise, just to start a bit of friendly chat, just to settle the resentment in his belly. "You know, you haven't told me what you'll be doing for the Resident, in Kabul."

"You haven't asked."

Well, no, he hadn't. He didn't know many English, and couldn't guess what might come across as prying.

But Holyoke had apparently decided to answer Jefferji's question, to impress Jefferji, maybe. "We hear that the Russian agent with whom Dost Mohammed Khan was treating has not abandoned his ground and field, and I'm to be Burnes's point man in the pursuit and observation of the same. Man named Viktevish. Vikovitch. Something like that."

"That would be the famous Captain Sir Alexander Burnes?" Jefferji asked. "The man who went to Bokhara, and got away to tell of it? I understand he's published a book."

Not a topic Holyoke was interested in pursuing, apparently. He scowled. "Yes. Well. Right place right time, lucky, and hit the public at an opportune moment. Such men must be found a place." The tone of voice in which Holyoke spoke of his new superior did not presage well for the development of either cordiality or mutual respect. But that was Holyoke's business, Jefferji supposed. "I'm to have a somewhat different role. Real work. Behind the scenes affairs."

As the road crested a little rise, the trees dropped with the hill's contour to give an unimpeded view of a flat plain with a little river. The bottom was not in cultivation; a deserted farm, perhaps, but the little cluster of buildings Jefferji could see between the road and the river looked like a temple complex, not a farm. There weren't many temples on the road from Ferozepore to Peshawar. This was Khalsa country. Sikhs didn't hate Hindus as much as they did Mohammedans, but they hated Hindus enough.

The sight of the little temple filled Jefferji with a sudden and poignant longing for home, for Tengarpore and the Hirpa temple and Sri Krsna. He wondered how Myamah was. He wondered how Jaisal Singh was, and how Jaisal Begum was faring, how his foster brothers and cousins were spending their days. Traveling to Peshawar was all very well, adventurous, romantic, fine; but just at this moment Jefferji wished he was home.

"I don't think you've particularly mentioned why Captain Fontenoy wants you in Peshawar, for that matter," Holyoke said suddenly.

Jefferji suppressed an impulse to say *You haven't asked.* He'd wondered at first about Holyoke's apparent lack of curiosity, but then he'd realized that Holyoke took little thought for things not immediately pertinent to him.

"He's investigating the market in antiquities." There wasn't much Jefferji could say because he didn't know much. "I'm to be his interpreter, though I'm sure he over-values my abilities."

The road had sunk to field level once more. There was an old-fashioned tank with a sunken well, its stone walls in relatively good repair. While Jefferji was trying to decide whether to mention the Mahabharata, Holyoke surprised him by dismounting again. Coriander twitched her ear at Jefferji: *I don't know about you, but if it was me, I'd be getting bored with this person, and tell no one, but I am in a position to know that Gunnery is.*

"I could do with a bit of a nap, don't you know," Holyoke said, yawning. "Recruit the animal spirits, refresh the energies. That caravanserai we stayed in last night, the bedding was positively teeming with insect life." So soon? Hadn't they just gotten started, scant hours ago? "I didn't get much sleep. I envy you your stoic temperament, Tamisen. What about lunch?"

It didn't pretend to be a question. "Thank you, no," Jefferji said. He wasn't going to sit down next to Holyoke. He was more annoyed than usual at the man's high-handedness. "I saw a little bit of something out by the river. I'll go have a look at it. Back in an hour or so."

He wasn't hungry. He didn't want a nap. He politely deferred to Holyoke on the issues of mealtimes and rest periods, most of the time, so it was Holyoke's own fault if Holyoke presumed that they were his to decide. How was Jefferji going to correct their course? There had to be a dance somewhere in his repertoire, one he could study for guidance in breaking out of this awkward situation. Standing in the middle of the road feeling dissatisfied wasn't going to solve anything.

Turning Coriander's head toward the river, Jefferji rode down into the valley with his mind full of sour thoughts. These fields had once been cultivated, but it had been years ago, to judge by the settled compaction of the unplowed earth and the luxurious crop of weeds that grew all around him. There'd been a road marked out with border stones; there were still some to be seen, here and there, almost lost in the long green grass.

The flagstones of the near approach were angled crazily in the dust with the effects of time and roots. There was a gateway but no gate, and mildew-blackened once-white-washed walls now worn and eroded by sun and wind and damp. The courtyard was in tolerable repair, however; the encroaching weeds of the lush green jangal still kept clear of sacred ground. There were the remains of cooking fires here and there, though none of them seemed very recent.

Coriander's hoofs struck echoes on the stone pavement. There was no other sound. The courtyard wasn't deep, perhaps thirty, fifty paces. At the far end of the forecourt, shallow steps worn to a gentle concave led to the river. Dismounting, Jefferji led Coriander down to the water, stamping his feet as he went to ward off snakes. Coriander hated snakes. Jefferji didn't particularly care for them himself.

It wasn't much more than a stream, but the current ran clear. The water was sweet, and tasted faintly of wholesome mud. Straightening up from a drink, shaking the water away from his cupped hand, Jefferji called to anybody who might be within earshot. "Hello. I saw the temple from the road and came to pay my respects to the god. Is anybody here?"

No answer, just a little wind stirring in the tall reeds. There'd been a pathway along the river bank once, as well. All that remained was a narrow aisle of red sandstone flags disappearing into the reeds, and a canopy overhead of vines leaping from the topmost reeds on one side to the other. Twining her reins loosely around the saddle pommel so they wouldn't drag Jefferji left Coriander to resume her interrupted snacking and went back into the courtyard to look into the temple.

It was an old-fashioned temple, with a narrow internal corridor running along its perimeter, and a domed great room with a free-standing sanctuary under a stone canopy toward the back, where the god lived. The entryway was low, and it was dark inside. Drawing a flint from his bits-and-pieces pouch, Jefferji relit a partially consumed branch from one of the abandoned fires to use as a torch, and went in.

Slowly and thoughtfully Jefferji paced the ambulatory corridor surrounding the holy place, circling the sanctuary to show his respect. It was quiet, and almost cold. The interior ambit was cleaner than he'd expected. Where travelers came and went—especially in other peoples' temples—there was often a natural buildup of scraps, trash, discarded rags, rodent excrement, the dried-up corpses of frogs. These corridors were as tidy as the best-swept houses.

He couldn't see the carvings on the walls well enough to tell which god-form was served here, but when he opened the wooden doors at the front of the great room he found no carved lingam within. So Lord Shiva was not in-dwelling. Here inside the great room, though, there were dead leaves on the ground, the presence of which seemed to speak of some hidden purpose.

Approaching the god's dwelling beneath its stone canopy, Jefferji reached out to open the shutters across the sanctuary and see who was there, but stopped himself. He had no offering. It would be the height of rudeness to wake the god, if god there was, and offer no refreshment.

Remembering that he had a handful of Kashmiri apricots in his saddlebags, Jefferji turned away to find them, suddenly eager to open the shrine, see who was there, and worship omnipresent Krsna in the empty space if no one was. The half-burned branch he'd lit had begun to flicker and grow faint. He was going to fix himself a fresh torch before this one failed him.

He frowned to see Gunnery standing in the courtyard as he came out. Not because he didn't like Gunnery—he did, and so did Coriander—but because where there was Gunnery there was Holyoke, who would undoubtedly be very superior about apricots and indwelling gods who might not be there.

Coming out onto the stone porch, Jefferji was startled by a sharp and sudden sound behind him. Flinching by reflex he half-turned, feeling the breeze as something flew past his face more quickly than his eye could follow and struck the doorframe very near his head. It was old wood, and dense. Turning, Jefferji could see the object, only half imbedded. It was a pistol ball.

"Warning shot," Lieutenant Holyoke said, tucking the spent pistol into the bosom of his jacket and drawing a fresh one from his belt. One in each hand. He'd been carrying three all along? "Don't think the second one won't drill you through the forehead. End of our comradeship, Tamisen. Give me the money and the jewels and I won't kill you."

Jefferji's first instinct was that this was a joke, one in poor taste. He almost laughed. But there was the bullet, and Coriander was unhappy. Holyoke wasn't joking.

"St-stop it," Jefferji stammered, in disbelief. "British Lieutenants don't rob. This is a stupid joke, Holyoke."

He started forward to take Coriander's reins. Holyoke pointed one of his pistols at Coriander.

"Careful," Holyoke said. "Never done this before, first time for everything, very regrettable if a pistol went off. I'll shoot the mare, Tamisen, I'll shoot her in the belly. Then you can either kill her yourself or just sit there for two or three days watching her die in agony. Do you take my meaning?"

"I understand."

Holyoke had gone mad.

Jefferji knew how to travel across the dance floor without

seeming to move. No detectible muscle tension, feet that moved too slowly and subtly to catch the eye of almost any man. He floated across the flagstones of the temple's porch, feeling no sensation of weight or friction where his feet met pavement "Don't hurt her. I'll do anything. You know I will."

Drifting like a ghost, he shifted closer to the ornamental post that anchored the stone fence marking the temple porch off from the courtyard, fumbling at the knot that secured his money pouch to his sash belt to draw Holyoke's attention away from his traveling. "Money. All the money I have. The jewels. Here, here, take the money."

Holyoke wasn't fooled, more was the pity. Didn't tuck one pistol back into its holster at his belt to reach for the money pouch that Jefferji offered in two hands trembling with only slightly exaggerated fear.

"On the ground. There. Then back up till I tell you to stop. And now the jewels, Tamisen. I'll shoot the mare. I will."

He's going to shoot Coriander anyway. The uncomfortable conviction sprang full-grown into Jefferji's mind and terrified him. *He might shoot me, too.* Unless he could think of something right this minute, he was as good as dead. He'd found his mark at the railing, as though it was his place on a dance stage. He could see his avenues, his axes, where he could leap and where he could fall. What was he going to do with it?

Oh, darling, he thought at Coriander, as hard as he could. *Run away.* Pulling the leather jewel pouch out from underneath his shirt he worked at its bound neck with trembling fingers. "I just—I can't get—"

Fortunately for him, Holyoke was new at this, and didn't suppress a reflex gesture of exasperation—rolling his eyes, wavering in his aim at Coriander, shifting his weight. "Just put it down on the ground, Tamisen, slowly and carefully."

Jefferji had a better idea.

When Sri Krsna, as a naughty boy playing pranks, stole the milkmaids' clothing while they were bathing in the river, he made them believe there were men in the bushes behind them by throwing stones that stirred the leaves in the jangal. Jefferji held the pouch out in his open palm for Holyoke to see. There could be no physical clues, nothing to warn the audience, or Holyoke. The pouch had to seem to move of its own volition.

Gathering all of his energies into a single channel running from the great toe of his left foot to the middle finger of his right hand Jefferji flung the pouch deep into the dark of the temple. The shadows swallowed the sound of its impact. Holyoke tracked its flight by instinct, but with his head turned toward the temple his aim—Jefferji hoped—might not be true.

"Go!" Jefferji shouted to Coriander. She knew the drill; he and Coriander and every cadet and war-horse of Tengarpore had practiced it. *Run away now, quickly. Leave the field and wait for my call.* Using the imperfect cover that the low railing of the porch provided Jefferji rolled across the stage to its far end in one long extended movement. He had to get away from Holyoke.

The bullet struck the post of the stone railing, chips and chunks of alabaster exploding into the air and in his face, temporarily blinding him. In his very best and newly invented *I'm shot I'm shot there never was a man so shot as me* dance step Jefferji flung his arms out above his head and fell heavily full-length on the ground.

That was two. Holyoke had three pistols, but he'd fired two of them, without a pause to reload. He had another at the ready: but Coriander was safe, she'd run away as she'd been told. It was up to him to give Holyoke so much to worry about that he wouldn't take a long shot at her from pure frustration.

Jefferji listened with every ear he had for the sound of a pistol hammer being cocked or a footstep approaching. His right arm, his shoulder, the upper part of his torso, all lay in Holyoke's direct line of sight, and the bullet didn't have to find his heart to kill him if it let enough blood.

He heard footsteps, but the sound was traveling across the porch with slow deliberation, not toward him. It was the tread of a man who knew where his priorities lay: the jewels were in the temple, somewhere in the dark. Jefferji had only meant to distract Holyoke with his ruse, but he'd won a chance to get away.

Holyoke's rifle was in its scabbard, laced to Gunnery's saddle. With a rifle the odds were much more even. Jefferji had little training as a marksman; there were few guns in the household of Jaisal Singh—they weren't that wealthy. But there'd been enough to share around for basic training in all of the weapons of war.

Would Holyoke know that? No. Jefferji's potential marksmanship, Jaisal Singh's armory, would have been far beneath Holyoke's attention, and Holyoke had never even been to Tengarpore, as far as Jefferji knew.

Gunnery was unhappy with Jefferji's approach, ear-twitchingly nervous. *Are you sure you should have that? I don't know if it's yours.* Gunnery's cavalry training kept him fixed where he stood even with pistol shot going off so close to his ears. Jefferji patted Gunnery's neck reassuringly, breathing a thought as he lifted the rifle out of its scabbard. *Don't worry, old man. No blame to you. And I won't hurt him unless I have to, but he threatened to harm Coriander.*

Jefferji checked the rifle: a flintlock, primed and loaded. Approaching the dark doorway from the side, his back flat to the outside wall, Jefferji listened hard, blocking out other distractions. Audiences made noise. A dancer had to know when the drums changed tempo, he had to catch it at the very point of transition, because it was time-honored tradition for drummers to try to catch dancers flat-footed. He shut out the sound of the sky, the river, Gunnery's anxiety, and concentrated.

Holyoke wore boots with soles of hard leather. The heels were new, sharp-edged. Where was the sound of those boots on the ground? There were the dried leaves that were strewn across the sanctuary floor, Jefferji could hear them, faintly rustling as they were trodden on or pushed aside. Holyoke hadn't stopped to light a torch; maybe he'd struck a Lucifer match. There was the faintest scent of hot wax, a suggestion of soot: he'd lit a candle.

Closing his eyes Jefferji counted slowly for five repetitions of an old bhakti praise-chant, preparing his eyes for the dark. Those jewels were his inheritance, and Holyoke had threatened Coriander with torture and death. Pivoting noiselessly on his heel Jefferji slipped inside.

Had Holyoke noticed? No. Jefferji could hear Holyoke in the sanctuary, swearing under his breath. *Got to be here someplace, damned if I'm leaving without them.* It had been a lucky toss to have gotten that far—but the point wasn't the jewels, now. The point was Holyoke. Holyoke was unlikely to be familiar with the architecture of a Hindu temple: advantage Jefferji, even in the dark.

Picking his way carefully, rifle held close and upright, Jefferji felt along through the corridor that ringed the sanctuary. There *was* a light, very faint: sunlight, filtering in from a fault in the domed roof. Jefferji could see. Dimly, but well enough, and he had to move quickly, because as soon as Holyoke found the pouch he'd leave. Jefferji intended to see Holyoke didn't get away with it.

He was mid-way down the right wing of the ambulatory now, where there was an entrance—small and meant for the priests' use only—at a respectful distance from the shrine. The doorway was deep but the door itself stood open, though Jefferji hadn't noticed that earlier. It was rude for anybody not a consecrated acolyte of Brahmin status to approach the god from the side on which the god's wife and children would stand. But surely the god would excuse him, because needs must where the devil drove.

After the dimness of the ambulatory corridor, the light shed by Holyoke's stub of a candle at the foot of the shrine seemed to flood the sanctuary chamber.

Stepping forward Jefferji raised the rifle. "You can stop looking," he said. "They aren't yours. You'll answer to the authorities at Peshawar for this."

Holyoke's face was demonic in the weird shadows cast upward from the candle. "Damn you!" Holyoke shouted. The fluid grace with which he raised his arm to point his pistol was mesmerizing, and Jefferji realized too late that he was being shot at. The blow came first, and then the paralysis of pain, traveling up his upraised arm with astonishing speed into his shoulder, spinning him around to slam him face-first into the sanctuary wall.

He knew what bleeding felt like, the always-surprising warmth of his own blood on the wrong side of his skin. There seemed to be a lot of it. Frantically Jefferji willed himself to move. He was helpless in the presence of his enemy.

But his enemy, presumably in possession of the jewels he sought, fled out and away.

His arm felt like it was broken, burning, and sliced open

from forearm to shoulder, all at once. He couldn't help himself. He closed his eyes and sank down to the floor, unconscious.

▲

When pain roused Jefferji to consciousness once more he was being dragged along the stone floor of the temple by the wadded-up fabric of his shirt. What had got hold of him? He was sure he knew what it was from the brushing against his skin of something hot and wet and inexpressibly soft; something that smelled like a horse. And not just any horse. Coriander. What was she doing here, in a temple? The god's dignity would be outraged.

She was pulling him out.

It was cold on the floor of the temple and so was Jefferji, almost shivering. Hadn't one of Jaisal Singh's old soldiers, ancient of days, told the story of his maiming at the battle of Panipat, when the Maratha forces had broken the back of the Afghan invaders? Hadn't he described the cold he'd felt as he lay wounded on the field of battle? Jefferji was shot, so he was cold. With one hand he clung to the rifle as though it was his most prized possession. With the rest of his body he hurt.

"Stop it," he said. He would have batted her beautiful pink and black nose to get her to let go, if he'd had the strength. "You're making it worse."

She loosened her grip on his collar with an emphatic and generously moist snort. *Listen, I'm getting you out of here. Are you going to get moving? Because I will drag you. Well?*

Rolling over on the floor, Jefferji pushed himself up onto his knees, using the rifle as leverage, reminding himself that it was loaded and that he didn't want it going off in an enclosed place. Stone walls. Ricochet. Or was it loaded? Had he discharged it at Holyoke? He couldn't remember.

Once on all threes—all fours was not to be considered, he was shot—he pondered his predicament. He couldn't use the rifle in his right hand for leverage; it hurt too much. If he stood up he was going to fall down.

Coriander snorted in a concerned and threatening matter.

"All right," Jefferji said. "Keep your shoes on. I'm coming."

Crawling awkwardly on one hand and two knees Jefferji made his way past the god's alcove and came out, scraping the rifle across the floor in his right hand as he went. Halfway across the floor something snagged against his hand, and he pulled it along with him, impatient to be out in the sun.

How had Coriander gotten in? The doors were wide, but not high. She'd been taught to dance as well, that was how. Equestrian dancing was part of the finishing of educated Rajput horses and their riders alike. She'd crept though.

She crept out now, following him. Maybe she was afraid he'd get lost. He could see the light from outside, blindingly brilliant through the open doorway. He could feel the heat of the sun-warmed stones radiating into the cool darkness of the temple. Being warm was a good idea.

He reached the threshold. He wanted to just lie there for a while, a very long while, but there was a horse in the sanctuary behind him, and he was between her and some forage. In the course of time she was certain to break wind or make water, and either would profane the sanctity of the temple.

Bracing himself against the doorframe Jefferji crawled forward wearily till Coriander could clear the doorway and come out. *There. That's good. Are you going to get this saddle off me? I was afraid not. You lie there and rest for a while, but not too long. It'll be night soon. We'll want a fire, and it's your job to make it.*

She could be such a tyrant. Wearily Jefferji put his back to the wall, soaking up the sun. His entire body ached as much as when he'd had fever, and been almost despaired of. He'd been shot at twice today, the first time in his life that had happened, and it had to be twice on the same day when he could just as happily have done without being shot at all.

His fingers seemed to be set like iron, curled around the rifle's stock. He raised the rifle with an effort, seeking to use the pull of gravity to loosen his grip; as he did so, something dropped from his hand to the ground, the thing he'd picked up on his trek across the floor. It was his neck-pouch, the one with his inheritance in it, its strings wound around his wrist. Hadn't Holyoke been hunting for that?

Grateful to be warm and not moving, Jefferji put his head back against the wall and went to sleep.

▲

You came into my house, the young voice chided, with the cadence of an adult despite the youthful sweetness of its music. *You didn't so much as greet me. I've been waiting to see you for months. You never come to see me anymore, why?*

Jefferji shifted his weight uneasily, aware of a throbbing ache in his shoulder. The action caught wrong. He gasped in surprise at how much it hurt. The voice reached out to touch him like the hand of a beautiful young child on his shoulder, and the hurt fled away to a far country. It left its address at the market forwarders, but as long as he stayed away from the city he was probably safe.

This stubborn heart. The voice was changing, slowing down, deepening. Falling like twilight over the shady canals of the temple of the peacocks on the river Akloji, so beautiful as the light changed moment by moment that it took a man's breath away. *Why did you desert me, Jefferji? Why do you scorn your Krsna, who loves you? You grieve me.*

No, no, no. He wasn't the one who'd left Sri Krsna. Sri Krsna had left *him*, turning his back, refusing to utter a single word, not even showing his face.

"My branch was going out," Jefferji said. "And I wanted to bring you some apricots. They're good. I hoped you would enjoy them."

I don't want apricots so much as I want you. I miss you. You should come back to me, Jefferji. You are so beautiful when you dance that it always gives me pleasure to watch you. The voice arrayed itself in years like an adornment, the voice of a king garlanded in the exuberance of a youth. *Yes, you should come back to me, before I forget that I love you. As if I could ever forget to love you. But right now you should wake—*

"—up," someone said, from very close by.

Jefferji gasped himself awake, unpleasantly startled, pushing himself away from the ground with both elbows. Only after a moment did he realize that one of them was attached to his shot shoulder. It didn't hurt as much as he thought it was going to.

"Don't make me shake you. I'd rather not, but I will, because you need to drink something."

The pain had apparently found a good place wherever it had gone and had forgotten to write back. Maybe it owed Jefferji money. Blinking his eyes open Jefferji tried to figure out where he was and who was talking. He was having a hard time focusing.

The man who spoke was crouched down at his side. Jefferji had been lying on a bed of brushwood covered over with what felt like someone's sleeping rug. The sun was westering, from the shadows it cast. As Jefferji's vision slowly cleared he could see that the man's face was as dark-complected as niello silver, like the decorative shields on the walls of Jaisal Singh's audience hall that he'd sold during the famine years for rice to feed his people. There was one piece left. Jefferji had only ever seen the rest in pictures.

"Are you Sri Krsna?" Jefferji asked.

The man didn't look like any image of the Dark One that Jefferji could remember. He had round plump cheekbones, curly brown-black hair, no beard, no moustache, a full mouth with well-shaped lips. Maybe he was the child Krsna grown tall.

"No, I'm a doctor," the man said, and settled from his crouch to sit down crossed-legged beside Jefferji. As though he didn't know what Jefferji was talking about; as though he thought Sri Krsna was a local merchant, a vendor of rice and dahl. There might well be a Sri Krsna selling flour at the next market. Why not? It was a common name. "My name is Simon Jericho. How are you feeling?"

Reaching across his body, Jefferji felt for his arm. Pain's country cousin stopped at his front gate, but was too shy to actually come in. "A thief shot me. But he left me my wealth." Should he be telling a stranger that he even had wealth? Too late now.

The stranger nodded. "Yes, there was money all over the place when I got here. I gathered up as much as I could find, nearly three thousand rupees in gold. Does that sound right? And what do you suppose frightened him off? A thief is one thing, but robbery at gunpoint can lead to murder."

What *had* frightened Holyoke off? He'd shot Jefferji on instinct, and that would have left him with three pistols discharged. But he could have reloaded, or taken the rifle away from Jefferji and shot him again with that. Holyoke's had been the upper hand in any case. Had Jefferji's sudden appearance from the darkness startled Holyoke into flight?

Jefferji raised his hand to take the cup of water Simon was holding out to him, but he couldn't make it work. He already had something in his hand: the pouch full of jewels from around his neck, the fastening knotted tight.

"You wouldn't let go of it," Simon said. "See if you can put it down now, though, and drink something. You've had a shock. People need to have enough fluid in their bodies to heal efficiently."

He distinctly remembered throwing them, to keep them from Holyoke. He couldn't remember picking them up, but he didn't have the energy to worry at the problem. "Jericho." Jefferji dragged his fingers across his shirt to straighten them out. "That was a city in Canaan. My mother told me."

"I'm not from Canaan, though." With Simon Jericho's help Jefferji got the pouch's strap around his neck. "I've come from the medical school at Varanasi. I study pharmacy there. I was told I could find a mature plantation of the four-bladed variety of Ashtivir's Bandages in the river-bottom."

"How long have I been lying here? Do you know?"

Coriander had been keeping to the background, but she'd reached the limits of her patience and stuck her nose into Jefferji's bosom, demanding attention. Looking for a sweet. She'd gotten Jericho to undress her, Jefferji was glad to see. But he couldn't give her an apricot without finding his saddle-bags, and he wasn't sure he had the energy. Or the balance.

Simon watched him pet her, talking. "I got here last night. Afternoon. Following your horse down the river road. I didn't want to leave my harvesting, but I figured the herbs weren't going anywhere and why would a horse, saddle and all, be luring me down a road? I thought I recognized her from the Bharaj fair, too, all the way from Rajputana. And there you were, lying on the ground with blood all over. Gave me quite a shock."

"I need to report the thief," Jefferji said. Patting Coriander's nose one last time Jefferji chirped at her, *Go away. Enough for now.* "I need to report him. Can I get up and ride? Am I badly hurt?"

Simon shrugged, and turned back toward the fire. He was

baking bread, it seemed. The fragrance made Jefferji very hungry, suddenly.

"Your clothing, yes. You, not so much." Simon was all over round, shoulders, forearms, buttocks. Not fat; just rounded, as with muscle. "The ball went through your sleeve, that slowed it down for starters. Tore your shirt all the way up to your shoulder. Got into that a little bit but not very far. I cut it away with a knife just to check on damages. I owe you a shirt, I'm afraid."

A dish had appeared in Jefferji's lap. It was a stew, in a bowl made out of leaves; meatless, but remarkably good. Jefferji had been spoiled since the famine had gone away. At home in Tengarpore they had meat meals once a week, in these days of plenty. Even more often, sometimes, when there were guests. Here there were no guests. Here there were lentils, but these were delicious.

"Well, I'm going to Peshawar," Jefferji said. What had happened to the food? It was all gone. Jefferji tilted his leaf plate to one side and another, trying to find the trick of it, the secret compartment that would be concealing the stew.

Simon laughed. Reaching for Jefferji's leaf he refilled the makeshift dish and passed it back. Jefferji was very happy to see it. "We could ride together, if you're interested," Jefferji said. "I'll want to stop in Attok to report Lieutenant—ah, I mean the thief."

Should he? Holyoke had shot him, but apparently only lightly. Holyoke had meant to rob him and had fled empty-handed. Shouldn't he forget the whole thing?

No. He should not. Holyoke was a British officer, and the English—unlike other armies Jefferji could name whose names started with "Pin" and ended with "i" and had "dar" in the middle—had high standards for their officers. Holyoke had threatened Coriander. Holyoke had to be brought to account for that.

Simon twitched his shoulders with what Jefferji took to be the beginning of a polite rejection, but his body changed its mind and he nodded. "All right, yes. Why not? I'm on foot, though. I've no idea how to ride a horse."

Jefferji could deal with that. Maybe he hadn't been quite as shot as he'd thought he was, but he was still very adequately shot, in his opinion. He wasn't going to be moving very quickly any time soon. "In the morning, then."

Now he was tired. Yawning, Jefferji let his hand fall to the ground with the empty leaf plate on his palm. He could feel the soft brush of familiar lips against his skin—Coriander stealing the empty dish for a snack, with exquisite delicacy—and went to sleep.

▲

They went to the municipal guard when they reached Attok—two days on the road, days that were shorter because Jefferji was weaker, but they seemed long enough. He could move much more easily now, but he was still miserably sore.

They stated their case and were led to the office in the guardhouse, where a short man with a very tidily kept beard and a flat-topped blue cotton turban sat on a chair at a table in the European manner, scowling at his thumbs. "Describe this man," the officer said. "Leave nothing out."

So Jefferji closed his eyes and read off features and characteristics from the study sheets in his mind. *Tall as the corporal there, neck rises straight from his collarbones and he walks like a man whose toes are always absentmindedly turning toward each other. Hair the color of leaves rotted in a tank after they've dried up in the sun again. Light-colored eyes. Teeth crooked, always smiles with his lips together, when he smiles at all, probably self-conscious about his teeth.*

The officer listened to it all as the clerk wrote it down, resting his head in his hands with his elbows on the desk, staring at the papers before him with his eyebrows raised and his eyes haunted. *Wearing when last I saw him the field uniform of a British Army officer, lieutenant's rank, buttons tarnished. No notion of which unit, I'm sorry.*

When Jefferji was done the clerk set the written page down in front of the officer and stepped back. The officer picked it up. "That's him, all right," the officer said. "Stole my horse three miles from town two days ago. His was all in. Thought he'd make a play for my money as well, but I convinced him otherwise. Attempted theft, attempted murder, horse thief, what is his name?"

"His name is Holyoke." This was the tricky part. "Hard as it may be to believe, and with all due respect, he's an Englishman. Lieutenant Broderick Holyoke. Vouched for as such by a witness with reason to know, my courtesy-uncle, Captain Fontenoy."

It was excruciatingly awkward to accuse a British officer of common theft, so it was lucky that the watch officer had been robbed of his horse. Lucky as well that Holyoke hadn't bothered to change into civilian dress—maybe he hadn't packed any.

Maybe the officer was as glad Jefferji had been shot as Jefferji that a horse had been stolen: if two men accused a British lieutenant independently of each other, it was less likely that either of them was making it up.

"The horse he left behind wears a Crown brand, from Moorcroft's stud," the officer said. "A cavalry horse."

Gunnery. Jefferji was glad they'd found him. Coriander had been bored with no one to talk to.

The officer wasn't finished. "I can't keep him. Take him on with you to Peshawar and turn him over to the English there. I'll give you a copy of my report. Come with me."

"I think I know the horse," Jefferji said, as the officer led them out through the back of the gatehouse to the stables. "Can he carry? My friend is on foot."

The officer stopped, looking Simon up and down. "Your friend doesn't look over-heavy to me. It will be all right, so long as you keep to a walk. Ah, here's the horse himself."

Here came a groom, leading a tall chestnut horse out of the dark interior of the stables. Yes, it was Gunnery, Jefferji was glad to see, albeit moving a little slowly. Depressed. Holyoke had ridden him out, and then left him.

"He's a very good horse, though," Jefferji said firmly. Gunnery bobbed his head with anxiety; was he looking for Holyoke? "A warrior, honest and true. At least he was, before Holyoke did this. Both courageous and resolute, and deserves better than Holyoke served him."

Captain Fontenoy had told Jefferji to meet him in Peshawar, but hadn't set a date. Still, Holyoke's attack and Jefferji's wounding had already delayed the journey. If Gunnery could carry and Simon could ride, it would save them some time.

"How far is it between his back and the ground?" Simon

asked, sounding a little dubious—or maybe a little scared. "Bearing in mind that I am accustomed to walk."

"Be sure to fall off onto the grass, and you'll be fine," the officer said. Cavalry horses didn't go around letting people fall off their backs; part of their job was precisely to keep their riders in the saddle. Jefferji was impressed by Gunnery's sweet temper. To look at him you wouldn't think he'd heard a thing.

The officer turned to go. "Come back and sign for him before you leave," he said. "You can have a copy of the warrant as well as the report. We'll get it out as quickly as we can. That was the best horse I've ever owned, and I don't like what he did to this one."

So Holyoke's imprudent theft of the officer's horse meant that the entire security apparatus of Attok and its surrounding area was enlisted in a hunt for the fugitive. All in all Holyoke had lost much more than Jefferji had by his attempt. He hadn't gotten the jewels, and he apparently hadn't collected any significant amount of the gold either. It was a poor return for abandoning his career and his good name as a British officer.

"Thank you, sir, we will." The groom was still standing there with Gunnery, so Jefferji, beckoning for Simon to come with him, went forward to greet him. "Simon, there's someone you should meet. Gunnery, how are you? You're a good horse. This man is Simon Jericho. Will you bear him? He may not be as good a rider as you're accustomed to, in the cavalry. But you are equal to the challenge of making up the difference, I'm sure of it."

Gunnery didn't look quite convinced.

Simon stepped up to pet Gunnery's neck gently, which seemed to give Gunnery confidence. "Also I give bribes," Simon said. "Generously of a good sort, which this gentleman Jefferji will point out to me. I'm glad to meet you, Gunnery. I hope that I'll turn out to be an agreeable weight."

Coriander was coming into the yard now. There was whickering. There'd be no getting an intelligent word out of either of them for at least an hour—horse relationships being what they were—so Jefferji took Simon away to the bazaar to get some horse treats for the road.

It was a lovely spring night in Peshawar. The air in the garden below Fontenoy's windows was redolent of the sweet fragrance of fruit trees in bloom, and the nightingale sang with exquisite longing for... a man's desire to get some sleep.

Fontenoy had the best of reasons to sleep: the affectionate embrace of a young, pretty woman loaned on special recommendation from the household of General Avitabile himself. Now her voice in his ear woke him from his blissful drowsing, and he heard the sound of muted commotion in the halls below.

You must wake up, please, beloved Captain whose vigor delights as his knightly courtesy charms. Wake up. I must desert you too soon, don't think too harshly of me, I beg you.

From the fading of her perfume like a sigh of exquisite regret, Fontenoy knew she'd slipped out of bed and away. And scarcely had he had a chance to sit up and swing his legs over the edge of the bed before there was an urgent knock at his bedroom door.

"Your pardon, Captain Fontenoy. There are men to see you. One is injured. Please come down." It was Rashid, the general factotum detailed to Fontenoy for the duration of his stay. He was a good man, thorough, who took pride in his job.

"With you directly, Rashid. Do we need a doctor?"

"One says he is a doctor. The surgeon is sent for. Hasten please."

Injured men who showed up in the middle of the night almost never brought good news. Hunting around for his discarded pajamas, Fontenoy dressed himself quickly, took the candle Rashid had left on the table outside his door for him, and hurried downstairs. He was the only visiting officer in residence right now; no danger of waking anybody.

The room he'd made his office was well lit, doors open, with Rashid coming toward him with a huge tray bearing hot tea, hot fresh bread, dishes of relishes. As Fontenoy went in—clearing the way for Rashid—he saw a man he didn't know: middle height, travel-stained clothing, black as an African negro, leaning over someone slumped deeply in one of the bolstered European armchairs that furnished the room. The man caught sight of Fontenoy, and stepped to one side, speaking.

"Come, here's your friend, isn't it? Captain Fontenoy?"

The slumped-deeply person lifted his head, starting to stand up. It was Tamisen. Stubbled cheek, very pale beneath the sun's browning. Eyes pinched with weariness and possibly even pain brightened immediately, even so, when he saw Fontenoy.

"Captain Fontenoy, sir," Jefferji said. His voice sounded a little rusty, to Fontenoy's ear. "Very sorry to wake you, but we just arrived. Simon wouldn't agree to sleep on the steps until morning."

What had happened? Tamisen's face was scratched, puffy and livid in places. Closing the distance between them quickly, Fontenoy caught Tamisen half-risen and embraced him, testing him out. Tamisen was favoring one shoulder. He almost put his head on Fontenoy's shoulder, as if he'd been ten years old, but only almost.

"Good God, Tamisen. What have you been up to? I expected to see you with Lieutenant Holyoke. What's happened?"

Rashid passed a glass of brandy to Fontenoy, who passed it on to Tamisen. The other man, Simon, declined brandy with a nod. Tamisen drank, but the brandy made him cough. Not a drinker, Tamisen.

"I've been shot." Tamisen had a certain degree of pride in his voice. "No, sir, please don't concern yourself, rather mildly shot really, and Simon's a doctor. Holyoke tried to rob me."

There were echoes there of Ganders Tamisen that caught Fontenoy by surprise and nearly destroyed his composure. *Only very lightly tortured.*

"Clearly raving," Fontenoy said, looking to Simon to cover his momentary turmoil of spirit. If there was any quaver in his own voice, he declined to acknowledge it. "To whom do I have the honor? Can you tell me what's going on?"

"My name is Simon Jericho." Rashid had given Simon a cup of tea smelling of sugar and cardamom, since the brandy had apparently been not quite the thing. "I followed a riderless horse and found your friend lying in the yard of an old temple. There was a lot of money scattered around, like an interrupted robbery. No sign of a third party. And he's pushed himself, but he was anxious to get in."

"Shot at me while I was trying to hide behind a pillar, and scratched my face," Tamisen said. His scrapes had been carefully cleaned; Fontenoy saw no evidence of infection, though they were red and angry enough yet. He could readily imagine that they hurt. "He shot at me again, but then he left, without getting my valuables. Really very strenuously hoping to obtain a wash in hot water, sir, and to beg room for Simon, who came to a stranger's aid as a doctor and a friend."

Tamisen was obviously tired, but not unreasonably so, and while weary, he sounded like he was in good spirits.

Fontenoy looked around for Rashid, but the man had left the room: to heat water for bathing, unless Fontenoy was very much mistaken.

"I'm obliged," Fontenoy said to Simon. "Significantly in your debt, needless to say. Do you have someplace to be in Peshawar? Because you're very welcome to stay here, as my guest."

Fontenoy was traveling as a private person on personal business, but he was still English enough in the eyes of the Bengal British—and sufficiently well placed in Jaswant Rao Holkar's military establishment—to be given the freedom of the Residency's guest premises. There was plenty of room.

Simon Jericho bowed his head politely. "Thank you, sir, I'll be very glad of a place to light for a day or two. May I attend your surgeon's examination? I'm a medical student, not a doctor. Excuse me please for any exaggerations. I should be glad to learn by observation."

"Tamisen won't mind," Fontenoy said, with a hearty clap of the hand on Tamisen's good shoulder. Tamisen flinched anyway. "He's used to an audience. Please. Have something to eat."

Fontenoy meant to be there, too. Why hadn't it occurred to him that harm might come to so very young a man as Tamisen? Jaisal Singh's tutelage and Tamisen's native intelligence could only go so far to keep him safe on the road. Fontenoy had trusted in Lieutenant Holyoke to escort Tamisen safely to Peshawar, and look at where that had gotten him.

By the time the doctor came—Heathstead, a veteran of the Pindari wars himself—Tamisen was well into his bath, sitting on the stone bench in the bathroom patting soapy lather tenderly over his arm and shoulder for Rashid to rinse away with a carefully gentle stream from the bucket. He was beautifully bruised from his forearm to his shoulder and a little down his side, as though he was wearing one enormous purple-green epaulette. With long, long tassels.

"Holyoke found out that I carried gemstones with me. From Jaisal Begum," Tamisen said, after introductions all around. Heathstead's man helped Tamisen dry off his injured arm; care was evidently required. "He was there when I showed them to Old Fanum at the Hirpa temple, though I thought he wasn't paying attention. And then also at the jeweler's in Churu. I should have been more circumspect."

Yes. He should have been. But Jefferji was eighteen, and a young man wasn't always as careful as an older man might wish. Holding the neck pouch he was keeping for Tamisen as he bathed, Fontenoy tossed it gently in the palm of his hand. It was agreeably heavy. He knew Ganders had left his bride provided for, and the jewels wouldn't have lost any of their value over the years. And Tamisen's half-mad grandfather Daoji had had a little trove of his own.

Now Rashid set down his rinsing bucket to help Heathstead's man group lamps close, so Heathstead would have ample light.

Tamisen waited patiently, talking. "Old Fanum's brother gave me three thousand rupees in gold at Churu, and a referral to a good jeweler here in Peshawar who could keep the gems on my account. We were on the road between Taxila and Panch Abdal. I went to look at the ruins of a temple, because I was homesick. He surprised me."

There were many ruins on the road from Ferozepore to Rawal Pindi, and thence to Peshawar. Fontenoy could easily imagine Tamisen turning aside from the road to seek the presence of God in the person of Sri Krsna. It was more difficult to understand Holyoke's behavior, and yet Tamisen's evidence was incontrovertible. Fontenoy would swear his oath on it.

"First he threatened to shoot Coriander—my mare,"

Tamisen added, for Heathstead's benefit. "There's a trick you do with a stone, in some of the Krsna-lila. I threw the pouch into the temple, and tried to get away. When he shot at me I tried to make it seem that I was badly wounded. It hurt enough."

Heathstead was tapping the side of Tamisen's face and neck, listening without comment. Checking for any still-embedded chips of stone, Fontenoy guessed. Simon Jericho seemed a little anxious; about whether Heathstead would find anything he'd missed, maybe. The skin was obviously still tender. Tamisen bore it patiently, if not without distress.

"He'd left his rifle on his horse Gunnery, though. He was in the temple looking for the jewels, and I snuck in after him with his rifle. I can't really remember. I know that he shot me, but when I woke up he'd left, and I still had the jewels." Tamisen nodded at the pouch in Fontenoy's hand. "Maybe I shot him too, but there's no blood. We found Gunnery in Attok. Holyoke apparently stole himself a remount."

Heathstead had finished his checking for stone chips. Lifting his head, he looked around for Jericho, and addressed him. "Would you care to assist me here, sir? I'll want your history of the wound."

There was something diffident in Jericho's demeanor as he came forward that suggested he was blushing, though it was hard to see a blush on the face of a black man in a candlelit room. Heathstead's aide was perfectly competent, Fontenoy knew, else he would not be Heathstead's aide, but Heathstead had apparently found Jericho's course of treatment acceptable, so far.

Taking Tamisen's bruised arm by the elbow, Heathstead raised it to shoulder height. "When you found Mr. Tamisen, was his arm stretched out, like this?" Heathstead clearly wanted to get a sense of the track of the bullet. Tamisen just as clearly would rather Heathstead did not.

Putting the neck pouch away in the pocket of his robe, Fontenoy stepped forward to take Tamisen's hand. As Tamisen very naturally grasped back, Fontenoy pulled the arm straight; Tamisen grunted—very softly, to be sure—but held on.

"No, sir," Jericho said. "He was outside the temple when I got there. Lying on his left side, rifle in his right hand."

Fontenoy knew that Tamisen was left-handed. But Tengarpore trained all of its young men to shoot with their right hands, regardless, and considered it an advantage for a man to emulate Equal-Armed Arjuna—the paradigm of archers—in that as in so many other ways.

"It was Coriander's doing," Tamisen explained. "She wanted to be unsaddled and have her supper. So she dragged me out. I couldn't oblige her, I'm sorry to say."

From the look Heathstead shot Fontenoy over Tamisen's head it seemed clear the doctor didn't quite believe the motivation that Tamisen attributed to Coriander. Fontenoy shrugged. Maybe Heathstead didn't know any Rajput horses.

"Flex your arm," Heathstead suggested. "As you held the rifle."

Tamisen gave it his best effort, but Fontenoy could see that the stance would have been out of alignment, so he corrected the elevation of Tamisen's elbow, and the extension of his arm. Tamisen grunted again, a little more loudly this time.

"Sorry about that," Heathstead said, then turned to Jericho. "The bullet went into the muscle here, just the fraction?"

"He was unconscious, so I was able to squeeze the ball out without too much damage. With the muscle relaxed, you see." An appealing note of modest pride had crept into Simon's voice. "My first surgery. Pharmacy is my area of study, actually."

The wound was very red, and somewhat swollen. Fortunately Tamisen was young, and had a surplus of animal spirits. An older man might have been much more seriously disabled. *An older man like, oh, me, perhaps*, Fontenoy mused.

"It's handy when they're already unconscious," Heathstead said. "They don't writhe about as much. Still this was well done, Jericho. I'd say the powder was a little old, too, or the muscle might have been shot through. How much fever?"

"Intermittent," Jericho said. "It's been four days now. He slept through one. And we've had to travel slowly because the horse we've brought from Attok is in recovery." And Tamisen was clearly not up to a full gallop, but Fontenoy felt it was tactful of Simon to put it on the horse.

"Hakim Jericho, my congratulations on your course of treatment," Heathstead said, with a nod. Fontenoy noted the title: *Doctor*. "Captain Fontenoy, your friend Tamisen has received excellent care, and can confidently be left in Hakim Jericho's good hands. Feel free to call on me should anything change of course. I expect you'll be prescribing a few days' rest, Hakim?"

Heathstead was working as he spoke, scrubbing gently at Tamisen's scrapes. His man had clean linen bandages. Simon Jericho watched Heathstead's work closely. "Yes, sir." From the tone of Jericho's voice Fontenoy could guess that no one had called him "Hakim" before. If Heathstead approved Jericho's work, Fontenoy was happy to honor the title. "I'd like at least a week for the swelling to retreat. Thank you."

"Seven days it is," Heathstead said firmly. "Kumar, perhaps you'll help see Mr. Tamisen up to bed. Captain Fontenoy, could I have a word with you?"

Rashid had clean pajamas for Tamisen, and was helping him into them, but Jericho could not be abandoned to his own devices. "Get the night porter to go with you," Fontenoy told Heathstead's man. "Rashid, where are we putting our guests?"

"Second door to your bedroom, sahib," Rashid said. "Next door to that for Mister—for Hakim Jericho. You may leave Hakim Jericho to me, sir, with his permission. I will see to everything."

It was always easier to bathe when there was someone to pour hot water for you. Some of the house staff had been roused by now; a laundry boy was here to gather road-seasoned clothing for immediate attention, and Rashid had personal effects under personal observation.

Pausing long enough to replace the leather pouch on its strap back around Tamisen's neck where it belonged, Fontenoy followed Heathstead out of the room, making way for Heathstead's man with Tamisen directly after.

Heathstead waited till they'd gotten a little way down the hall to speak. "You should have no problem," he said. "Powder old, charge light. He could have gotten much worse. But 'Tamisen,' that's not a common name. Should I know him?"

"That would be his father. Ganders Tamisen, 2nd Lieutenant, 3rd Mahratta Horse. We were knocking around near Sinhgarh whilst your lot came up the banks of the Nira, as I recall."

From the quick light in Heathstead's eyes it was clear Heathstead had made that connection. "Oh. *That* Tamisen. Really? I'd heard he'd gone missing years ago. Still on the rolls, of course."

Yes, of course. Missing in the line of duty and presumed dead to within ninety-nine hundredths of one last degree of certainty, lacking only a body and a convincing provenance thereof. But not absolutely proven dead, not yet.

"He'd gotten married just before he got his orders. Tamisen's been raised by a mutual friend in Tengarpore; I can't think of a better place to be a boy." Well, maybe he could and maybe he couldn't. Jaisal Begum had made the question moot. "I'm taking him out on a trial run to test his paces. You might just begin to think about Ganders Tamisen's son with respect to any interesting opportunities that may come to your ear."

Yes, he meant for Tamisen to come back from adventuring a wealthy man, but it was always a good idea to arrange for a fallback position.

Here were Heathstead's man and the night porter, coming back downstairs. It was two flights from the bathroom to the bedrooms, but Tamisen had clearly found his way to bed without mishap. Fontenoy hoped Rashid had provided Tamisen with a tray, in case he woke up hungry before breakfast. Rashid was good at guest management, though; Fontenoy put his concern away. He remembered being Tamisen's age—albeit vaguely—and being hungry all the time.

"I'll speak to the General," Heathstead agreed. "He may remember Tamisen's name as well. Come and see us when you're back from wherever. Bring Tamisen with you. We'll introduce him around. Good night, Fontenoy, food for thought."

"Thank you for coming," Fontenoy called after him. He wanted to go find Simon Jericho for more details, but he wasn't on terms of intimacy with him, and wouldn't feel quite comfortable talking to Jericho while Jericho was bathing. Under the circumstances, he should almost certainly leave Jericho alone to get to bed. He had to wait.

It was time for him to go back to bed himself. Tamisen was his own man and didn't need a good-night kiss from any courtesy uncle. Hadn't for years. Tamisen could get his own good-night kiss from whomever he liked, with plenty of whomevers to choose from. Fontenoy could pump both men for more details over breakfast in the morning. And then he could speak to Tamisen about plans.

Chapter Six
Treasure Hunt

Jefferji felt he had good reason to be pleased with himself. Yes, his shoulder hurt, but it had been only a week since he'd been shot. Just two days in Peshawar, well fed, well rested, he wouldn't have minded lazing in quarters for another few days. He meant to do just that, but there were some issues to attend to that had been nagging.

For Simon Jericho, that meant presenting himself for Kushak Singh's audience, letters of introduction in hand. For Jefferji, it meant seeing the jewels he'd been carrying all the way from Tengarpore safely under lock and key at last, in a trusted establishment. He had receipts notarized and cross-signed to send back to Churu with monies owed, and to Old Fanum all the way back in the Hirpa temple to provide a record of deposit. He had a personal receipt in hand, and a goodly sum of gold in his pocket.

The receipts were for a sum that astonished him. He could buy a farm, a good one. Perhaps that widow's farm that Jaisal Begum had taken under Tengarpore's protection. He could invest in opium or indigo. He could buy a house, a wife of good family, and an elephant, and live in modest luxury for the rest of his life.

Pausing in the shade of an awning close to the mouth of the jewelers' arcade in the Peshawar bazaar, Jefferji stood for a moment to take stock of himself. The transaction had taken several hours. There'd been lunch. Two independent evaluations; a negotiated value for insurance purposes; terms and conditions with interest payable to Geoffrey Tamisen of Tengarpore, with cross-signatures and beautiful certificates of surrender on demand handwritten in fine Persian script.

Now it was early afternoon, with dinner starting to rise agreeably on the horizon. The sun had shifted two hours past mid-heaven. So sharp and crisp were the shadows cast by the awnings of the bazaar that Simon Jericho might well have passed Jefferji by completely, had Jefferji not called out to him.

"Hi! Simon! Over here!"

From the expression on Simon's face he had more than the sun in his eyes to worry him, for all his cheerful tone. "Well met, Jefferji! I didn't expect to see you. Are you done?"

Simon's interview with Kushak Singh had apparently not gone as well as it could have done. "Business transacted, all satisfactory and correct. Just on my way back to the Residence. How about you?"

Simon seemed glad of the relative coolness of the shadows that the awning provided. Fetching out a hand cloth from his waist, Simon wiped his face with a vigorous gesture.

"No luck, I'm afraid. Unexpected change in circumstances, rich patrons just now dead with a country estate to absorb, establishment in Peshawar to be dissolved. No use for an additional doctor in attendance at this time. He made me a very nice present for my trouble, yes, right enough, but, Jefferji, there's no job."

Simon had known there was no guarantee. He'd told Jefferji as much, but it wouldn't soothe the sting to say so. Scanning the street for a suitable reply, Jefferji saw something that distracted him entirely.

"I'm sorry." Jefferji took Simon by the arm and turned him so that Simon faced into the street. "I must interrupt. There's a man just coming down the street on your right, behind you." Jefferji bent his knees as he spoke, sinking down gently out of sight. "It's all right, you can look, just don't catch his eye. That's the man who tried to rob me."

Holyoke.

Jefferji didn't say the name. The sound of a man's name could carry through a crowd in a remarkable manner.

"Man in a uniform?" Simon asked, as Holyoke walked by without a sideways glance. "Got him. See here, Jefferji, I'll go after him, and find out where he's staying. Meet me back at the Residence?"

It was good of Simon to put his own cares aside so absolutely, and instantly.

"Don't let him notice you. Hurry. I'll go tell Captain Fontenoy."

With a sort of a sideways skip and a wriggle, Simon slid into the current of street traffic without another word. Only when Jefferji could no longer see either the dark green of Holyoke's field jacket or the distinct wrap of Simon's turban did he feel safe from chance discovery. If Holyoke saw him, Holyoke would most likely do one of two things, one of which was to shoot him, and the other of which was to disappear. Maybe Holyoke wouldn't risk shooting Jefferji in public, in the street. But if Holyoke disappeared, he'd be getting away.

Jefferji couldn't run without the risk of overtaking Simon and Holyoke and queering the hunt, and he didn't know Peshawar's shortcuts if there were any. The best he could do was a subtle sort of hurry, keeping a sharp eye out for men in uniform. Through the bazaar. Down the tree-lined allée to the Bengal British residency.

Up the stairs of the guesthouse two at a time with a nod to the doorman, beckoning to Rashid as he passed. Into Captain Fontenoy's office, where Fontenoy was sitting behind a beautiful table of heavy black wood, one with its massive legs turned in a British fashion.

Fontenoy looked up, his expression shifting from mild surprise to keen concern in an instant. He'd known where Jefferji had been going this morning.

"Lieutenant Holyoke, sir," Jefferji said. "Simon and I saw him just now in the bazaar. Simon's following him."

Fontenoy's mouth made a "Holyoke?"-shaped grimace, but aloud Fontenoy said "Are you sure?—forgive me, of course you'd know the man who shot you." Sitting back down—he'd half-risen, as Jefferji burst in—Fontenoy reached for his pen and a sheet of paper from the sandalwood box near at hand. "Rashid, please take this to Captain Paston, at once. We'll get a squad."

Fontenoy wrote, he folded, he passed the note off to Rashid, who hurried out of the room. Picking up the paper he'd been working on when Jefferji had interrupted, Fontenoy waved it at Jefferji cheerfully.

"I've just been summarizing particulars. Paston will be keenly interested. Sixth Bluecoat Guards. He'll make sure Holyoke is properly handled. Very fortuitous. Hakim Jericho following him, you say?"

There was the sound of slippered feet running up the hall Rashid had just run down. The doorman's face appeared at the half-open door. "Captain Fontenoy, sahib, forgive, Rashid is gone. There is an officer to see you. He wishes to say Lieutenant Holyoke."

Jefferji was stunned. Holyoke here? Wasn't Captain Fontenoy the last person he would seek out, having tried to rob a man whom Fontenoy had entrusted to his care? Then Jefferji realized that Holyoke might not know that Jefferji was in Peshawar. He might not know Jefferji was even alive.

Captain Fontenoy was smiling. "Tamisen, the window," he said, with a nod toward the tall narrow glassed-in frame that separated the room from the outside ledge. "Wait outside. Thank you, Pann. Send the Lieutenant right up."

⛰

"I regret to say that your friend Tamisen parted company with me shortly after we left Amritsar," Holyoke said, at polite and precise parade rest in front of Captain Fontenoy's desk in the spacious office Fontenoy apparently rated amongst the British Residency at Peshawar. This was all Fontenoy's fault, and Broderick could have strangled him. "It seems he had his own idea of how to come to Peshawar. I tried to dissuade him, but without success."

"Indeed?" Captain Fontenoy asked, with an expression of mild surprise on his face. Fontenoy wore field dress too, but Fontenoy's uniform was half-native and offensive accordingly. Why should such a man as Fontenoy be counted among honest Britishers at all? "That's troubling. There are thieves and bandits on the road between Amritsar road. I should very much regret it if any harm came to him."

Blinded by the muzzle flash and deafened by the echoing roar of the pistol, Broderick Holyoke had fled from the deserted temple on the road to Attok, conscious only of the fact that he'd just fired his last round and Tamisen had the rifle. Maybe Tamisen had been hit. Maybe Holyoke had actually had plenty of time to reload, and make sure of both his victim and his prize. He hadn't stopped to find out.

In the five days since then, Broderick had come as close to despair as he cared to call to mind, hiding out in back ways and bywaters, forced to abandon the good horse he'd taken outside Attok for fear of it being recognized. At least he'd brought along his own saddle when he'd taken the black horse, which meant he still had his kit. Some articles of uniform. A small sum of money.

If it hadn't been for Fontenoy, Broderick wouldn't have been burdened with a naïve traveling companion in the first place. That companion wouldn't have turned out to be carrying a fortune in gems, Broderick wouldn't have decided to try to take them for himself, he wouldn't have been reduced to abandoning Gunnery and stealing a remount. Fontenoy had a lot to answer for, and the five days it had taken Broderick to reach Peshawar—with all of their attendant annoyances and inconveniences—were no small part of the whole.

Broderick had been watching very hard for any sign of increased police activity every step of his way here, and had seen nothing. So one of two things was the case. One was the possibility that he'd killed Tamisen, or at least wounded him to the extent that Tamisen hadn't been able to give an alarm. He'd never shot a man before, but how hard could it be? You pointed the gun and fired it, and the closer you were, the better your chances of making it count.

The other possibility was that Tamisen had turned around and slunk home to spend all that money and enjoy life. That would have been sensible. Why put himself to the trouble of making his way alone to Peshawar, now that he was a rich man?

There was a third possibility, one that Holyoke liked least of all. Tamisen might both have survived and be determined to see his adventure through. But Broderick had a strategy for dealing with that as well. All he really needed to do was get safely through Peshawar, past Jellalabad, and into Kabul. He'd unquestionably have been in a much better position with Tamisen's valuables than without, but once he got to Kabul he knew how to improve his prospects.

There was no shame in taking a bribe from some petty tribesman so long as it didn't touch the interests or honor of the Bengal British. And who was to say that tendering small tokens of respect was not to be encouraged as proof of a tribesman's goodwill toward the Crown? And among the useful things that money could buy was an early warning of any hints of trouble in the offing from the general direction of Tamisens, or Fontenoys, or anybody else.

He had to get to Kabul. Rumor had it that Colonel Sir Alexander Burnes was a keen judge of character with a certain weakness in his own. Broderick could flatter.

He had to avoid attracting any undue notice on his way there, though, so—having been detailed by Fontenoy to escort Tamisen—he obviously had to report to Fontenoy on the execution of his mission and present a plausible, or at least not blatantly improbable, explanation for its failure, to forestall being met with embarrassing inquiries when he got to Kabul.

"He met some people at a temple in Amritsar who befriended him. Had I realized the class of people he was mixing with on his tour of the local rites I certainly would have discouraged it more strongly. He felt the company would be more congenial if he came on to Peshawar with his newfound friends. There was a man named Ali Hassan, I think. And one named Mir Singh."

Each name as common as Smith or Edwards. Broderick was confident that any search for two such men would turn up so many likely prospects that it would take months to get through them, by which time Broderick would be safely away.

He didn't have to stop at Kabul. He could get himself posted through to another station, a scout outpost, where he would find himself—make himself—so essential a link between the mission in Kabul and some influential but hitherto unsuspected warlord, that any questions about inconsistencies in his story would have to be set aside for future discussions. Which would never come; or not in time to touch him.

"Hmm." Captain Fontenoy had walked past the desk to stand behind it, examining some papers that were laid out there. "It says here that there are very recent reports of lawless activity on the Peshawar road. Around Attok, it seems. A very valuable horse was stolen."

"Surely not an unheard-of occurrence, Captain Fontenoy. More's the pity." It *had* been a valuable horse. Broderick had been very sorry to part with it, but he'd had no choice. "Are there other recent robberies? I suppose a horse theft need not pose too much concern for Tamisen's sake. I understand his mare is not deemed to be a particularly good specimen."

"Yes, I'm sure you're right," Fontenoy agreed, picking up one of his papers. It looked like native court production to Broderick, letters writ large in brilliantly green ink with a full brush. "How about yours? A tall chestnut gelding has been taken into care, found wandering loose near Attok, Crown brand, Moorcroft's stud. Here, take a look."

Holding the document out with an inquiring gaze Fontenoy waited.

Broderick knew he didn't have much time to come up with a good story. Taking the document he looked it over, not bothering to turn it right side up.

"Sorry, sir, can't make head nor tail of their script. No, Gunnery fetched up lame a few miles out of Attok. I gave a local man some money for board and keep and came on with a hired nag. I wonder that the story's got so muddled, if it is my horse."

Muddled it had got. It was very unfortunate that Gunnery had been identified, even tentatively. A man wanted more time to build up his picture, but he'd been too busy working up the story of Tamisen's nonappearance to have had time to spare for lesser issues. It was the most appallingly bad luck. He should have shot the damned horse when there was no more good to be had from him. Someone would have butchered the carcass—he could have sold the carcass—and Gunnery would have disappeared into the meat curries of Attok with no one ever the wiser.

Shrugging, Fontenoy put the document down on his desk

behind him with his back to it now, his hands braced against the desktop's lip. "It is indeed a muddle. Even a confusion. A man came into my office very early this morning with a warrant for the apprehension of a British officer identified as Lieutenant Broderick Holyoke on charges of horse theft, armed robbery, and attempted murder."

"That's outrageous." Anything less than an immediate, emphatic reply would be suspect. "I trust swift measures can be taken to refute this slander, sir?" Nobody could connect him with the theft, nobody who knew his name. So someone had come after the fact to point the finger. Someone who could also identify Gunnery.

Only Tamisen could have accused him of attempted murder to Captain Fontenoy and made it stick. Broderick didn't have time to ponder the unfairness of it all. He needed an escape plan now. He would curse Fate later.

The door behind him was closed, but not locked. If Fontenoy had been prepared for a confrontation—and he must have been, damn him, toying with Broderick like a dog with a noose around its neck, wriggling frantically to escape—there would logically be someone watching there. He'd have to get through guards, and the hue and cry would go up.

Alternatively, there was bound to be a servant's or merchant's gate into the embassy compound. He hadn't managed to secure any of Tamisen's gold, but he'd sold the fine horse and gotten nearly half of what it was worth—the dealer had pretended to have suspicions but had bought the horse anyway, thereby proving himself corrupt. So Broderick had money on him.

Now for the first time Fontenoy showed signs of diffidence, even sympathy. "It doesn't appear to be a slander," he said, gently. *Confess now and it will be counted in your favor.* But it was never counted in favor. Never truly. Never enough to make a difference. "There are two separate witnesses that describe the same man. One of them is in an unchallengeable position to put your name to the crimes."

The Bengal British law held in this compound, and under British law if Broderick was taken prisoner much more than just theft of a horse and shooting some Englishman's orphan would be laid at his door. Usurpation of identity. Impersonating an officer. That would be only the beginning.

"I demand to confront this false witness immediately," Broderick said firmly.

But he knew who it was. He did genuinely want to see Tamisen, for two reasons: one, it might give him a diversion; and two, he needed to know how badly Tamisen was hurt, both for personal satisfaction and so he'd know how much more effort it would take to finish the job.

Swallowing back a sigh of apparent regret—had Fontenoy actually expected him to "come clean," confess all, take his punishment like a man?—Fontenoy raised his voice. "Tamisen, my boy," Fontenoy said. "Come in."

There was a sound at the tall window in the outside wall of Fontenoy's office. Holyoke's sense of self-preservation kicked into the highest of many efficient and well-adjusted gears. Tamisen was outside the window.

The building was adjacent to the Residence proper; adjacent, and much closer to the compound's side walls, along which servants and low-caste menials would creep to seek their own level at the bottom of the dung heap. There were almost never armed guards outside kitchens, laundries, latrines. But were there guards with Tamisen, likewise waiting outside?

The window opened in. It was tall for a window, but not for a door—Tamisen would have to bend his head to get through—so Broderick knew he had to wait till it was at least halfway open, or any rush on his part might just push it shut again. If he'd ever lied successfully in his life he had to do it now. He could take a step forward and draw a deep breath, yes; Fontenoy would expect a reaction. But anything more than that might hint too broadly at his intention.

The window opened wide and Tamisen stepped over the sill into the room. As Tamisen straightened up—as the words "Hello, Holyoke" began to form in Tamisen's mouth—Broderick raised his voice in fury and charged. "You lying bastard! You swore you were taking that horse back to its rightful owner!"

Tamisen's face was cut and bruised, left side, that would have been the first bullet. But it was his right side Tamisen favored. Broderick saw no hint of other bodies outside, shadowing the window. Throwing himself forward Broderick reached for Tamisen's throat with both hands; Tamisen flinched away, toward the right, just where Broderick wanted him.

Pushing past Tamisen, shoving him as hard as he could into Fontenoy's path, Broderick was through the window in seconds, pulling it closed behind him. It might win him the fraction of a second. He looked around. One lone water carrier in the courtyard below looking up from his water cans in mild curiosity. Low wall between the courtyard and the perimeter wall that defined the compound. Could he possibly make it?

The intermediate wall was half the distance to the ground, less than a yard wide at a quick estimate, but he'd get over to other side directly. He didn't have time for more than the quickest of estimates, because Fontenoy was already coming through the window and Tamisen would logically be close behind.

Running a few steps down the broad ledge, out of reach of a grab for his jacket, Broderick jumped, landing atop the wall with a bone-jarring impact. He couldn't make it work. He couldn't keep his balance. All he could do was fall to the outside of the wall and hope for the best.

The momentum of the jump carried him over and beyond, but he got the back of his shoulder turned to the fall so that the force of the impact rolled him over but spared his head a hard knock. His knee hurt so much he could hardly think, but his life was at stake and his knee would work, so he ran.

Behind him he could hear Fontenoy's voice—*Stop that man, stop him!* —but the servile instinct of the underclass was too strong. They gave way. And when two men—house guard, perhaps, chowkidars on personal time—stepped in front of him with obvious intent to grapple, Broderick climbed a stack of wicker produce crates awaiting return, sending them crashing down into the heads of his would-be interceptors behind him.

He was through the back gate and into the alley. Problem: logically the guard would be running even now to seal the alley at each end. He needed a horse. No, a horse would only make him conspicuous. He could lose himself in the labyrinthine warrens of the city, but all the pursuit would have to do was go two by two to the gates and wait.

There were more ways out of the native quarters than the gates. Native quarters it was. Fontenoy would need permission from the local authorities to send troops in after him. He was unlikely to receive permission to stop everyone at the gates who might be Broderick Holyoke, and all Fontenoy had was a written description. Broderick would be out of the city and miles away before Fontenoy got authorization.

No. Let them seek him outside the gates. Fontenoy's reasoning would be sound enough. Any rational man would expect him to flee, to get as far away as possible as quickly as possible. If he left the city, how was he to discover the details of Fontenoy's planned excursion with Tamisen? And without knowledge of the details, how was Broderick to follow them?

Follow them he would. Fontenoy was going north for antiquities, Tamisen had said, and they would logically be valuable, marketable. Now that there was no hope of going to Kabul, Broderick needed a new plan.

Tamisen had brought him to this pass, and when Broderick saw his opportunity Tamisen would pay, Tamisen and Fontenoy together. One way or another they would requite him for his pains, and if he did not profit from earned revenge his name was not Broderick Holyoke.

At the end of the day, Captain Fontenoy sat at the great desk in his office, writing a report to forward to Calcutta with a copy for Madras. He wondered what they were going to make of it all, a British officer turned thief, and now renegade. There was a knock at the door; Tamisen, fresh from Doctor Heathstead's re-examination, in the shirt and loose cotton trousers that made the national dress of Rajputani men from high to low. The differences were all in the quality and costliness of the fabric.

"I'd like to talk to you, sir." Tamisen closed the door behind him. "Something happened today that I don't want to lose amidst all of the excitement."

"Please." Fontenoy gestured at a chair.

Tamisen sat down with the careful formality of a man more accustomed to couch and bolsters. He'd been absolutely frustrated with himself over losing Holyoke earlier today, but Fontenoy didn't think it could be Tamisen's fault in any way. Holyoke had taken them by surprise. If Holyoke had only been an honest man and faithful to his salt, he could have been a real strength as a tactical officer; he could certainly think on his feet.

Smoothing the fabric of his long-tailed shirt across his thighs, Tamisen seemed to consider his words thoughtfully. "The thing is, Simon's interview didn't go well. Now he'll have to go back to Varanasi. I don't think he wants to do that. I've gathered that he has some frustrations with his teachers."

Fontenoy had spoken briefly with Jericho about his interview over dinner. Hakim Jericho hadn't pursued the opening, so Fontenoy concluded that Jericho didn't want to talk about it. He could easily respect such a feeling, and there'd been a very great deal to discuss in mulling over the discovery and flight of Broderick Holyoke.

"No one's making him go back to Varanasi, are they?" Fontenoy asked. "But wait. Does he need a loan? I'm sure we could send Gunnery with him, at least. The cavalry won't touch a horse once it's been overridden like that, nerves never the same."

Tamisen's eyes were dark and thoughtful in the dimness. "No such rebuke is to be brought against the sirdar, sir. Simon's been well recompensed for his time and travel. But we've talked. He did abandon some promising wayside research into the medicinal herbs of the Attok tablelands on my account. Might I, with your permission, suggest that he make a virtue of necessity, and accompany us into Badakhshan?"

Ganders Tamisen had been a quick judge of character, who when he erred, did so on the negative side of the balance. Tamisen was young; he couldn't be expected to know how to take the measure of a man. Still, his father's son, and there was his musical training to consider, sensitivity to nuance in voice, carriage, and expression.

"Can he be trusted? Based on what you know?"

Tamisen looked down, aside, and then back up at Fontenoy so quickly that a blink would have obscured it. "I've considered the question, sir, after my experience with Holyoke. I like Simon a great deal better, but that's no measure." Well, it could count for something. "He might not have known about the jewels, because I was holding the pouch fast in my hand. But he'd gathered up the money Holyoke left behind. It was by far the better part of three thousand rupees in gold double mohurs. Allowing for what I think I'd spent already, everything."

Simon had found Tamisen unconscious. There'd been nothing to stop him from secreting some or all of that gold, and laying the theft at Holyoke's doorstep. If the measure of a man's character was what he did when nobody was looking, Simon Jericho might prove out to be an honest man.

Fontenoy wished it was daylight, so that he could see Tamisen's face more clearly. His eyesight wasn't what it had been, and the dark was darker year by year. Rising from his desk, he walked around from behind it to stand in front of Tamisen.

"We've got a bit of a rough ride ahead of us," he said. "You were raised Rajput, Geoffrey, and a fine athlete it's made you. We don't know if your friend has the endurance for the enterprise."

Up the Chitral valley over paths impassable for camels, along the turbulent banks of the river where cold winds blew throughout the year and ice lingered even in mid-summer. Picking up pre-arranged escort in Chitral, Lehna Singh and his men, to cross the Dora Pass. Fontenoy didn't know Lehna Singh. But he came well vouched for by people Fontenoy trusted.

Up to Fayzabad, then a quick jog south across the Panj and up the Wakhan valley from Ishkashem. There was an old Siaposh Kaffir fort, Deravass wrote, north of a tributary of the Wakhan River. It could be dangerous. Some accidents could happen any time, any place; others occurred with more frequency in the vicinity of mountains. Falling rocks. Landslides. Still others were general hazards wherever there were men but no law.

Tamisen took a moment over his reply, clearly considering his words carefully. "I think he would take a considerable pounding. He's not a practiced rider, but Gunnery teaches as he goes."

Not saying *Twenty years younger than you are, Captain Fontenoy*, even though it was true. Who knew which of them would fall behind, and which go on? All that was necessary was to meet up with Deravass Khan on the road to Tashkurgan.

Hakim Jericho was a student of medicine, of whose ground-level doctoring Heathstead had approved. The experience of other European travelers in wild high places was that the presence of a medical man opened doors in the most suspicious of neighborhoods, quite apart from the usefulness of having someone knowledgeable at hand if someone accidentally fell off a mountain or something.

"Well, my boy." Fontenoy gave Tamisen's good shoulder a gentle squeze little shake full of affection. "No harm in asking. Then, if you catch his interest, we can talk. I can give you both the briefing at one time, or just between ourselves. All right? You should go to bed."

Tamisen stood up. "Thank you, sir, I'll do as you say. Good night, Captain Fontenoy. We should both go to bed, sir."

"Yes, of course, you tiresome puppy. By all means let us both go to bed." There had been times—especially after the death of Tamisen's mother—that Fontenoy had wondered what it would be like if Tamisen were his son, rather than his adopted nephew. It was sheer greed on his part. "I'll see you in the morning, then. Good night."

He was really looking forward to introducing Ganders's boy to Deravass Khan.

Yesterday, Jefferji and Simon had seen Broderick Holyoke in the bazaar, on his way to the Bengal British residency for an interview with Captain Fontenoy. Last night, Jefferji had asked Fontenoy whether Simon might come with them to Badakhshan on their excursion in search of artifacts.

This morning, Jefferji had proposed the idea to Simon; and

now, two o'clock in the afternoon, scarcely twenty-four hours since the excitement with Holyoke, here they were. He, and Captain Fontenoy, and Simon. And Rashid the major-domo, who was supervising the laying of trays for a hybrid sort of luncheon—cold roast, pheasant, kebabs, curried eggs, rice, a splendid sherbet to drink, grapes. Bread and butter. Yoghurt thinned with milk and sweetened with honey. It was a sumptuous feast.

When Rashid had closed the doors behind him Captain Fontenoy spoke, helping himself to kebabs and cucumber. "Last night you told us that your hopes for employment have been disappointed, Hakim Jericho, am I right?" Simon nodded, so Fontenoy continued. "Tamisen tells me you know a little of his business here, and our plans. I thought this might be an opportune time to discuss them."

To Jefferji it seemed lucky, in a sense, that they'd had the uproar with Holyoke's escape. Holyoke couldn't be found; Jefferji wasn't sure Fontenoy expected him to be. It was too bad. Jefferji had decided that he genuinely resented being shot at, and would have liked a chance to yell a little about it. But it had been a distraction for Simon, and seemed to have taken the edge off the blow he'd sustained.

If Simon came with them to Badakhshan now, he wouldn't have to go back to Varanasi with nothing to show for his absence. The suggestion had seemed to be a welcome one, when Jefferji had proposed to him over breakfast.

"Tamisen keeps his business close, sir," Simon said. "I only know that he's come to Peshawar to assist you in an expedition to Badakhshan. As you say, my plans have changed. I'd be very interested."

The kebabs were good. The sherbet was good, too. Normally Jefferji would save the sweets for after the meat course, but iced anything was too good to be wasted even this early in the summer, and the meal was, after all, set out for them in all its glory all at once. Service *a la francaise*, Jefferji thought. The table that Fontenoy had brought in for the occasion was fortunately a large one. Jefferji ate steadily and in silence.

"The route will take us north through challenging terri-tory all the way to Fayzabad," Fontenoy said. "and a little distance east from there—I don't know exactly how far. I suppose the flora may present some novelty. Previous English travelers have restricted their interests to game, and frankly there haven't been many of them."

"Several references exist in the master library," Simon said, musingly. "Nothing worth mentioning within the past thirty-five years. It would be interesting to see whether Panshi's Powder herb still winters over. It's very hard to find ones that have survived the five years that it takes for the root to really develop."

Captain Fontenoy grinned. "I'll be frank, Hakim Jericho, Tamisen. Nothing in life is safe, and the journey will present its dangers. I have some acquaintance that may work in our favor: the Mehtar of Chitral; one or two old political connections that may have held up over twenty years. There's one man in particular, an old and very dear friend, who is well placed to offer us significant assistance."

After a moment of polite silence Captain Fontenoy picked up his narrative again. "Now, you're both young men, with your places to make. I'm not a young man. I'm proud of my service to Holkar but there are far fewer places for colonels than captains, for generals fewer still. I mean to start a new career to keep me in my old age. Antiquities. I mean to deal in antiquities."

"I know nothing of antiquities, sir." Simon sounded cautious, reserved. "There's not much I could contribute to your enterprise, I'm afraid."

"A misapprehension, if you'll allow me, Hakim Jericho. For one, you are a student of medicine, and such men smooth the way wonderfully." Fontenoy stood up, with an air of holding too much excitement within his bosom to quite contain. "There is a little more to it than I first revealed, however. Shall I explain how you can put my mission forward materially?"

Jefferji felt a sudden thrill, a prickling at the back of his neck. Something more? A secret mission? Were they going to be spies? Myamah would never have allowed it. Maybe Captain Fontenoy hadn't told her. Maybe he had, and she had. "Yes, please," Simon said; for both of them. "I'm very intrigued."

Captain Fontenoy sat back down. "Well, it's like this. The British in Bengal are concerned about Russians north and west of the Kun-Lun mountains. They want maps. They'll pay money."

Then they could just ask anybody, traders, expatriates, pilgrims. Couldn't they? No; mapmaking was an art and a science, and required more than casual observation.

Jefferji reconsidered. If Badakhshan would not come to Bengal, the only alternative was to send Bengal—or a representative—to Badakhshan.

Simon looked a little uncertain, however. "And how do I play into this, sir?"

"I intend for Tamisen to help me make a map—clandestinely, to avoid suspicion of being a spy. None now exist; the Bengal intelligence services say so. I'm told they have confirmation of a reliable nature from Delhi, Mysore, and Pune alike."

Two of whose intelligence services would have an only academic interest at present, but the point was made. A map of a route through Badakhshan would be valuable.

"How am I to do that, sir?" Jefferji asked. He couldn't sketch. He was a good judge of distances, but only within the limited dimensions of a stage, or a firing range. He was not among the more successful hunters of Tengarpore. "I have no cartography in me."

Leaning over the table Fontenoy patted him on the arm, clearly mindful of the fact that Jefferji's shoulder was sore. "You have musical notation, and you can write a Persian script. I've worked out a cipher, Jefferji, and together we'll make all the notes we need as we travel. If you're willing, Hakim Jericho, you'll supplement the record in proper Devanagari writing. I doubt anybody in Badakhshan reads the Vedas, and you can improvise a recitation if necessary, perhaps?"

Notes as musical notations in the Persian writing, something innocuous and familiar even to people who were themselves illiterate. Notes as well in the Sanskrit devanagari script. Captain Fontenoy might make notes in English, in Roman script, or not. Jefferji could see the logic in it.

Captain Fontenoy leaned back in his chair. "And there's a

third share of sixty thousand rupees in it for each you, if you're willing. Maybe even more, if we sell the finished product to other interested government agencies as well."

Twenty thousand rupees. It was enough money to command anybody's serious consideration, and Simon—so far as Jefferji knew, at any rate—had no stash of patrimonial jewels.

Simon's voice held a little quaver. "It's a very pretty purse." But not one easily gained, Jefferji knew. Reward never came without risk. He had to admit to a certain degree of apprehension, but the intrigue of the idea was more than sufficiently engaging to tip the balance in his mind. At least for Jefferji, at least for now. He wasn't in a position to speak for Simon, whose words were very much to the point as Simon continued. "But are we to hazard our lives? And what about our honesty?"

Fontenoy seemed to consider the question carefully before he replied. "I can pledge on my honor that the map is secondary to my primary purpose—antiquities to sell. The appetite for maps is a long-standing one, and serves no immediate strictly political purpose that I know of. You need neither participate in nor countenance the enterprise by coming with us, of course. I'd ask you to keep my secret until our safe return, one way or the other."

Simon had apparently been thinking hard and fast. "I'll have to show a record of where I've collected samples and made observations," he said, thoughtfully. "And that becomes public knowledge through the Varanasi libraries. If that will earn me a share of sixty thousand rupees, it will be very useful to me."

Simon wanted to go. Jefferji could hear it. "What if we're thought to be enemy spies, sir?" Jefferji asked. There was that risk-reward equation to be considered. "Is Simon in danger of guilt by association?"

Fontenoy shook his head. "No one will be watching for us. We might lose our notes, I might lose my antiquities. I can't say there isn't any danger of embarrassment over potential misunderstandings, Hakim Jericho, but I wouldn't risk the life of my friend Ganders's son for any amount of money. And we have friends who will be watching out for us."

Jefferji blushed, and was glad to be spared exposure. Captain Fontenoy had told Jefferji stories of his father, but almost always lighthearted and affectionate ones. He was uncomfortable when Fontenoy got serious. He didn't need to hear Fontenoy say "I loved your father, and you for his sake" to know that it was true.

The room fell silent. In the waiting quiet, the sudden knock at the door startled Jefferji halfway out of his chair, but it was only Rashid come to take away the dishes. He'd brought fresh tea, and fruit.

When he'd gone, Simon shrugged his shoulders. "'Nothing ventured,'" Simon said. "Let's all go to Badakhshan, and each seek his own kind of treasure there."

Fontenoy raised his teacup. Jefferji touched glasses with him and Simon alike, with all solemnity. They drank.

"I'm glad," Fontenoy said. "Now I've got to keep an appointment with General Avitabile that may hold me until tomorrow morning, when we can put our heads together with respect to what we'll need by way of supplies. Outfitting is my ticket. The both of you, no argument with me on this if you please. I'll take it out of our proceeds when the time comes."

They were to make a map, and Captain Fontenoy knew where to get money for it. Money was treasure. That made it a treasure map. Didn't it? And antiquities were typically buried; that was how they survived to become antiquities. So they were going to Badakhshan to map out buried treasure.

There wasn't anything quite like it in the classic repertoire. Jefferji would have to write this saga up himself, to be danced in the best heroic style. Guru-ji had told him it was time he create his maiden piece of choreography. He could debut the adventure at the Bharaj fair. It would be a masterpiece of storytelling, only slightly embroidered and almost all true.

But first there was the rest of this meal to dispose of, or it would go to waste. Jefferji and Simon stood politely and bowed Captain Fontenoy out of the room, and then together, by mutual and unspoken consent, sat down to conclude the consumption of Rashid's provisions, with the happy prospect of adventure in their minds.

The room was dark and quiet, none too clean but Broderick was reasonably secure in its safety. It had been three days. There was no reward for his apprehension, not that his informant could report, and his informant was in a position to know.

"They're leaving two days after tomorrow," Rashid said, standing in front of Broderick at the plain wooden table that served as dresser, table, desk, dining room, and washing station all in one. "I didn't hear many details. Through Badakhshan to Fayzabad, at least to start, and yes, Captain Fontenoy has a map, though it is really a sketch, at this point."

Broderick had realized right away that if he meant to find out Fontenoy's plans he'd need someone close to Fontenoy who could speak English. Nobody in the native city seemed to care who Broderick was, or why he wanted to find out who worked in the guesthouse of the Bengal British residency. A few small coins was all it had cost him, in the end, to locate the exact man. But would Broderick be able to fully enlist him?

"Have you been able to get a good look, perhaps a copy?" Broderick asked. "We'll be much better off if we get there first."

Rashid was a well-paid man with a responsible job, but he was a Mohammedan in a city full of Sikhs who hated Mohammedans—especially those of Afghani extraction. A man whose attitude towards his employers was rational and independent, as well, a man who was open to suggestion where his self-interest was concerned. Ripe for exploitation.

Rashid shook his head. "Only once, sahib. But Captain Fontenoy is going out this evening to take leave of General Avitabile. They are friends. I have tracing materials."

The story as Broderick had built it up from Rashid's naïve reports was that Fontenoy was seeking buried treasure, ancient and forgotten, which was lawfully the property of the first man who unearthed it—as long as he could make off with it undetected. Naturally a map was required.

"Good man." Broderick could be honestly appreciative.

One step ahead of Tamisen every inch of the way, that was the way to do it, planning the best time and place to take revenge as they went.

"I will need a little money to send the night watchman out for snacks," Rashid said. "More to outfit you, Holyoke sahib."

Broderick nodded vigorously, of course. "Take my purse," he said. It wasn't all the gold he'd gotten for the horse, but it was enough to pass for the whole of a fugitive's store. "Use what you need. Outfit us both, Rashid. You're coming with me, aren't you? We have our fortunes to seek."

Rashid took the purse Broderick offered him with a deferential nod. Broderick could almost hear the machinery of Rashid's mind, testing the weight of the gold, considering whether the certain gain of money in hand outweighed the promised treasure Broderick had proposed to him, whether he could leverage a reward by betraying Broderick's presence in the absence of any official interest, whether he could explain his own involvement.

When Rashid replied Broderick knew he'd won the point. "Yes, sahib. I'll get a copy of the map." From now on, Broderick knew, Rashid was Broderick's man. "I have a reliable man to obtain supplies. I'll get it all put together as quickly as I can."

Until Broderick saw the map he had no way of knowing its level of detail. He didn't dare alert Fontenoy to his presence, as outright theft unquestionably would. No. Let Fontenoy do the heavy lifting, Fontenoy and Tamisen and that third party Tamisen had apparently picked up along the side of the road. All Broderick had to do was follow along behind.

If there was a treasure, he'd take it and go north to find the Russians whose threatened incursion into the kingdom of Kabul had so exercised Lord Auckland's apprehension. If there was none, he'd go east into Kistwar and seek service with Gulab Singh, a man to whom Broderick had much to offer, and one unlikely to be displaced from power by the death of Ranjit Singh. Quite the reverse.

In either case he'd be revenged on Tamisen, and anybody else who stood in his way. Killing in self-defense, that wasn't murder. And if the truth about Broderick Holyoke ever came out it would be the end of him.

If these then are mountains, Jefferji told himself, *they are welcome to themselves, and heartily so.* They were nothing more than glorified rocks with an inflated sense of their own importance, having neither beauty nor comfort to recommend them: bare and black, and disagreeably icy, completely lacking in the lovely red and pink that had made Jaipur the queen of Rajputana.

Neither of a noble and up-reaching form or of a soft and rounded one, they were wounded and scored with gashes and great spurs of bare, sharp, cold, and altogether uninviting rock. All of the same color. Jefferji could get no sense of scale. There was nothing to use as a benchmark to measure these rocks against but more rock, and every time he climbed up yet another rise to seek the welcome view of some green valley it was only to be faced with yet more rock. More rock. And then again, more rock.

The water wasn't blue, it wasn't white, it had no green and creamy tint of indolence and white marble bottom, no small plants to wave languidly in the gentle current on a temple grounds as beautiful as agates. It was the color of mud. A river of slate grey mud, brown ground mud, grey and ugly pebbles on a grey and ugly river, and taken all together, he was very much out of temper with mountains already, and they had only been *en route* for a week.

Which only made it all the more annoying of Captain Fontenoy to love them with all his heart and of Simon Jericho to exclaim over one bit of frankly unattractive scrubby sort of herb after another and make sketch after sketch in the uncertain light of a fire in the evening.

"Beautiful evening," Captain Fontenoy called back over his shoulder. "This is the life, eh, Tamisen?"

Jefferji waved a hand as cheerfully as he could in token of having heard, but there was rebellion in his heart. It wasn't his idea of the life. He didn't like these rocks.

Oh, there were green places here and there where little rivulets ran down from rocks into the river valley to nourish little fragments of villages at which a man could buy eggs and apricots. They simply could not compare with the forty-seven different varieties of grapes that he'd heard were to be found in the great bazaar of Kabul. They'd skirted Kabul, because Captain Fontenoy feared being ambushed into socializing. Jefferji wasn't sure he'd tasted more than seven kinds of grapes since then.

Still, for all the fault he had to find with the rocks, he had to admit that when fruit was to be found, it evoked the luscious plenties of Paradise. It was surely early for there to be fruit in such abundance, stone fruit, as though the trees felt they had to hurry to bring their work to a successful conclusion before the weather started to change again.

Under the sparse shade of a half-bald tree set well back from the road, with its own semi-circle of rocks to conceal it and its own trickle of a little stream, Captain Fontenoy dropped the reins of his good horse Farouk, dismounted, and started the unsaddling. Unburdening the hairy little pack ponies, the ugly little yabus whose short legs belied their phenomenal stamina, Jefferji shooed them onto a sheltered patch of earth where little tufts of forage would provide them with something to snack on.

Coriander's turn next—a man couldn't play favorites, and there were more of the yabus than there was of his darling girl—and then once at her ease Coriander put her nose to the little stream and drank before she went to gossip with Farouk for a bit as though they hadn't already spent every moment of the past ten days together night and day. Marigold, the beautiful black mule they'd brought from Peshawar to carry their camping kit, gave Jefferji a little nudge by way of conversation before she followed the yabus upslope just a bit to seek her own appetizers.

She didn't care for what Jefferji had laid in store, and it made him self-conscious to have his best offerings rejected. So there was that, on top of everything else. Everybody was in a good humor except for him, and it was the fault of the rocks, Jefferji was sure. Yet another reason that he didn't like them.

The homely hills of Tengarpore in winter could be as bleak and bare as those of the river valley they were traveling up to Chitral; Jefferji had determined *that* within a day of their departure from Peshawar. But these Chitrali hills were so much higher, and the river bottom did not stretch away toward the blue horizon of the great Thar desert, but ran into an abrupt barrier of mountains. Captain Fontenoy insisted these were mere hills compared to Himalaya, but if these were hills what did mountains look like?

It was mid-May. In Tengarpore the heat would have begun, the great baking that turned the entire country into oven-dried brick and made the architecture of breeze management the exalted art it was. There would be a great carrying of charpoy beds up onto the roof of the bachelors' quarters for the catching of night breezes, if there ever were any.

Patiently, Jefferji fed the nightly fire as it settled into its rocky divan, twigs, little branches, a few shavings of bark. They had firewood, no problem about that. The road was well traveled but not over-frequently so, and there was adequate brushwood for the finding.

"Four days, perhaps, and we reach the fort at Chitral," Captain Fontenoy announced, changing his boots out for camp slippers to the sympathetic approval of Jefferji's toes.

Jefferji could ride, almost as well as ever, but until his departure from Tengarpore he hadn't ridden all day every day for days on end as his shoulder continued to heal. His feet were used to more freedom, even if his boots were well broken in.

There was no dancing in these camps. That was a problem too. The ground was too rocky, and time didn't allow any preparation of a suitably flat space.

"Are there flat roofs?" he asked over his shoulder, from his fire-starting duties at the ad hoc hearth. The sun was going down. The sharp line of the hills wore a glorious tiara of gold and amethyst. But it was too high a line, too sharp. It made him homesick, even though it was beautiful. If there were flat places in Chitral fort he could dance on them, and that at least would be a comfort.

"You shall have flat roofs and open places. But you might want to be careful, Tamisen. Guests who make themselves too welcome sometimes find themselves unable to leave when they like, and the music can get a little monotonous."

Well, fine. No dancing, then, for fear of becoming too interesting to be let go. He would miss out on the adventure, if that happened. And there was more adventure to be had than Simon could use up on his own, Jefferji was certain of that.

"I'll go for the rest of the water," he said, resigned.

The fire was well ablaze, the kettle simmering briskly. Simon was cooking dinner; he was so much better at it than Captain Fontenoy and Jefferji combined that the chore had devolved to him, and to the mutual benefit of them all, he had not shirked it. At least that way he got a decent meal out of it, he said. So Simon cooked, Jefferji carried water, and Captain Fontenoy tended the horses and Marigold, and talked about philosophy.

When Jefferji came back up the gentle slope from the clear tributary stream beside which they'd pitched camp, Simon had dinner on. Gunnery and Coriander and Captain Fontenoy's good grey Farouk—as well as the lady mule Marigold, an admitted beauty with wonderfully soft ears and an unexpectedly sweet temperament—were browsing in the underbrush.

Simon was talking to Captain Fontenoy about the future. "Will we be taking on more mules or camels in Chitral, or trusting to luck to hire in Fayzabad?"

Right now they had only Marigold. She and Gunnery had struck up a friendly acquaintance early on. Her dam had been an English horse, Jefferji thought, to judge from her conformation and her height. Coriander had been jealous, but she was working past it. Farouk hadn't paid a great deal of attention to any of them. So far as Farouk was apparently concerned, being Captain Fontenoy's horse was a calling sufficient unto itself.

"Ah. Well." Fontenoy's tone of voice was interesting; Jefferji had heard it before, his *your question is good but somewhat wide of the mark, did you but realize it* tone. "Let's talk about that."

About what? Jefferji wondered. Oh. Right. Fontenoy was answering the question Simon had asked him, just now, beasts of burden to be found in Chitral or Fayzabad. Jefferji set his leather buckets of water down beside the fire. The animals had all watered at the stream. One bucket was for washing tomorrow morning, because the water—while as sweet and good as any Jefferji had ever tasted—was very,

very cold, and he continued to hope that it would benefit from the company of the lingering fire as the night wore on.

Dinner smelled good. They'd gotten some eggs and a few surplus chickens at a little house beside the road earlier today, the chickens very obligingly plucked and gutted on demand. Tough aged chickens for dinner; eggs in the morning. Jefferji crouched down on his heels to gaze into the fire at what Simon was preparing, interested.

"Can't carry many inscriptions with one mule," Jefferji said, to Simon and the fire alike. "Coriander won't tolerate hauling. She minds me enough as it is, and dust makes her sneeze."

"Well, there's artifacts, and there's artifacts," Fontenoy said. He'd lit his pipe. A good corner of Marigold's pack was in tobacco; it made a very useful item in trade, though neither Jefferji nor Simon used it as habitually as Fontenoy did. "Uncle Zafar's interests focused on the less bulky sort. Yes, we'll hire pack animals, possibly in Ishkashem. Camou-flage."

"But statuary," Simon protested, his attention divided between his evident curiosity and dinner. There was bread baking on the rounded surface of their second kettle, which was overturned at the edge of the fire. "Pottery. Coins. Books."

"Exactly, coins," Fontenoy said, very agreeably indeed. Jefferji turned around to face him. This was becoming more interesting than dinner, which was in itself a novelty. "Think smaller, lighter. Three years ago, some interesting articles began to trickle down into the Delhi markets through Amritsar. One or two gold coins yes, but of most interest a piece of gold plate as big as a man's palm. There were inscrip-tions."

Fontenoy was having fun with them. Jefferji was delight-ed: Fontenoy had clearly been holding a treat in reserve, and Jefferji didn't know quite what it was yet, but he knew he was going to like it. Because this was Captain Fontenoy talking. *I've brought you something that needs your looking after, Tamisen. This is important. Can you be very good and careful? It's a parrot. Its name is Almaviva. You can teach it to talk, if you promise not to use bad words.*

"What did the inscriptions say, sir?" Jefferji asked.

With a final flourishing stir, Simon set the communal pot on its makeshift tripod beside the fire, and passed the bread around. Joining Captain Fontenoy on the rug beside the fire, Simon picked a small black cinder off his bread, waiting—as Jefferji was—for the chicken to cool enough to eat.

"That appears to be subject to controversy. The correspondence was of large volume, and very heated. Different hands saw the artifact, different hands transcribed it—one scholar actually took a rubbing, but the text was so old that the process apparently destroyed what was left of the inscription. What interested me most was the discussion of the difficulty in deciphering the text. It was inscribed between and around five fine spinel rubies."

A rug big enough for all of them to sit on had been discussed and discarded as too heavy. As it was, the sitting rug doubled as bedding for Captain Fontenoy, since it was the largest and thickest one they had. Jefferji sat on his own bedroll, settling in with chicken on flatbread in hand. This was getting more and more fun by the moment. "Rubies, sir."

"And the rubies themselves inscribed. Here. I have one." Digging deep into an inside pocket in the long shirt next to his skin Captain Fontenoy drew forth a paper packet and unfolded it carefully, holding up the contents to the light. It was as large as any of the stones Jefferji had left in security in Peshawar, and each of those had been worth a handsome sum. Where it caught the firelight, it shot a gleaming lance of blood-red light into the darkness to muddle against the side of Marigold's pack where it lay.

Simon set his bread plate down carefully in his lap, receiving the gem as Captain Fontenoy passed it to him. "They pried the stone out of its setting?" Simon asked with a note of incredulity in his voice, turning the ruby to admire the light in it.

Captain Fontenoy nodded. "Quite so, and there were recriminations. Some said the piece should have remained intact, others that its pieces should be distributed as widely as possible, to determine their source and meaning. In the end it all came down to money, and Uncle Zafar had much less of that once he obtained this, but still enough left over to trace the artifact to Fayzabad and the jeweler who'd sold it."

Simon passed the ruby to Jefferji. If he squinted, he could barely make out faint lettering within its red glow, but he didn't know the script.

"I'd like to see it again by daylight." Jefferji returned it to Captain Fontenoy. "Could nobody make it out, the inscription?"

Fontenoy had said controversy; that implied alternate meanings.

"Some read 'Arjuna cast aside.' Then they fell into disagreement between 'glorious indifference' versus 'sorrow and mourning.' Please don't ask me to follow the translations. At least one other scholar read 'even-handed fate deals,' or drops, or throws, and no hint about what was dropped or dealt or thrown. And one voice was convinced it said 'arrow of good strike,' if I'm remembering it right."

Arjuna and *even-handed* could be interpreted together, ambidextrous Arjuna.

"That's how many people know about this, sir?" The meat was cool enough to eat, now. It wasn't as tough as Jefferji had anticipated, and he ate with vigorous appreciation, waving a denuded thigh bone at Simon in salute.

"Six men formed the syndicate. Unequal shares, because they're of varying means, one or two so poor they're members almost by charity. Impoverished in the cause of knowledge. I have to admire their dedication, which is why I took a share as the seventh, rather than hire for this expedition."

Surprise stuck in Jefferji's throat; it was with difficulty that he managed to swallow his mouthful of chicken. "Syndicate, sir." There'd been no talk about paid expeditions, and shares, and so forth. And yet while Captain Fontenoy apparently had a comfortable life, had anybody ever said he was independently wealthy? He'd paid to outfit Jefferji and Simon alike, undertaking both provisioning and stores. "The map's to be made for the syndicate, then."

Fontenoy nodded his head left and right, yes and no. "One particular portion of the map only for the syndicate, a small area of no political interest. It'll be a study to see how best to arrange that. We can't have all the intelligence services in India coming after what I hope to find."

In Tengarpore, Fontenoy had said antiquities. In Peshawar, he'd said maps. En route to Chitral, he spoke of a treasure trove of ancient jewels. What would it be the next time someone asked? But Jefferji didn't think he was worried. It did all fit together. Nothing Fontenoy had said had been actually untrue, in any important sense.

"The map remains a commercial item?" Simon asked, thoughtfully. Jefferji wondered if Simon's mind was running in the same direction as his own: if there was money, was all of it to be shared three ways? There were investors. He and Simon would share the work—would they also share the proceeds?

Folding the ruby up into its wad of paper wrapping Fontenoy put it away. "Yes, you may be assured of that. The map will be commercial. As to any other possibilities, I'm not empowered to say, so with your permission, I'd rather not speculate."

The sale of a map to British intelligence was Captain Fontenoy's private business, and he'd generously offered to share the proceeds of that. His money, in a sense. If he found an antiquarian treasure it was on behalf of the friends and acquaintances of his Uncle Zafar. Jefferji understood. Clearly Captain Fontenoy could in honor make no representations without consultations.

But the potential was there.

It added spice and savor to his dinner, as Jefferji sat and talked with Simon and Captain Fontenoy about Chitral.

The very next night they stopped at an old dilapidated cara-vanserai to treat themselves to an evening with someone else to do the cooking. Jefferji knew that the beds were likely to have a life of their own—he'd communed with the small annoyances of the earth often enough in his dancing career. Still, it would make a change. It was cold at night, and could be unpleasantly so by day, as well. The shade of the rocks kept sunlight from warming the air during the earliest and latest hours, and comfort fled from the air as though it didn't like the mountains any more than he did.

"Thank you," he said to the man who brought them hot bread and a big bowl of yoghurt—the man responsible to whatever civil authority might be keeping an eye on the good treatment of travelers, by the good quality of his clothing. "This is good." Just because Jefferji didn't like rocks that had too good an opinion of themselves, there was no reason to be impolite. He wouldn't like to emulate these mountains, tall and brusque and ugly and of no use to anyone. "Do we come close to Chitral?"

The proprietor was a little puzzled by Jefferji's accent, Jefferji could tell. He had to work on some of his inflections, which were more varied and musical than those of the mountains. This dialect was as sharp and keen-edged as the rocks whose attitude he did not like.

"Three days to Chitral," the proprietor said with a nod. "Do you stop there?"

They were all together at a single table, he and Simon and Captain Fontenoy, but then there was only the single table— a long broad plank rectangle with benches along one side, stools along the other, miscellaneous chairs making up the seating at both ends.

Captain Fontenoy was eating yoghurt on a piece of bread, with raisins. Fontenoy could follow some of the conversation, but didn't speak enough of the language to try to speak it yet himself. Simon was frowning at his latest sketch. Jefferji shook his head, speaking quickly before Simon could decide to go sift through the forage for herbal treasure.

"We go on to Fayzabad to meet my brother. He's promised us a load of fine silk to sell in Kabul."

There'd been some embroidering on their story since they'd left Peshawar. The yabus had to be explained, but nobody needed to know that Fontenoy was making a map.

"I had a brother once." The proprietor brought pitchers of milk and dishes of nutmeats. He nodded at Simon, mean-ingfully. "We had different mothers too. Mine was a whore, alas."

The offhand remark surprised Jefferji, and he laughed. "God save me from suggesting that his mother was—anything but pure," Jefferji said, with one hand to Simon's shoulder to bring him in on the joke whether or not he understood it. "The hakim and I have neither mother nor father in common. *He* is our sister's husband's uncle. And owns these beasts." Jefferji nodded at the yabus.

The proprietor shrugged and went away. Fontenoy waited for a moment, until they were more or less alone at the table under the tree. "About three days, am I right?—I'm right. Gratify an old man, Tamisen, let me imagine I remember the road, after all these years."

Jefferji certainly hoped that Fontenoy remembered the road, because Jefferji didn't have more than a vague notion of where they were going. Yes, Captain Fontenoy had shown him maps and discussed routes, and Jefferji had had schooling in reading maps. The fact that Fontenoy remembered where he was meant something more to him, Jefferji guessed. A way to claim, to reclaim, the man that he'd been twenty years ago when he'd been younger and stronger than today.

If Fontenoy were any stronger, Jefferji didn't think he could have kept up. Fontenoy wore him out well and truly as it was. But then Fontenoy liked the mountains, so maybe they liked him, and were channeling some of the strength of their ugly bare rocks into his body.

The proprietor came back again with a dish of boiled potatoes and another wooden stool, setting them both down on table and ground in turn. Joining them for a little gossip, Jefferji decided, and why not? The man didn't seem overwhelmed with customers just now, though there were people wandering up and down the eight or ten booths on either side of the road.

"There was an Englishman through here not long ago," the proprietor said, reaching for a boiled potato. There was a pile of salt heaped up in the middle of the bowl, and the proprietor dipped his potato in it before he took a bite. The salt looked dirty—local product, perhaps—but did the trick well enough. It was generous of their host to bring it. "Tried to conceal it, but you can't mistake that smell of beef. With a servant, both of them on horseback, too. As fine as these, yes, truly."

Their weakest link in their loosely constructed three-poor-merchants story was exactly this point: good horses, not to speak of Marigold the mule. This was where the Peshawar part of the story came into its own.

"Oh, but we've only the use of these, my cousin," Jefferji said. "Would that they were mine to sell. And only till we reach Fayzabad. We're not supposed to be riding them, but who's to know? They'll go out of condition if they have no work. The whole world knows this to be true."

The joke succeeded; the proprietor laughed. It was interesting to Jefferji to see how truly horrible the teeth of these people were, blackened and cracked and leaning in their mouths like wheat stalks knocked awry by a horse passing. Perhaps it was in solidarity with the mountains.

"What account did they give of themselves, these men?" Jefferji asked, adjusting the tonal phrasing of his voice carefully to encourage the flow of the narrative. *Thus spake Malika's maid to draw the cherished secret out of the young maiden's pure bosom.*

"Well, the English horses were very hard-ridden. They might well have wanted fleet horses to outrun Gipur the One-Eyed, but I haven't heard any gossip about any fine plunder or horses to sell in only very slightly used condition. So they must have escaped the danger."

Jefferji stopped with a piece of salted bread halfway to his mouth, to show his interest in this news. "And we, how are we to avoid this prince among the mountains, who takes his prey like an eagle takes a young goat?"

The proprietor laughed with a gesture that was almost flirtatious. "Oh, Gipur is drawn off to the west, to seek Dost Mohammed Khan. Only we didn't tell the English that. They say the Emir is in Bokhara."

That's what they'd been saying in Peshawar, as well. Fontenoy would be interested in the story, once Jefferji had a chance to share it—Fontenoy had recognized the name, clearly enough.

The proprietor saw as much as well, and leaned forward over the table with a conspiratorial air. "It is a time of portents. English in Kabul. Foreigners in Fayzabad. Armed men, not traders. The cousin of the brother of my nephew's new wife's uncle has seen women riding on horseback with lances. Women."

He nodded as if to emphasize the truth of his claim, so Jefferji—understanding that he was expected to be completely astonished, as well as impressed—put on an appropriate face, wide-eyed, slack-jawed, the expression of the mean-spirited brother discovering that his sister was visited by a god, not a goatherd.

For his reward the man gave him a wink, rising to go tend to a new customer. "So be on the lookout if you go to Fayzabad. What would it be like to bed such a woman? Oh, could I but have the chance to find out."

Jefferji's mother had read to him about Amazons in the Greek histories, although she'd said they were just a story. His teachers had described the martial valor of Rajput women at war, and nothing he had heard would indicate that they bedded any differently than other women, except perhaps that they might accidentally stab one in a moment of amorous abandon if one hadn't taken the precaution of removing sharp objects from the place of repose prior to initiating the engagement. Any firearms, as well, because there was no sense in taking chances.

Captain Fontenoy was waiting patiently, eating raisins. "Two men came through recently, one of them English," Jefferji said, quietly, in the basic Urdu dialect that all three of them had in common to a greater or lesser extent. Speaking English was too much of a risk, especially since the topic of mysterious Englishmen was on the table. "The local bandits have gone to take employment with Dost Mohammed Khan. Who would the English have been?"

"No idea." Fontenoy kept his responses short, when they were in public; it was one way to minimize the attention he drew to himself. No one would take Fontenoy for Chitrali or Afghan, he didn't have a mountain face. But so long as he said little there was no reason for people to suspect him of being English rather than the claimed Punjabi. He wore Afghan costume comfortably enough. "Holyoke? Hard to guess."

But it was a strange road, and there were mountains. Any anomalies were unquestionably the fault of the rocks. Three days to Chitral. They'd find that English there, perhaps. And armed women on horseback besides. Why not?

"Amazons, too, he says," Jefferji said, and Simon looked

up from his sketch, clearly startled. Jefferji nodded. "Yes, female warriors, just like the Maharaja's bodyguard." Which Maharaja it was who was supposed to rejoice in an all-female guard Jefferji couldn't immediately call to mind, but Simon and Fontenoy would take the general point. Jefferji knew that Captain Fontenoy would find that thought intriguing. "In Fayzabad. I hope there may be fewer mountains. Or at least mountains of a different color."

Whether Fontenoy's laugh was over Amazons or the color of mountains Jefferji couldn't tell.

"Do I smell kebabs?" Fontenoy asked quietly, in a halting sort of what Jefferji thought was a Hyderabad dialect. One that might be less likely to be understood northeast of Kabul. "If there's lamb, we might need to spend the night. No offense to your excellent chicken, Hakim Jericho, just that a man likes the occasional change. We could hear more about those English, maybe." Or more about the Amazons.

The server came back to the common table with a platter of meat skewers and more hot flatbread, bringing his new customer with him. Captain Fontenoy's eyes lit up—at the prospect of the food, and the prospect of someone to pump for information Jefferji supposed—and he resigned himself to kebabs and conversation. There'd be no leaving for them before morning.

So long as they were stuck here, he might as well make the best of it. "This English, took he your store of fodder for his horses?" Coriander would expect some consideration, and the question would bring the subject back to the Englishman. "Because we'll have trouble with my brother's rich friend Mohandur if the horses are too lame. And the mare bites."

The proprietor's expression gladdened—a chance for more money, and also more gossip. "He paid in silver, meagerly enough. But he wouldn't stay long enough for the beasts to eat their fill, so as the English has already paid for it I'll sell you the leftovers for half price. On the other hand, you have more beasts."

Jefferji didn't know the hairy little yabu ponies very well, but they unquestionably had worked very hard, and uncomplainingly. Fontenoy's Farouk was worth his grain as well, even-tempered and hard-working as well as beautiful;

powerful and strong, silvery grey from his nose to his nettles, with his hind legs white from hock to hoof as though they were wrapped in puttees. All the mounts had earned a good feed and a little rest.

"Excuse my friend Fonjeny, he hears well but doesn't speak well. It embarrasses him to show his clumsiness to others," Jefferji said, to the man who'd just joined them. Jefferji didn't want people wondering at Fontenoy's taciturnity, or mistaking it for rudeness. "I am Hari-Prasad the dancer, called Prasad. Currently unemployed, alas. May we know your honored and respected name?"

"Dancer?" the man said, exchanging intrigued and eager glances with the proprietor. "I visit farmers for the lord of Chitral, on my way to report my news to the Mehtar. I love dancing, as does the Mehtar. If you would honor us with a demonstration of your art, I would feast you tonight with thanks, and your companions and beasts as well."

The proprietor looked a little, just a little, worried about that, but the newcomer's nod seemed to reassure him that nobody was proposing to give away any of his goods. In Tengarpore the man who visited farms for Jaisal Singh to keep up to date on how well the seed was sprouting or the grain growing was called a farm agent. In larger-wealthier-states than Tengarpore such men frequently had money. This one was offering to pay room and board.

Jefferji had hardly had time to more than run through his exercises, morning and evening, since they'd left Peshawar—and his map, of course, the secret one, the one neither Fontenoy nor Simon were to know about until he could reveal it in all of its splendor and glory. And his notes were pertinent to his music, if anybody noticed them, if anybody asked. So this was all in support of their concealment in plain sight.

"It's southern dance," Jefferji said, by way of warning. "In the style of Delhi. I'm very out of practice, I'm afraid, but if there's a drummer to be found I'll do my best to make for you a tamasha." Tamasha, any kind of a spectacle to be wondered at; excitement, a show, a burning, a fete, a flooded river in full spate. Anything to break the monotony. "Is there a place where I can arrange my clothes?"

He couldn't dance in boots. At least he'd never tried it. In camp he changed into the felted fabric camp slippers, and finding a flat place was a challenge. The road wasn't flat, but since there was apparently grain here there'd be a threshing ground, and that would do.

"Go and tell everybody," the farm agent said with an expansive gesture. "Tell them that their friend Mohammed Mishram invites them to a show. And to bring drums, those who have them."

That was a daunting prospect—a collection of amateur drummers, each with his own drums, each drum at its own pitch and timbre—but if they could all stay on beat, any beat, it'd be all right. Jefferji could play the music in his head. He knew all the music he would need by heart.

Captain Fontenoy was looking at him with a curious expression: fond, respectful, and admiring, approving of his action. His ploy. All of the news to be had would come to them. Fontenoy clearly felt that Jefferji had done well. That realization made Jefferji unexpectedly happy, and the mountains all around seemed just for now a little less grey than they had before.

Chapter Seven
A Curse on Coins and Rubies

It had been three days now since Tamisen had declared himself to be a dancer, and successfully, as well. His performances over the past two nights had been well attended, and generously rewarded in gifts of fruit and clothing. Hakim Jericho in particular had been the beneficiary of samples of herbs and medicinals. He was making careful record of folk remedies, so Tamisen's stratagem helped cover Jericho's note-taking as well.

Sitting in the privileged place he'd been granted on the roof, Fontenoy looked around him. This wasn't the first time he'd seen the fortress of Chitral, and it hadn't changed much in twenty years—unless, perhaps, the precarious bracing that held up the walls looked even more precarious than before.

The noble house of the Mehtar of Chitral was as low-ceilinged and soot-blackened as that of any landed peasant, only somewhat larger. Small rooms were easier to heat. It could get very cold in Chitral, especially when Chitral was buried under three feet of snow. The Mehtar held his audience on the rooftop; it was the only place within the fortress walls where numbers of men could congregate, and people on nearby roofs could see too.

In the middle of the Mehtar's roof where space had been cleared for him, Tamisen was dancing. He hadn't carried any costume with him, but people had been bringing him bells since he'd first announced himself to be a dancer, and good-natured women young and old had sewn them onto long bandages for him to wind around his ankles. There were three drummers, none of them on the same cue. Tamisen apparently found some rhythmic pattern there to follow even so, or perhaps he'd shut the drummers out of his mind entirely.

That Tamisen was dancing something specific and internally coherent seemed clear to Fontenoy, and apparently to these others—Tamisen's audience—as well. He'd tied a red shawl around his waist, and scraps of colored fabric around his legs just above the knee as well as around his arms above the elbow. His hair fell in four long braids, two behind, two before.

Tamisen's long hair was not, after all, the problem Fontenoy had feared it might be. He was counting on Tamisen's ability to pass for native to keep him safe, if anything went wrong. And why not? Tamisen's grandfather had been nurtured in the court of Tipu Sultan. His father had placed him, if by proxy, in the care of a Rajput prince before he was even born; Tamisen *was* a native, although with European blood. But he was much more than that.

Fontenoy had thought only of Tamisen's upbringing and his ability to learn and speak new languages when he'd convinced his contacts that Tamisen was the man for a mapping mission, one to be watched with an eye toward recruitment as a confidential agent for all manner of specialized tasks. Tamisen's ability to dance put those qualifications, valuable though they were, into the shade. It was astonishing. It was such a simple thing, and so extraordinary.

Tamisen's hands drew perfect scripts of god-praise in the air, and the discipline with which he used his instrument—his body—was that of a virtuoso. Stripped down to what amounted to his underwear, he seemed taller than he actually was, and everyone around him was sitting down, so he seemed larger than any mortal man could be, all alone in the dancing space.

It made the sheer athletic power of his dance all the more impressive, not least because it was so precisely contained. No matter how ferocious his approaches, or the leaps he made as he fought an unseen foe, his energy was confined and contained within the boundaries of the rug that had been put down for him. Tamisen danced barefoot, and made the bells around his calves ring on one beat or another as though he and the drummers had practiced with one another for years.

There were men here who could almost certainly leap higher than Tamisen, jump more quickly than Tamisen, demonstrate more martial skill with sword and shield than Tamisen. But none—Fontenoy was sure—could do any of it with Tamisen's almost frightening degree of control, the halts so sudden and so perfect, the body so composed even in mid-air that it almost looked like Tamisen was levitating.

If it hadn't been for the fact that some of the strands of Tamisen's hair that had worked free from his braids had been captured by sweat on his face and stuck to the skin of his cheeks and forehead, there'd be no visible signs of actual physical effort there at all.

Fontenoy didn't know the story Tamisen was dancing, but he had enough vocabulary to understand from the way in which Tamisen stopped at the bottom of a final figure—sinking from the top of one last joyful spin onto one knee on the rug, hands held palm-to-palm, head bowed, perfectly aligned in a posture of respectful conclusion—that he was finished.

The drummers fell abruptly silent. Tamisen's pose spoke more clearly than words. *This is the end of my story. I offer it to you, my host, with my sincere respect. I hope it's pleased you.* Tamisen didn't need to give a signal. He was one.

In the established and sophisticated palaces of native princes, in the temples great and humble alike of Rajputana, dance was as much a part of artistic entertainment as singing. Fontenoy had always enjoyed watching Tamisen dance because he loved Tamisen for his father's sake. But he hadn't really understood how good Tamisen actually was at it until now that he saw Tamisen isolated, as it were, from the culture in which the idea of dance was part of the language.

Fontenoy didn't speak the dialects of Chitrali language. Tamisen did—at least Tamisen could communicate well enough—but Tamisen didn't have to. Tamisen's body spoke. That language was universally comprehensible. With Tamisen with him to dance, Fontenoy could go anywhere.

Tamisen stood up and pushed his escaped hair up out of his eyes, smiling at the Mehtar and his audience. Nobody threw coins or sweets as they might at girls at a party, Fontenoy was happy to see. Nobody even approached Tamisen until Tamisen moved. And as a token of respect in this communal society Fontenoy couldn't think of anything more powerful than leaving the space around Tamisen empty, for his exclusive use.

But when Tamisen turned to his left to salute the drums and the drummers the noise went from loud to wild. Surrounded by a clamoring crowd, Tamisen was as much drawn as escorted to a thick cushion on the best rug next to the ruler of Chitral. Men clustered around with food and drink and gifts of fabric to lay across Tamisen's shoulders.

Fontenoy stood up. The people gathered around the Mehtar let him through to take a seat somewhat behind Tamisen— definitely below the Mehtar, needless to say—to share some of the delicacies presented for Tamisen's enjoyment and approval. Fruit juices flavored with expensive spices and cooled with snow, for all that it wasn't noticeably warm. Fragrant cups of strong tea, and that which was pressed on Fontenoy had been sweetened with almost frantic generosity.

Something moved past Fontenoy's field of vision at its periphery, a man, a face. The place was packed with men. They all had faces. What was different about this one? Fontenoy turned his head, but all he saw were Chitralis with friendly smiles. Searching the crowd with his eyes, Fontenoy tried to find one anomalous face out of many. Failing, he shrugged, and settled back on the cushion.

Tamisen's brilliant idea had given them an unprecedented degree of access to these influential tribesmen, and every assistance was eagerly on offer to put their travel forward. The only potential problem that Fontenoy could foresee was the possibility that the Mehtar wouldn't let them leave, but keep Tamisen on as an honored prisoner, showered with gifts but unable to get away.

Still, if that happened, Deravass Khan would know where to find them. Fontenoy sipped politely at his achingly sweet tea and gave himself over to enjoyment of the privilege that had been granted to them, in this wild place, because Geoffrey Tamisen could dance.

There were apparently immutable laws of Chitrali hospitality
that absolutely mandated an escort for an honored guest for
some several stipulated days of travel from one's door.
Jefferji hadn't decided whether he was honored or intimi-
dated. They meant to see him clear to Fayzabad, but Captain
Fontenoy didn't seem to be concerned. Jefferji supposed they
could always wait a few days in Fayzabad until the Chitralis
started home and double back, if it came to that.

The cold and inhospitable slopes of the Dora Pass had the
additional attraction of dirty ice to add to their ghastly gray
charms. Coriander didn't like it and neither did Jefferji. He
worried about her in the cold—Fontenoy said it could get very
cold—but how could he have left Coriander out of his adventure? With the sun high in the sky it wasn't very much colder
than a winter night in Tengarpore. The Dora Pass being
called "pass" clearly implied that there was a descent to
lower ground on the other side. That would mean warmer.

Amid the rocks and miserable scrub and dirty ice, Lehna
Singh—the captain of their escort, six men all told, three
pack ponies—drew to a stop and sat on horseback, watching
something approach. Jefferji saw nothing, but they kept him
in the middle of the group, an honored guest—or valuable
commodity. Captain Fontenoy rode beside him, and to
Captain Fontenoy, Lehna Singh turned and waved: *Come
forward.* Jefferji was as curious as the next man. He came too.

There was a single man coming slowly up the road, struggling with evident effort against the handicap of a bandaged
leg. "I think we know that man," Lehna said. "He went out
with a party of like-minded men to find some plunder. It
doesn't look like he found much."

Clearly then, he hadn't suffered from a weak leg when he'd
left. Lehna Singh hadn't dismounted, for all that he said he
knew the man. Jefferji saw Fontenoy scan the road, the rocks.
Potential ambush. Perhaps if a man didn't find plunder away
from home, it wasn't considered impossible that he might
strike for a nearer target. Lehna raised his voice and called out.

"Son of Ajimal Bani. Where's your horse?"

The man hadn't noticed them; he'd been concentrating on

his feet, head down, shoulders hunched. When the man looked up, Jefferji could see his face was black with bruising, his cheek and jaw swollen. He seemed to want to wave, to speak, but lacked apparent strength to do so. One of Lehna's men hurried forward on foot to help Ajimal Bani's son close the distance. After another long moment and a careful survey of the skyline, Lehna dismounted. Fontenoy did too, so Jefferji followed.

Close up, the man looked worse. He had a long deep running gash from his forehead to the base of his nose that seemed to only just miss his lips. His leg was wrapped around with a knotted cloth, dark fabric, so there was no way to tell if there was blood. Simon had dismounted to hurry forward. Bani's son's friend helped him to sit down beside the road, leaning against some rocks.

"Greetings to you, Lehna Singh." The man winced as Simon probed his knee gently. His voice was hoarse. "This isn't how I imagined my return. I thought it would be in triumph, with rich booty. Werin is dead, Fasad too. I don't know about Hevis."

If there was going to be a surprise attack, now would be a good time to spring it, Jefferji thought, with everybody gathered close.

One man helped the injured man to drink some water-thinned yoghurt, which seemed to refresh him. "Tell us what happened," Lehna said. "We're going to Fayzabad. Is there something we should know?"

Bani's son shook his head, raising his hands in a gesture of defeat that seemed to give him physical pain. "A man came last month and said Deravass Khan wouldn't be escorting Panner's caravan. Camels, some loads of silk, Russian goods. Panner's rich. He could spare them. We thought, well, this is our chance." It was clearly difficult for him to speak, but it seemed to be important to him to tell the story regardless. "On the Fayzabad road. Panner had an escort, but who? We didn't know. Kavkazki. Shikander Beg. It meant nothing."

Not to Lehna or his men, but it apparently did to Captain Fontenoy. Another layer to Fontenoy's motives for going north? This was suddenly much more interesting than just a chance meeting with an unsuccessful would-be raider.

"But you had Nagreb Narval," one of Lehna's men said.

"A famous fighter. Nagreb surely must have got at *some* plunder, and yet gave you no share for friendship's sake?"

It took Bani's son a moment to gather his strength to reply, swallowing a few bits of milk curd with careful deliberation. "He got six feet of earth for his part. There were soldiers. We thought, boys, they looked like boys, on horseback. People said women. Maybe. I was lucky. I was one of the first to run away."

It was the bitter candor of a defeated man. Jefferji knew how much Captain Fontenoy wanted to ask questions, pump the man for information. There didn't look to be much hope of getting any more out of him, though.

Those of their escort were consulting among themselves. One came forward to communicate with Simon, mostly by signs and nods and pointings; another had turned to Lehna Singh. "He's hurt," the man said. "I could take him on my horse. Take a fresh horse, rejoin you as quickly as I can."

It was a natural instinct to take their comrade home. Lehna Singh turned to Fontenoy. "What do you think, Fonjeny?" he asked. "The road may be safer, cleared of raiders. Or more dangerous. We know who Deravass Khan is. I've never heard of Shikander Beg Kavkazki." But he wanted to help Bani's son, who clearly seemed exhausted as well as wounded, possibly starved. It was a long way from here to the nearest house for a man in his condition to walk.

Lehna had given Fontenoy an opening, though. "You know best, Lehna Singh," Fontenoy said, taking evident care with his language. Really, he was learning, but Jefferji knew Fontenoy was still struggling to understand and make himself understood. "But tell, please. Did he see this man? If we met, on road. How would we know him? Be on our guard."

Bani's son nodded. Each successive nod brought his chin down lower to his chest. He seemed to be rapidly losing the strength to keep his head up. "Fair-skinned as a Feringhee. Strange horse. Upright of stature. A matchlock's twist with a burning ember, in his mouth."

But a pistol's match would fall against a man's chin if he tried to hold it between his teeth. Maybe a sagar? No. A cigar, that was the word. English smoked cigars, if few Rajputs. Jefferji had seen Fontenoy do it.

"We're safely in your care," Fontenoy said to Lehna. "This man will die of cold from one more night."

Quite possibly.

"Take him back to Moroe's place," Lehna told the man who'd made the suggestion. "Send us more if you can. Now we're going to hurry, and you hurry too. We all want to be well clear of the pass before the sun goes down."

While the sun shone on the grey rock, clothing warmed across the shoulders and the ice hid in the shadows. When the sun was eaten by the western rocks, the cold crept out into the road to hunt for warm-blooded prey. They made fires of green pine and scrub willow to keep the cold away, but it was there, just waiting for its opportunity.

Jefferji was glad Bani's son wouldn't spend the night in the dark—even if he was a robber. The ice was everybody's enemy. Mounting back up on Coriander's back, Jefferji hastened to get away from as much of it as possible before nightfall.

Because he had Rashid and a copy of Fontenoy's rough map, Broderick knew Fontenoy was headed north on the Fayzabad road. Because Broderick had treated a party of alum merchants to a little mutton stew in Malakhand, he knew that the river on Fontenoy's map was a tributary of the river that ran east of the Panj at Ishkashem before joining it halfway to China.

Fontenoy apparently knew people in Chitral. When Broderick and Rashid got there the place had been in gala mode, with space and supplies both at an unpleasantly steep premium. Rashid had spotted Tamisen by his height, in Chitral's bazaar—a narrow escape for the both of them, because if Tamisen was there Fontenoy was too. Indeed Broderick had picked Fontenoy out almost immediately, and ducked into hiding. A familiar face could be a beacon in a crowd of strangers.

Tamisen might not recognize Rashid at a glance, but Fontenoy would, and neither of those men was likely to have forgotten Broderick himself, even changed as he was by travel dirt and dilapidated native costume. They'd been forced to lay very low indeed to save their common purse and avoid the danger of being spotted, and that had meant parting reluctantly with the merchants whose company the mutton stew had bought.

Then they'd had to wait for the next party going north that was willing to have them. That put them three days behind Fontenoy at least. There were twenty of them in all: three distinct groups, banded together for mutual support and safety in numbers as they crossed the Dora Pass, on their way to Zebak where the road went north to Fayzabad or east to Tashkurgan.

If Chitral, by its reputation a seat of power, were so plain and pitiful, Zebak would doubtless be more of the same—a miserable excuse for a town, a mere collection of villages. Would the prices on produce be more unreasonable than they'd been in Chitral due to a relative reduction in the amount of goods available? Or less so because with a smaller population it would be more of a buyer's market? Broderick needed resupply badly. They were still almost a half-a-day short of Zebak when sundown had overtaken them, though, cold and black and unyielding.

The party made camp on the thin and flinty soil beside the road, in open defiance of Broderick's best efforts to move them forward by just a few more miles, and here they sat for another night of singing and eating up provisions while Broderick brooded and Fontenoy got further and further away. Not actively, no—he had probably stopped for the night as well—but conceptually. Inexorably. Damnably.

During the tiresome process of cooking a thin watery batter into unleavened bread for their evening meal, a stir in camp alerted Broderick to the arrival of a new contingent, an event that created obvious anxiety amongst Broderick's traveling companions.

"Twenty men," Rashid whispered in Broderick's ear—in English, because it was the only language Broderick could understand well enough to be confident of his grasp of what was said to him. "All mounted, and one of them at least may have a pistol. They may be bandits, or even worse."

What could be worse than Rashid's breath, rank with the

pungent fragrance of cumin and onions from the neighboring campfire's stewpot? Slavers, perhaps?

"Find out their story," Broderick said.

No, he didn't want any of that stinking stew. Yes, as a servant Rashid could move easily from campfire to campfire and gracefully accept ladlesful of stew by way of hospitality where his master would never be expected to unbend so far from his dignity. And there was no telling whether Parsis would eat barley flour stew anyway.

But it was provoking to be reminded that Rashid had a bellyful of hot food while Broderick sat alone waiting for his bread to burn. The story was that Broderick was a Parsi from Mumbai, because Parsis weren't Moslem. So Broderick wouldn't be expected to prostrate himself five times a day in prayer, or otherwise conform to universal expectations of which he was ignorant anyway. He was a holy man; that explained his shabby appearance, and his general air of traveling on the cheap.

Rashid went away, leaving Broderick to sit with a wretched pot of tea-tinted hot water and several slabs of blistering bread blackening over their pathetic little fire. He had several concerns on his mind, some more immediate, some less. After a short time Rashid returned, bringing with him in childlike innocence a potential, if only partial, resolution to at least one of Broderick's issues.

"They offer themselves as protection to Zebak, and on to Fayzabad. They only want a present in return for this valuable service, whether or not their service is accepted."

Shakedown money. *Pay us for helping you or for leaving you alone, but pay us.* Broderick understood the proposition. Sound business practice. "So you've come back to collect our share. How much is it to be?" And how good would Rashid prove as a negotiator?

Rashid frowned anxiously, as if aware that the news would be unwelcome no matter how lightly the impound would lie. "Perhaps an ounce of silver, elder brother." Rashid spoke carefully and softly, so as not to be easily overheard. "Elder brother" was as close to an honorific "sahib" or "Lieutenant" as Broderick had been able to work out for the brief conversations he was unable to avoid with Rashid. "I pled our poverty as hard as I could, but less than that they would not accept."

"Who is the leader?" Since they were levying contributions, Broderick knew they were for hire. "Please ask him to come and honor our humble fire. Tell him we may have more than a mere ounce of silver to repay his interest, and keep it quiet."

Rashid seemed shocked to hear Broderick's instruction; even frightened. They were only two people, in a strange land. There was obvious risk in making it known to even just one man that they had a little—even if it was very little—money.

Yet they'd be paying their insurance money for protection, wouldn't they? *In for a penny, in for a pound, my lad,* Broderick admonished himself. Or perhaps it was *might as well be hanged for a sheep as for a goat.* Hanged either way.

For Rashid a hanging would be unnecessarily complicated. A knife was more along the lines of Broderick's thinking, or better yet an unexpected flight off a precipice. An accident. It could happen to anybody. It happened every day. But that was in the future and sufficient unto the day was the evil thereof.

Closing his eyes, Broderick inhaled deeply of the stew with cumin and onions that was on the neighbor's fire and imagined a plate of mutton with gravy, potatoes, hot bread, a glass of cold beer.

Rashid came back with a man who was comparatively well dressed, clean-shaven, wearing a flat Herati cap; that was a hint, perhaps. Herat was renowned for its predators. A man who wished to make a quiet point about the care with which his word should be weighed and measured would be well advised to wear a Herati cap.

"This is Mirza Cassim," Rashid said, in simple bazaar language. "He is a protector of men."

"Peace to you, Mirza Cassim." Broderick could manage that much on his own before he had to turn it over to translation. Closer to the firelight, Mirza Cassim had an agreeably sharp and alert expression, and didn't smell any more than any man who went about on horseback might honestly wear a perfume of sweat and leather around him like an aura—all points in his favor.

"'Peace also to you,' he says," Rashid translated, though Broderick could gather that much for himself. "He greets you respectfully. He's interested in silver and how to get it."

Since leaving Peshawar, Broderick had spent many hours meditating on what he was going to do when he caught up with Fontenoy. Time and again his projections foundered on the crucial question of exactly how Fontenoy was to be persuaded to share the treasure. Tamisen might be in the position of a nephew or he might actually be Fontenoy's bastard son, but Broderick was neither. He needed leverage. And here was a lever, presenting itself to hand in a cordial convenient manner, ready to be turned to use.

"Tell him that the gods reveal an enormous treasure waiting in the mountains, and that we need help to discover it." Rashid was obviously surprised, so Broderick made up a reassuring explanation. "Captain Fontenoy will surely need our help, with bandits everywhere. We'll set a bandit to protect us against bandits, at least until we've found the treasure. Tell him."

Rashid seemed reluctant, but Broderick felt sure his evident discomfort would be more rather than less convincing. The message was received with obvious interest. Mirza Cassim took a moment to digest it before replying.

"He's intrigued." Broderick didn't need Rashid's help to figure that out; the intent was clear. "He wonders how he is to pay his men if there is no treasure, what he will be paid for his help if there is, and why we would lead a band of armed men to a treasure and trust us to not simply take it all."

All good questions. After a minute's thoughtful silence Broderick spoke to Rashid again. "If there's no treasure Fontenoy will pay him, out of his expense money. We will pay one part in five of our share of the treasure. And we trust him not to take it all because he's a man of honor, as I am a man of God and a sorcerer. Don't worry, Rashid. I have it all under control."

Broderick still knew next to nothing about Fontenoy's treasure—just a mark on a map, and a logical conclusion—so it didn't matter how much of it he promised away.

"He says it's a risk," Rashid said. "Our partner might have no money at all. But we're clearly pious and holy, and he's respectful of all faiths, so he's willing to take us under his protection, since he is, as you say, a man of honor."

Broderick looked searchingly into Mirza Cassim's face for a long moment. The firelight was an uncertain lamp, but from what he saw in Cassim's expression he was sure that Mirza Cassim was as honorable a man as Broderick himself. They understood each other, even without words, better than Rashid understood either of them. Broderick nodded with satisfaction.

"Very good," Broderick said. "Can we leave at first light? We have time to make up." Men with a mind for money could be counted on to keep the prize fixed firmly in view and pursue it with determination. Now, at last, finally, he was getting somewhere.

The lord had ridden long this morning on the Cherkess stallion, because stallions when not worked sometimes grew moody and brooded, and such behavior was not to be tolerated in the lord's household. Therefore a good lord took care to remove the potential cause for bad behavior. Also it was a pleasant valley in its own way. The rocks and hills were not like those of the home they'd left, but home was where the lord was.

And now he was in one of the stalls under the house next door, grooming Cherkess. So home was here with Birkit, washing her fine chestnut face. The village of Old Fort had no camels here. Shelter was being built outside its old stone walls. The earth had moved at Tilted Slope. Where one earthslip was, there often came another. There was no knowing when they'd be able to get home.

There was a shadow at the doorway. Birkit didn't like shadows. Boy looked to see who it was. One of the children of one of the men whose caravan they had rescued, who had brought them here. That had been a good event, because it meant there was good shelter to give the lord security for his goods and chattel. For that reason, Boy did not drive the child away.

"Can I have her?" he said.

Boy had learned the languages of the caravans, because it was something serviceable to the lord. She knew what the child was saying. She couldn't make sense of his meaning, nonetheless.

"I have money. How much?"

Birkit had her ears fixed on the child, wary. Boy patted her neck in reassurance; as if Birkit could be had for any amount of money. "No. Go away."

When Boy had begun to bleed, Second Wife's women had taken her away from the lord's tents, dressed her in women's clothing, and arranged her hair. She'd been terrified. Then they'd made a wedding feast for her, which had been absurd. She wasn't one of the lord's wives. She was only the bodyguard of an angel. Afterwards they'd let her go back to her accustomed dress and her accustomed place, but the sepahis had given her wedding presents that she liked. Horse furniture. Birkit.

The child hadn't gone. "Take," he said, stepping down into the straw-strewn darkness with his hand outstretched. "Not enough? How many? I want."

The child had a handful of gold coins. Boy picked one up to get a closer look, turning it from side to side as she held it up against the light. It felt the right weight for its size. Maybe it was real. There was no reading any news on either side, though. There was a sort of a picture, but it was too worn to look like anything. Boy dropped it back into the child's palm.

"No," she repeated. "Go away."

This time he did. Boy took up her chamois cloth to smooth the feather edges of Birkit's ears. Birkit had been a gift from matchmaking sepahis who'd admired the mare's quality and her red color, and had taken her as spoils after successfully driving off a caravan raid. Birkit worked harder than any horse Boy had ever ridden, except the Cherkess stallion who bore her weight only out of humility because they both served the lord. Boy doubted she would ever have as good a partner.

The child was back. "You give it to me," he said. "I can pay, you must take. Look."

He had a doll of gold metal, with red eyes. She'd never seen anything exactly like it, but she knew an idol when she saw one. These people were heathens.

"I'll beat you," she said. "Go away. You can't have her. She serves the lord, you don't." Therefore, obviously, the child couldn't have Birkit.

Would the lord give Birkit away to someone, if he was asked? Boy thought about it, combing out Birkit's mane. It was thick and strong. Birkit was in good health. Birkit served her well, and she wouldn't be able to serve the lord as well without Birkit. Boy was glad she'd thought that through. She felt better.

Here was the child again. Both hands full. "Look. I trade you these. They're good."

Little scales with colored chips that caught the light, green, yellow, white. These were jewels. Where had Lamish's child gotten jewels? He was right; they *were* good ones. She'd studied jewels, because the lord had some he kept about him, like the blue stone ringed with tiny pearls that he used to fix a spray of feathers to his turban.

"Where did you get them?" Boy asked, but she didn't want him to tell her. She wanted him to tell the lord. "Come."

She didn't touch the jewels, for fear of accidentally selling Birkit. Holding the child fastidiously by the wrist, she took him with her to find the lord, which meant going out of Birkit's stall into the courtyard and then back into the place beside it where the Cherkess stallion was kept. The other horses were here as well, the short-legged savage steppe ponies the sepahis rode; they were unafraid even of the Cherkess stallion, and could quarter with him.

She saw the lord coming up out of the stall, wiping his hands. "This child wants to buy Birkit," she said. "Look what he offers me. He may not have her. I don't want any of these."

She had no use for jewels, except the ones the lord gave her. There was a pair of bracelets in Captain Katische's kit that were for her, but Boy wasn't supposed to know about them yet. The stones were as blue as the lord's eyes, and as the eyes of the son he'd given her also.

"These are indeed a rich offering," the lord said, crouched down to see what the child was carrying. "Does your father know you have such things? Let us go and ask."

A good opportunity to ensure Birkit remained clearly Boy's horse. She followed the lord and the child to his house—not anxious about Birkit, just prudent—and she also wanted to know where rich gems lived in such a place as Old Fort.

Sifting through the contents of the small chest, letting gold jewelry play against his fingers, Shashka listened to what Lamish was saying with increasing concern. This was bad.

"He was going to call for a scholar to come up from the south, from Delhi. I was to keep them until the scholar came, and be paid for guarding them until then. Well, if I'm to be paid then, why shouldn't I advance myself a little? Where's the harm in that? I'm an honest man, I've kept receipts."

Shashka had no reason to doubt it. Someone had come into the valley looking for ancient artifacts and found treasure. So far so good. Left it on site rather than carry it away and destroy the provenance of the articles, Shashka could understand that too; a man would want security, before he traveled with such a sum, and was the entire village to disappear? There was an inventory here, with Lamish's mark made against each item, line by line.

"So you took some gold and went to Fayzabad to spend it." And someone had noticed, and the caravan had been followed by the robbers whose attack the sepahis had interrupted. That in itself was encouraging—the robbers had not, apparently, understood that there was a greater treasure at the end of the road, had they only followed it to its end. "Only gold?"

There was a chance, if it was only gold. The coins were clearly old by their wear, but a prudent merchant melted his gold down immediately to destroy its identity if it turned out to have been stolen. These jewels, however...

Lamish seemed a little uncomfortable with this question. "Well. Yes, lord. We only spent gold, and the time before, we didn't know anything about this treasure. It was in my father's things, from his father. What good is an old piece of metal to anybody? And a few rocks. My grandfather said only that he'd found them. He looked, but he never found any more, and after a while he gave up. As did my father. As did I."

People buried hoards. Time and weather did its work, and they came to light, were broken up by frost or flood, or lay forgotten. If there was anything left of this particular hoard to find, Lamish would have his hands on it by now. That was not the problem.

"You sold a piece in Fayzabad, then."

"Yes, but three years ago. One like this." Picking through the pieces in the chest Lamish drew out a palm-sized piece of gold, with four gems. "We bought wool. Sugar. Medicine."

Opium and charras, Shashka suspected. Lamish was full of charras right now, or he surely would've noticed his son scrabbling under the bed for the treasure chest earlier.

Opium and charras were honest medicines, but a man could grow accustomed, and imports of luxury goods were expensive. Someone had noticed. And with a new discovery of hoard gold entering the markets of Fayzabad, someone would almost certainly be taking an interest. "You use the same dealers, I suppose."

"Honest men all. Did I do wrong, lord?"

Shashka closed the small chest, holding it out for Lamish to take. "That's between you and the scholar from Delhi, whoever he may be. As you say, you have receipts." Lamish was not as suspicious as he might be, but that was no reflection on his honor. "But we may have other visitors from Fayzabad, because of this."

Peri had left Shashka's side some minutes ago. Now she was back with Captain Katische, before he'd had a chance to send for her. Peri was efficient that way. "The gold is good," Lamish said. "The coins were tested. We paid fairly."

Yes, that was the problem. If Lamish were not tipsy with drugs he'd have seen that as clearly as Shashka did. "I've no doubt that it is, friend Lamish. You have dealt honestly, I think. Thank you."

Turning to go, Shashka began to speak to Captain Katische, but Lamish spoke before Shashka had a chance to say a word.

"You keep it, lord." Lamish held out the chest. "So long as you are here. I'm embarrassed by my son."

Shashka hesitated. Peri did not. She took the chest, so the thing was decided.

"Keep the inventory safe," Shashka told Lamish. "Now I will take leave of you. We have work."

Since he'd been here he'd built cattle pens, repaired roofs

over rooms to use as wares houses for the packs, set the outside gate in order, cleared away debris from around the walls. That wasn't going to be enough. Old Fort needed to be defensibly arrayed, because the next time someone came from Fayzabad they might come in greater force, and he would not be here to intervene.

Broderick Holyoke walked slowly down the narrow streets of the Zebak bazaar with his eyes fixed on a point overhead where the sun shone, somewhere beyond the sepia smoke of the kebab vendors' fires. The kebabs smelled good, so good it made his mouth water, but he couldn't buy one.

Oh, he had money, but he'd told Rashid that there was only the common purse, and if he suddenly turned up with gold in his pocket it would be a blow to his credibility. He was as far from a hot, steaming, juicy lamb kebab—generously basted with drippings and garlic, with chunks of onion and potato skewered between fat cubes of meat—as he'd been as a child without a single anna to his name. It was not a reminder he appreciated.

He was otherwise in a good mood, though. Since he'd been traveling with Mirza Cassim they'd made excellent time. They'd picked up one or two bits of news about Fontenoy on their road, and all in all Broderick had good hope for the enterprise.

Someone behind him nudged Broderick in the shoulder and he turned around casually, unconcerned. He had nothing to steal, nothing any casual bump-and-run was going to be able to discover. It was a boy with a pair of kebabs, and Rashid behind him.

"Take," the boy said—Broderick assumed; the gesture of offering was universal. "Eat."

"We've said you are a holy man," Rashid said. "The boy wishes to make a donation, in hope of a blessing. Say something, elder brother. Please."

If he was to sustain the deception he was clearly going to have to swallow his pride, and the kebabs. Broderick took a deep breath.

"Oh, roe, the rambling bog," he began, opening his arms wide with his palms upturned. Then he reconsidered. They were in the middle of a bazaar. Who knew whether someone here by ill chance knew enough English to detect a lack of sincerity on his part? Broderick changed his approach.

Sergeant Halloran, now, had had a thick accent. "Me mind bein' too airy to drap it sae low," Broderick said, slurring the sounds from one word to the next to help muddle the meaning." Even other English-speaking men had failed to puzzle through Halloran's dialect. "And in multiplication in truth I was bright." Taking the kebabs with a dignified nod, Broderick made three cryptic passes with them in the air over the boy's head. "Ahgas fahga mayshoe mori doisha."

Looking to Rashid, Broderick nodded—*Get this boy out of my sight.* Rashid stepped up quickly and took the kebabs. It was surprisingly hard to let them go. They'd get cold. The fat was congealing in the murky air, but somehow that only made them more appetizing, and not less.

"This way, elder brother," Rashid said, looking to a little alcove beside a tea wallah where a man stood obviously waiting for them. "News of Fontenoy. Cassim needs to know."

There was a table, and a bench. The man took delivery of two glasses of tea from the tea-seller's stand, and sat down with them. Taking one of the kebabs back from Rashid with a firmness that brooked no opposition, Broderick sat down to eat.

The man across the table was not a local, judging by his dress. He kept an eye on bazaar traffic as he spoke, suspicious, wary, alert. Broderick had noticed more than one of his like in Zebak, men whose irritated air spoke of restlessness without a ready outlet. Useful men. "Peace to you," the man said.

There was only room for two at the table, and Rashid had to stand, which made a useful screen between Broderick and the street, and provided a little privacy. Rashid bent low to speak in Broderick's ear, confidentially. "He says three men and a mule came past three days ago."

Broderick's heart sank. How could he still be three days behind, as hard as they'd had been traveling? This was not the news Broderick had hoped for, but at least it was information. "And he wonders why we ask." The man sat drinking his tea, still keeping a look-out for who knew what threat from people in the street. Waiting for Rashid to finish passing information to Broderick. "He says it might profit us to tell him."

Was that a threat? Broderick noted with dismay that the kebab was half gone; worse, the man had noticed that Broderick was eating like a starving man. The man pushed the glass of tea closer to Broderick with a polite nod, drinking from his own glass encouragingly.

Broderick needed to keep the man talking, in case there was yet more solid information to be gotten from him. "Give peace to him also, Rashid. Say that one of them is an estranged kinsman of mine, whom I seek to give welcome word of an inheritance. Thank him for the news."

Broderick reached slowly for the glass of tea, and drank. The tea was lukewarm, but it was so sweet that Broderick could have eaten it as an ice. Sugar. Mountains of clear, white, pristine, sparkling sugar. He'd fill a room with sugar. He'd take off all of his clothes and roll stark naked in it.

"Ask if we can assist him, in any way."

The man sat down and leaned closer. "They say," he said—to Rashid, who translated for Broderick. "Two years ago there was a man in Fayzabad bazaar with gold things, plates. Like a goblet smashed open. Heavy as a stone and as thick as a new horseshoe, with rubies the size of the yolk of an egg."

The jewels Tamisen had been carrying hadn't been so large as that, but they'd been toothsome enough. Broderick still thought about them, and wondered whether Fate would be kind enough to bring them here for Broderick to reclaim from Tamisen's dead body.

"Tell me more of this." He sipped his tea, taking the second kebab back from Rashid just in time to prevent him from absentmindedly biting into a chunk of potato.

"Three months ago more gold coins came into the market at Fayzabad, very old coins. Their faces were worn as smooth as glass. Coins of Iskander the Greek, they say." The man straightened up on the bench where he sat at the table, tapping one finger on the plank surface as if to say *Tell me what you think of that.*

Broderick wasn't sure he liked where this was going. His plans for the treasure depended on his ability to control the story so that he could shape it to his own ends. Still, this was his first hard evidence of the nature of the treasure Fontenoy sought; as such Broderick welcomed it.

"Say that surely this is a marvel. But why tell me? Is there a sorcery in these coins that he wants me to exorcise?"

Their companion grew visibly impatient with Broderick's apparent slowness, leaning in almost nose-to-nose with him. "Three men come through Zebak, going east. You come asking about men going east, and you a Parsi enchanter."

Rashid spoke low-voiced, softly, very close to Broderick's ear. Broderick felt he could fill in the details easily enough; the man was still talking. "Mirza Cassim is in the market, buying supplies for a long trip. Where is he going? Does it have anything to do with your kinsman, or that gold of Iskander? I have connections. You should know that."

Broderick hadn't foreseen that people would take note of Mirza Cassim's comings and goings. It was exactly contrary to what he wanted. He had to turn this quickly.

"I can't conjure that knowledge," he protested, in an insulted and frightened tone of voice that would supplement Rashid's translation nicely. *I would never dare steal from your kit, sir, and what use would I have for your soap? Please, sir. The sweeper must have done it.* And that had been perfectly true. Broderick had had no use for the lieutenant's soap, but it had smelled like him. "The ordinance of God forbids me to look into the mind of any man."

Not that the man had suggested any conjuring. The conversation seemed to Broderick to be headed in a direction more along the lines of *I know you know something so you'd better tell me because I'm prepared to threaten you.* As Broderick had hoped, though, the deliberate misdirection of his reply brought his host down to the main point at last.

"But you can see treasure in the earth. Can't you? It is known. And there's no holy ordinance against discovering buried riches so they can be put to righteous use, charity, good works." Having to hear it all second-hand—by way of Rashid's translation—and how was Broderick to know how accurate that was?—was a frustration. But there was no help for it, and the delays gave him valuable time to think. "I'll pay you well. I can have twenty brave lads together in a day, two days. What do you say? Both of you will be generously rewarded."

Broderick rubbed his rough-bearded chin vigorously to keep his grin from showing. This was funny. But it could lead to trouble. "I'll have to take the auspices," he said solemnly. "Tonight is no good, it has to be at sunrise."

"Tomorrow, then," the man said with a grateful smile. "Come to the coppersmith's shop on the metalworker's street, two streets that way, the only man in town with Russian goods. Ask for Asher. I'll be waiting." Pushing himself away from the table, the man stood up and put a few coins on the table for the clearing away. "You'll come? God be praised. Say nothing to anybody else, or you ruin everything. Tomorrow."

Once Asher had gone Rashid sat down, picking over the coins on the table as if he had the same thought Broderick did. *I could use that money better than any tea boy.* But Rashid didn't pick them up.

"What do we do now, elder brother?"

If Broderick hadn't already enlisted assistance, this would have been brilliant. But Cassim knew too much about where Broderick was going, and was in a position to give chase. Besides, Cassim was a known quantity; Asher was not.

Broderick took a moment to collect his thoughts, drawing little story maps on the table with his index finger for a pen. Never ran out of ink.

Then Broderick raised his head and looked Rashid in the face. "We tell Cassim we're going north to consult an oracle. Then we'll double back." People had noticed Cassim; he might be followed. They had to get to Fontenoy before anybody else did. It meant poor roads, rough travel, slow going, but delay was better than pursuit and discovery. "We'll need to disguise ourselves, Rashid, so that no one sees a Parsi man leaving with Cassim in the morning."

They could be an English lieutenant, and a Moslem adventurer who was out to change a steady job with the Bengal British in Peshawar for a chance at a glittering treasure. He'd made disguises work for him before. Only a few days, surely, it would only be another few days to Fontenoy, the treasure, and security and safety at last and forevermore for Lieutenant Broderick Holyoke, Madras Palladian Horse.

⛰

Tamisen, my boy, Fontenoy thought, desperate with frustration. *Heir to a decent portion of my worldly goods, son of my friend, whom I have seen grow from infant to child, boy to man. If you don't stop singing I am going to kill you.*

The map showed a road beside a tributary stream branching away north away from the river. There were no obvious indications of a well-traveled byway. But they *were* four days along the river from Ishkashem, and this was the first trace of a stream-bed they'd seen all morning.

Dismounting, Fontenoy opened up his satchel. He'd picked out the route on the fabric lining of the flap for quick reference on the road.

"We should follow this stream-bed. For perhaps three miles, I think," he said. "We may be near."

And Tamisen, thanks be to all-merciful Heaven, shut up and got down off Coriander to have a look. He'd been singing the same tune day in, day out, since they'd left Chitral, composing a new praise song to Sri Krsna, he said. And here Fontenoy had thought that Tamisen and Krsna were on the outs, and could find it in his heart to wish they'd stayed that way.

There weren't even any words, it was all nonsense syllables. And there wasn't an ounce of malice to it. Tamisen just kept on coming back to it at odd intervals as if absentmindedly. Fontenoy thought he would go mad.

"Look," Simon Jericho said, dismounting in turn and pointing at some bit of shrubbery. "Biscar's Fingers. Beautiful. I must make a note of this. Let me just get my sketch book." On his knees in the scrub, Jericho sketched a leaf out in his journal, taking a careful clipping to layer between the sheets of linen he used as his temporary press during the day to keep his specimens for a more complete examination later, when they made camp, before the light went.

"Wheel tracks," Tamisen said. "Look. Carts. Horses. Camels, even. Possibly." The narrow stream-bed that the side road accompanied still showed damp and a little muddy from the spring runoff, its white bleached skirts showing the height of its spate. That made it easy to follow. As the path curved north with the stream-bed, a little valley came gradually into view, the green of cultivated fields very grateful to the eye—the mark that men were here in community. A weary traveler could hope for eggs.

The three of them drew up abreast on the road looking out to where a village with a little lake pooling at its base stood atop a rocky hill halfway up the valley.

Captain Fontenoy nodded. "I think perhaps we're here."

The hill was not of the lofty and towering variety. It was no more than two hundred and fifty feet high, but it was crowned by a stone wall of peculiar construction—stones stacked rather than faced, chinked and smoothed with mud—that rose another forty feet or so to a crenellated finish. The fort sketched on Fontenoy's map, then, built on a natural base, its feet washed by the lake. Deravass Khan had said it was a small position, but defensible. An antique Siaposh Kaffir hill fort.

A mile down the valley the road branched, and began to climb up to the fort on a natural spur improved with pounded earth. The stone walls showed signs of recent repair. Someone had been at work here, but there was no sign of Deravass Khan, whose pennant would be flying were he in residence.

"Something is odd," Fontenoy said to Simon and Tamisen beside him. "Let's be careful."

The tall gates that opened across the road were decently hung, respectably forbidding. Deravass had written of a small farming settlement. Where would they have come up with the surplus manpower to build such a gate, let alone the expertise required? The closer he got to those walls the more questions Fontenoy had. He halted them all fifty feet short of the walls to take stock of the situation.

"To your right, sir," Tamisen said. "On the walls."

The glint of sun on steel told Fontenoy exactly where Tamisen was looking. The sentries with their rifles aimed appeared to be wearing a species of uniform. Definitely not Deravass's men.

Nor did the costume of the man walking calmly through the gates to wait for them in the road place him among Deravass Khan's company. He wore a woolen coat of light blue with braided trim the brilliant white of which spoke of careful and frequent cleaning. The turban he wore was built in the Turkish fashion, right down to the spray of pheasant feathers that he wore pinned into the folds of his headgear with a brooch that flashed the lucent sapphire of a gem of the first water.

His dress and deportment, the stance he took in the middle of the road with his hands on his hips, were that of a war leader, but he was certainly not Deravass Khan. Who was he? Where had he come from? What was he doing here? And—most importantly of all—how much did he know?

"Wait here, why don't you, while I find out if our way is clear," Fontenoy said. Climbing down from Farouk's back, he started forward, to see what he could see.

Patiently Nartshu—the farrier—stood, tongs in hand, ready to clip the bent end of the horseshoe nail and pull the last of the pony's shoes. Three hoofs bare, one still shod, and a full set waiting, beautiful new shoes expertly fitted and most suitable. The pony wouldn't lift her leg. Her foot stayed stubbornly flat on the ground, with its full share of the pony's weight on top of it.

Nartshu shook his head. "She's usually patient with me," he said. "I'd better wait until Satsi gets back."

Taking in the expression on the pony's face—eye rolled back and showing white, lips tense, ears flat—Shashka nodded. The sepahis's ponies were phenomenal brutes, almost supernatural in their strength and their endurance. Their ability came with a temperament as savage as the sepahis themselves, and sometimes it was best to let the sepahis deal with them.

"Don't risk losing a piece of your arm. We need it whole. And all of your bones unbroken."

The makeshift forge stood up against the curve of the old wall. There was all the room a man could want for building between the old fort wall and the village, but most of the northern sweep was full of scaffolding. They were building a proper gate into the village.

Now the pony snorted, and its face relaxed as if to say *Oh, all right, very well.* Nartshu moved carefully, keeping a careful eye on the animal's ears. The pony gave Nartshu its foot. He pulled the worn shoe, but straightened up and put his tools aside.

"Thank you, beast," he said, and nodded to the boy to lead the pony away. "I think it best to wait for the new shoes, lord. All of these beasts seem to be on edge."

Shashka had noticed it as well. There were a dozen ponies in the pen for shoeing, all of them restless, none of them satisfied with its place or its companions for more than a moment at a time.

"I think they put their heads together and concert it, just to make us wonder," Shashka said. Had there been a quarrel amongst the ponies? Some sort of a scandal?

Grinning, Nartshu opened his mouth to reply when something behind Shashka caught Nartshu's eye and silenced him. Turning, Shashka saw one of the sepahis waving from the top of the wall, and hurried to climb up the wooden stair join her, with Peri following.

"Satsi's signal," the sepahi said, and nodded toward the wooded hill west of the mouth of the valley where Captain Katische had placed a sentry post. "Someone is coming, lord."

Shashka waited. Behind him he could hear the creaking of the ropes as a work crew hauled a bucketful of earth up from the ground below the base of the wall. Out and away across the valley, fencing was going up to secure pasturage for steppe-ponies shod and unshod alike. There was the faint perfume of bread and roasting mutton in the air. It was a beautiful day, and still the unease the animals displayed had communicated itself to him in some way.

"There, lord," Peri said, pointing.

Shashka squinted at the road: three mounted men and a beast of burden, riding up slowly in no particular order. Lamish's expert in artifacts, perhaps?

"Let them approach," he said, turning to climb down to ground level once again. "Open the gates. Peri, I'll go change my coat. Tell Captain Katische. And someone let Lamish know, in case these are his visitors."

Opening the gates was a moderately complicated business. There was a small everyday coming-and-going pedestrian entryway cut into the gate itself. But Shashka—now settling the creases of his Circassian coat into proper order—was the protector of this place, while he was here. When Shikander Beg came to confront these strangers of unknown intent the gates were to swing wide for him. It was the theater of lordship.

Two each to a side, his men pulled the bolts and pushed the great wings open and out. Once the visitors were within a reasonable range, Shashka stepped out into the road to see what they would do. Captain Katische was there with four archers at the ready and two rifles on the wall, and the headman Mekmout. Just around the edge of the gate Peri would be scowling and thinking cross thoughts: *They could be demons.*

Three men, three horses—one of Arabic lineage, one with English lines. One brown and white of breed unknown, but surely with the blood of an Arab in it by the elegance of its ears—scimitar ears, crescent-moon ears, Shashka had never seen their like for perfection. And a tall mule.

Several yabu ponies, better fed than the common run, well to the rear. The older man wore a short blond moustache, and the contours of his face were those of much campaigning; Shashka recognized him as one of the brotherhood of men in command.

Of the two others, one was tall and one was not. The latter was an indifferent rider—from the city, perhaps. An antiquarian, his tall young apprentice, and an associate, perhaps? None of those horses were tradesman's mounts, and the mule was a genuine beauty. Maybe she was for sale.

At a respectful distance all three stopped and sat for a quiet moment. Dismounting, the older man walked forward with a deliberate tread. Once he was well advanced toward Shashka, the others stood down into the road, politely. When he was within arm's reach the stranger stopped and looked Shashka in the eye with courteous frankness. What language would he speak?

"Peace be with you," the stranger said. Bazaar Persian—a purer language than the local dialect with its Turkoman loan words and rough grammar. Shashka had run caravans through Persia east and west for five years and more. He could manage this. "My name, Fontenoy. I come to meet Deravass Khan. You are not he, lord."

No, but he'd heard the name. They were in the same business—caravan security and related services—though Shashka was traveling on his own behalf this time. "Peace also to you. I am Shikander Beg, waiting here until my road is open to the east. What is your business with Deravass Khan, if may I ask?"

What are you doing here?

It was a moment before "Fontenoy" replied. He was apparently considering his words carefully—and with what Shashka thought he knew of his errand, Shashka could understand why. "Old things for market in Amritsar. You know of these, lord?"

This was a delicate situation. Did Fontenoy know that the "antiquities" were gold and jewels? If he did, he might well wonder whether Shashka's presence would interfere with his business. Any man might take a tax from the treasure as a reward for declining to take it all. But it wasn't his, and Shashka didn't take things he didn't need or couldn't use.

"There's a man who can talk to you. Enter in, and be welcome as his guest." To claim host privilege would be to agree to hold this place, and Shashka had no intention of doing so.

At a wave from Fontenoy the other two came up, the tall one with the mule in hand. "Hakim Jericho, lord," Fontenoy said, bringing forward the shorter man. Hakim, a doctor. Shashka would welcome his presence—with reservations. Jericho was black, like an African; but his turban wasn't Berber. "Tamisen, the son of my friend."

Jericho, Tamisen. Shashka nodded to each in turn, and was respectfully acknowledged.

"Medical student, you say?" He'd studied medicine in St. Petersburg, but neither deeply nor long. Maybe Jericho would open a clinic while he was here. Caravan and village were in good health, but everybody liked to see a doctor. "This is

Mekmout, the headman. He'll bring you to Lamish. Perhaps you will come and see me, Fontenoy, when it suits you."

If Deravass Khan was coming, he could be responsible for the jewels and the people alike. Maybe Shashka could feel Fontenoy out on the subject of the peril to which Old Fort was exposed by such antiquities. But for the moment he left it all to Lamish; and went to visit Ismara and his infant son.

Chapter Eight
Old Things Come to Light

A feast of welcome had been laid on a carpet on the roof of Lamish's house. Jefferji sat cross-legged on the rug covering the flat, smoothed earth with Simon to one side and Captain Fontenoy on the other, squinting in the sun and enjoying the cheerful chaos of children, goats, and chickens.

"No, I've heard nothing from him since he left," their host, Lamish, was saying. "This letter is the first news."

Lamish had the letter in his hand, the warrant Fontenoy had brought that identified him as the man Deravass Khan had sent to take charge of the trove. The chest of jewels sat open in the very middle of the carpet; the inventory rested with Fontenoy.

"He's been delayed, then. I thought to meet him here. The lord Shikander Beg, he's not of Deravass's party."

It was a question, howsoever politely phrased. Fontenoy had reverted to a more usual dialect for him, a Persian of Bombay not necessarily completely intelligible north of Kabul. From what Jefferji could tell there were enough common words there for Lamish to correctly take Fontenoy's meaning.

Lamish responded readily enough. He shook his head with a wide smile, waving both hands at once and scattering the wine in his cup liberally over all. He was a cheerful man, though apparently invalid. He hadn't stopped smiling since their arrival, not even when one of his bearers had slipped on the ladder and nearly dropped him.

"No, God himself sent the lord to Old Fort to rescue us. Our caravan was attacked on our way home from Fayzabad. I was wounded. You see." Lamish made a vague gesture toward his body, but whatever wound he'd suffered was not evident. Jefferji was beginning to wonder about Lamish's good cheer. He'd have to ask Simon's opinion, later. "And it pleased God to destroy the lord's road to his lands, so he has condescended to stop with us for a little while. See all that he's given us."

Jefferji had remarked upon the new construction. It wasn't the kind of activity he'd expect from a short-term sojourner.

Captain Fontenoy clearly had similar thoughts. "A man takes care of his own house," Fontenoy said, and took a mouthful of mutton rice. A sheep had been killed in their honor almost as soon as they'd passed through the outer gate. "Will he honor the agreement you made with Deravass, now that he's lord here?"

The question apparently surprised Lamish, whose reaction seemed delayed in a sense to Jefferji. Not because Lamish was thinking about it; more as if it took an extra moment for him to finish listening to what he was hearing.

"He hasn't touched a single stone. No." Or, in other words, yes, Shikander Beg meant to respect Fontenoy's prior right of ownership. "You'll want to take away the other things, as well?"

"Other things," Fontenoy repeated. "Oh, the cave." That would be the cave where the antiquities waited for them, Jefferji guessed. "Yes. Of course. Who can show us the way?"

"One of my boys will take you," Lamish said. "My son Elker. Or my son Boaz. Or any of them. Oh, good. The musicians have come."

There were three of them coming up the ladder from Lamish's house, with instruments and fancy dress of admittedly worn and somewhat shabby silk embroidered in tarnished tinsel thread. There wasn't any room for dancing here, not with the feast spread and the space crowded with Lamish's family and friends. But Jefferji had noted the cleanliness of the grounds between the outer walls and the village, and his feet had designs on several promisingly flat places.

"Is it far?" Fontenoy asked, raising his voice a little to get the question on the table before the music started. "How long will it take us to get there?"

"Halfway up the valley." Lamish said. "Old things. We've kept everything safe, as I promised the great khan Deravass."

Jefferji knew enough about antiquities to understand that "old things" could be worth much more than mere gold, to the right collector. Which meant all that much more gold for them. If all the beasts here were the Beg's caravan, how were they going to find carriage to make a baggage train? They had only brought four yabus, unsure of how many would be needed. Maybe Deravass Khan would be bringing extra animals with him.

Fontenoy was looking up at the sky. It was mid-afternoon. The feast would run into the night, not because they were such distinguished guests so much as that they *were* guests and an excuse for a party. People would be drinking; at least Lamish would be, that seemed certain. There'd be a question about how long it would take Lamish's household to get itself started in the morning, and a prudent man didn't start a relationship with expectations that were only going to be disappointed. It set a bad precedent.

"Not tomorrow, I think," Fontenoy said. "We've come a long way to see these wonders. I'll want to be rested. Though I can hardly wait to cast my eyes on the old things myself. First thing in the morning, then, the day after tomorrow? First light?"

"In praise of old things," Lamish cried, and lifted his goblet. His other guests all cheered. The musicians began to play. Fontenoy toasted the sentiment in turn.

Jefferji turned to touch mugs with Simon, who was drinking tea. "He has taken medicine," Jefferji said, under cover of the music's opening bars. "It makes him cheerful."

"I think he smokes charras," Simon whispered back. "Look at his teeth." How could he tell? Lamish's moustache seemed to cover all. But if Simon said so, Jefferji believed it.

What did Shikander Beg make of Lamish and his luxury? Shikander Beg wasn't from around here. He was more fair-skinned than the Turkoman natives of Badakhshan. Jefferji had heard it said that the Kaffirs of the Hindu Kush were as white as Europeans, but so far they hadn't seen any Kaffirs, apart from a slave or two in Chitral. And the Beg's Persian accent had seemed a little peculiar, while that of Lamish and the headman Mekmout and their establishment were of a piece with that of Fayzabad.

But now the singer had started, and Jefferji had a professional interest in hearing the story. He put Shikander Beg and his people to the back of his mind and concentrated on the music and the sweetmeats of the feast.

In the early morning Jefferji awoke in the guesthouse, an open room with a fire on the central hearth and a broad sleeping ledge running all around that was warm and sonorously musical with Captain Fontenoy's snoring. What time was it? Not time for breakfast yet, or his stomach would let him know. So it was time to practice. A solo dancer was expected to present his own compositions on occasion. Jefferji had been working on something special ever since they'd left Peshawar.

His slippers were waiting for him. Putting his cover aside, Jefferji made a loose knot in his braided hair and wrapped his turban around his head to go out. He didn't want to wake either Simon or Fontenoy, so once he was decently covered, Jefferji snuck out as quietly as he could. It had been part of his training from his first steps as a dancer, moving with the silence of a shadow.

He'd scouted a good area yesterday, under cover of a latrine break from the party: grass growing between old worn paving stones; a decently sized court neatly delineated by old fitted-stone walls. And if someone passing the place should chance to glance over and catch him at exercise, the worst that could happen was an audience.

He stretched slowly, without thinking about it. It was a habit, a morning ritual learned over long years of training. Warming up his muscles. Pulling the body together. Softening his joints into fluidity, and integrating the entire armature of his body with wide sweeps of his arms and legs—the injured arm was reluctant to move as it must, and needed remedial work—with the precision of the entire range of gestures the language of which was all-important to the art. And he prayed. It was habit, it was training, it was teaching- it was hope.

I worship at your lotus feet, Beloved, and pray that all I do may sing your praise. You are the universe and everything that is in it. There is nothing in the world that is not Krsna.

There was only silence. Emptiness. Jefferji told himself firmly that it didn't matter. He had other goals to accomplish that required his attention.

It had taken him several days of trial and error to come up with his personal private mapping strategy. The drum tempo could be used to indicate distance. There were elements of choreography that were specific to stage position: two steps front of center, three steps left of right, east by northeast, south-southwest. The song itself could be arranged with words to match the tune to hold the details of the route.

It wasn't perfect, but he thought he had a solid grasp of his procedure, now. Captain Fontenoy might map on silk in French with Roman script; Jefferji himself on a music-roll in Urdu with nasta'liq script; Simon on paper in Sanskrit, devanagari. Silk could tear and paper burn. Maps held in the mind were safer from most forms of physical destruction.

They'd left Peshawar and traveled to Alladand by way of the Malakund pass, almost unimaginably higher into the mountains than he'd ever been in his life, yet Fontenoy insisted that the white peaks Jefferji had seen from Attok were giants to these. Getting those first days down had been hard, because the best tune was a love song, but the drumbeat one more fit for songs of war.

By the time they'd crossed the Punjkora river in Talash, things had run much more smoothly. Some of the stages between Dir and Chitral had challenged him, but there was relatively little to occupy a man's mind when he was on the road—one's body did the work of staying on the horse, watching the sky, knowing when to stop and rest. He'd had time. He was glad he'd started with a love song. It was a comfort to sing about the Beloved even when it was just a way to make a map.

Beloved, my brother scolds me, he rebukes me.

There'd been a lot of snow on the way to the Nuksan pass and they'd had to walk over ice, even though it was nearly May. It had been a fascinating experience. Coriander hadn't cared for the cold.

I don't care. There is a nightingale in the jasmine, surely it brings me a message.

The apple crop at the confluence of rivers at Zebak was very promising this year, which was an unexpected sort of love letter but there'd been no other way to capture it. And the old song *did* have apples in it, so it might have been a love letter. Of a sort. In a manner of speaking.

Muscle had memory. Poetry was more easily remembered than plain text, and singing strengthened the channel of the word. Moving at half-tempo, concentrating link by link, Jefferji danced his song of the route from Peshawar to Old Fort with care, testing each phrase to make sure that the connecting phrases still matched seamlessly, that there were no places where a note could be dropped without calling attention to its absence.

The Mehtar of Chitral had been a friend of Captain Fontenoy's. There'd been a party. There'd been places on the road where they'd dismounted and gone single file, leading the horses, because what was a good road in Chitral would be a marginally respectable footpath in Tengarpore.

The last leg of the journey required a particularly complex marriage of tone and tempo to capture the course of the river and the exact place where they'd turned off. Jefferji was confident of it regardless, because the steps were made memorable by their absurd juxtaposition of Queen Amrita and dung patties, pancakes and the Moghul army.

He'd only just arrived at Old Fort in his dance when he saw that someone, two someones, had stopped in the open space between walls to watch him. It was Shikander Beg, in a plain turban and a well-fitted coat of an unfamiliar pattern that suited his figure admirably. And with him, the woman who seemed to be always near, beside him, behind him, just coming in, like an attendant spirit. The village called her "Miss Boy," Jefferji thought, but he wasn't sure of his trans-lation.

"Namaste, lord," Jefferji said politely, with hands pressed

palm-to-palm together at chest level in front of him. "I salute the god in you."

Shikander Beg didn't give him namaste back, but he wouldn't, would he? There were no Hindus here. Shikander was almost certainly Moslem, Shia perhaps, Jefferji thought. Instead of returning a morning greeting, Shikander bowed in a perfunctory manner, nothing more than an abrupt nod, really, and came onto Jefferji's dancing ground with a stiff-legged formality, swinging his arms with precision to raise fist to chest as he walked. It was an unnatural step, but that—Jefferji realized, with a sudden surge of delight—was exactly what it was. A dance-step. A processional.

Within three paces of Jefferji, Shikander did a quick controlled spin that ended with him facing Jefferji, hands dropped to his hips. So Jefferji gave him one in return, and added a knee bend. Shikander took a few steps side to side, there and back again, with a thoughtful look on his face as though he was selecting from a programme, and went into a traveling step such as Jefferji had never seen before.

He had to concentrate. What was that, what was Shikander doing? Making a complete circle around Jefferji in an acrobatic style Jefferji had never seen before. The top of one foot brushing the ground, brought forward to support the entire weight of Shikander's body crouching on one leg while the corresponding foot swept the ground on the other side so close to the paving stones that he almost knelt.

Where, exactly, was Shikander's center of gravity, Jefferji wondered? How was he even balancing his weight? Was it on the fore part of his foot? Was it actually on the point of the toe? To dance on pointed toes like that required the ultimate of a man's muscles, both in strength and in control. And Shikander wasn't posed and poised, it was a complex dynamic fluidity of movement. Jefferji had thought only Rajput war dancers did that. What was *he* going to do? It was his turn—

The answer came to Jefferji in a flash of inspiration—not the answer to what step it was that Shikander was dancing, but the appropriate response. Equal-armed Arjuna, ambidextrous, resuming his armor after a year spent disguised as the eunuch Brihannala, rejoicing in his reclaimed weapons.

Jefferji leaped up from a crouching position, pulling an arrow from one of the two imaginary quivers across his back to fit it into the great Gandiva bow and draw. One arrow skyward, and an eagle came out of the direction of the sun with the arrow in its claws, rejoicing in his good fortune in meeting always-victorious Arjuna. One arrow east, one west, announcing his presence to the spirits of the land.

One arrow tipped with gold and inlaid with a praise song of lapis and ivory, sent from the top of a somersault into the earth beneath his feet, tribute to the goddess. Then three arrows collected as they came back to him, to be returned with the one the eagle had brought to his quiver.

Then Jefferji collected Arjuna into himself again, and stood grave and devout in front of Shikander Beg with his palms together once more. *I hope you have enjoyed my story. Truncated though it was.* Shikander Beg was smiling broadly, showing his teeth; it gave his countenance an open, surprisingly youthful appearance. It struck Jefferji that Shikander Beg was an attractive man.

"Bravo, Tamisen," Shikander said, reached out, and put his hands to Jefferji's upper arms in a sort of a restrained and friendly embrace. "Perhaps we can match steps again, though I have not your mastery. I excuse myself, I have things that need seeing into, and your breakfast will be cooking. Again later, Tamisen, again bravo."

Miss Boy stepped to one side to allow her lord to pass, giving Jefferji a long sideways glance before she followed him. It made him feel as though he was a young boy in his first days of martial training under the sharp gaze of one of Tengarpore's cadre. He had been put on notice, not because he'd done anything wrong or made a mistake, but because she'd made up her mind to keep an eye on him just in case there was mischief. It made him feel oddly proud of himself, for no particular reason.

What had Shikander said? Breakfast?

With a short but very fervent prayer of thanks to the ground, the god, and Guru-ji for the successful conclusion of his practice, Jefferji slid his feet into his camp slippers, snatched up the coat and tunic he'd laid aside, and went with decision and dispatch to find his morning meal.

Never had the ability to sleep in the saddle served Captain Fontenoy so well. Tamisen and Jericho were awake, but they were younger men. The uncivilized hour at which Lamish's boy had come to guide them to the treasure cave was not so much a shock as a mere challenge to their systems. It was his own fault. *First thing in the morning*, he'd said, so the boy had awakened them as soon as it was light enough to see. Altogether too early.

Dozing off and on, only just awake enough to retain his grip on the apple he was working on for breakfast, Fontenoy followed the little boy on his donkey as it jogged energetically north along the stream-bed toward the far end of the valley. The air smelled of morning but the dawn birds were either still abed or feeding closer to the river, perhaps; it seemed too still. Yet they'd only just got here the day before this. They knew nothing of the local birds' eating habits.

A break in Farouk's rhythm roused Fontenoy to a greater awareness. The boy and his donkey had turned up onto the slopes of the hill beneath which they rode, but he'd apparently made a mistake—he came down immediately and hurried on, without explanation. The boy clearly had instructions, but no very firm idea of the place. It was a good sign. The boy, and by implication the rest of Lamish's people, hadn't been to the cave recently or frequently enough to be able to go straight to it.

Finally the boy turned upslope and stayed there, standing on a rock to wave and call. "Here, we're here!"

Farouk knew how to climb, and a Marwari was equally as agile, as horses went. Fontenoy dismounted anyway, with Tamisen following his lead, because there was no good reason to risk either animal to mischance, especially as they didn't know exactly what they were to be climbing into. It wasn't easy going. Tamisen took the lead; as the tallest among them he had the best vantage point for picking out the trail. Jericho had pencil and paper in his portfolio, so Fontenoy brought up the rear to ensure speedy recovery of any essential recording supplies that might by misadventure drop.

When they reached the spot, they found that the little boy had tied a large dead branch to the donkey's neck and was trying to get the donkey to drag it away. The donkey wouldn't move—nor could Fontenoy blame it; the branch was twice as big as the donkey—so he and Tamisen took over.

It proved to be the once-leafy top of a felled scrub tree. The donkey, once relieved of its burden, went briskly downslope to grab some breakfast forage with the horses. Jefferji and Fontenoy cleared the tree away. Under it there was an apparently loosely piled layer of rocks that, when moved aside, proved to conceal a careful, clearly man-made sort of stone depression previously masked by the dead treetop.

They took a break to eat some cold bread and dried apricots, drinking milk-thinned honey-sweetened yoghurt that the boy had carried with him on the donkey, and then went back to work. Underneath a thick layer of fist-sized stones—the boy was handy with the smaller ones—they found a final layer of rough-dressed tree trunks, and when they lifted those away Fontenoy could see the cave mouth, steps leading down and away into the hill.

The sun had cleared the mountains, flooding the valley with light the clear brilliance of which angled deep into the cave. One hand to the last of the shifted—aside stones, Fontenoy climbed down the stairs carefully, testing the steps as he went.

They were as flat and true as though they'd been cut within living memory, but the cave's chamber had clearly been buried or concealed for much, much longer than that. It was large enough for eight or ten men, high enough toward the back for even Tamisen to stand upright, and its walls were lined with paintings of spectacular color and execution.

Fontenoy had never seen such things, not in Tamil Nadu in the south, not in the Elephanta caves, not in any temple or relic of the Hindu gods. No miniature miracles of Moghul painting were these, but life-sized, of surpassing grace, smiling and beneficent. If they were Hindu gods, they were gods drawn by people with an uncertain grasp of the iconography, and perhaps that was a hint. They looked almost Greek.

Jericho stood at the foot of the stairs, staring in rapt

wonder. "I've seen things like this," Jericho said. "Chinese paintings, silk. Like these, but—but not like *these*."

"Look, this one," Tamisen said. "Could that be Ganesh? And here, Durga, maybe."

Jericho stepped closer as Tamisen pointed at one figure with the body of an athlete draped in something like a toga. The head seemed too long and narrow for an elephant's head, surely, but there were the ears of an Indian elephant, tusks and a trunk and an expression of benign serenity. And tumbled to the floor, there in the dust—small stones? Lamps? Votive offerings?

"This way," the boy said from beside Fontenoy and, taking his hand, led Fontenoy through to the back of the cave.

Two statues stood half-shadowed in the dark, their brightly painted limbs still vivid with pink and blue. Coral, perhaps, Fontenoy thought. Powdered coral and lapis lazuli from the mines of Badakhshan. The spinel ruby that Uncle Zafar had left him was of surpassing clarity and richness of color—also from Badakhshan, or Fontenoy missed his guess.

Fontenoy pulled back, alarmed, as the boy walked into the wall; surely he'd crash into the black wall between two statues? No. Through. There was more than one room to this cave. Lighting the candle, Fontenoy raised it cautiously and followed.

The little boy gestured. "There, sir."

The walls of the second room were carved from floor to ceiling with figures, larger than life. A giant figure in relief was carved into the low ceiling, its feet at the entryway's stone lintel, extending the entire length of the room, ending with its head almost touching that of a life-sized corresponding figure in similar relief that stood upright, facing Fontenoy from the far wall. Fontenoy couldn't quite make out the faces, but they seemed to move and breathe in the flickering candlelight. *I've been waiting for you. You took your own good time.*

Shaking off the eerie illusion, Fontenoy moved into the room to get a better look. He felt an object underneath his foot, crushed by his weight almost before he had a chance to register the fact that he'd stepped on something. Alarmed, he retreated a step and squatted down to the floor to see what harm he'd done.

It was just a clod of earth, now turned to powder. There were bits of dried mud littering the floor, and as he passed his candle close to the floor in front of him its yellow gleam caught an answering spark amidst the rubble. Picking through the dirt he found the source: a yellow diamond. Or perhaps a citrine, or a topaz, but a jewel.

Frowning, Fontenoy stood up. "Gentlemen? In here."

When Hakim Jericho and Tamisen joined Fontenoy, the increase in candlelight made it easier to see the carvings. Just to Fontenoy's right, a recumbent body was carved in deep relief into the wall, a woman with the melon-round breasts and lotus-stalk waist of the classic Hindu beauty. She lay on a long low bas-relief couch with her arms outstretched, her hands poised gracefully in the air like the trembling of early leaves in a strong wind, her fingers as long and slender as ribbons. And there were inscriptions carved into the walls all around her like a garland of flowers.

Jericho squatted down with his candle held close to the portion of the lady's inscription that was nearest him. It was something neither Fontenoy nor, he suspected, Tamisen could read—Sanskrit script, devanagari.

"'The noble lady of matchless dharma'," Hakim Jericho read aloud. "'The only shadow on her spotless virtue.' There's no name, though."

The sculpted figure wore armbands, necklaces, jewelry in her ears and hair. Where had the yellow stone come from? The figures had been painted, once upon a time; traces of red, of blue, of brilliant gold remained, shining behind the woman's head like a halo. Rock was hard to paint, and these carvings were old, very old. How came the color to persist?

Tamisen wasn't looking at the inscription. "Carved in stone," Tamisen said, pointing at the woman's sculpted nose ring. "But finished with plaster, to take the paint." He touched the carved jewelry; his finger came up color and dust, and where he'd touched the wall a dull gleam in the candle light betrayed the presence of a jewel of gorgeous green.

The implications were both exhilarating and perplexing. There were gems in the wall for the taking. But they could only be taken by shattering the plaster that clothed the carvings. It seemed a shame: the carvings were beautiful. But jewels were jewels, and who knew what might be carved on these, waiting to speak their secrets after who knew how many centuries?

"More," Tamisen said, taking a half a step to his right.

Jericho followed the light as Tamisen held the candle, Jericho's face just inches away from the wall. Brushing the dust of centuries away from the carved text, Jericho read the words in tones of increasing wonder.

"The dharma king Yudhisthira best of men, the chariot of Indra down from heaven."

It sounded like Mahabharata to Captain Fontenoy. He knew only a little of Uncle Zafar's studies, but what Jericho was reading seemed to confirm that this was the place from whence the original artifact had come. It was reassurance Fontenoy hadn't realized he'd been waiting for.

"Look, Jefferji," Jericho continued. "Here's the dog. But aren't they out of order?"

They didn't need him, and he had logistics to consider. Fontenoy ducked back into the outer chamber to consider the challenges they faced.

The statuary would be relatively simple; pieces that were too large to remove intact could be sawn apart and reassembled later. The wall paintings, well, he'd heard of a technique of pulling paint away from stone walls with specially formulated plaster. The actual paint was preserved that way, a mirror image back to front, safe and protected from the stresses of travel and handling.

These were too wonderful to be left, unknown and unappreciated, in the wilds of Badakhshan, where only the few travelers willing to brave a tiring and potentially dangerous journey would ever be able to admire them. They deserved to find the audience they merited by virtue of their age, their artistry, their stunning beauty.

He was the man who was going to make that happen.

And if the paintings proved to be too brittle with age, there were still the jewels. They were all going to be very, very rich.

The sun had risen higher in the sky. The outer room was full of light.

"Hakim Jericho?" Fontenoy called. Jericho and Tamisen were having some sort of a mild controversy, in the inner room, *This is absolutely revolutionary* and *No, look, there's more.* Whatever it was, they could sort it out later. "You might want to make a full schematic, first thing, to start. While everything is fresh."

There'd be plenty of time to sketch by candlelight later on. In the sunlight the colors of the paintings on the walls were breathtaking—but who knew whether these ancient pigments would fade, exposed to sunlight? He'd heard about such risks, from Uncle Zafar. He wanted Hakim Jericho to take notes on the pigmentation right away.

"Of course," Jericho said, coming back out into the light. He sounded a little breathless to Fontenoy—the cumulative impact of the wonders they were seeing, perhaps. "Look what we've found, Captain." He had scraps of paper there, carefully arranged on an open page of his sketch book. No. Not paper. Fontenoy had seen things like these before. Thin slices of wood, the ink black and sharp even though the edges of the wooden slips were round and soft with time.

"My God," Fontenoy said. "Can you read it? This is astonishing." He'd thought they'd happened on a treasure eight hundred, perhaps as many as a thousand years. But what he'd read about the wooden books preserved in the hidden temples of Ceylon could push the age of this trove back to centuries before the birth of Christ.

"It's going to take work. But I think so." Jericho closed the page on the wooden fragments reverently, tying the book open at the next blank sheet to secure them in place. "It's amazing. And there are more. They're scattered all over the floor, in amongst the votive rubbish. But first things first. Can those rocks outside the door be cleared away, Jefferji? I want more light."

Tamisen didn't answer immediately from the inside room; maybe he hadn't heard. Before Fontenoy could raise his voice to reinforce Jericho's call a sun-blocking shadow suddenly interposed itself between the cave and the outer world.

"Hello," someone said, in English, but continued in what Fontenoy recognized as the Turkified Persian of Badakhshan. "I would like to see, may I come in?"

Fontenoy hurried to the stairs and halfway up. It was Lamish's guest, the lord of the caravan people, Shikander Beg.

Fontenoy blinked in surprise. "You speak English?" he asked, wondering as he did whether he'd shared any secrets with Tamisen in that language, in the mistaken belief that no one here would know what he was saying.

Shikander shook his head, squatting down on his heels politely to save Fontenoy's neck the strain. "I can say hello, and thank you. But very little else. It has been a very long time." His English was thickly accented, but Fontenoy couldn't place its flavor. "I have more French," Shikander added, in that language. "If you prefer."

Shikander's French was much more fluent than his English. His accent was gentlemanly. Fontenoy had worked with many Frenchmen in Holkar's service, and knew what an officer sounded like.

"I can say hello, and thank you," Fontenoy replied. He wasn't going to embarrass himself in front of a man whose command of the language appeared to outreach his, so he switched back to local dialect.

"Come in, welcome. We're blocking the light. We need a sketch of these rooms just as they are, before we do anything else."

Shikander Beg's presence complicated matters considerably, for all Lamish's naïve confidence. Shikander Beg was here in force. He had men, and Amazons as well. It was probably best, Fontenoy decided, to be as open with him as possible.

As soon as Shikander Beg had cleared the stairs and the sunlight shone through unimpeded once more, Jericho started to sketch with furious speed, blocking in panels and statues, framing the scene.

"These are heathenish things," Shikander said, staring around him. "How old is this, do you know?"

Heathenish indeed. It occurred to Fontenoy that they didn't know where Shikander Beg came from, or what his religious sensibilities were, except that the hapless refugee they'd met at the Dora Pass had said that Shikander Beg was called Kavkazki. Moslem, at a guess; almost everyone in this part of the world was, of one sort or another, and not even all Russians were Orthodox of any description. Shikander's caravan was traveling west to east, but from how far west, exactly? Fontenoy hoped Shikander wasn't an iconoclast, like those of Aurungzeb's time.

"It may be older than I'd been led to believe," Fontenoy said carefully. "It may be two thousand years old. It may be even older than that."

"Icons," Shikander murmured, folding his arms across his chest contemplatively. "Like the ones in the cathedral, smothered in jewels."

A thrill of danger ran through Fontenoy's body to have his suppositions confirmed. Shikander was fair-complected and blue-eyed. His English was unusually accented and he spoke French. He'd seen icons in a cathedral. Shikander Beg was a Russian. That had been Sanders's assignment. *Look out for a Russian named Kavkazki.*

What would a Russian be doing with a caravan, going into the wild places of the high Pamir—unless he was a spy? There'd been Russian spies in Kabul. That had been why the Bengal British had forced a regime change there, to protect their sphere of influence and maintain a buffer zone between British John Bull and the Russian bear.

He'd have to be careful. And also see if he couldn't get a look at what, exactly, Shikander Beg was carrying with him in caravan. Fontenoy opened his mouth to reply. But before he could speak the earth jumped beneath him, trembling violently with sufficient force to send him sprawling.

"Watch out!" Shikander cried, reaching for Jericho, pulling him away from the statues.

A thick yellow haze filled the air, making it impossible for Fontenoy to see anything. Where was Tamisen? He'd been inside the second chamber. Would the shaking never stop?

Then there was quiet, broken only by the little rain of debris pattering to the ground. Fontenoy could hardly breathe the dust-thick air.

"Tamisen!" He couldn't see his hand in front of his face, but he couldn't wait a moment longer. Tamisen had been inside. Tamisen wasn't coming out. There was only a slow billowing cloud of settling dust. "Jefferji!"

A cold wind came up from deep inside the cave, blowing the dust away through the open cave mouth. There was no answer. Fontenoy rushed forward into the dark to see what harm had come to the child that he loved, the child of his friend, the boy he'd brought all the way to Badakhshan for the sake of some things that Deravass had found of his dead father.

Simon had gone out into the first of the two rooms to start sketching the walls and the inscriptions. The light was better, there. Simon would want to bring more candles when they came back, or at least time the sun's path in the sky for its period of maximum penetration.

Left by himself in the dark interior, Jefferji looked around, studying the carved figures with wonder and confusion. The five Pandava brothers were all there: Yudhisthira on the left, the twins—Nakula and Sahadeva—and Bhima on the right, peerless Arjuna opposite the doorway, and Krsna, kingly above all, gazing down on the face of his friend with serene affection. How could the iconography be so precise and correct, when the picture was all wrong?

The story of how the Pandavas went to heaven was clear. First Draupadi fell behind in the final pilgrimage, as King Yudhisthira and his brothers walked away from the world in sorrow to seek the peace of final renunciation. Then the twins, then Arjuna, and wolf-belly Bhima, until only the eldest, Yudhisthira, remained, with a yellow cur dog as his only companion. Lord Dharmaraja, in the person of an unclean beast.

But whoever had made these figures had put Arjuna in the place of honor, above his older brother, in violation of right conduct. And there was more. The inscriptions claimed that Arjuna stayed on in the world for many years, ruling the western Kambojas as Rama had Ayodhya, and with the same perfect dharma.

Whoever they were, their veneration of Arjuna had been sincere. As Jefferji walked slowly toward the very back of the inner chamber—trying desperately not to step on anything—he could see long slender rods split for fletching like arrows, scraps of gilt leather brittle with age that had probably been portions of a quiver, and white stone horses, beautifully carved in miniature, that would logically have been harnessed to a model of Arjuna's chariot, the one that Krsna himself drove for his friend during the great war.

Of the great Gandiva bow there was no sign, but Arjuna had surrendered it to red waters when he and his brothers started out on pilgrimage, thus returning the gift of Varuna. Why were the arrows here, but not the bow? Theological confusion.

Stooping to the ground, Jefferji picked a shell up out of the trash of votive offerings crumbled into dust at Arjuna's feet. A sacred conch, the size and shape of a large mango, that shone white in the sepia darkness of the candlelight. He'd seen old trumpets in temples; this one—he was surprised to see—was a true dakshinavarta shankha, a right-turned conch, the conch of Vishnu-Krsna. Such a rarity was a treasure in its own right, and not out of place in a room where diamonds and sapphires had been lavished on Draupadi's jewelry.

Something stirred the air, too subtle to be a breeze; a little shifting sound, as if sand was falling through a crack between the stones as the sun warmed one before the other. Jefferji raised his head and looked back over his shoulder, distracted, but it was only the caravan's lord, Shikander Beg, come down to see what was here. Captain Fontenoy would handle it. The rumble Jefferji thought he'd heard was only the echo in the rock of Shikander's voice, as deep as the night sky.

The shankha felt pleasantly cool, satisfying in its weight, its bulb resting comfortably in the palm of his hand while the long column of its aperture reached just beyond the tips of his fingers. Devadatta, the conch of Arjuna. Jefferji raised his eyes to face Arjuna-on-the-wall, whose carven countenance was more joyful than weary—because he would see Krsna again. Unlike Jefferji, who despaired.

The beauty of the carvings and the religious quiet of the cave betrayed Jefferji to his own loneliness suddenly, without warning, and with an impact so immense that it brought him to his knees in the dust. He'd prayed and prayed to silence, and the echo in his heart was terrible.

Arjuna had known what that pain was like, bereft in his

heart after Krsna laid mortal costume aside and passed out of the breathing world. If Arjuna were here in person rather than in stone, Jefferji could touch his feet and ask, *What have I done wrong, that I should be abandoned? What must I do, to see Krsna again?* Overwhelmed by sorrow Jefferji leaned his forehead against the wall, pressing the conch to his heart in both hands, trying to ease the pain he suffered there.

A roar so loud its impact was physical sent Jefferji sprawling, threw him back from the wall with a force like lightning. Lying on his back, staring up into the darkness, Jefferji lay stunned. It was utterly silent, and he couldn't see—the sun was partially obscured behind some clouds suddenly come up, or he'd been blinded by a blow from an angry God, struck by an outraged divinity. For what? For touching a wall?

The ground rose up beneath him, belling out like a silk tent blown in the wind. Rolled onto his belly by the rising of that swell, Jefferji fell on his face and curled into himself, holding the conch to his chest like the pearl of an oyster.

Not for touching a wall. Jefferji heard a voice deep and powerful, but it wasn't Shikander Beg. *For stubbornness.*

The earth would not stop shaking him about, and strange flat scales of rock rained down on his head. Some of them were heavy. Jefferji stopped thinking, for a little while.

He woke with the taste of dust in his mouth and the smell of mud in the air, choking on its sharp-edged fragrance. Coughing, he tried to push himself up, away from the floor, and as he did he heard voices that seemed to come from far above him.

"Jefferji! Jefferji, wake up, breathe, boy, breathe!"

One voice dove out of the sky like a kite on a hare, closer, louder, familiar and unexpected at the same time. Captain Fontenoy. Where had *he* come from? The other room, yes, of course, Jefferji could understand that. Taking a breath sent Jefferji into a spasm of retching, while Fontenoy pulled him up out of a pile of rubble and pounded him between the shoulder blades to help expel the dust-choked air from his lungs.

Someone beside him put the open mouth of a flask to his

lips, saying in a voice like echoing rock *here. Spit. Swallow.* Jefferji wasn't sure about the words but he took the meaning, rinsing his mouth to clear it of dust and spitting out the slurry, swallowing the second time to rinse his throat. It was strong tea, black and sweet, and it worked wonderfully. It didn't clear his lungs, but he could breathe in through his open mouth without turning his stomach inside out.

Reaching up, Jefferji took the flask with a hoarse word of thanks, sipping the drink as he gradually regained control of his breathing. The flask was as light as leather in his hand, and yet metallic; how could that be? Raising it to eye level in the murky darkness, Jefferji tried to understand.

"Called 'aluminum,'" Shikander Beg said. "Now, before you move, take inventory. Is anything broken? Carefully."

Fontenoy was brushing Jefferji off, his back, his shoulders. Jefferji had lost his pagri somewhere; Fontenoy dusted his head as well, as lightly as a paternal caress.

"Left arm intact," Jefferji said, because he was holding Shikander's flask in it. Handing it back to its master Jefferji turned his attention to the other side. "Right arm—"

He held the shankha in his right hand. Was it all right? Quickly Jefferji felt it with both hands. It felt smooth and whole. He tucked it away in the folds of his shirt, bulky though it was, where its presence against his chest heartened him.

"I think everything's correct and accounted for, thank you, lord."

"The earthquake has certainly shaken things around in here," Simon said, standing at Jefferji's back, holding his candle high in the dusty air. "Look at this."

The entire floor of the cave was covered with a fresh layer of debris, now. Gently curved shards and plates, one side mud-colored, one painted in gold. Shikander picked one of them up, and Fontenoy brought his own candle closer. Not gold-colored; gold.

Simon turned slowly, full circle; there were saucers of mud-backed gold all around. Shikander was looking at the ceiling; there was no carving left. It had all come down on top of Jefferji. The mud layer of the piece in Shikander's hand flaked away, and exposed a layer of blue—a slice of lapis lazuli. Krsna's color.

"Up with you," Fontenoy said, his arm around Jefferji's back. "We should get out of here. Get some air." There was a breeze blowing from somewhere, cold and pure and pleasant, but it was summer. Any breeze coming from outside would be warm, so there was some sort of respiration in the rock, which, taken together with an earthquake in the area, meant *leaving in an expeditious manner would be prudent.*

Scrambling to his feet with Fontenoy's assistance, Jefferji joined in with Simon to gather up an armload of gold saucers and stagger toward the cave mouth. The statues? At least one was still upright. There was sunlight across the stone stairs, so the roof of the main chamber had not caved in. That was lucky.

Jefferji didn't like earthquakes. Coriander didn't particularly care for them either. Had that been why she'd been so nervous since they'd got here? Why did he never think to connect a coming earthshake with her nerves until after the fact? Were there not enough earthquakes in his life? That couldn't be the reason. There were already as many earthquakes in his life as he cared to have, plus three hoarded away in case the rains failed.

Something rumbling in the rock behind him made Jefferji flinch, but it was only Shikander Beg talking to Simon. "Yes, I'll help you carry them. Come away now. I insist."

Outside the cave the rocks seemed just the same to Jefferji. Maybe it was dry enough that a dislodged boulder left no obvious track. Fontenoy helped Jefferji and Jefferji helped Fontenoy clamber down over the rocks, with the boy's willing if less-than-able assistance. Out past the hem of the hill Jefferji could see the horses farther out in the valley: Coriander, Farouk, Gunnery, and the others would be Shikander's stallion and that strange woman's red horse with that strange woman—Miss Boy—astride.

Picking his way with care, Jefferji carried his burden of gold down into the valley, setting it down on a convenient rock well clear of the new-tumbled stones as the boy and "Boy" brought the horses in.

"It's all right, darling," Jefferji said to Coriander, who came trotting in Farouk's wake—perfectly happy to let another horse go first, since there was an earthquake in the neighborhood. "All done." She nudged at his bosom for a treat, bumping her nose against the shankha Jefferji had tucked inside his shirt. Jefferji showed it to her, so she'd know it wasn't something to eat. She lipped it in an experimental manner, just making sure.

"What've you got there, Tamisen?" Fontenoy asked, nodding at the shankha.

Now that they were all out in the open Jefferji could see that Fontenoy had been badly shaken—by fear for Jefferji and Simon, possibly, because Fontenoy was otherwise relatively indifferent to peril, by report.

"Votive offering I picked up off the floor, just before the quake hit. I thought of taking it back to Hirpa temple. It's valuable."

Fontenoy rolled it over in his hands with mild interest before passing it to Simon. Simon knew the difference between an average conch and a dakshinavarta, and smiled at it appreciatively before offering it to Shikander in turn.

"What is it?" Shikander asked.

"This is a trumpet that they use in temples, lord. There's the mouthpiece, see?" Merely a smoothed aperture, but one burnished in red gold. "This is the rare right-turning form of the shell, and most desirable. You blow into the end, there."

Shikander blew, but only dust came out.

Jefferji bowed to the lord, reaching out for the shankha. "I've played shankha from time to time at festivals. There's a trick of breathing from the bottom of your stomach. Let me try." Taking a deep breath, he puffed at the aperture at the base of the conch to clear it of as much dust as possible. When no more dust flew out, he closed his eyes and thought himself back at the Hirpa temple on the god's birthday, and concentrated on air flow, gentle and sustained. *Krsna*.

The sound rolled out of the bell of the conch beautiful and round and majestic, as deep as Shikander Beg's voice. There was the comfort of a remembered joy in that sound, a moment's return to the wonder Jefferji had lost, the sense of being at home forever in the presence of the god. Jefferji exhaled long and slow. When his lungs were empty he stood for a long moment with his eyes closed, knowing that when he inhaled he would be back in Badakhshan, bereft. But he had to breathe eventually.

He opened his eyes to see Shikander staring at him with an expression of astonished delight that changed, suddenly, to one of concerned surprise, as Shikander turned his head back the way they'd come from to look at the hillside behind them. Then Jefferji heard the rumbling. But Shikander had seen the plume before the sound had traveled—a spear-point jet of dust rising from the hillside. From the cave that they'd just left.

Putting the shankha down quickly atop stacked plates of gold, Jefferji followed Fontenoy back up the hill. It was easy to find the cave, now, with a dust plume for a beacon. There were the stairs cut into the rock, but they were broken off in mid-air, hanging over the collapsed crater of a deep pit, a rubble-filled fissure that ran back into the rock for fifty feet.

Simon threw himself full-length on his stomach on the stairs, reaching down as though to call up the treasures of the cave by force of levitation. "No! The books—those inscriptions—crushed, gone, destroyed—"

Jefferji caught hold of Simon's shirt, and pulled him back before he could fall headlong into the pit. "Maybe not," he said, anxious to coax Simon safely away. "We could get lucky. But there's nothing to be done about it now. We're going to need a lot of hands to clear things out again."

He could feel Simon's despair, and deeply sympathized. Those thin panes of wood were history, more valuable than solid gold—priceless, if they cast new light on the Pandavas' final pilgrimage, with their astounding claims of Arjuna's later kingdom. At least now they knew what they were looking for. And Simon had made some notes.

"The cave protects itself," Shikander said, musingly. "At least we need not fear for pilferage, until your friend Deravass Khan arrives." That was a point, Jefferji supposed. "If all is well I'll leave you here, and ride ahead." Shikander would want to get back to Old Fort. He had his family there with him, a wife, a child.

"Thank you for your help, lord," Captain Fontenoy said. "It's lucky for us you stopped by. I apologize for dropping the sky on you. It was unintended."

As Shikander took his seat in the saddle, Jefferji could see him smile. It was a very attractive smile, honest, open, and unguarded. "I only ask that your tall friend not sound his

trumpet within the walls of Old Fort," Shikander said.
Turning his horse's head, he rode away down the valley,
leaving them to pack mud-fronted plates of beaten gold
across the donkey's back and make their own way back to Old
Fort with slow and careful steps.

The sun shone warm overhead, but the heat was pleasant. A
little breeze flapped in the crimson panels of the tent,
pitched outside the village well clear of the tower walls.
Shashka could hear a baby crying, the soft voices of women,
the laughter of a child mollified and tickled of toe—his son.
And his newest wife, and her women, turned out of quarters
into an open-air enclosure while Shashka's men inspected
the tower for any damage.

"All of the people in the fields found and numbered, lord,"
Lamish's head man Mekmout said, respectfully. "That
accounts for all of Old Fort's men, women, and children. The
fences you put up held, and the animals are safe as well."

It was good news. Shashka wished that all earthquakes
could be as careful of life and property. There were no children crushed beneath the weight of a fallen wall, no women
scalded by an overturned cooking pot full of boiling water,
and only a very few bruised or broken bones.

There also seemed to be no serious concern on Lamish's
part for Old Fort's welfare. He seemed sublimely confident
that his help was unwanted and unnecessary. To give the
man credit, he had asked after his guests, his family, and
Shashka's people, in that order. But Shashka had left him
reclining at his ease on a bed in the sun in front of his house,
singing tunelessly to himself and waving a fly whisk at
random intervals as if he thought he was keeping time.

"You have inspected," Shashka said to Captain Fontenoy,
who approached him from the tower with his assistant
Tamisen in tow. "What do you find?"

The English were good at fortifications. Shashka wanted
more reassurance than the mere absence of any clearly
splintered beams before he put his wife and her women back
into the tower with his child.

The pavilion they'd set up was open to the sky; but they were far from Ismara's home in Persia, so perhaps no evil djinn would know to bend a malicious eye on them. The local djinn could hardly be expected to care whether Shashka loved his child more than a prudent man should and admired the courage of its mother to an improper degree.

"I'm not engineer, lord. But towers have I seen. This one— good as any in my life. It has been here for a long time. It has lasted." Fontenoy spoke as a man aware of the importance of the question. He clearly knew who was living in the upper story of the tower.

Shashka beckoned him closer. "Before I send my family back, it might be well if the things you brought out of the earth today were placed within, on the upper floor, until Deravass Khan's arrival." Gold plates shaped to the contours of carved heroes, set with jewels and then covered with mud. How had they held to the ceiling before now, so that it took an earthquake to shake it all free? "You will be free to come examine them, at any time."

People were curious, Old Fort was their home, and nobody could truly protect possessions, no matter how personal, from the innocent curiosity of the wonder-starved. The plates and fragments of worked gold were too heavy and too bulky to be carried on one's person. Captain Katische kept a sepahi guard on the tower, day and night. Shashka thought his proposal good, but would Fontenoy misinterpret his motive?

"We shouldn't need much time to list," Fontenoy said, and his tone was perfectly calm, holding no subterranean current of suspicion that Shashka could detect. "Yes, it would be best. Thank you, lord."

The unspoken message was crystalline in its clarity. Fontenoy held Shashka to be a man of honor. Shashka appreciated Fontenoy's confidence, and nodded his own thanks.

Then he shifted his attention to Fontenoy's assistant Tamisen. "How are you feeling, now that you've had a chance to let things settle?" Shashka found Tamisen a little comical because of the candid openness of his expressions, but he carried himself gracefully and well.

"Thank you, lord," Tamisen said. "I have no cracks in my

walls, if some of my bracing may have shifted around a bit. I fell into a tank once in dry weather, and that was worse." Good, because Tamisen was an engaging young man, and it went without saying that the fewer were injured the more were able to work. "I could happily keep custody of this, though."

The shankha trumpet. "So long as there is no discharge of the weapon within walls." Shashka didn't think it would tempt someone to steal. It was just a shell. "Captain Fontenoy, I ask for your further assistance in inspection of the outer walls. Tamisen, I must visit my outpost. Meet me at the gate."

Tamisen had been buried in rubble when they'd found him, and men who'd been knocked on their heads stood in need of observation for a little while to ensure nothing had gone wrong. Everybody else here was busy. Shashka decided that he would look after Tamisen himself, and play the doctor's helper.

Peri stood by with the Cherkess stallion. Tamisen ran off to fetch his mare. Skewbald, ears like scimitars; the Cherkess stallion had particularly remarked on them, and wondered whether the mare was seeing anybody.

Peri held Shashka's stirrup so he could mount. She wouldn't meet his eyes. She was cross at him for making her stay, but he needed her to partner with Katische—to manage triage and repair, and represent him to his women—and she knew it.

The sepahis knew a direct route into the hills where his scouts were posted. He would hurry.

Climbing into saddle Shashka raised his voice. "And you, Mekmout, if Fontenoy consents he will instruct you toward the repair of the walls. There will be more work to do. I'm sorry."

When he left, he'd slaughter some sheep to feast them, maybe a camel. They were working hard and willingly at his direction, though it was in their own self-interest. The thought made him feel a little moody as he rode out towards the gates. The ironware they'd had available to hang the wooden wings of the gate was old and unsatisfactory. Nartshu had done wonders, but the hinges were only adequate. If it had been his gold he would have spent it on iron, not opium.

Katische had sent Dacha to guide him; she was waiting at the gate, mounted and ready. As Shashka rode up, something behind him apparently caught Dacha's eye and made her smile. Shashka turned his head to see what it might be. Tamisen, that was what. He hadn't taken the time to saddle his mare but rode her half-naked in her quilted saddle pad with a simple girth, which meant there were no stirrups for his feet. His reins were a mere rope looped through her halter nose-strap.

Well, Shashka told himself, *if he falls off and hits his head, we'll know he's concussed for sure.*

The sepahi led them down the long ramp of the outer gates to the valley floor at a fair clip, branching away from the road almost at once to cross a fallow field heading for the scrub well to the west of the valley's mouth. It wasn't long before they started climbing.

Shashka began to talk, in part to allay his concerns about whether or not Tamisen could keep his seat. "Your mare climbs mountains, Tamisen?" Her pace was sure and her manner confident. Shashka hastened to explain himself. "Those of Kabardia are mountain-born and -bred. Cherkess, here, is of an old and noble family—and perhaps over-proud," he added, hastily. He hadn't meant to boast, just make conversation. The steppe ponies, Dacha's for one, were supremely self-confident, and could not be bothered by any assumed superiority on the part of the Cherkess stallion.

"She climbs such mountains as we have in Tengarpore, yes, lord." He couldn't hear the slightest bit of any uncertainty in Tamisen's voice, though he was riding up an increasingly challenging slope without a saddle. "Ours are a little rounder, and less tall. Coriander comes from an ancient and honorable line of warhorses, but my parents have no Rajput pedigree."

Cherkess jerked his head the slightest bit, whether at a minute shift in his balance or out of surprise to hear this fact Shashka couldn't tell.

"Rajput—what is that? And how came you by her, that she carries you so well?"

"There are many famous fighters you will know of, lord. There are Sikhs, Marathas, Pathans. All of them have been defeated by Rajputs. Even the British, yes, and the French. Akbar himself sought princesses of Rajput blood." Tamisen spoke wistfully as of departed glory, loyal to honored memory. There was something else in Tamisen's voice as well—what was it?

"I was raised in Tengarpore, which has never fallen to siege or attack. My foster father's valor is too great. Also Tengarpore is small, and neither rich nor important."

Tamisen was homesick, Shashka decided. How would Tamisen feel if his home had been destroyed with no chance of ever going back, and his people murdered by that foster father of whom he spoke with such evident love?

"Jaisal Singh gave my mother shelter, and me his fond protection. He raised me as his own, and granted me the noble beast of royal heritage who now consents to bear me."

The path had widened. Tamisen and Shashka rode side by side. Tamisen patted the mare's neck with pure affection as he spoke of her, while she murmured gently at him in response. He rode as well upslope with nothing but a girth to secure a saddle pad as many in saddle on flat ground. If the Rajputs were not world-famous as warriors, Shashka decided, some of them were unquestionably good horsemen.

Still, there was a problem. Tamisen's narrative reminded Shashka of his own history. "I was fostered as well, Tamisen." The path narrowed as it continued to climb, a thin thread between red-grey boulders brushed with green. They rode single file. Shashka couldn't see Tamisen's face. It helped.

"I loved my foster father with all my heart. I was bereft when he sent me to Russia, but I did all that I could to do him honor. And for a gift at my homecoming he set the Cossacks on my villages, and slaughtered the family into which I was born so that I could not defy his authority or resist the usurpation now that I was a man. Because it was all waste land, and me without anybody left to work it."

Every time he spoke of it he saw the fires and smelled the stink of burning flesh. He shook his head to shake the memory back down into the depths of his mind. "So I killed him and his Cossacks, and came away." Why was he telling Tamisen? Because he was the one who'd started the conversation. And because Tamisen sounded homesick.

Tamisen rode on silently for several minutes, during which Shashka entertained himself by imagining what might be going through Tamisen's head. *Yes, a filial son avenges his father's death*, to which Shashka could reply *A foster father is as sacred to a man of my family as a natural sire, and I killed one for the murder of the other.*

Or perhaps *Vengeance must pursue you*, by which Tamisen might mean *And that's why your caravan is moving east*, to which Shashka could truthfully reply *I killed my foster brothers as well and left no one to pursue.* Oh, maybe some obscure cousins would come after him some year, it wasn't impossible. Just—considering the circumstances under which Shashka had left his home Caucasus—just very, very unlikely.

They were approaching the crest of the hill. Shashka could see the skyline, close ahead. "Here, lord," Dacha said, and pulled aside.

The guard post was well sited. Perfectly obvious once he was there, but there'd been no clues on the way to hint at its presence. Shashka dismounted; with Tamisen at his shoulder, Shashka climbed the makeshift stair of rocks to look down through the concealment of the trees and study the river below.

"What's happened to the water?" Tamisen asked. Down in the valley, the riverbed shone clay-brown and rocky in the afternoon light. There was a stream of water in the channel, but no more than that—a fraction of the water's breadth when they'd first come this way. Was it seasonal, or something else?

"After the earthquake," Dacha said. "Within a few hours."

Shashka could extrapolate. A rockfall or an upheaval somewhere upstream had blocked the water, or turned it aside. It had been ten hours now since the earthshake. If he'd taken a measure of the stream's rate of flow, he'd know how far upstream they had to go to find out where it was obstructed. Had the landslip on the way home endangered his bridging party? He'd send three men out to bring back news.

"All is well else here?" Shashka asked. "Anybody hurt?" He knew already that none of the sepahis had suffered a serious injury, but he always had to ask.

The sepahis didn't look at one another, but they were so obvious about it that Shashka knew at once there was a secret. "None hurt, lord," Linye said. "We had some damage to our shelter. And we've been inspecting the sight lines, clearing them up. No other damage to report."

Damage, no, but something. Linye was blushing with a grimly clenched jaw, and Dabye and Guna were both white-lipped with the effort of not smiling.

"I'm glad to hear it." Someone had been squatting in the brush relieving herself when the earthshake had come and soiled her garments, perhaps. "I'd like a cup of coffee. Is there water?"

Dacha had brought powdered coffee beans in her saddle-bag, along with thick lumps of sugar. There was only one cup, so they had to pass it around. They brought it to Shashka first; he sipped at the thick broth with pleasure before giving it to Dabye, who was officer of the watch. She passed it to Tamisen. Shashka realized with bemused surprise that the sepahis liked Tamisen's looks.

Tamisen made no attempt to disguise his surprise at his first taste. The sepahis made a strong cup, and Shashka had no idea how coffee was prepared amongst Rajputs. His second sip Tamisen took slowly, as if carefully considering the flavor of the brew, its texture in his mouth. His third and final taste was clearly appreciative.

"Thank you," Tamisen said, handing the cup back respectfully, with both hands. "This is truly a cup for the brave."

Truly for the brave, as in *it takes a strong stomach to deal with this*. Ghosts of the women they'd once been were in their eyes as the sepahis laughed. It was a rare thing to see, and a precious vision.

After the coffee had been shared around three times, it was time to go. Shashka stepped up on the back of the Cherkess stallion, while Tamisen leapfrogged up and across the mare's back to straddle her. It was a trick to mount a horse without a saddle, especially with any semblance of grace; Tamisen clearly had practice. The sepahis liked that, too.

Should he say anything to Tamisen? *Take care how you offer impertinence to the sepahis, they will kill you?* Maybe they wouldn't kill him. Maybe they'd give him a ride to remember. And maybe—Shashka decided—it wasn't any of his business one way or another, as long as nobody took a mortal injury.

They left Dacha to unload the supplies she'd brought up with them. Linye would return to Old Fort later, in the changing of the guard. He was alone with Tamisen, and once they were half a mile away and in no danger of being over-heard Tamisen spoke.

"There's surely a story to go with your Amazon soldiers, lord."

The phrase made Shashka laugh, but he didn't want Tamisen to get the wrong idea. "Another part of the same story. Cossacks came without warning and burned the villages." While his foster father had delayed him with wedding festivities. It hadn't been the bride's fault; Shashka was sorry she'd killed herself. The sons of such a woman might have been heroes of iron. "Not all of the women died. My Hell-riders live to revenge themselves on the world for that injustice."

Tamisen was an intelligent man. He could extrapolate, Linye with her scarred face, Guna with her limp, Dabye with a piece of her jaw missing. What would he make of it all?

They rode together in silence for some time, the blue sky, the warm breeze, the smell of horseflesh and hoof-bruised vegetation.

"A Rajput kills her children and then herself as her men ride out to die and the house burns around her," Tamisen said finally. "I like the sepahis's approach better."

Shashka laughed again, which made two times today. "I once was told that it was better to be a live jackal than a dead lion." Shashka remembered long evenings in his foster father's house, sitting on a rug, listening to the musicians. "But I'm not sure." His foster father's treachery had made all of Shashka's childhood insane in retrospect. How could he ever have been genuinely loved by a man capable of so fiendish a betrayal?

They were well down into the valley now, on their way toward Old Fort. Peri was riding toward them with some others.

"Thank you for your company, Tamisen," Shashka said,

and nudged Cherkess to hurry. "Come back at your own pace. I'll see you later."

He'd seen no indication of confusion in Tamisen, beyond that natural to a young man clearly unacquainted with evil in the face of such a story as Shashka had to tell. He was a little ashamed of himself for having burdened Tamisen with it.

Tamisen could be safely left to muse as he liked. Any man who could ride a horse bareback up and down a hillside would have no difficulty with the road back to Old Fort. For his own part Shashka had had an enjoyable few hours in Tamisen's company, but now it was back to work.

Chapter Nine
The River Shahiva

It was as dark as damnation. Broderick sat as close as he could get to the pathetic fire Rashid had built, rubbing his arms and trying not to think of how quickly morning would come. Cassim was determined, and his men almost too well trained in the art of getting up and on their way at any hour.

There'd been an earthquake yesterday, four days after they'd left Fayzabad. Cassim had known what to make of Broderick's report. His iron drive forward made it difficult for Broderick to consult the map unobserved. Even his hygienic retreats were carefully monitored, at a respectful distance.

Did Cassim think Broderick would try to get out of their deal? He had no horse. He had no weapons. He couldn't speak the language. As far as Cassim knew he had very little money, and inadequate provisions, which were supplemented out of Cassim's stores—generously supplemented, Broderick could grant that—but only in single-meal increments.

They'd found what was left of the river yesterday. Somewhere upstream the earthquake had forced a diversion, Broderick supposed. It made finding clean drinking water an unexpected challenge, and the damp fog that rose at night was somehow colder and wetter than Broderick had ever imagined it could be.

He remembered that it had been hellishly hot on the banks of the Nerbudda, its foglike haze of fever-laden air as heavy as wet wool drawn into his lungs. They'd been crossing from Madras on their way north to Bombay—that had been what? Four years ago, perhaps? Another time, another place. Another life.

The later they camped, the more difficult it was to find enough suitable firewood to make up a decent cooking fire, since a man had to climb up the riverbank to find sufficiently dry fuel. The bread would be half-raw, half-burned again tonight.

It was a grievance in Broderick's heart that Rashid couldn't do better. It made them look bad. Broderick was a Parsi sorcerer. Shouldn't he be able to conjure a brilliant crackling fire out of damp earth? Wasn't his special deity the sacred fire? And yet, even if he'd had dry wood, if he'd had proper kindling, Cassim would frustrate his quest to get warm anyway. Cassim had the cooking fires banked as soon as the meal was prepared, for fear of drawing attention.

Suspicion and paranoia were admirable traits. They made a man manageable. In this case, however, Cassim's caution left Broderick cold and hungry, as well as exhausted, but he knew how to do cold, hungry, and exhausted. He'd learnt it at a very young age. His years of privilege and plenty had dulled the memory, but it all came back to him quickly enough. He didn't like it and he wasn't enjoying himself, but he could manage.

Fontenoy had left Fayzabad six or seven days ago. Maybe in the morning when the sun came up, Broderick would have a chance to check the map. He'd studied well on the road from Chitral: five days from Fayzabad to the little road with the "X" at the end of it. There couldn't be much more than three days between him and his goal, if the map continued to prove out.

There was a risk that Fontenoy's map carried a secret code that only Fontenoy knew. But they were on Fontenoy's trail. Fontenoy had unquestionably come this way. Cassim's scouts said several men with large horses had been on the river recently, the traces of their passage undisturbed on the dry road that ran along the river's recently wave-washed banks. Once they found the road that led north from the river, they would find Fontenoy.

And Broderick had several alternatives in mind when they found him, one for each possible situation. Fontenoy might be alone with Tamisen, relying on secrecy and stealth for his success. Fontenoy might have met armed men. He might have expected to meet them, or not. Broderick's catalog was as comprehensive as his cunning could devise.

But that was meditation for daylight hours, when the body was in motion and physical energy was not so sharply focused on the cold, bad food, hard ground, and hunger. During the night other subjects were more agreeable, schemes and conjectures that heartened a man against adversity, contemplation of a future state in which all his present discomforts would be in so distant a past as to have acquired the hazy and imperfect outlines of a particularly pointless and unhappy dream.

There'd be warm dry clothing, clean linen, luxurious Kashmir shawls to wrap carelessly around his waist for cummerbunds. He'd never sleep in a hard bed again, not even on shikar. He'd hunt in as noble a style as the Sultan of Mysore. Whole cities would accompany his every move. Auckland's progress to Simla would be as a distant shadow to his state.

He'd have hot food waiting at all hours, whatever he might want, whenever he wanted it. The fragrances of white-flour bread, delicately scented pilaus, sugary sweetmeats, roasted pheasant and wild boar with gravy that was thick and salty and rich with butter, would all perfume the air outside his tents. Within his tents it would be champagne, and the fine French colognes of the most beautiful women that money could buy.

If he closed his eyes and wrapped his arms around himself tightly, he could make a thin envelope of still air around him for insulation, and imagine he was already there. He'd have bonfires that would crackle and leap in the night, their resinous incense proclaiming his presence for miles around. He could smell the bonfires now, and the smoke of a feast as well. That would be his shikaris, perhaps, celebrating the day's sport, a rude counterpart to the refined elegance of his own repast.

The sound of someone in a hurry jolted Broderick out of

his reverie. One of Cassim's men, saying something low-voiced and urgent to Rashid that made him start to pile up earth on top of the fire immediately. Broderick only just snatched the half-baked bread away before Rashid buried the fire, food and all.

He started to object. Then he realized suddenly that though his daydream had been destroyed he still smelled smoke and cooking fires. It wasn't very strong and he could hear nothing, but there was no mistaking the message of the scents of pine resin and roasted meat: someone else was on the river, encamped not far away. Fontenoy? No. Fontenoy had surely reached his destination by now, and that lay north, away from the river.

Cassim's men began to move, silent as ghosts, walking the horses forward along the level damp mud banks between the river's edge and its high-water mark where the soft damp earth muffled the sound of shod hoof striking stone. From his place in the procession Broderick could hear voices a little way off, faint and indistinct. There were cooking fires, but well back in the trees, a place where men might stop to camp and watch the river to see who came and went between its banks and the stony hills.

The trees saved them. If there were night guards posted they might yet be found out, but as the column made its careful way forward, Broderick heard no alarms. The moon was rising, and it was waxing full, but they would have the protection of its shadow for an hour or three still.

Broderick felt no fear for himself. He was the sorcerer; he was the magic man. It was Cassim who was in danger, whether of attack or of acquiring an unwanted business partner. Let Cassim find himself with competition. Broderick was content. He was confident of his ability to make it work, to find a way, to make himself sole master of Fontenoy's treasure. Additional contingency planning might be required, that was all.

They had hours of moonlight to travel by along the road, north by northeast across the river from Zebak, following Broderick's visions, following Fontenoy's map. When they stopped to rest it would be in the welcome warmth of morning. It was weary to walk after so long a day on horseback, but Broderick for once could find no resentment in his heart for the discomfort. This only put him closer to his goal.

Were there others? Had more than one merry band of adventurers decided to travel up the river looking for Cassim? All to the good, Broderick told himself with satisfaction, and went forward with as light a heart as he had known for days.

It was the day after the earthshake. Jefferji had experienced them before, mostly of the small and modest kind. It wasn't the earthshake itself that had reached deep inside of him to change him.

He had held the great conch trumpet Devadatta, though it bore little resemblance to the pictures in which it was something the size of a melon or a coconut still in its green husk. He had heard it sing in a voice both strange and familiar, resonating with the pain of Sri Krsna's abandonment in a way that had made him thirst to feel the pain, because it was at least a kind of Krsna. The voice of the Beloved had been in his heart as he had never heard it before—because it had sounded, as it had seemed to Jefferji, like the voice of Shikander Beg.

As at all times of perplexity in his life, Jefferji had to dance to manage his emotions, to process them through in the working of his body, to gather his scattered thoughts and sensations together and knit himself whole again. He had no drummer here to be his guide, but he had the voice of his teacher in his ears to measure out his steps.

He runs for his life, Guru-ji sang softly. *Raja Rathor, once mighty in battle, hunted like a wild stag in the forest.* It was a strange story filled with violence, and Jefferji's body was sore—from head to foot, as it seemed to Jefferji—but he'd danced injured and he'd danced filled with sorrow and he would dance now.

Raja Rathor. Proud, haughty, wicked, brought to justice, hunted in the semblance of a deer as he had hunted the sacred abhibhaavak stag, the prince of the forest, the beloved of Krsna. The secluded courtyard at Old Fort dissolved. Jefferji ran through the ancient and holy Chanderminen forest with the fear-filled leaps of a desperate man, reaching for freedom with hands outreached clawing and beseeching, neck stretched to gasp for air to ease an aching chest—all instinct, no strategy.

Running so hard in place on any practice floor was almost as much work as running in fact, all of the weight of his body concentrated on one point of his flexed feet one after the other, the muscles of his thighs absorbing the energy of a constantly arrested fall. It had to look convincing; that made it harder. The audience had to believe that he was fleeing through the forest in sheer terror.

The fallen trunks of the trees he cut down in his pride seek their revenge. The granter of justice, the avenging king hot on his trail, presses him hard. He hears the dogs of retribution behind him, singing for his blood like the voice of the demon king coming for him.

Looking back over his shoulder as he ran, Jefferji danced a symbolic tripping hard over an invisible tree trunk, crashing heavily to the ground with an apparently bone-jarring impact. He broke his fall with a short quick push back against the earth, muscles tensed and relaxed in swift succession one after another, his knees, his forearm, his shoulders.

Coming within a dry leaf's width of striking his head against the bare stone with stupefying force, Jefferji used the grimace that the effort to control his fall evoked to mime Raja Rathor's panic fear before an unseen audience. Scrambling to his feet, exhausted, stumbling, Raja Rathor fought his way through a thick forest full of branches that seemed to thirst to catch him hand and foot, vines to trip him up.

But the noble king has caught the prey of justice. One arrow flies from bow pulled by serene righteousness. The arrow finds its mark. Shot in the back between the shoulder blades, and with such force it knocked Jefferji down. There'd be a costume arrow for the performance, but the timing went by the drum. On the beat Jefferji stopped, his arms flung wide, his face raised slack-jawed to the skies in a mask of anguish.

On the beat of the music in his mind, he fell to his knees, over onto his back, turning to one side as the arrow pierced him through. Face turned to the front of his practice floor Jefferji held the pose, unblinking, open-mouthed, dying in inglorious fear, for three long beats, then closed his eyes, letting his body go limp on the ground.

Then there was the lion of the grasslands, suddenly, not the song of Raja Rathor that Jefferji knew, and a voice as deep as thunder saying "Tamisen, are you all right? You seem to have been shot with an arrow. What dance is this?"

Jefferji opened his eyes, startled out of himself, so confused and disoriented that for a moment he wasn't sure where he was and what he saw. Shikander Beg. Shikander Beg was there at Jefferji's side, down on one knee, a hand to Jefferji's face solicitously. Jefferji blinked, and swallowed.

"Exactly so, lord, but it's only Raja Rathor." Why had he said that? Jefferji wondered. Why would Shikander Beg know anything of Raja Rathor? He was pleased all the same that Shikander had seen him shot with an arrow, because if a man who didn't know the story could see that as plainly as Shikander seemed to have done, it meant his body was telling the story convincingly whether or not his brains were possibly a little addled. "No cause for alarm."

"If you say so." Shikander took his hand away, with what Jefferji thought might have been a gentle caress with his thumb against Jefferji's cheek. "You died very beautifully, and I would like to talk to you about it. Later."

Peculiar, and promising, in some sense. Shikander was on his feet again and hurrying away. There was an anticipatory tension in his shoulders, Miss Boy was not in evidence, Jefferji heard the voices of the sepahis calling to one another on the walls, and something was clearly happening. Pulling himself together, Jefferji ran after Shikander to find out what it was.

There were three horses standing unburdened in front of the guesthouse facing the central courtyard square by the time Jefferji got there. Captain Fontenoy was just coming out of the guesthouse, his turban showing signs of having been donned in haste.

Catching sight of Jefferji, Fontenoy beckoned him with a wave. Jefferji was very happy to hurry to Fontenoy's side: first row seats to whatever show this was going to be. There was a clearly newly arrived rider, very dusty from travel. Shikander Beg was there, and yes Miss Boy, and as Jefferji watched

Shikander waved the sepahis away. No threat, apparently. One of the women of Old Fort had brought the new man a pitcherful of milk, and he drank from its earthen lip very thirstily indeed.

Wiping his milky moustache on his sleeve, he lowered the jug and spoke. "Thank you." He spoke another version of the language Jefferji had been hearing since they'd crossed the Dora Pass—its own distinct sort of Persian Urdu, with many new words to learn and a slight, but still distinct, variation in the accent. "Peace to you, lord of this place. My name is Runji, a messenger from Deravass Khan with a letter for Captain Fontenoy. Are you Lamish Khan?"

Lamish "Khan," that was a good one. Still, any man could call himself what he liked, until someone who objected to the self-assigned title presented a cogent argument for alteration. Mockery worked as well as cudgels.

Shikander Beg shook his head. "Lamish Khan lies invalid in his house. You shall be taken to him if you like. But this man is Captain Fontenoy."

The courier Runji didn't seem to doubt it. "Deravass Khan sends his warmest greetings, Captain Fontenoy. He sends his apologies for the delay." Runji had taken his dispatch case off his saddle, and had it draped over his shoulder. Now he unfastened the leather flap and pulled out a plain thin square of folded paper, extending it for Fontenoy to take.

"Nothing of concern, I hope?" Fontenoy asked, turning the envelope over to look at the seal.

Jefferji couldn't read the inscription. If the script was Persian, the calligraphy was bad. Boldly lettered, though. Energetic. Admirably black ink.

Runji smiled, but with respectful reserve. "Not any longer. Business led us farther north than we had planned. We're coming over the hills from Ferghana, not by the Fayzabad road as expected. So he sent me on ahead to let you know."

"There's a road out of the valley, there, to the north?" Shikander asked. "You've startled me, Runji. I've no watch set for visitors from the mountains."

Another smile from Runji, this one rueful. "It's an old road, lord, and not mapped. The door may be unlocked, but it is hidden."

Shikander nodded, smiling a little. "Thank you." The messenger was an intelligent man, who could guess the concern behind Shikander's question. "If the road is long I trust you rest with us a while. Captain Fontenoy, your guest and mine."

Miss Boy cocked her head in a beckoning manner, and one of the boys of Old Fort came forward to take Runji by the hand and lead him away to food and drink. Fontenoy bowed his head to Shikander and went after Runji. Jefferji would have gone too, but Shikander surprised him, taking him by the arm in a friendly manner.

"No, hold back just a moment, if you will," Shikander said. "Just now. I saw a great antlered stag pursued by hunters. I wished to be one of them." His tone of voice was perfectly cordial, his hand on Jefferji's arm casually intimate. Jefferji could still remember the touch of Shikander's hand on his cheek. "What is the story?"

There was no need for him to run after Fontenoy immediately, Jefferji decided. He could hear all about it later. And what was there to hear? Deravass Khan's men were delayed; they'd already known that.

"Raja Rathor must die, lord. He does not repent. He isn't sorry. There is no redemption." The arrow was earned. Generation upon generation of children had seen, and rejoiced in justice served out to the wicked. "A kind of prayer, for retribution against the profane. I'm glad you saw the stag, lord. I'm out of practice. I've been neglecting the exercise."

"My people dance on feast days." Shikander sounded a little surprised. "Or used to. And there are mystics who dance to offer up their suffering. But mostly we would dance to show ourselves off to the young women."

"That too," Jefferji agreed happily. All of those things, but he couldn't think about it, not here, not now. He would follow the more universal thread. "At festivals, for the entertainment of the god and his worshippers. One represents the Beloved, or his Beloved, to bring joy to those who watch. Who sometimes extend the play, but privately."

Jefferji hadn't danced at love-play for more than two months. He wasn't sure he knew how, any longer, without the Beloved in his heart. Surprisingly enough the thought brought him no pain, only a wistful longing, almost nostalgia. If the Beloved had spoken with the voice of Arjuna he had a different form, and who knew how one was to best please him in the dance?

The confidential pressure of Shikander's hand on Jefferji's arm had begun to lift in a very subtle manner, as if Shikander had started to think about the next place he needed to be. Now Shikander drew him closer, almost imperceptibly, a mere whisper of increased interest.

"You dance both roles?"

Jefferji wondered suddenly if he'd made a mistake, said too much about himself. "Yes, lord." But there was nothing in Shikander's body language that spoke of distaste or revulsion. Jefferji knew how to read body language; he was a dancer. "Do I lose your respect?"

Now Shikander did release Jefferji's arm, stepping back by a very little bit to put his hand on Jefferji's shoulder briefly. Almost a friendly pat of reassurance.

"I am only surprised," Shikander said. "And also, if I may say it without insult, encouraged. Perhaps you would honor me and dance something to entertain my family, at some convenient time."

He didn't have any costumes. He didn't have any bells, and there were no drummers. Shikander's family wouldn't know Jefferji's stories. They weren't from the same lands.

Jefferji stood silent for a crucial moment, trying to decide which reason he should select from the list. In that moment Shikander Beg nodded and turned away, with the confidence of every lord whose will was law to his community. The absence of "no" was "yes."

He could do a pantomime, Jefferji supposed, one that didn't depend on knowing who the characters were for it to make sense. Shikander's family? Wife, women, and child, by report. He felt obliged to Shikander for not insisting that the conch be kept with the gold even after Jefferji had explained that it was valuable. One favor for another—why not?

Captain Fontenoy could help him. And he wanted to know if there was other news Fontenoy had to share of Deravass Khan. Jefferji went to go find Fontenoy and breakfast in the guesthouse, with the sound of Shikander's "I am only surprised" an unexamined note of inexplicable encouragement in his mind.

Another day of resting, with too many puzzles in his mind for Jefferji to concentrate on any one of them. He danced his map. He thought about Shikander Beg, and wondered about Miss Boy. He thought about who could have built Old Fort and how old it really was, because the way in which the walls were put together was peculiar, stacked slate-like tiles worn glassy-smooth. He went down to the river with Simon to pick flowers, herbs, roots.

In the early afternoon light, it was warmer on the river than Jefferji had anticipated, and the dampness of the riverbed rose in an unpleasant and surely unhealthy miasma under the powerful rays of the sun. There were no trees to cool the air out here, standing with Coriander in what had been the middle of the river's channel.

"I never rode across a river like this," he called to Simon, on the far bank. "I've forded rivers, yes. Swum across rivers, yes. Walked? No."

Captain Fontenoy had left the day before yesterday with the messenger Runji, to accompany him for a little of the way and see where the road was. So he said. If he also meant to have a private word with Runji on the subject of Shikander Beg it was Fontenoy's business, Jefferji supposed.

Simon had stores to replenish in his medicine box, and Jefferji had wanted to see the river. It was an eerie scene, reminiscent of the way things looked when the floodwaters receded after the monsoon and the Tengarpore river settled back into its course. But these banks had been carrying the river for years, not weeks. They were smoothed and shaped by water much more beautifully than the floodplains of home, which were broken for planting as soon as the mud would bear the plow.

"Amazing opportunity," Simon called back, from the far banks. A root of legendary efficacy against fever grew in the muck of the shallows; with the water gone what herb Simon didn't harvest would go to waste, rotting where it lay in the drying mud. The good mule Marigold was with them, browsing on the near bank, and Gunnery, with whom Simon had become friends. "This side of the river—absolutely pristine."

The river's name was Shahiva, as Captain Fontenoy pronounced it. Not as big as the Panj river to which it was tributary, but its own respectable slice of a mile wide, four days ago. Now there was nothing but mud. It was an interesting view of a river's contours, the wide cut and deep banks carved by the spring runoff, the gentle slope down toward its summer stream.

Now even that was down to slurry. Coriander didn't like the feel of it beneath her hoofs, and could Jefferji blame her? Thick black mud drying in the sun with a perfume of decaying vegetable matter. Good stuff for manuring the fields, though, or it would be, if the labor of transporting sodden muck the distance to the fields could be managed with so few men and beasts as Old Fort held in inventory. Shikander Beg had everybody he could enlist busy at wall mending anyway.

Coriander shifted her weight restlessly, which gave Jefferji the opportunity to look up and down the river. He could see much farther downriver from the middle than they'd been able to do from the banks, and the place where the stream joined the river from Old Fort's valley was much more obvious. How far upriver could he see?

"Just going upstream a bit, Simon, all right?" Jefferji called.

Simon just waved. He was happy. There were no traces of human traffic on the south bank of the river, no foot traffic to disturb the undergrowth. As far as Simon was concerned it was Eden untouched.

There was a strip of level sand between the high-water mark and the dry-season banks that seemed likely to be firm beneath the weight of Coriander's hoofs. Jefferji pointed Coriander at that to see how she liked it, and she humored him so far as to walk on without objection or grumbling, picking her way over and around mud-caked river bottom and old dead wood.

Half a mile east, the river's turn led to a fine long stretch of maybe three miles, at Jefferji's estimation, before it curved around the spring-green hills and out of sight again. There'd be more of that herb Simon was so happy to find, there for the taking. Without the river, the water plants would dry up and die anyway, so he did nobody harm by harvesting. Maybe they'd regrow, but by the banks of the now-much-smaller stream. There was *some* water left there in the channel, just not enough to make a rivulet.

Coriander put her nose down toward the middle part of the river where the water was. She hadn't had a drink since they'd left Old Fort this morning, watering at the well there that Shikander had had cleared out and restored between the outer walls and the village. If she could find a little puddle where some water had collected and settled out, so much the better. But when she got to the middle of the channel she apparently reconsidered, curling her lip in disdain and turning away.

Dismounting, Jefferji crouched down on the mucky surface. He wouldn't have minded a drink of water himself. He hadn't brought his canteen with him. He'd tucked the shankha into his saddle pouch and hung it where his canteen would be, neglecting to think twice about the fact that you couldn't carry water in a conch trumpet until they'd been well away.

Once he got down to the ground and saw for himself he understood Coriander's decision. This wasn't clear water by any means. It was as turgid as Turkish coffee. He wasn't about to test its flavor for any further points in common.

Straightening up, Jefferji stood in what would have been mid-stream, looking upriver, wondering where this newly revealed road would lead. It would be easier for Shikander Beg to move his caravan, and that was surely a benefit—as long as there was fresh water to be found along the way, not just the noisome mud that trickled underfoot. How far upstream had the river been diverted? Was there a new lake to be negotiated farther east, perhaps? If so, that might destroy the usefulness of the new road, unless there was an easy way around.

Feeling the disagreeable suction of wet mud against his feet, Jefferji turned to remount. He didn't want to get his feet wet. He'd underestimated the volume of that wet mud trickle;

there was more of it than he'd realized. No, there was more of it than there'd been. It had been the merest whisper of a tiny rivulet, no thicker than his little finger. There were two fingers of water running there now.

Maybe he was thinking of the place in the river where he'd left Simon. Climbing up into saddle he turned Coriander back downstream, and she was glad to go. She didn't like it here, it seemed. Maybe she was just annoyed about the mud.

It seemed to Jefferji that the smell of wet decay and damp clay was getting stronger. Was it just the sun? That didn't make sense. Why would a scant five minutes' extra warmth bring up the stench of the river bottom?

He could see Simon on the far bank, Marigold and Gunnery browsing where they'd been asked to wait. This was the place Jefferji'd been just fifteen minutes ago. There hadn't been a little rill of water running through the very center of the riverbed. Not one finger; not two fingers. Certainly not as wide as the palm of his hand.

"Simon," Jefferji shouted. "I think we should call it good for now. Let's go back to the village."

Simon didn't turn around, so his voice came muffled by his body, but his words were adequately clear. "What for? I need to collect as much of this as possible. You could come and help me if you're in a hurry to get back, I can show you how."

And of course Jefferji would be very willing to do that. He'd helped Simon gather herbs off and on during their journey from Peshawar. He enjoyed the opportunity to pick up a little knowledge of herb-craft. He couldn't explain why he didn't want to get involved with serving as Simon's apprentice here and now, but he knew he wanted to get away from the river.

"No, really, Simon, we should go. Something is happening. Pack up."

Simon didn't want to. There was a clearly annoyed set to Simon's shoulders, and he looked back at Jefferji with a frown. "Plenty of time for you to dance later on."

Coriander shifted her weight uncomfortably, turning her head to catch Jefferji's eye. Her own eyes showed white; she was unhappy. He could see the water rising in the riverbed at his feet, now. It was a finger-stretched handspan of a stream, but a moment ago it had been a palm-broad cord of brown water coming down. And why muddy? Was it only because it was running through the mud? What if it wasn't picking up mud? What if it was coming down muddy?

Then he knew. He was a long way from the fields of Tengarpore, but still he knew. Simon needed to bundle up his harvest. They needed to leave. It wasn't a tributary stream. It was much more serious than that.

Jefferji pointed Coriander to the far side of the river; she didn't want to go, but he couldn't wait any longer. Hastily he dismounted at Simon's side, and gathered up the drop cloth with its carefully stacked harvest of green herbs.

"Hurry. There's water coming. We've got to get out of here."

Simon started to disagree, to push him back, but something silenced him and he froze, staring behind Jefferji. Jefferji looked back over his shoulder. There was a larger stream there now, and it bubbled and boiled with a sort of restless energy that touched off a wave of near-panic in Jefferji's mind.

"You may be right," Simon said. "Let's go."

Jefferji was too happy to have Simon's cooperation to argue about how sure he was that he was right. Remounting, he pulled Simon up onto Coriander's back behind him. The stream was rising. The mare hurried back across the riverbed, through the angry mud-black stream, lifting her feet as though there were snakes in the water. The stream was rising much too quickly. If an earthquake-created dam was giving way, four days' worth of water would be coming down the river on top of them, and there was no way to tell how soon it was going to get here.

Coriander had to scramble through the barricade of drift-wood and debris normal to the boundaries of rivers, but she was clever and canny and they were both in a hurry to reach the shore. Jefferji let Simon down at Gunnery's side and whistled for Marigold, who raised her head and came as she was bidden.

"Go on as fast as you can. Faster. Get everybody up into the village. Tell them the river's coming." Was it his imagination, or did he hear an almost subterranean roar, somewhere to the east? Jefferji tied the bundled herbs to Marigold's pack saddle without dismounting and caught her lead rope up in his hand, tossing it to Simon. "Hurry!"

The stream was widening as he watched. The roar he heard was getting louder, moment by moment. He'd heard that sound once before. A man never forgot the sound of the animal rage of an insulted river escaping from captivity.

He knew what flooded rivers did to their tributaries. The river would back up along the stream-bed with explosive force as the floodwaters rose. Simon and Marigold were clear, were man and mule together well on their way toward Old Fort-but they wouldn't be able to warn everybody, not in time.

There were people in the valley bottom, some of them harvesting kitchen gardens, some of them driving the grazing animals from one pasture to another. And that was another thing. The animals. But the sepahis on lookout communicated with the sentries on the walls of Old Fort by means of visual signals. If he could get *their* attention, they would see what was happening for themselves, and raise the alarm.

He had the shankha. He'd planned on practicing with it out here, far enough away from Old Fort that nobody but Simon would be bothered by any wrong notes. It made no difference now whether the note was pleasing so long as it was loud enough. The rumble in the east was getting louder, and it sounded angry. It wasn't the fault of the people of Old Fort that the river had been unjustly imprisoned, but the river wouldn't care. There was no reasoning with rivers. You got out of their way and hoped for the best, and that was all.

Fumbling with the ties that secured the mouth of the bag Jefferji reached for the conch as Coriander twitched nervously beneath him. *I think we should run. If you don't do something about this river, I might run anyway, because you don't seem to be paying attention.*

He didn't have time to discuss it with her. Taking a deep breath he filled his lungs, and blew the trumpet. Nothing. An embarrassing squeal like someone breaking wind. The breath had to come from the bottom of the belly and it had to come steady as well as deep. He tried again, and this time it worked: a clear round bell of warning. *Look*, Jefferji thought fiercely, blowing the conch trumpet, hearing its voice fierce and demanding of attention. *Look.*

No, Coriander said, taking a nervous lurch sideways. *No more looking. Run.*

Muddy water splashed in the riverbed so violently that Jefferji saw the spatters on the ground beneath Coriander's feet, and the roar of water coming from upriver was as loud in his ears as a monsoon rain. It was more than enough for him. He tucked the shankha close against his chest inside his shirt and leaned in as Coriander took off like a pheasant startled by the dogs.

A quarter of a mile, galloping up the road. The angry roar of the river wasn't coming any closer, but it wasn't dying back into the distance either. Half a mile—wasn't he being a complete idiot? How could the river be chasing him? The river didn't even know him. But he'd seen the floods, and those had been monsoon rain floods, not those of a river dammed up for four days and angry about it.

A mile and a quarter, and the road turned to bend into the valley between brown hills. Stopping Coriander with shifted weight and a word, Jefferji twisted around in the saddle to look behind him. The sound was terrible, a giant walking through the brush, tearing up scrub trees, kicking up boulders.

He could see frantic activity on the walls of Old Fort, so the sepahis had sent a signal; but what about the people in the valley bottom? The herders and the women and children who worked their kitchen gardens? He couldn't stop to make a rational analysis. He pushed Coriander through the stream-bed to the west bank, blowing the conch trumpet and yelling, "Get to high ground! The river is coming! Run! Head away from the water!"

Coriander ran, because that was her job. Jefferji blew the trumpet. She carried him into the fields that lay across the stream-bed. He could see people running for the high ground of Old Fort and it looked like they were going to make it. The river could come up the road between the rocks but it couldn't flush out the entire plain, could it? Could it? Far ahead of him, Jefferji could see frightened animals, camels, horses, stampeding toward the hills. All to the good. They'd be safe. As long as they could get out of the way they would be safe.

The treble note of a small bird piping on the ground in its distress cut through the bass growl of the river, and instinctively Coriander turned an ear toward it. If it was a bird it could fly up, but the sound Jefferji heard was frightened and fixed. Not a bird. A child. Someone's boy or girl, crouched there on a garden path with an overturned basket of abandoned greens and its hands cupped over its ears, keening and terrified.

Jefferji looked back. There was a great roiling cloud coming up through the valley from the river, billowing with brown and grey. It would eat this child up without mercy. He reached his hand down with a beckoning nod: *Come up, come up*, but the child was too frightened to move. The water was coming. He slid down out of saddle and picked the child up.

Coriander stood still, but Jefferji knew how hard it was for her by the way she trembled. She hardly waited to feel the weight settled on her back before she bolted up the valley as fast as he had ever known his girl to run.

There was no finding his stirrups. The child clung to his neck, possibly screaming, but Jefferji couldn't hear anything above the roaring of the river, now. With the child held close, Jefferji emptied his mind of unnecessary thoughts and willed them all safely, swiftly, up the valley, and beyond the reach of now-freed and ferocious river.

Cassim's scout had returned from his morning reconnaissance run at mid-day, not that anybody stopped for lunch and Broderick would have objected had they done so. They'd lost enough time getting out of Fayzabad. One might have thought that following a dried-up river would be easier than riding up the banks of the existing river, but no—water had to be dug for, every time they made camp, and it took all that much more time to fill, and draw, and water the animals.

"It curves around left, then straightens," Rashid translated low-voiced, but Broderick hardly needed Rashid's help to interpret a simple line drawn in the mud. "That's where he stopped to return with his report. The river follows a fairly straight course. There's a place—here—where the vegetation falls away, maybe a pond or a stream."

"Does he say how long it will be before we get there?" Broderick did his best to keep the excitement out of his voice.

Trying to find the few landmarks there'd been on Fontenoy's map was like trying to read a word on a beer-soaked page the outlines of which were swollen to three times their original width—because the river was no longer a line, but a trough. If the scout had seen a stream-bed, it could be the place where the road branched off. Could be. Could be.

"Now Cassim says they'll hurry forward, because if it's a stream we could get fresh water which we would all very much appreciate."

Over the course of these past several days, Cassim had fallen out of his initial habit of consulting Broderick on the route, keeping him informed, asking for his opinion and generally deferring to him as an employer, if not a sorcerer. The time had come to assert himself, Broderick decided, because if they didn't find the junction he was going to have to lead Cassim off the river anyway in order to make good an escape.

His story was stretching very thin. The problem was not so much whether Cassim and his men believed Broderick to be a genuine Parsi sorcerer; the problem was that Cassim and his men were getting bored with the search for a treasure the trail of which had apparently gone cold. Broderick needed to get away before Cassim decided to return to Fayzabad and cut his losses, meaning Broderick himself. As well as Rashid, Broderick supposed.

Broderick let drop the wedge of cold dry bread he'd hidden away from breakfast for his lunch, opening his arms wide and raising his face to the sky. "Praise be to God the almighty, the king of all nations," Broderick cried loudly. "Tell them that I can see the golden trace of the Sun on the horizon. Say we must be there by sundown or lose all."

The wretched pony Cassim had provided for Broderick to ride stood away from the river in the brush, trying to find something to eat. Broderick hurried toward it, declaiming loudly as he went. "Tell them I'm impelled by the voice of God to hurry forward, or perish in the fiery wrath of sacred fire. Now get on your horse and follow me."

The river road itself was fairly blocked by Cassim's party, but Broderick's pony, when beaten hard enough, found a way to bypass the obstruction. Broderick kicked the pony again, chanting at the top of his lungs in what he hoped would be interpreted as religious exaltation.

"I showed him where to find it! I showed him where to go, amidst the bushes! And the brambles! Where the wild cuckoos grow!" It had worked for him in Fayzabad; it would work here. "But once he had discovered it! He would not let me rest till he'd ruffled! Up the feathers! Of the cuckoo's nest!"

That was him. He was the cuckoo. He was feathered and nested comfortably here, with Cassim, in the person of a Parsi sorcerer. He'd been Lieutenant Broderick Holyoke and no one ever the wiser. If the pony slipped and broke a leg Broderick didn't care, so long as he reached his goal first. He could hear the horsemen behind him, but he wasn't trying to escape them now. He'd do that later, when he didn't need them anymore.

He pushed the pony hard, concentrating on the map in his mind and the one he'd just seen in the mud. The river turned north by a fraction of a degree, then it ran straight. There'd be a stream that joined it from the north. The all-important road up from the river to the place where a wall was drawn and a few words written, and an "X" on the map marked the spot.

But the scout, the mother's husband, had drawn the course of the river just wrong enough. Broderick could see the bend in the river, but not the place in the bank that would indicate the bulge he'd clearly seen in the mud schematic. As he puzzle-studied the problem Broderick heard a sound of urgent hoofbeats coming up behind him, but why? Was it the scout on horseback trying to overtake him, in order to cover up the man's error with the map by persuading Broderick that the river was doing exactly as the scout had said it would?

Cassim was following, with all of his men. Broderick could hear the noise of their horses, hoofs pounding, branches crackling as the men crowded each other in their eagerness to be with Broderick when he found the road. The ground shook, the mud shore of the river amplifying the impact of each horse's footfall like a drum. Just around the bend in the river. So close that Broderick could almost see it, he did see it, but what else was it that he saw?

There at the limit of his eyesight's range, the blurred figure on horseback on the bank of the river? Could it be—Broderick asked himself, in a near-delirium of a fond wish realized—could it be Geoffrey Tamisen's skewbald mare, and that tall splinter astride her Tamisen himself, a beacon to guide Broderick to his goal?

Then something happened. The indistinct figure that might be Tamisen seemed to gesture toward the sky, and there was a sound, huge and horrible, so loud it could almost not be heard at all but felt, a sound without tone or pitch but with a clear unspoken message that said *run*.

The impact of that sound was so strong that Broderick lurched in his saddle, nearly unhorsed by an unseen blow. He hung on by pure instinct as the pony turned and fled back the way they'd come, climbing the steep slopes of the riverbank as it went faster than it had ever moved under Broderick's stick.

Breaking from the road, the pony scrambled frantically up the rocky slopes of the valley. It stumbled in the loose gravel, and Broderick only just managed to jump clear before his leg was crushed beneath the beast's weight. The pony found its feet again and staggered forward, going ever faster as it found its balance. Broderick lunged for the reins, but he was too late.

Steadying himself with both hands entangled in the pony's mane Broderick looked around. On the other side of the riverbank he could see some of Cassim's men running away. He didn't see Rashid. There was no sign of Tamisen. There were just the hills and the scrub, and a handful of men and horses scattered across the slopes trying to get away as far, as fast, as they could. What had happened to them, just now? Broderick remembered the terror that had seized him, but what had that sound been?

Something peculiar was happening to the river. There was a ribbon of black mud crawling down the middle of the dry course like a trickle of thick blood from a morbid wound. As Broderick watched, it strengthened into a stream, and then a drainage ditch, carrying floodwaters away from the streets of a city.

He could hear a crashing noise, like the steps of a clumsy giant splintering wood and spurning rock as he came. Broderick didn't believe in giants. He stood and stared in fascinated wonder as the black ribbon of muddy water rose with incredible swiftness and the clumsy giant's footsteps came ever closer.

The roaring in the air grew louder. A black cloud blew up from the east over the river as fast as a monsoon storm on the Nerbudda, the one that had ruined him, the one that had made him. He could see sticks and pebbles roiling in its mass, spanning the riverbanks side to side, overflowing its banks, climbing the hills as it came, huge and horrible. But they weren't sticks and pebbles. They were boulders, entire trees, grinding against each other in the surge of a giant wave that came on like the day of Judgment with vengeance and damnation.

The ground trembled beneath his feet. He could smell water in the air. The river came on at incredible speed, and he realized too late that it was much closer than he'd realized, misled by the massive scale of the monster into taking it for farther away than it was. Instinct alone preserved him. Without thinking, blind with panic, Broderick turned up the side of the hill and ran and crawled and climbed and didn't stop until he couldn't move any more.

Chapter Ten
Three Meetings under the Moon

At first light yesterday morning, Fontenoy had left Deravass's scout Runji at a passage in the rocks of the Shugnan foothills to travel back to Old Fort with the news that Deravass could confidently be expected within eight to ten days of his return. That would ease Shikander Beg's mind. Once the gold they'd clear from the now-collapsed cave was gone, the people of Old Fort need fear no more from Fayzabad raiders.

Especially so if Deravass left some people behind for a year or two, so that the other valuables—the ones not of gold or rubies but of painted walls and inscriptions and statuary— could be carefully protected and removed, if any of them had survived the cave-in. The cave-in had been peculiar. There'd been no discernable aftershocks reported by anyone else in the valley. Had some old gods intervened to protect their shrine?

Crossing the low saddle into the valley late in the afternoon Fontenoy rode down the path of the little stream that fed Old Fort's pond, whistling cheerfully in anticipation of a good wash. And a warm grain feed for Farouk, who was very patient about the whole thing, but to whom one scrubby slope apparently looked very much like another. Captain Fontenoy had to redirect Farouk's footsteps more than once. When not in immediate danger of death or injury, Farouk could retreat into his own little world. What he did there Fontenoy had no idea—compose poetry, perhaps—but certainly not pathfinding or geography.

As Fontenoy dropped down into the valley, though, a little abstracted in mind himself—looking up at the waxing moon rising and the lucent sapphire of the twilight sky—the road, cresting at a vista of the valley, took a turn with a clear view down to Old Fort. Fontenoy saw such a scene of chaotic destruction that he drew rein in instinctive dismay and sat there, staring, trying to make sense of what he saw.

Had he taken a wrong turn? Was he in the wrong valley entirely? There were no well-ordered plots along a well-behaved stream running into a placid waterfowl-bejeweled lakelet at the foot of the great wall of an old fort. There was a tangle of splintered wood and shattered boughs strewn from Old Fort to the valley's mouth, a long tongue of destruction that looked like the aftermath of an elephant stampede through the forest.

Farouk turned his head to catch Fontenoy's eye, apparently unmoved by the devastation. *Are we going down, or not? I'm tired, and I want to eat.* Could they even get to Old Fort? The valley bottom was a swampy mere of splintered brush and jumbled rock, as if a fleet of wooden ships driven by the fury of a monsoon storm had crashed into the reefs. That was a clue, and suddenly Fontenoy thought he knew what had happened.

"All right," he said to Farouk, giving him rein. Nodding with apparent satisfaction, Farouk started down the path once more, while Fontenoy tried to figure out where Farouk thought he was going. Farouk took the trail down into the valley, but took the fork that led out and away across to the far slope of its western flanks, rather than the eastern branch that would take them to Old Fort. Fontenoy let Farouk walk on. Farouk was more likely than not to have valid grounds for his behavior. He wouldn't be walking away from Old Fort and supper without a persuasive reason.

A light appeared, cheerful and yellow, from a clump of trees upslope. Fontenoy remembered seeing a small grove of walnut trees out across the valley from Old Fort. He'd been told there was a little spring there, too. As he approached he saw a fire, and—shining between the trunks of trees—a ghostly shade wandering eldritch and inchoate in the deepening dusk.

It was Tamisen's mare Coriander, her white spots weaving through the brush like a spirit from another world. That explained Farouk's behavior. He preferred Coriander's company to that of the Cherkess stallion and those steppe ponies, though he would never admit to it in so many sneezes.

"Who's within?" Fontenoy called, with Coriander in view. Tamisen would have heard him coming, no doubt, and there was only very little chance of there being Coriander without Tamisen. "And what have you done to the place since I've been gone?"

Tamisen materialized out of a thicket of willow wands to stand at Farouk's shoulder. "Good to see you, sir," Tamisen said, politely not noticing Fontenoy's involuntary start. Fontenoy was tired. Tamisen was good at moving silently. Stages could be creaky, and dancers were expected to be seen and not heard unless they were using jewelry for percussive effect. "It seems that the river was dammed up by the earthquake, and the dam broke. It's made a bit of a mess, but we've got a nice fire here, and plenty to eat if you don't mind mixed vegetables."

So, Fontenoy told himself, *he'd been right about the river.* "How do you come to be all the way out here?" he asked, dismounting to follow Tamisen toward the fire, where a small boy crouched at work. Cooking, maybe. There was the spring; Tamisen had made camp on its rocky lip. Something smelled very much like food, and Farouk wasn't the only one who was hungry. "Tell me all you know."

Coriander's saddle was braced on the ground across a fallen tree trunk. Farouk had a long drink of water, then Tamisen helped Fontenoy undress Farouk as far as was decent and appropriate so that Farouk could go find Coriander, who could be relied upon to have a good line on the better quality of wild grass. Clearly Tamisen didn't expect to be leaving any time soon. But it was a warm night, the sky was clear, the moon was rising, and there were far worse things to be doing at the end of a long day's riding.

Escorting Fontenoy courteously to a bit of level ground with a horse blanket overspread, Tamisen waited until Fontenoy had settled himself comfortably to beckon for the boy to pass Fontenoy a dish of roasted potatoes on a leaf plate. "This is Berni," Tamisen said. "He knows all the plots and what's growing there, luckily for us."

Potatoes, long onions, roasted green peas. It was good. Tamisen would have had salt in his saddlebags, of course. Too bad he didn't make a habit of carrying pepper and ghee as well. The boy fed the fire. Tamisen sat down facing Fontenoy, and the boy settled against Tamisen very confidently as Tamisen continued.

"Simon and I went down to the river to harvest medicines, so we were right there when the water started to rise. We were lucky. We realized something was wrong in time to give an alarm. When the flood surge hit the west side of the stream-bed's cut, it followed a path of least resistance, and things got exciting."

The boy pulled some more roasted potatoes out of the fire, arranging them artistically beside Tamisen's foot. There was a pause in Tamisen's narrative as he and the boy ran through a little bit of a play, wordlessly—*You eat it... No* you *eat it... No I insist... No I insist*—until Tamisen cut three potatoes in two and divided the halves between them, which seemed to satisfy the little boy. Passing his share of the potatoes to Captain Fontenoy Tamisen watched the boy eat, protectively, before going on.

"Berni and I found each other along the river, and came up here. Haven't seen anyone else, and we didn't see our way clear to fighting with the water. By three or four o'clock it stopped rising, and I think it'll start to drain away by morning. I'm sorry there's no coffee, sir."

"These are good potatoes, though," Fontenoy said to the boy. "Thank you." Were there any casualties? Tamisen probably didn't know. Berni wasn't a casualty, but where were Berni's parents? "I've slept in much less comfortable places, Tamisen. Have you a cup of water? Thank you." Leafware. The boy again. The cup was woven of willow cunningly lined with whole leaf. It leaked, but only a little.

Fontenoy could easily have eaten all the food on his plate,

but he had no way of telling how much of their mutual stores he might be running through. And he'd had a perfectly adequate lunch, though it was probably going on ten hours ago.

"Excellent meal." Fontenoy handed the plate back to the boy, who received it solemnly. "Coffee not at all missed, Tamisen."

But he couldn't help yawning. He'd ridden from sunrise to sunset two days running, and he wasn't as young as he used to be. How old was it, that smuggler's path?

"I'll wake you for your watch, sir." Tamisen rose to his feet as he lied, dusting his rump with one hand to rid it of bits of bruised grass. They both knew that Tamisen would do no such thing, and claim to have mistaken the hour. That was a great unspoken tradition between young men and their elders, one Fontenoy could not in this instance much resent.

When he'd been Tamisen's age he'd done the same. When he'd been Tamisen's age he would have ridden nonstop over passes and through valleys, pausing only for a change of horses, until he reached his goal. It had been him and Ganders Tamisen and Deravass Khan. Deravass Khan had something to show Tamisen. It wouldn't be long now.

"See that you do," Fontenoy admonished Tamisen with hearty insincerity, and went to sleep.

Jefferji had no real apprehension about sleeping out on the slopes of the valley. The river had no more rise to it, and everything he'd learned from Lamish's people pointed to peaceful and under-populated surroundings. But there was a fire, which he meant to keep burning at a low flame, because a chill could sometimes come up from nowhere on even a warm night. Since there was a fire, there had to be a fire-watch, and no son of Tengarpore could be so heedless of his education as to trust in open spaces under alien skies without reservations.

Jefferji found a good leaning place amongst the trees to stand his watch. A pleasant breeze came up around midnight. The moon shone full and fair in a cloudless sky. Across the small valley from where Jefferji stood his watch he couldn't see any lights on Old Fort walls, no cloud-caught reflection of cooking fires below. All was calm and serenity; and somebody riding across the middle slope of the hillside towards Jefferji's camp, whistling softly.

Jefferji listened. Did he recognize the voice? He knew he was glad to hear it. Craning his neck, he checked on Coriander and Farouk. Coriander switched her tail but seemed otherwise unworried, so she knew the horse. When the whistling stranger was quite close, the sound of a horse traveling in the grass stilled, and whomever spoke.

"Come not nigh which is harmful to man." Jefferji put a welcome name to voice within the first two letters of the word: Shikander Beg. "Be conjured by heaven. Be conjured by earth."

It seemed a strange thing to say, but Shikander Beg was a mysterious man. "Peace be to you, lord," Jefferji said, suddenly and inexplicably cheerful. A wistful image rose unbidden in his mind, not to be realized, but nice to cherish in the imagination: Fontenoy not to wake, and Jefferji to dance something mildly ribald with Shikander Beg as an appreciative audience. It could be Krsna and Radha. It could be Krsna and Arjuna in a wrestling match. "Come and warm yourself. Are you alone? I'll just see if Captain Fontenoy is prepared to receive you."

Fontenoy was already awake, however, calling out from the campfire some yards removed. "Good, you are awake for your watch, Tamisen," Fontenoy said cheerfully, the old joke about who was sleeping and who awake. "Peace, lord Shikander. Have a potato."

Berni was awake as well, rubbing the sleep out of his young eyes even as he dipped fresh water out of the spring-fed pool.

Shikander sat down and ate a bit of cold roasted potato with apparent relish. "Berni, is it? I'm glad to see you. Your parents are frantic, but I find you in good hands."

The remark was to the point. "You've come from Old Fort, surely," Jefferji said, and Shikander nodded, his mouth full of potato. "Is Simon all right? Are any more missing?"

"Your alert was very timely," Shikander said, with a little smile that looked feral in the campfire light. Jefferji was not ready to put a name to the way that made him feel. "Thanks to you and Jericho's encouragement, everyone who was working outside the village took warning in good time. Some herdsmen are unaccounted for, but the beasts seem to have stampeded safely. No bodies in the water, either, not yet."

That was a relief. "Berni and I looked for any others on this side," Jefferji said. "We didn't find anybody. It seemed best to wait till morning before we tried to cross the valley. I'm sorry we've distressed Berni's parents."

Shikander shook his head and started to speak, but just then Jefferji heard Coriander swing her head around where she stood in the dark, and snort meaningfully. Jefferji knew that snort, and put a finger to his lips.

"Someone's coming," he said, low-voiced and quietly. "Over there. Are you expecting a report, lord?"

"Come in," Shikander said, without raising his voice. "Tell me."

It was one of the sepahis, silent as a ghost. Jefferji saw her move but heard no sound of her footfall. As a professional he could admire her technique.

"We have one." The sepahi's grasp of the local dialect was not so good as Shikander's but, in response to his evident will, she did her best to report in words they could all understand. "He comes alone. He says things in some language."

"The sepahis saw people coming up from downriver," Shikander explained. "There were few pack animals and no women, so we suspect bandits. They were warned by your signal as well, Tamisen. They ran away, but I doubt they've gone far. Shall we see if we can discover anything from this man, Linye? Maybe he knows Lamish's people."

"Two things he says, lord," the sepahi—Linye—replied. "They are names of Lamish's guests, those with you. Font-tan-no-eee. Tamm-eh-sin."

Jefferji felt the skin crawl between his shoulder blades. "This is a puzzle," Fontenoy said to Shikander. "Deravass Khan comes from the north, not by the river, as the lord knows. Should we see this man now?"

Rather than taking him to Old Fort, that was.

Shikander nodded in agreement. "Bring him. Have no doubt of any danger, Captain Fontenoy. You can trust my Hell-riders with your life, as I have often done with a good outcome."

The sepahi smiled, which was a little unfortunate because she turned out to be the one who was missing a good piece of the jaw on one side of her head. The effect was obvious even in the small light of the little fire, but Berni didn't even flinch.

In moments she was back with two more sepahis and a dirty, ragged man who broke free from the sepahi's restraining hands, rushing forward into the circle of the camp with his hands outstretched. For a moment Jefferji thought he was going to fall down on his knees.

"Thank God," he said, in English. The sound was very strange to Jefferji's ear, here in the middle of the night in a wild valley. "I thought it must be you on the river, Tamisen, so could Captain Fontenoy be far? You're in great danger. Very great danger. But I can save you both."

The man's voice was beginning to stir a vague odor of recognition in Jefferji's mind—an odor that sharpened into a sudden stink as his ear made the connection. "Holyoke?"

Captain Fontenoy hadn't recognized him. But Fontenoy had spent far less time in his company, and sang neither formally nor well. He had no training for catching a tune or cadence.

Holyoke seemed offended by Jefferji's failure to recognize him on sight, and replied with a transparent annoyance that was outrageous, under the circumstances. "Yes, that's me. Who else would I be? I've got news that could—"

Shikander Beg interrupted, his tone one of mild curiosity. "Does this person speak the city language of this place? I can follow only some of his English. It has been many years, and he speaks quickly."

Fontenoy looked to Jefferji for the answer. Jefferji had spent the better part of three weeks with Holyoke, after all, before Holyoke had tried to rob him. Fontenoy clearly felt Jefferji was in a position to know Holyoke better than he did.

"I shouldn't think he does, lord," Jefferji said. "Not much Urdu either."

The pained impatience in Holyoke's voice confirmed the fact. "See here, Tamisen, I'm trying to tell you something of the utmost importance! Just between us, you and me and Fontenoy. Do these people speak English? And this fellow from the fort, get rid of him, he and these—viragos."

Shikander gave no sign that he understood, reaching into

his short coat for a cigar. The gesture helped to mask his face and conceal any inadvertent betrayal of comprehension.

"Not a word of English," Jefferji said, to answer Holyoke's question this time. Shikander's show of ignorance was a gesture of trust, and Jefferji meant to prove it well placed. "He was just asking whether you could speak Persian. How did you come to be here? How are we in danger?"

The little boy brought Holyoke some water, but Holyoke dashed the cup away. "He has no manners," Shikander said to Berni. "Shame on him, not you. Fetch me a coal to light my cigar, please."

Holyoke talked over Shikander, urgently. "It doesn't matter how I got here, only that I know there are fifty men on the road coming here to find some kind of a treasure. They have a map. They'll torture whoever they can find until they get it, and they'll kill everyone here just to cover their tracks. If we can get it out of here before they arrive there may be hope. It's our only chance."

This was much meat to be digested. Shikander had lit his cigar and was smoking it calmly, gazing into the fire with apparent indifference.

"Just what we feared from Lamish's naiveté, spending money from the hoard," Shikander said in Broderick's direction. He was clear enough on the general outline, apparently. "What do you think he means to do?"

Fontenoy turned back to Holyoke, *I'll find out.* "Chance of what? What treasure?" Fontenoy asked. In English, of course. "Aren't you in enough trouble already, thief, deserter, attempted murderer, and so forth?" And hadn't Holyoke just said these men would torture the villagers until they got what they'd come for? How was leaving Old Fort in the hands of Pindari marauders *hope?* "Why should we trust you, Holyoke?"

Holyoke leaned close, blinking rapidly. Men frequently did that when they lied, but Holyoke was already an accomplished liar so it was probably just the smoke from the campfire. The wood was rather green.

"Take me to the fort. We'll find the treasure. I'll smuggle word back—remember Rashid, from Peshawar?—and tell their leader that we'll open the gates, and so forth. There'll be a good deal of confusion, naturally, and we can escape with the treasure. Otherwise you're sure to be killed, Captain Fontenoy, I swear to you on my life."

"Are you getting this, lord?" Fontenoy asked, his head turned to look at Shikander. Holyoke would think Fontenoy was making the arrangements to bring Holyoke in.

Shikander looked up from the fire. "Probably not all of the detail." Shikander's speech was steady, giving no hint of outrage or concern. "But *open the gates* and *sure to be killed*, these things I hear. Clearly you know this man?"

"Yes, we do. And not to trust him." Fontenoy's bazaar-Persian had really gotten much better, Jefferji thought, with admiration. It was so close to being perfectly fluent that the difference hardly called any attention to itself. "If we bring him to Old Fort perhaps we can use his knowledge. But he'd be as likely to betray us all at the first opportunity, if he feels it's to his advantage."

Holyoke was waiting none too patiently while Fontenoy and Shikander spoke. "What are they talking about?" Holyoke asked Jefferji. "I'm telling you, Tamisen, this is deadly serious, I'm your only hope. I know we got off to a bad start—"

That was an understatement that Jefferji would have gladly discussed further, but Shikander rose to his feet and Holyoke shut up.

"I'm willing to take a serpent into my bosom if it's to *my* advantage," Shikander said. "But I won't have Lamish's people put at risk. Enlist him if you can, Fontenoy, as you like. I do not admit him to Old Fort. Tell him."

Shaking his head Fontenoy turned back to Holyoke. "Sorry, Holyoke, he's not having any of it. Says there isn't any treasure. The headman found a few coins and spent them all in Fayzabad months ago, but that's all there was. Place is poorer than a city cow."

Even in the flickering firelight Jefferji could clearly see Holyoke's shocked expression. "It can't be true," Holyoke said. "Cassim is determined. What am I supposed to tell him? Come on, Fontenoy. You can't have come all this way for nothing?"

That was an odd thing to say, surely. Jefferji filed it away for further consideration.

But Captain Fontenoy was unmoved. "No help for it," Fontenoy said. "Go back and tell your Cassim he'll find no treasure here. I'll stake my life on it."

Both things were true; so much was obvious from Fontenoy's tone of voice. There *was* no help for it: Cassim would find no treasure, because he'd never live to seek it. And Captain Fontenoy undertook to put himself between Holyoke and Cassim and the accomplishment of their goal.

That Holyoke would not accept the message was clear. "He's crazy," Holyoke said to Jefferji. "You don't want to die. Talk to him, it's your only hope. Cassim's lost his stores, he's hungry, he's desperate. Please, Tamisen. They'll kill me."

If we're lucky they'll kill you anyway, Jefferji thought, but felt it more prudent not to say so out loud. Let Holyoke believe that they could still be talked around.

"There's nothing I can do. Captain Fontenoy is telling the truth. Make Cassim understand, Lieutenant. We'll help you if we can, but there's no treasure for him here."

Shikander stood up. "Bury the fire," he said to Berni, who hurried to obey. "Go and get your horses, we'll leave." Shikander didn't name any names that Holyoke might recognize, but Jefferji knew what was meant because there were only the three horses here, after all. Shikander hadn't finished. "Linye, you and Dabye stay with this man until we've reached the ford, and then come after. I want everybody back within the walls of Old Fort before sunrise."

Jefferji whistled for Coriander and she came walking up calmly out of the night woods, her white patches like flickering ghost lights. She brought Farouk with her, Farouk apparently expecting he might be wanted if she was. Another of Shikander Beg's sepahis brought Shikander's horse—the Cherkess stallion—from where she'd apparently been keeping an eye on him, stallions being so easily distracted.

"He means to hold you here until we've gone," Fontenoy told Holyoke, with a nod in Shikander's direction. "If I were you I'd do everything in my power to turn this Cassim around, and go back to Fayzabad. This may be a farming community, but they know how to defend themselves."

Between the three men, two sepahis, and a boy, the horses were saddled with swift efficiency. Jefferji put the boy—

Berni—up on Coriander's saddle. He'd walk her down to the river. She liked someone to follow when she wasn't sure of the road.

Fontenoy mounted, and spoke to Holyoke once more. "If you succeed, I'll take your assistance into account when I report to the authorities. That'll be all, Lieutenant."

"Lieutenant" was more than Holyoke was worth. But Jefferji could see what Fontenoy was trying to do—persuade Holyoke that his best interest lay in alliance with Fontenoy and Old Fort. Jefferji didn't think it would do any good, but he could agree with Fontenoy that it should at least be tried.

"You're making a terrible mistake!" Holyoke called after them. Jefferji shut his ears to Holyoke and concentrated his energies on the unlit path.

The moon shone blue across the valley, so brightly that the walls of Old Fort cast a clear black shadow across the flooded lake. The sepahi led them back toward the valley mouth, which seemed strange to Jefferji—surely the water would be deeper and wider, the closer they got to the river?— but as they approached the swollen stream someone stood up from the tangle of tossed-up brush to greet them, and Jefferji saw a line of thin white batons in the water stretching from shore to shore. A ford, marked out with willow wands.

"The others have returned, lord." It was one of Lamish's people, by the accent. "Seven people have passed in all. Five have yet to cross, including you."

"We have three more with us," Shikander said. "We found Captain Fontenoy, and Tamisen had this boy with him. Linye and Dabye are coming behind. When they get here, you cross too, and pull up the markers as you go. Then come into the fort, and receive my thanks."

Jefferji started to strip. The boy would cross on Coriander's back. Jefferji considered it unlikely that the boy knew how to swim, and midnight in floodwaters at the end of a long and exhausting day was not the time to see how quickly he could learn. Jefferji would swim alongside Coriander. Fontenoy handed him a rope; Jefferji tied a slip-knot around the boy's waist. Anchoring Berni in the saddle, but allowing for an emergency disconnect, if they needed one.

The water was cold. There'd be fires at Old Fort, and more

to eat than roasted potatoes, welcome as those had been. Fixing his mind firmly on those pleasant prospects Jefferji struck out across the flood at Coriander's side, and tried not to think about Broderick Holyoke's unwelcome appearance.

Shashka counted them as they crossed the water one by one: Tamisen, Fontenoy, Berni. Though Fontenoy was apparently Jefferji's superior and would therefore have precedence, Shashka put Tamisen next to him to go into the fort. It was important that Tamisen be given the place next to his own, riding in with the boy whose life he'd saved.

In the deep open space between the outer gate and the blind wall of the village, a bonfire burned tall and bright. Captain Katische was waiting on horseback with several concerned parties in her company: the doctor, the parents of the missing child, Peri.

Perversely the boy, who'd been imperturbably silent all of this time, started shrieking at the top of his lungs the moment he saw them, *mama, papa.* Tamisen was too far off the ground to set the child down, but the parents were at the mare's side within moments to receive Berni with tears and open arms. They stared at Tamisen for scant seconds before they turned to carry their son away. Shashka met Tamisen's somewhat confused eyes, and smiled. It didn't matter. These people would never forget who'd brought them back their son.

Peri brought mulled wine in a mug. Shikander drank it gratefully, thankful for the comfort of sugar and sweet spice. The mug emptied quickly. She topped it up from a steaming pitcher she held wrapped in a cloth, and raised her eyes to his with The Gaze, *I wish only to know your will to see it done and if you don't know what your will is I'll just go take care of it for you anyway.* Shashka nodded.

She carried the refilled mug over to Tamisen, who'd dismounted and stood now absorbed in animated conversation with Jericho. *I'm astonished I held on. Yes, several minutes, and then there was the noise, but everybody got in except Berni. No, we've got scrapes and sprains, but everybody's found, now—except some of the herdsmen—and we have good hope.*

Tamisen took the wine without seeming to question its appearance, and drank with the numb acceptance of an exhausted man.

Beckoning Fontenoy to him, Shashka spoke to Katische and Fontenoy at once, low-voiced. "Meet with me in the tower," Shikander said, using French for efficiency. Katische would wait for Dabye and Linye to come in, but it would not be long. "We'll talk. I can offer dry tobacco."

Fontenoy smiled. "Turkish black? Thank you, lord. Directly as I see Tamisen dried and warm."

Reasonable enough. Nodding, Shashka rode away around the blind wall into the village, through the newly constructed gate into the square. They'd built as good a gate as could be managed with the material at hand, thick-walled, mud brick and mud-plastered scaffolding; narrow, to control access, high enough for a man on horseback to ride through. It smelled of water: the cladding was not yet fully sun-dried. It would have to be done over, when they had time.

Alone for a few moments, he let Cherkess walk at his own pace. For Cherkess the night's work was over. Handing Cherkess off to the waiting groom, Shashka went up to the topmost level of the tower without stopping to change. They'd know he'd gone out across the river. Ismara would be worrying and waiting.

One of her women—Caide—was asleep at the top of the stairs. Normally he had a sepahi there, but tonight he'd needed all of them in the valley on business. Coughing as he came up the stairs to wake her, Shashka nodded to Caide in greeting. "I'd like some coffee," he said to her. "Is your lady awake?"

He didn't wait for an answer. He went through into Ismara's outer room, insulated from the bare stone tower walls with embroidered felt tenting. Ismara met him at the door, lifting the flap for him to enter.

"Good evening, my lord." She was very young, for all that she was nubile and had proved it. "I hope you're well?" Too thin—this journey with a young baby had been hard on her—but strong-boned, and the large brown eyes in her round pale face looked on the world directly and without illusion.

Inside her tent, she lived as though they were in camp, with furniture made up of piled rugs and cushions on the floor. "I've asked Caide for coffee," he said. "Is there something to eat? I can't be long. I've only come to say we're back within walls, and a boy who'd gone missing is found safe."

The women had kept the water ready to make coffee for him, late or early. Ismara's father had sent old women, little valued, to serve Ismara in exile. That had been yet another demonstration of her father's lack of judgment. Her women were well worth their keep. Shashka felt himself lucky to have them.

"There's rice," Ismara said, guiding him to the seat of honor on the best cushion she had despite his river-soaked trousers. Shashka liked to sit there and hold Azul, but he didn't want Azul now; he had to think about war. "We're glad you're back. All's well?"

It had been more than a year and a half since her father had made a slave of her over a matter of honor. Twenty months, and she still treated him with polite reserve.

"No, not really." He didn't want to alarm her unnecessarily, but he wasn't going to lie to her either. "It's to do with the things from the cave. It may come to shooting. I hope not." *I wish you were away from here, and someplace safe.* He wouldn't say that, though. Honesty only went so far.

Now would be the time for a woman of her class to lament and mourn. *You should have left me in my father's house, bitter was my fate the day I was given to you.*

"Thank you for telling us." Her voice was both firm and a little frightened. "Is there anything that we can do, to help my lord?"

Caide had brought a hot dish of mutton and rice, seasoned with saffron and rich with raisins. The raisins had been added just for him, not cooked as part of the original meal; he could tell by the firmness of their texture. Ismara was frugal, though not parsimonious. He wished she'd feed herself more of her own raisins.

"I had a cold roast potato for dinner," he said. "This is much better. Thank you. I want you to stay safely here, and look after Azul and yourself."

"I was raised to be useless, my lord," she said, without bitterness. "But these women have many skills, and I hope to learn from them to help in tending the wounded, God grant there are none."

As little as Shashka liked the idea, good lordship required him to honor her intention. "If that time comes, I'll let the doctor know to call on you, and them." Then he leaned forward, speaking close to her ear. He could see a muscle in her cheek twitch; she didn't like being too close to him. "There are no useless women here. Trust in me to know this."

He couldn't stay. People would be gathering for him downstairs.

"I'll know it better when I *feel* of use," she said, also very quietly and privately, because it was not submissive and wifely to push back at him. But he'd liked it in her from the beginning. She wasn't rude, she wasn't foolish, and she knew the place for which her father had prepared her. But she had a sense of herself that transcended rules and roles to make of her a warrior in her own way.

"Let it be so." Putting the much diminished dish of mutton and rice off to one side Shashka stood up from his cushion. As he did he had an idea. "Send down the treasure that the English found," he said. "It is the cause of our difficulty. We should have it there so we may scold it for its mischief."

There was more to it than that. If it came to the worst, if he should fail, he couldn't leave those things where they could be found. He had to get them away from Old Fort. If a marauder found gold he'd look for more. If none was found there were better odds that despoilers would shrug and go away, and leave Lamish's people to bury their dead and repair their lives.

If he could get Fontenoy and Tamisen and Jericho to go away, he could get them to take the treasure with them. That would be two birds killed with one stone. He thought he'd taken Fontenoy's measure, Tamisen's as well, so he didn't have much hope of success in sending them away. But he could try.

Shikander Beg's tower room was lit with half a dozen resin torches that spat and fumed fitfully in the air, not unpleasantly. There was an enclosure on one side of the open floor, felt panels, like a tent pitched indoors.

Captain Fontenoy, dried and dressed, stood warming his hands at the charcoal brazier—a cubit across, well filled with hot coals—that stood between the trestle table and the windows to help dispel the coolness of the night air.

Captain Katische stood opposite to Fontenoy smoking a cigar, her face in shadow, her posture the relaxed and watchful slouch of a tiger waiting for a goat. With her she had one of the sepahis, one Fontenoy had seen out in the grove earlier tonight. Also there was Mekmout, Lamish's headman.

Neither Tamisen nor Jericho had ever stood in council of war before. Fontenoy felt they had a right to observe, and he was the man who had brought them here, endangering them thereby well past the benign parameters of random accidents and unplanned dunkings in cold rivers and the challenges of eating tough, elderly chicken.

Shikander Beg came into the room from his women's quarters one flight up, glancing at Tamisen and Jericho before he met Fontenoy's eyes—but only for an instant, before shifting his gaze. He apparently didn't want to look at Fontenoy, who realized by that token that Shikander meant to send them off, and didn't want any argument from them.

"Let us take Linye's report, Katische," Shikander said. There was a map laid out on the table, like a covering cloth. Fontenoy examined it with curiosity. The river Shahiva. The stream. Old Fort. The road leading north to Deravass Khan had been sketched in lightly with a splinter of blackened wood, as befit its uncertainty.

Captain Katische nodded to the sepahi, who—stepping forward—stood straight and tall with her eyes fixed fearlessly on Shikander's face. "Here, lord," she said, pointing to a place on the map a little west of the valley's mouth. "A few more than twenty men, but followed by two parties, and we think one more. We counted thirty-five in all. They were hiding from the foremost. They were not as close when the flood came down."

"And now?" Shikander asked.

Katische nodded. "Since then there has been gathering. Tonight we saw fires across the river and six large ones on this side. Forty men by best count."

The sepahi clearly knew the answer. Fontenoy could see

that Shikander didn't like it. Nor did he. "Speak of what arms you saw, Linye," Captain Katische suggested.

She answered to Shikander direct. "We saw twenty rifles, lord. More pistols than that, we think, but we can't be sure."

Pistols were much more difficult to count at night, and at a distance. But the information was of critical importance. Twenty rifles meant at least twenty rifles, for instance.

"Thank you, Linye," Shikander said. He sounded grim indeed, to Fontenoy. "Katische, present my compliments to the sepahis, and say we will have fighting before long."

Fontenoy looked at Tamisen out of the corner of his eye, not wanting Tamisen to catch him looking. To anticipate was one thing; to hear the words spoken out loud, another.

Tamisen seemed a little pale, but he'd had an exhausting day topped off with a swim through cold floodwaters. Fontenoy couldn't catch enough of Simon Jericho's expression to be sure, but his best guess was that Jericho was apprehensive but determined.

The sepahi retreated to the door and stood there, listening. To take a full report to her company, Fontenoy supposed, and rightly so. They were Old Fort's primary line of defense.

"About Old Fort, Mekmout," Shikander said.

"Twenty-four men, eight of them old," Mekmout said. He was a good headman. He'd come prepared. Not the first time a headman had been a better lord than the man with the title, Fontenoy mused. Lamish might as well have been an absentee landlord, for all the interest he took. "Fourteen boys," Mekmout continued. "All the rest women and children, lord, numbering in all one hundred and six. No rifles. Two pistols. Only so much powder as will load them two or three times."

"Katische," Shikander said, looking at the map, both arms braced to the table with elbows locked. The torches cast shadows across his face; Fontenoy couldn't read his expression.

"We have twenty-two rifles, counting three in your hands. Powder and shot in good supply. There is a lot of wall. And noncombatants. Farmers cannot shoot." And while farmers could be taught to shoot with relative success, teaching people how to kill one another almost always took rather more doing.

Shikander Beg had two dozen sepahis, the few men of his caravan, and a village full of agrarian folk. Ordinarily they'd be able to rely on the advantage of the defense, but there were an unknown number of reinforcements on the road. There was no knowing how many of them could be honestly compared to Shikander's sepahis. Fontenoy had seen the sepahis ride and post watch. He had an idea they were very effective warriors.

"I hope you include me in your inventory, lord," he said. "Three rifles, six pistols, some experience at defending a field position against brigands. At your service, and that of the people of Old Fort." He sensed the reaction in young Tamisen, behind him, a surge of pride mixed with an apprehension almost physical. "Tamisen and Jericho shall go, to seek out Deravass Khan. He has thirty horse, and may be as few as seven days away—he will strengthen your position."

It was unfortunate that there'd been no chance to discuss this with Tamisen beforehand. Fontenoy could feel the body heat of Tamisen's indignation rising as fast and fierce as the power of a young man's passion could impel it. He didn't have to look over his shoulder to see the outrage in Tamisen's eyes. It was clear enough in his tone of voice when he spoke.

"I'm not going anywhere," Tamisen said. "There are women and children here. I am a son of Tengarpore. I stay."

Please don't tell me to go, Captain Fontenoy. Fontenoy could hear it as plainly as though Tamisen had spoken out loud. But also, although Fontenoy didn't hear *because I won't* in so many words, Fontenoy knew his man. For perhaps the first time in his life, Tamisen was ready to defy him.

"I do not include any of you." Shikander's voice was very firm, his expression hard and unfriendly. It wasn't going to work, but Fontenoy would be surprised if Shikander didn't already know that. "Get out of the valley now, tonight, before it comes to confrontation. Take these two with you, I've no—"

Use for them. But before Shikander could finish his words the sepahi coughed suddenly in warning, and a parade of women came in procession through the open door from the landing. One bore trays laden with coffee and pastry the sweet fragrance of which made Fontenoy very, very hungry.

Three more carried heavy bundles of gold from the cave into the center of the room, setting them down on the floor. Then there was food and drink on the table, treasure on the map, and four silent waiting women withdrawn to the door, standing to one side as another woman came through into the room.

Shikander was clearly startled to see her, and Fontenoy inspected the woman with increased interest.

She was young, and dressed with rich simplicity in Turkish trousers, a long coat with tight sleeves and silver buttons from collar to ankle-length hem. She wore a rich silk scarf of generous length wrapped around her waist that had enough left over to drape over her hair. Her coat was open at the throat, and her blouse buttoned up to her chin underneath was white.

Like the other woman, she was carrying a bundle in arms, but this one was child-shaped and of a weight—to judge by her holding of it—to be a very young child indeed. One who did not seem happy where he lay.

"My lord sent for the treasure from the upper floor," she said. Her voice was clear and strong, very determined. Her Persian was like none Fontenoy had heard except from wandering scholars and poets who came to court as guests from time to time. From Persia. "I've brought the most precious of them all. Shall I put it here, lord, with the other treasures?"

Walking forward as she spoke she held her bundle out, uncovering the face of the baby in her arms. Less than a yearling. More than six months. A healthy-looking child, and in the torchlight—uncertain though it was—Fontenoy knew in an instant that the child was Shikander Beg's.

"No, Ismara." Shikander Beg's voice sounded both surprised and regretful. "Let no man try to part you from your child, and live. Go back to your house."

He clearly wasn't angry at her, though it was in Fontenoy's opinion an audacious stunt. She had no business coming unbidden into her husband's presence when there were strange men in attendance.

"I hasten to obey my lord." But she turned to go away slowly enough to ensure that Fontenoy, and Tamisen and Jericho and Mekmout as well if he was looking, had a clear view of the baby.

Shikander watched her go with an expression of mixed affection and regret on his face, and when she had left the room he spoke again, picking up his thread where he had dropped it. "If the worst should come, the gold must not be found, or more will be expected. Pack up your things. The sepahis will escort you out, and take this—" gesturing at the treasure piled on the table— "away with you. I don't want any of you underfoot. You will, I must say this, only be in the way."

It was a fine line Shikander trod, Fontenoy felt, between insulting them to a degree that would persuade them to cut their losses and leave in disgust with a fortune in gold and jewels, and provoking them into digging in their heels and refusing to go. For Ganders Tamisen's sake, Fontenoy hoped Shikander had managed the former. But because Tamisen was Ganders's son, Fontenoy had little hope for the more prudent and conservative outcome.

"You may justly deny me the honor of defending your wife and child, Shikander Beg," Tamisen said, surprising Fontenoy by the calm determination in his voice. "But not scriptures. You have no way of knowing what we found in that cave that was neither gold nor jewels, and more valuable than either. I must defend it, whether inside or outside of your walls."

What would Ganders Tamisen want for his son? An early death on a quixotic quest, or a long life founded on a prudent decision to turn his back on a village in danger because the quarrel wasn't his? What would Fontenoy himself want for *his* son, if he'd had one? And if they ran away, and met Deravass on the road, would Deravass welcome Tamisen as the son of his father, or as an unworthy pretender to the title?

Shikander Beg waited, apparently feeling that Fontenoy as the older man had the best hope of telling Tamisen what to do. But the next words were from Hakim Jericho, also here with Fontenoy, also an outsider, also marginal to the fight Old Fort was faced with.

"You have no doctors." And Jericho wasn't one. He was only a medical student, and of pharmacy—an unquestioned fact that could easily have excused his retreat, had he been willing to. Clearly he was not. "Where there are rifles, doctors are needed, sooner or later. I can't leave Old Fort without a doctor. I should stay."

Shikander Beg was angry, but for good reason. He was lord here, and two bachelors—unseasoned, untried, ignorant—had just defied him. "Clearly out of the question for me to leave without them, lord," Fontenoy said. It didn't seem to help.

"If you are killed here, Tamisen, you will forfeit any good that you might do other women, other children, forever after, and Tengarpore will never even know. And you, Hakim Jericho." Shikander gave every indication of being willing to dig in his heels. "I send you away from here, tonight. If I see you in the morning you'll have stayed, to your undoubted cost. Do as I've asked the both of you, and taken these things away when you go. Now leave."

Shashka turned his back. Boy pointed at the door. Captain Katische left with the sepahi, as encouragement. Fontenoy gave Tamisen a push. Jericho went out with Tamisen, but as Fontenoy started forward Shikander reached out, snagging Fontenoy by the upper arm. "If there's no other way, I welcome your support," he said. "But you're neither of my caravan, nor of Old Fort."

Fontenoy could respect Shikander's position. Deeply. "Neither of us would walk away, lord," he replied. "We can't blame them. Or wish them different."

Nodding, Shikander dropped his hand, and let Fontenoy go. Shame about making the women bring all of that treasure down, Fontenoy thought. They'd only have to move it all back upstairs, in the morning.

And now it was past time he got to sleep.

There was a proper fire, a blazing bonfire crackling with bone-dry boughs that popped and spat. Broderick had a close place, so near he could scorch himself if he liked, but he couldn't get warm. He rocked himself by the fire, back and forth, knowing he looked like the idiot boy of the cantonment but unable to keep his body still. He needed rhythm to help bring the chaos of his mind into order.

Someone nudged his elbow, and he smelled meat broth. It

was Rashid, with a bowl of soup. For once Broderick didn't think twice about the number of greasy mouths that had besmirched the lip of that bowl. He wasn't hungry—the shock he'd sustained sat in his gut like a lump of undigested dough—but he was thirsty, so he took the bowl and drank the broth, choking down its bits of meat and potato whole without chewing.

Fontenoy was lying. There had to be treasure. Broderick had come all this way. There were armed men at his back who expected treasure. He'd promised treasure. If they found out there wasn't any they'd tear his flesh off his bones with red-hot pincers and serve it up to him in this same bowl.

"People are worried, elder brother," Rashid whispered. "Say something. Reassure them."

Cassim had built his fire on the hillside well above the angry roiling river. Even now as the sun was rising it was a beacon, and men who'd scattered in flight from the floodwaters came stumbling in with their clothing torn and their eyes haunted—not all of them Cassim's, Broderick gathered, but suffered to warm themselves at the fire regardless.

Had any of them found themselves on the north side of that hill? Had any of them been snatched up off of the ground by harpies on short-legged hell-beasts with shaggy coats, and carried off? He'd told Rashid nothing about meeting Fontenoy—and as for as the harpies, he'd been saving revelation for the appropriate moment to demonstrate his sorcery.

"I've seen things." This might be the moment. "Soldiers like women, with scarred faces. A man in a blue wool coat." He'd seen the castle where the treasure lay, a great rock in the middle of the valley with an outline too regular at the top to be natural: a stronghold; a fortified place. "The treasure lies within an iron box atop a hillside in a house made by giants."

He waited as Rashid translated for the others. After a moment's discussion Rashid was back. "Now Cassim asks you to interpret what you've seen. Men are coming to the fire that aren't his men. He runs the risk of being overwhelmed. Give him something to maintain his authority."

How was he to avoid raising Rashid's suspicions? He'd have to speak at least some of the truth.

"I got over the hill last night," Broderick said. "I saw females with lances on horseback, and a fire in the valley where a man in a blue wool coat took their reports. There's a fort on a hill. Now put all that in visionary terms as best you can, I'm tired."

The man in the blue wool coat had been fair-skinned enough to be a European. He'd been smoking a cigar, and Broderick had never known a native to do that. Some of those Indo-Europeans, yes—half-breeds, trying to make themselves out to be more British than British. Fontenoy smoked cigars, from the stink in his study in Peshawar. Maybe he was one of them.

Thank God Rashid went away again. But then came back.

"Cassim asks for your advice," Rashid said. Really? It was about time. Cassim wasn't stupid; Broderick knew that, and had allowed for it in his planning, because men who weren't stupid were more difficult to get rid of.

"We should make up an embassy to the man in the blue coat," Broderick said. He had to see Fontenoy again, and talk sense to him. "Tell Cassim that you and I must be there. If we can reach Fontenoy, we'll persuade him to admit us." Then they'd be out of Cassim's immediate reach, but still in a position to influence his actions, even to claim to be working on his account. "Fontenoy will take us in, we'll go from there. Now I'm tired. I'm going to go to sleep."

He needed time alone, and the closest he could get to privacy was to close his eyes and pretend to be unconscious. There was only one more thing he needed to do before he lay down—because once he did, he knew he'd lose consciousness in fact. There were new people here, men unused to pretending to believe that Broderick could see visions. There was a possibility that he could lose control of the only piece of information that still provided him with leverage. He had to destroy any evidence that he was just an ordinary man with a secret.

Once Rashid was gone, Broderick reached into the innermost layers of his clothing, next to his skin, where he held his greatest treasures. Where he wore his money belt. Where he kept the thing that had brought them all here. Tearing the fabric into manageable pieces, Broderick burned the map, bit by bit, in the bonfire.

Chapter Eleven
First Blood

It was the morning after the flood, and the valley bottom was still underwater. From Jefferji's vantage point on the south walls he could see across to the flat roofs of the village, one long platform enclosing the square. Shikander Beg had work crews there, clearing away the coops and pens and storage crates that were the usual contents of those open-air attics, so that he could raise barricades along the perimeter.

Shikander Beg climbed the ladder like a man coming up a staircase without a handrail to stand with Jefferji at the wall. "The day is mild," Shikander said. Last night Shikander had told them to leave in strongly worded terms. Today, there was no hint in his demeanor that any such interview had taken place. "A man could forget his troubles under so clear a sky. Do you see any signs?"

If Shikander wasn't going to mention last night's interview, Jefferji wouldn't either. "Water, some birds, trees. Clouds there to the east. Nothing else, lord." He wasn't on sentry duty; he'd just come up to catch the breeze. When a man kept his braid tucked up beneath a pagri turban he had to unwind himself from time to time to shake his hair loose and let his scalp breathe. He'd have a time with tangles in the evening, but Jefferji was used to that.

"Natural advantage of terrain. It's a fine position."

Shikander was looking east where the ground fell away into a deep cleft in the rock. The nearest vantage was more than a bowshot away. But there was cover now at the bottom of the ramp road that climbed up to the gates, a tangled barricade of splintered wood cast up by the river yesterday. Nor was the foot of the west slope clear. A small army could hide in that wrack, planning a surprise attack.

Jefferji could tell that this frustrated Shikander by the frown of vexation on his face as he leaned out over the chest-high embrasure, looking down. "A fine defensive position indeed, and yours for the taking, lord," Jefferji pointed out. "Should you care to accept it."

Indeed so far as Jefferji had been able to tell the people of Old Fort seemed hopeful that Shikander would. Shikander himself, however, shook his head as he straightened up, still scowling.

"I have no people I can leave to hold it, so I can offer them no protection." It was clearly an issue that weighed on Shikander's mind, so that he hit on anything for a distraction. "But who would have guessed you had such a mane tied up in your braid, Tamisen? It would be the envy of any woman. And not a few men, I suspect. Have you found it so? I admit I found it particularly attractive myself, the first time that I saw you uncovered."

That would have been five days ago, now. The day after the earthquake.

"My brain gets snarls." Jefferji was glad of something trivial to talk about. "One has to let the sun bleach out the sillier notions, from time to time."

Shikander laughed. "Does it work, then?" He lifted his turban up and away, not so far as to allow its folds to slump into disorder, raising his face to the sun and squinting as he lost the sliver of shade the white linen folds had given to his eyes. He was blonder than his beard, on top, and looked much younger than Jefferji had taken him to be. "So direct a sun might make a man drunk with the warmth. Better not to risk it."

Setting his turban straight on his head once more, Shikander relaxed against the cut in the wall, leaning on his elbow. "I revert to a topic that I found of interest," Shikander said, after a moment. "How long have you played lover, in your dance? Because I have no doubt you do it well."

Shikander's hair was trimmed as short at the back of his neck as an Englishman's. "Since I was eight. Eleven years," Jefferji replied, musingly. His mother had trimmed his hair once a month until she died. When she'd died, a dark man—as black as the men of the South, as beautiful as an angel—had come to Tengarpore, and taken him by the hand to the Hirpa temple where he could find comfort in his grief. "That was when first the Dark One came into my heart, and I knew that I loved him. And that he liked my dancing."

Jefferji hadn't understood it in quite those terms at the time. He'd only known that from the moment his teacher, his Guru-ji, had shown him his first steps, Jefferji had felt a joy matched only by that which he felt when making love. Which had been some years in the future yet, when he'd been eight.

"The 'Dark One'?" Shikander asked. "An idol? I've heard of a Christian one, an icon. The Black Virgin, they call her. Chestakova. That one was of no help to me when I would have cried out to her, however. I would say it is all superstition, Tamisen. Excuse the impertinence."

This was amusing. Even as Shikander spoke of idols as superstition, the shape of his body as he stood—his weight on his right elbow, hipshot, left hand to his hip, one foot flexed to rest on its toes in front of the other—mirrored that of the sacred women Jefferji had seen carved into temples, divine dancers, servants of the blissful God. As though Shikander himself were a dedicated dancer, married to Sri Krsna.

How do you call the God you serve? he could ask. Did calling an icon "Christian" imply that Shikander was not? What kind of Europeans weren't Christian? Shikander was as fair-skinned as a Persian, in Jefferji's limited experience. Jefferji had never met a Russian, but Fontenoy said there were some in these parts, spying on behalf of the White Tsar. Was Shikander one of those? But if he was Russian, wasn't he a Christian, of a sort?

He could have asked the other day, Jefferji supposed, riding out to see the guard post. The horrors to which Shikander had confessed, done to and by him, had made Jefferji reluctant to spend any more time with Shikander's history, so he'd lost his chance. And now when he could have asked again they had more important issues to address.

"Look, lord. Riders. There."

Several men on horseback were approaching from the south. They were on the east bank where the stream round its way between hills to the river, Jefferji saw with regret. It meant they'd gotten across, somehow.

"I see," Shikander said. "All right. We'll have a show." Putting his hand to Jefferji's shoulder as he spoke, he gave Jefferji a friendly shake. His mood hadn't changed, oddly enough. He still seemed perfectly cheerful, although there was a subtle tinge of the wolf beginning to show in the white of his eye, and the glint of teeth when he smiled. "You can come down if you like, but you'll get a better view from here. Just keep your head well back."

Looking back into the great yard as Shikander climbed down the ladder, Jefferji saw sepahis gathering, and Captain Fontenoy, who waved up at Jefferji smiling. Captain Katische was there, and two camel-guns that Shikander had been carrying in caravan—mounted on caissons that had been bulked up with wood to look larger than they were. Stage dressing. Jefferji understood that. The crowd of men from the caravan and the village collecting behind them were the extras, to represent an army.

He'd never seen a show like this go off in real life, whatever it would turn out to be. Tengarpore was at peace, and dance stages could accommodate only a fraction of the number of men who were approaching the gates. Mindful of Shikander's admonition to keep his head out of sight, Jefferji quickly rewrapped his pagri turban, and squatted down on his hams with his forearms crossed on the flat embrasure in the wall to watch. Not all the sepahis were in the formation below; there were four on the wall standing clear against the sky with their rifles steadied on snipers'-forks, making themselves obvious.

As their visitors climbed up the ramp road, Jefferji counted seven men on five horses. When they dismounted, well short of the gate, he recognized one of them as Holyoke. He thought he recognized another man as well—Jefferji just couldn't place him. His body language was familiar. It was a dancer's business to know a man by his carriage.

Three of the men came forward, while Holyoke hung back with the others. "We were caught in the flood on the river," one man called, to the closed gate. "My name is Mirza Cassim. I have twenty men on our way to Tashkurgan. There are men gathering on the river whose looks I don't like, twenty at least. Open the gates, let us in. We crave sanctuary."

Shikander gave a signal. The villagers manning the gate pushed its two wings open, but not by more than two or three yards. Wide enough for Shikander to step through with Fontenoy at his back. Jefferji remembered the first time he'd seen Shikander Beg, in much the same place, in much the same pose, his hands on his hips and the blue gem in his turban catching the light. He walked down the road as far as the road was level, stopping at its crest. The men backed away politely, keeping a reasonable distance.

It wasn't altogether far from the top of the wall to the gates below. Jefferji could hear it all clearly. Mirza Cassim used the sort of bazaar-Persian common to caravans and travelers, and apparently had a bit of education, as well. He spoke confidently, with assurance, with a more precise and comprehensible accent than the people of Old Fort.

"Peace to you, Mirza Cassim," Shikander said. "But if that's your name, I heard something different about your purpose here. From him. Last night."

Mirza Cassim turned and looked at Holyoke, and though Jefferji couldn't see his expression clearly from above, Cassim's posture was that of a man taken by surprise. The man Jefferji had thought familiar actually took a step back from Holyoke's side. Jefferji was beginning to focus in on where he'd seen that man before. Not recently. But not in Tengarpore. Not on the road to Chitral. Someplace between Churu and Peshawar. No. Not between; *in* Peshawar. Who was he?

Holyoke raised his voice and shouted. "Fontenoy! For the love of God listen to me, I'm your only hope!" In English; to be secret with his meaning, clearly enough.

Cassim turned back to Shikander. "You know of the Parsi?" he asked. "How?"

"Tell them about the treasure!" Holyoke cried. "They'll kill us all. It'll be on your head. Tell him about the treasure, we can do a deal, I can get you out of this."

Fontenoy shook his head, and Holyoke fell silent. The man who seemed familiar raised his head, suddenly, as if taking stock of his situation. Then Jefferji got him. That was the house-master from Peshawar, the man who'd taken care of him and Simon in the guesthouse where they'd stayed with Captain Fontenoy. Rashid. What was he doing here?

"He's not a Parsi of any sort," Fontenoy said, choosing his words carefully. Day by day Fontenoy was more confident, more at ease, with his bazaar-Persian dialect. Now, under the influence of outrage that inspired him, he was nearly fluent. Shikander half-turned to Fontenoy, ceding temporary authority for Fontenoy to speak.

"He's a thief, a renegade and a deserter," Fontenoy said. "An Englishman, I'm sorry to say, certainly not a Parsi. I don't know what lies he's been telling you, but after what he told this lord last night, we are determined not to open the gates to you or any of your men."

"That's right, Fontenoy," Holyoke said. If there'd been any doubt that Holyoke had very little language other than English it was proved transparently now. "Tell him you need his help. Promise him a share of the money. He knows—"

Rashid interrupted, stepping up close to Holyoke to take his arm, speaking urgently into his ear. Holyoke shook him off at first, but Rashid persisted, and Holyoke suddenly froze. Rashid had told him what Fontenoy was saying, then.

"I admit that you confuse me," Mirza Cassim said, grimly. "And I do have more than the word of the Parsi for the existence of a treasure to be had here. I was hired fairly, but there are others. Open your gates and receive us, lord. Let us help one another. As I am a man of honor, I will serve you well for a portion of the treasure in return."

That would have sounded reasonable, if Holyoke hadn't told them what he had last night. Shikander Beg nodded, and for a moment Jefferji wondered whether he was going to adjust his strategy on the fly. *Don't do it*, Jefferji thought. *If Mirza Cassim is a man of honor he's bound to his employer. And that's Holyoke.* Cassim had said so, hadn't he? That he'd been hired fairly? And who else was to have done it but Broderick Holyoke?

"I've heard your name, Mirza Cassim." Shikander's tone

of voice was reasonable in turn, but unyielding regardless. "You may have perhaps heard mine. I am Shikander Beg, called Kavkazki. And because some of what I've heard of you may not be true, I'll make you a fair offer of my own."

The villagers were pushing the gates open wider. Looking down into the yard Jefferji saw that every available body had been called to swell the crowd. Shikander was still talking, clearly confident that things were being done exactly as he had arranged them behind his back. He was lord. Jefferji admired his self-assurance.

"Leave, and take your men with you. Do that, and I'll have no quarrel with you if we should meet again. I'll deal with any others from the river on my own, with thanks for your offer. I consider myself well served in offense and defense alike."

Jefferji tried to imagine what it looked like from Cassim's point of view. A solid front of armed sepahis in uniform. More soldiers behind them, some of whose rifles were actually wood and scraps of metal but well mixed amongst the genuine weapons—and from a distance who would know? That was why Shikander had taken his position where he had, Jefferji realized. Mirza Cassim and his men were slightly below the level of the gate, and unlikely to be able to see over the heads of the assembly to realize it was only three men deep.

"If there is no treasure to protect, why are you here in force?" Cassim asked. It seemed a reasonable question to Jefferji. "We came from Fayzabad for a share, and mean to have it. Use us to your purpose, lord, it will do you good in the long run, and cost you less."

Shikander Beg had said he'd heard of Mirza Cassim. Whether that were true or a bluff Jefferji had no way to tell, and there was more than one way that it could be true. *I know of you by name* or *I know what kind of a man you are*. Either way Shikander had clearly made up his mind about Cassim, and Shikander Beg was a man of war. Jefferji trusted his judgment. So did Captain Fontenoy, and that clinched it for Jefferji.

"Fontenoy! Let me in!" Holyoke had pushed his way to the front and Cassim didn't stop him. "Don't let past misunderstandings come between you and your survival. These men are lost, we must save what we can!"

"And you can have *him*," Cassim said to Shikander. "I

don't want him anymore. He got me here. As far as I'm concerned, he can go."

There was Rashid at Holyoke's back, translating. It had been a shock to encounter Holyoke, but Jefferji found Rashid's presence even more perplexing. Rashid had taken good care of them, in Peshawar. He'd had a responsible position. Jefferji had left him a good tip. How could he be here, with Holyoke?

"But we don't want him. I have no room for cowards, thieves, and deserters. Go back to Fayzabad, Mirza Cassim, and leave me to deal with these men you warn me about as I did the others."

What did that mean? Then Jefferji remembered. Shikander was lord of Old Fort because he'd rescued its caravan from marauders on the road and buried their bodies by the river.

Mirza Cassim nodded. "Then I consider us fairly opposed, and will take what I can. Good bye, Shikander Beg."

As Cassim turned his horse's head to go, Holyoke broke away from the group, running desperately forward with obvious intent to force his way into Old Fort whether he was welcome there or no.

Jefferji heard the gunshot, and saw gravel explode from the ground at Holyoke's feet—a warning: *No, you're not coming in.*

Cassim turned at the sound of the shot, a pistol in his hand. Then he saw Holyoke recoiling to fall flat on his back in the dust, and put his pistol up.

"Rashid, see to your master," Cassim said.

Rashid hadn't followed Holyoke's sprint, and hung back now. Jefferji could well understand why a man would be reluctant to continue his association with Holyoke once exposed. How much of the truth had Rashid known?

Jefferji had little sympathy for Rashid, even so. There was only one way Holyoke could have gotten here, and that was by following Fontenoy's map, and that meant Rashid had copied it. When Holyoke had said "Cassim has a map" it was because Holyoke had provided it.

Could he blame Rashid for wanting to pursue a buried treasure? If it was buried, couldn't anyone claim it, honestly and honorably?

No. It was Fontenoy's map. And nobody had said anything about buried treasure while they were in Peshawar. Unless Holyoke had been trailing them step by step, hiding in the bushes to overhear their every word. Holyoke had come to his own conclusions about treasure, and whether it was Holyoke's fault that men had come—Shikander had been expecting trouble since before Fontenoy had even arrived here—Holyoke's intervention had clearly complicated things.

Shikander and Fontenoy passed through the gates; the gates were closed behind them. Jefferji climbed down the ladder to see what he could do to help defend Old Fort against Mirza Cassim and Broderick Holyoke and anybody else who sought to do it harm.

Cassim's men had given Broderick a good place close by the fire to warm himself and dry his clothing after the fording of the flooded stream. He'd stayed drier than the rest because he'd stayed securely on horseback as the nag swam, drawing up his knees. He didn't so much need to dry out as drive away the chill that the shock of it all had given him.

Tamisen had lied to him outright about whether the fellow in the blue coat could understand English. Either that or Tamisen and Fontenoy had been filling Blue Coat's ears with slanders, and that was just the same as lying, because Broderick had spoken frankly to them both under the clear understanding that what he had to say was for their ears only.

Now Holyoke's life was in danger and Rashid's as well, though Rashid had done nothing to deserve such treatment. How could Rashid be faulted for copying a map? What was worse, Rashid blamed *him*, now, for the position they were in, rather than directing his resentment in its proper direction toward Tamisen and Fontenoy.

They hadn't given Holyoke a place by the fire out of respect. They'd put him in the middle of the camp so that they could keep an eye on him. Now Cassim was here with three of his men, and Rashid. Rashid was wearing a new overshirt: obviously a bribe. So he'd gone over to Cassim's camp.

"What do you really know of treasure, sahib?" Rashid asked. Cassim hadn't spoken yet, so it was Rashid's question, and when he said "sahib" Broderick didn't like the tone of voice at all. Still he appreciated its significance. And he *was* a sahib, Rashid's natural master. Rashid should remember that.

"Only what you told me in Peshawar." Maybe it was true that he, himself, Holyoke, was the one who had put two and two together, but it hadn't been because he knew anything more than Rashid had told him. All Tamisen had said was "antiquities." Rashid had told him about the map, and made a copy. Rashid had done the marketing for provisions and equipment. "We're in this together, man, for good or ill. Stick with me, and I'll get us both out of this alive and rich."

Rashid shook his head, mulishly stubborn. "When you sought me out in Peshawar, you said there was a treasure, Fontenoy sahib was going to dig it up, and you had certain knowledge. I believed you. Now tell me the truth."

Tiresome. "I have. About the treasure and about the peril we're in. What does Cassim have to say to me, and what have you said to him, Rashid?" If Holyoke let an edge into his words, he had more cause for his contempt than Rashid for "sahib" Holyoke.

Rashid was right about one thing. It was Broderick who'd made it all happen, Broderick who'd gotten them safely from Peshawar to the place where treasure lay. Broderick had done it all. Rashid had merely followed along, doing the occasional spot of translating. For that Rashid believed he had a right to a share of the treasure, and to take an aggrieved tone with an officer in the service of the Crown.

"I've told him you're a deserter, and have been lying to him about being a Parsi. That I've shared in the lying, which I now regret." So Rashid believed Fontenoy when he said there was no treasure. More fool Rashid. "Now Mirza Cassim would like to know if there's any reason he should not throw you in the river to drown."

Broderick still knew things they didn't know—about the gold he'd carried safe and undetected all this way, for instance. "Tell him it's all the same to me. I know where the treasure lies and I will have a share. Tell him that. If he wants to lose a share for himself he's welcome to cast me aside." He wouldn't repeat the "throw you into the river" part. That might be interpreted as a challenge. "Tell him, Rashid."

Now, finally, Rashid turned to Cassim to speak. Cassim asked a question; Rashid answered it. Another word from Cassim and Rashid turned back to Broderick.

"Give us the map," Rashid said. "If he's to keep you and protect you he should at least share in what you may actually know."

Broderick could almost have sneered. He'd thought of this already. He was three steps ahead of Cassim all the way.

"I've burnt it, Rashid. So all you've got left is what you remember. I'm guessing not very much, am I right?"

Rashid had made the copy, originally. But he'd hardly seen it since. Broderick had made sure of that, and his caution was well rewarded now.

Rashid spoke to Cassim, who shook his head and said something. Three of Cassim's men came forward; two of them took Broderick's arms, lifting him bodily off the ground. It was a sudden reminder of unpleasant experiences from his childhood, but *that* history was dead, burnt on the banks of the Nerbudda. Let them search him for the map. They wouldn't find it.

But they'd find his gold. What had he been thinking?

Now Broderick began to struggle with all the strength that blind panic could muster within him, shouting "Rashid! No! I can redraw the map! Stop them! I'll make a map, I'll make one!"

Cassim's men stripped him anyway. Could he blame them? Would he have trusted himself to redraw the map under these circumstances, and not leave something out? Layer by layer of lousy cloth they tore and took as Broderick struggled.

"Tell them to let me go," he begged Rashid. "Tell them I'll pay them. I'll pay you. I was saving for the return trip, saving for an emergency—you never know when you might need a bribe—"

No good. They got down to his skin, and they found his money belt. They took it to Cassim and tore it open at his feet; Rashid turned away with his hand over his mouth.

What was that disgusting sound Rashid was making? He

was retching. Broderick didn't pity him. Rashid had allowed himself to be tempted too easily. He had nobody to blame but himself if he felt betrayed. How did a man get to adult age, and remain so uneducated, not to say stupid?

All of those beautiful, bright coins. All of that heavy gold. Broderick had carried it step by step from Peshawar and not minded the weight for the comfort it had given him to have it near and know he'd be all right whatever happened. Now it was gone. Cassim had it.

Putting one arm around Rashid kindly, Cassim beckoned someone over to give Rashid a drink of tea to rinse his mouth. Nobody paid Broderick any further attention. He warmed his clothing against the fire and dressed himself piece by piece. Things were torn. Somebody owed him for damages.

If he was to be cast out here in the middle of nowhere with four days' walk back to Fayzabad and no money for food and shelter, he was going to need a full kit, or his death from starvation and exposure would be on their heads. It was not a name to be taken up lightly, murderer of English officers. There would be consequences.

"Mirza Cassim says we've bought our freedom," Rashid said. There was a distasteful note of gloating in his voice that did not become him. He had several pieces of Broderick's gold, and was putting them into his neck pouch. He'd thank Rashid for keeping it safe for him, Broderick decided. It was, after all, Broderick's gold.

"If you want to stay, you must fight bravely. He doubts you have the stomach, but is willing to give you the chance to prove yourself. I will not stay. I have permission to take refuge with the other English if they will allow it."

Rashid would throw himself on Fontenoy's mercy as a poor silly native begging for forgiveness, *ma-bap*, "you are my mother and my father." That way he could succeed to at least part of the treasure, or hope for a portion of it as a tip. There hadn't been a reward for Broderick's apprehension in Peshawar. Why should Rashid be rewarded for abandoning him now?

"Suit yourself." Just because Broderick could understand Rashid's train of thought didn't mean he had to approve of it. Weak as water. A sodden flaccid reed of a man where an oak was wanted, or even just a willow, which after all had strength in flexibility. "Give me back the gold you've got around your neck, and good riddance. You'll be sorry."

Rashid shook his head. "It's Mirza Cassim's gold now, by forfeit. He gave some to me out of charity, which I accept gratefully in the spirit in which it was given. For this I praise him, even while I hate my need. Good bye, Holyoke sahib, may you receive the reward you deserve."

He'd have it, too. Only not the way Rashid expected. Broderick was still in the game. Cassim knew he was a British officer, now, howsoever compromised, and that meant Broderick had leadership and strategy at his command. What if one fellow in a blue wool coat held the fort, with soldiers and hand cannon? Broderick would have the treasure. He'd have the fellow's blue coat, and the blue jewel in his turban. The name "Shikander Beg" might impress Cassim, but not Broderick Holyoke.

There was no man on earth who was his match for scheming and survival and coming out on top. Rashid would beg his pardon on bended knees, before Broderick had him stripped and beaten and cast away naked and penniless to find his way if he could.

The enclosure behind the outer wall was strange in the moonlight. Where there'd been animal pens, storage sheds, workshops, only barricades remained: untidy structures standing at intervals between the great gate and the village, designed to funnel an attacker into killing lanes and string them out for destruction one by one as much as possible.

Anywhere an intruder might find shelter had been ruthlessly sacrificed for lumber. The barricades were up on the village rooftops, blank walls of rough-planed lumber salvaged from the destruction of the outbuildings to provide cover and vantage.

Jefferji hadn't studied much siege-craft at Tengarpore. It wasn't that there were no famous sieges or heroic stories of the defense of Chittorgarh or Gwalior; only that the young men of Jaisal Singh's establishment had been trained up as field soldiers, men whose first priority was to acquire property and *then* defend it. Jefferji could see the sense of Shikander Beg's dispositions, but the look of the small once-comfortable village dressed for war depressed him nonetheless.

Shikander Beg had been working on fortifications and defenses since early this morning, and the only rest he'd allowed himself or any of his people had been that little bit of pointed flirtation on the walls, and when Mirza Cassim had come to the gate to demand entrance. Since then, he'd driven them even harder. Jefferji, Simon, and even Captain Fontenoy had done a shift or two.

Now it was night, though the moon granted some illumination. Being up on the walls on guard was less work but more nerve-racking. The two sepahis in whose company he stood watch spoke little. With no hope of carrying on a conversation, all Jefferji could do was watch and brood.

The view from the parapets over the valley in moonlight was an enchanted one, like a scene painted as a backdrop on the stage where he danced at the Bharaj fair. The water was ebbing back toward the river. Out in the valley bottom there were occasional glimpses of men around their fires, but Shikander Beg had forbidden the firing of pot-shots as a waste of ammunition on a target out of range.

Captain Fontenoy had warned Jefferji to strict obedience of Shikander's orders. *It's his plan of action; you serve it. A soldier's honor is to be disciplined in ranks. You'll have your chance at heroics if and when it comes to that, my boy.*

The sepahis carried lances, wicked long poles taller than they were and tipped with some of the ugliest steel Jefferji had ever seen: long slender blades the shape of an iris leaf, whose steep honed shoulders were smeared with grease to keep their edge. Lances and a rifle each. Jefferji had been provided with a long stave for beating back any man so incautious as to try to scale the wall.

He had his pistols in his belt, primed and ready. Flintlocks, plain of ornamentation and somewhat old-fashioned in design, but they were his and had brought him fourth prize at a marksmanship match once. He was an only adequate shot by Tengarpore's standards, but Fontenoy had promised him that he was good enough for their current purpose.

The air at the foot of the wall was murmurous with whisperings as the water ebbed. The breeze ruffled the surface of the swollen pond, and small nocturnal animals—rats, half-wild dogs—scavenged for their suppers. There were wolves and wildcats, he understood. It was too cold for snakes.

Coriander would approve if he'd had a chance to discuss it with her, but she'd been working too. All the horses had been called into service to drag timber and haul beams, pulling primitive block-and-tackle frames to raise building materials to the village roofs. It was beneath her dignity, but to her credit she had given it her full attention, with the Cherkess stallion himself working alongside her.

The reeds rustling in the night made Jefferji long for the homely music of the water-margin in the hills of Tengarpore. There should be lovelorn nightingales singing of their sorrow over the absence of the Dark One. There should be little boys with nets out to trap frogs to provide a chorus for some rich man's water garden in Udaipore to the north. There should be the perfume of jasmine in the air.

One of the sepahis nudged him gently with the butt end of her lance, and tilted her head sharply to the night-music once she got his attention. The other sepahi was standing in the shelter of the crenellation's merlon, head down, as if listening carefully.

There are no water reeds in the pond, Jefferji, he reminded himself. Any existing vegetation had been flattened by the force of the flood, and what breeze there was up here on the wall was not enough to shake reeds and make them rattle if there'd been any. Someone was climbing up the wall.

Taking his cue from the sepahis, Jefferji turned one shoulder to the stone merlon and listened. He'd trained for years to listen and to hear things—drums, the silk-draped movement of another dancer's body, the little bells strung in a silver net across the top of a dancer's foot that spoke of which step was in use and what would come next. He could do this.

Once his ear had caught it, Jefferji could identify three melodic lines, which meant three men. Breathing, fabric dragging across rough surface, climbing hand over hand, finding footholds as they came, two in the lead and one behind.

Jefferji drew one of his pistols out of his bosom, holding

it up close to his face. The motion of the sepahi's hand as she gestured alerted him, and he looked to see her shaking her head. *No.* She showed her lance, with an emphatic stabbing motion, up and down: *Use your stick.* Oh. He was to wait until someone cleared the embrasure to climb onto the parapet, and bring it down on their heads to stun them so that they could be taken prisoner?

Putting his pistol away, he took a firm two-handed grip on the long stout staff they'd given him. One of the men was close, between him and the sepahi on his right. She inched her way closer to the sound, her lance in readiness—poised to strike with the butt end. Saving the spear's well-sharpened blade for backup?

Head and shoulders of a man rose into view. Jefferji faded back into the shadow of the wall, well out of sight. *Learn by observation.* The sepahi was focused on her prey, and gave no sign of wanting Jefferji's assistance. He'd catch the man when the man fell forward, head ringing with a blow from her spear, and... what? Dangle him down the inside of the wall until someone came to tie him up and take him away?

The man looked left and right, cautiously, but the sepahi was as still as death and Jefferji stood in shadow, head down, eyes hooded to prevent the whites from showing. Laying his hands flat on the crenellated wall's embrasure, the man hoisted himself up to gain the parapet. At that moment the sepahi stepped forward swiftly and planted the butt end of the spear in his chest, pushing him backwards with a vigorous shove. The man didn't make a sound. His body fell away from the wall into the darkness, and that was all.

Not taking prisoners. Not wasting shot. Not risking the loss of a valuable spear. Jefferji nodded to himself, pretending that he really understood.

There was another man. Jefferji had heard three; one had come up on the left of the leftmost sepahi. She hadn't been completely certain of where he was, apparently, or which of the remaining two would crown next. But as the man reached his head forward, as he crawled into the embrasure to peer around the corner of the merlon, the sepahi struck him hard across the top of his head, wielding the spear like a mace. Losing his grip and his balance, he too fell away.

That left the third climber. Jefferji was nearest. The sepahis held their spears at the ready—but they took no steps toward him. This one was his. Generously, they gave him the last one, like wolves teaching their cubs to hunt. *You've seen how it's done; now you try.*

He'd wanted to be a part of protecting Old Fort and its people. He'd wanted to frustrate Holyoke, and to ensure that the cave with its startling new information on the long denouement of the great Kaurava war would be protected as the priceless treasure that it was. He would indulge in no last-minute second thoughts about what it meant to do those things.

A hand came reaching up from out of the darkness. It was a left hand; the man would be looking right, then, after the man the sepahi had just sent off. Had he missed the first man's fall? Jefferji waited until he had a proper target, head and shoulders. He'd been taught stage fighting with staves, and the rules about where to never hit for fear of injury, so he'd learned where to hit a man wrong, too.

But waiting for that perfect strike had betrayed Jefferji to his enemy. He'd been seen, discovered, located where he stood. The man climbing up the wall might be hearing music of his own. Had he placed Jefferji by his breathing? By some sound cue Jefferji had been unaware of having provided?

The third man's right hand came up with a pistol in it, aimed at Jefferji's head. Jefferji hit him squarely in the breast-bone as the first sepahi had done, with all the power he could muster. The effort it took to push the man back and away from the wall astonished Jefferji. The man fell away, but this time he went screaming, and it seemed to Jefferji to be a very long time before the screaming stopped, with a soggy sound like a wet clod of manure dropped on a paving-stone.

The sound of the nothing after the screaming stopped shook Jefferji to the pit of his stomach. He'd seen the drop from the top of the wall to the foot of the rock, where the stream pooled. He knew how far it was: more than three hundred feet. He'd seen the carcass of a goat, once, that had fallen into the empty tank in the forecourt of the fort at Canrum, broken and bloodied, its body white with splintered bone. That was what he'd just done to a man.

The sepahis came to praise him wordlessly, striking him on the shoulder with genial approval. Did they remember? Had they ever had the sick feeling that came over him, to realize that he'd just killed a man? What had that man done to *him*, to deserve death at his hands?

Only evil intent, no harm. Because Jefferji had done unto him before he'd managed to do unto Jefferji as he'd clearly intended. No man who climbed up a wall in the middle of the night with a pistol in his hand could possibly have meant well.

Jefferji stood the rest of his watch heartsick and horrified, praying that no more men would climb the wall, as much for his sake as for their own.

In the morning Captain Fontenoy sat on a wooden box in the middle of the village square, taking the sun into his old bones, oiling his pistols, and watching Geoffrey Tamisen talking to his mare. Coriander had been working hard again on construction duty, but there was no more heavy lifting for her today, and Tamisen had been over her from nose to hind foot and back again three times when he should have been sleeping.

A horse did not pull in improvised harness without taking a chafe or cut. Farouk was stoic; Gunnery had been anxious until he'd had a chance to get the feel of things; the mule Marigold was resigned, which was good because she was surprisingly strong, even for one of her kind; and Coriander's feelings were between her and Tamisen.

The redheaded "Boy" that Shikander had with him day and night stooped suddenly through Fontenoy's peripheral field of vision to crouch at his feet, picking up one of his flints and squinting at it. If Boy was here, Shikander Beg stood close.

"Peace to you, lord," Fontenoy said, and Shikander returned, "How is your friend?"

Standing with his arm around Coriander's withers with his forehead pressed against her neck, just at present. Maybe he'd fallen asleep after all.

"Managing for now, I think."

Last night, Fontenoy had been told, Tamisen had done his duty on the walls of Old Fort, and repelled an invader. Tamisen hadn't said anything to him. When Tamisen wished to speak to him, Tamisen would. Fontenoy felt no need to intrude himself on Tamisen's feelings just to reassure himself.

"The first time I killed a man, I was too filled with rage to have any second thoughts. What might a dancer have in his heart, and this not even his quarrel?" Shikander sounded reflective, regretful.

Fontenoy could honor that in him. "*That* dancer elected the quarrel of his own volition, lord, and was raised as a cadet of Tengarpore and the household of a venerable warrior. Jaisal Singh and I, we knew his father."

Shikander stood silent for a few moments, watching Tamisen straighten up, kissing Coriander's cheek before he led her away to water. "Boy" sorted flints in the palm of her hand with rapt concentration, and since flint-sorting was one of the chores Fontenoy had yet to accomplish he was perfectly willing to let her do it for him. There was something he'd been wanting to ask Shikander.

"You said you'd heard of Mirza Cassim, lord?"

Scuffing the ground with one foot, Shikander spat. "Not a man to trust too far. Willing to trade in slaves if the price is right. No such man comes near my wife while I draw breath, and there are unarmed people here. I do not tithe to slavers."

It was contempt, not abhorrence, in Shikander's voice. Fontenoy considered the possibility that Shikander Beg was not above dabbling in the trade, if the terms and conditions were agreeable.

"Am I to guess he has no reputation as a fighter?"

"I've heard no particulars on that. But I'm only passing through. This valley offered security and forage for the cattle while I waited for my road to clear to the east."

Where from, lord? Fontenoy could ask. *Where to?* But those were not the questions of the moment.

"Twenty men, Cassim says, twenty others gathering. Forty men. You're spread thin, lord." Three fewer than there'd been yesterday at this time, but that wasn't enough to improve the odds, and Fontenoy had been thinking. "What have you heard of Deravass Khan?"

Shikander was silent, apparently pondering the question—or the question behind the question, Fontenoy didn't know.

"Never in connection with slaving. Had *he* come to the gates to offer troops for hire, I might have let him in."

Between the find that had started the adventure, Lamish's carelessness, and Holyoke's intervention, every useless man between here and Chitral had heard about a treasure trove on the Wakhan road from Fayzabad by now. "We can hope he hurries, then, lord. I hope for him in six days."

If Deravass arrived in good time, his men could decide the outcome of the siege that was to come. If he arrived too late, he would avenge their deaths, but that would be little comfort to any of them.

"Bitter reward for the rescue of a caravan," Shikander said. "But a man can't pass on the other side of the road when slaughter is being done. Not and be a man."

Or Shikander wouldn't be here at all. It shouldn't have mattered, either, because without Holyoke's intervention they wouldn't have this problem.

Fontenoy shook his head. "I wonder at inscrutable Fate, lord." The treasure they'd found was beyond Fontenoy's wildest expectations, but it was worth nothing to him here in Old Fort. "Something I can do while I see to my ammunition."

"I'm glad of your pistols, Fontenoy," Shikander said. Boy had set the flints back down in careful order on their red flannel cloth on the ground at Fontenoy's feet and stood up, so Shikander was leaving. "With you to vouch for him, I would be glad to see Deravass Khan too. Load well. We may have some more excitement tonight, but exercise is physic against anxiety. It relieves nervous tension."

So it did. Fontenoy was undecided which course of action he should undertake, hoping for a sign to force his hand. If it came to the worst, though, Fontenoy was sure that Shikander would know what to say to Tamisen.

Broderick Holyoke piled wood with the other men, hands blistered, back aching, ears and eyes awake for anything that might be happening. Rashid, faithless fool that he was, had spent the night by the fire as though he had every right to be there; had taken his breakfast, and left the camp without a word to the man who had brought him all this way and tried to make him rich beyond his wildest dreams.

That was too bad for Rashid. He'd have no hope of a share. But then, to be perfectly fair, he had a fair chance to live to enjoy his poverty, which would have been perhaps a little questionable had he continued on with Broderick.

At the same time, though, and much more interestingly, someone new had arrived in camp with some bodies draped over pack ponies. Cassim had had the bodies brought close in to the camp and laid out on the ground where people could admire them. Broderick respected his strategy, resent Cassim though he did.

The corpses themselves were disgusting: one whose stomach had been pierced with his own thigh-bones; one with only half a face left to his name—whatever that had been—what with the obvious impact of something rather hard all along his other side; and one simply cracked open in several places, broken skin, white bone showing, eyes hanging from their sockets and staring horrifically.

Clearly these were among the men who'd shadowed them on their march, the opportunists from Fayzabad hoping to slip in before Cassim could make his move and pre-empt his success. The point was obvious. *This is what will happen to you if you try for the prize on your own. Join with me and have a chance at a share. Go it on your own, and join these fellows.*

What had Broderick told Fontenoy, night before last? Fifty men? He didn't know what Cassim had told Fontenoy yesterday. Cassim had had only seventeen of his own at dawn—Broderick had had Rashid count them—though there had been twenty or twenty-five others who could be seen scattered at small fires here and there. More people had arrived since then as word spread down the river. Now there were easily forty-five men in Cassim's camp, *and that*, Broderick thought with satisfaction, *served Fontenoy right.*

They'd brought Broderick a pieced-together set of cast-off clothing to make up for the clothes they'd ruined, stripping him. One shirt in particular was actually almost not indecently filthy—one of Cassim's, perhaps? Small return for the gold they'd stolen. Broderick had taken the clothing without argument. The nights were cold, and his place by the fire was no longer one of privileged proximity.

This morning he'd been set to work to pile wood, and since they fed him with the others, he piled wood. It was in his best interest to stay close to Cassim and the action. Let them come to ignore his presence. He knew how to make being despised, being invisible, work to his advantage.

It was a lot of wood. By two hours past dawn it had been enough to feed a good bonfire all day and into the night; by noon it had grown well past any reasonable proportion, and Cassim had his men and those who'd offered themselves as volunteers out on the hillsides cutting everything they could find that would burn. There was clearly more to it than simply keeping warm through the next few nights.

Cassim was going to make it hot for Fontenoy, one way or another. As it happened Broderick had some experience in the construction of pyres. He could help. In the cleansing prophylactic fires he'd made on the banks of the Nerbudda River he'd burned the dying and the dead all together. He'd heard their screams.

He would enjoy listening to Tamisen, to Captain Fontenoy, to everybody in Old Fort burn.

Halfway on toward morning, when the night was as cold and black as it could get, the sound of shouting woke Captain Fontenoy from a light sleep at his place by the fire at the foot of the scaffolding between the gates of Old Fort and the walls of the village within. Pushing his thin blanket off his shoulders as he rose Fontenoy he fed a few dry branches into the fire, spoke-like, to catch a good spark. Since early afternoon this had been his post, between the great gate and the concave wall of interlaced lumber facing it that Shikander Beg had been building all day.

The first signs of Mirza Cassim's strategy had revealed itself in yesterday's early predawn hours, when a long wooden snake roofed in wet vegetation had come coiling up the ramp-road from the valley bottom, each man-sized segment depositing wood at the foot of the gate. They were building a fire. The sepahis had gotten a few good shots in, but without a way to tell exactly where the men were under those dripping reeds and wooden planks it was only a waste of ammunition.

They'd dumped some water on the growing pile to reduce its flammability, but it soon became clear that they couldn't keep it up for long before the wells failed. Mirza Cassim had piled up brush and branches all day, while the village boys had thrown down rocks on them to discourage them. It had done some good, but not enough.

They could have tried a frontal assault, scattering and perhaps killing the men who comprised the snake. But that would have meant opening the gates, and neutralizing their defensive advantage.

Shikander had a different idea, one designed to maximize the strength of their position. He'd built a wall. Not a strong one; not a solid structure, but several feet deep, interlaced with the heaviest timbers he could find, and with plenty of ventilation so that fire, once applied, could take hold quickly and spread.

It had meant a full day of backbreaking labor on top of days of urgent effort, but it was an admirable construction. A concave barrier wall of brush and debris of their own, chinked and padded with straw and scraps of cloth rags. Lamish himself had overseen the collection of the oil for the fires from stores in every household, as sober as Fontenoy had ever seen him.

Fontenoy's post was between the gate and the inner fire-wall. There was a rope ladder, well soaked in water, at the ready, and if he could get up it before the fire was in full blaze, he might very well get away from it in time. He knew there was a risk. He hadn't mentioned that part to Tamisen.

Now it was nearly three o'clock in the morning, judging by the position of the moon. Shikander said the gate would burn with enough heat against it, but that it was the hinges that would fail. The framing timbers set into the wall—the uprights on which the hinges anchored—were makeshift, new growth, not the same as the seasoned hardwood of the old gate. On that projection Shikander's plan depended. He meant to sacrifice Old Fort's outer wall in order to subtract as many of his opponents as possible en route to the more defensible perimeter of the village itself.

Fontenoy could hear the fire on the outer side of the wall, now, the sepahis on the parapet silhouetted against the leaping yellow light. They wouldn't be able to stand the heat for long, but Shikander had wanted them up there, both to keep watch and to assure the enemy that they meant to defend the gate by force of arms in a conventional manner. Much of Shikander's strategy depended on the element of surprise, but it was a very measured gamble in Fontenoy's estimation.

The fire at the gate was talking to itself, a muttering wind-born breath of giants. Fontenoy arranged his firebrands. Between the scaffolding and the village, people were still at work upturning rocks in the yard, building little traps for men who would come running in and—stumbling—open themselves to attack. The wind would be coming up from the valley bottom, fanning the flames. Shikander's plan counted on it: a fine fierce blaze, the prospect of an easy success to cheer the enemy and give them false confidence before disaster.

Fontenoy began to feel the heat radiating away from the great gates, not at all unpleasant in the chill night air.

Everything they could have done, they'd done. It was still an audacious risk. Much depended on whether Shikander was going to remain a lucky man.

The gates began to groan, long drawn-out screaking moans of protest against the torture they were in. Fire was starting to curl around from the outside, rising beneath the doors between the bottom edges and the ground, reaching flickering fingers through gaps at its jambs and the central seam where the two wings came together and were bolted across.

So much depended on where and how the gates failed. There was no guarantee the gate would fall true. Shikander had made models sized to scale, but small fires didn't make the roaring convection of large ones, and the fire at the gate of Shikander's scale model could only be a hint, not a prediction.

It was a safe assumption that Mirza Cassim would

concentrate his forces. Shikander's own forces were similarly concentrated at the gate to greet his guests when they came through, because he was a hospitable man.

Tamisen was with him. Fontenoy had thought he'd be the one to stand at Tamisen's side in his first battle; Shikander had taken his place. He begrudged it to Shikander, but not wholeheartedly. Shikander Beg was a leader of men—and Amazons—and an experienced campaigner. Shikander and Tamisen were not quite in love with each other, though neither of them seemed to have noticed yet; but it was enough. If it couldn't be Fontenoy himself to see Ganders's son through his final tempering, then Shikander Beg was as fine a substitute as could be wished for.

The gaps through which the hungry fire reached grew wider, and as Shikander had predicted, the wedge was widest along the outside of the gate's western wing, where the unseasoned wood and inferior old ironmongery were weakest. The heavy crossbars fixed against the gate kept the wings from leaning back into the yard. The gate was beginning to sag out and away, toward the road.

Now the question was how quickly it would fall, and how quickly Mirza Cassim's men would brave the heat to charge through the gap, in a rush to win the lion's share of the glory, before plundering Old Fort and dividing the spoils.

With lit torches in his hands, Fontenoy stood in the focal point of the concave firewall Shikander Beg had built, waiting for his moment. If he was too soon their attackers would see the danger, and avoid the trap. Too late and the stratagem would fail: the tangled wood would not hold Cassim's men for long enough, and they'd sweep through into the yard and then the village. It was up to three men, a dozen sepahis, and Captain Katische to stop the raiders at the outer gate.

The gate's hinges failed.

Its western wing fell open into the waiting night with a hideous shriek of splintering wood and iron scraping iron. Crashing down across the fire at its feet, it came to rest at an uneven angle, one corner propped up on a pile of burning brushwood and one buried in the ground. The crossbolts that had been wrenched free as the great panel had fallen hung at tortured angles against the other half of the gate.

Fontenoy nodded. This was good. The downed gate formed an open road across Cassim's bonfire and through to where Shikander Beg—and Tamisen—were waiting. Men were coming across it, running as hard as they could—thirty or more, indistinct but clearly all too numerous in the yellow smoky light.

Crouching low, Fontenoy torched the oil-soaked cords of straw and rags woven into the framework of Shikander's firetrap. There was a good breeze coming up, fire calling to fire. The tracks they'd traced so carefully from his small campfire into the scaffolding took the flame merrily, blazing up as the first of Cassim's raiders came through. It wasn't enough to stop their charge, but it hadn't been intended to.

It was Shikander's turn for fire now.

Chapter Twelve
Fires that Temper and Anneal

Jefferji stood waiting behind the chest-high barricade that ran across the great yard, wondering how the others—Shikander Beg, the sepahis, Captain Katische, some few of Shikander's men who knew the use of firearms—could sit, and smoke, share a few jokes, and even close their eyes.

The wide expanse of ground between the outer wall and the village had been razed, all of its structures gone, destroyed, sacrificed to build a wall that curved around as if to embrace the invaders when they came through the gates. The gate would give way at any moment. Captain Fontenoy would set fire to the wall. And then they'd come, and Jefferji would have to shoot them.

When he was out of bullets he'd have to fight with his sword, which like his pistols was of no exceptional pedigree or beauty, but had been his since he'd been old enough start being schooled in fighting. It had been Jaisal Singh's first sword, though Jefferji's foster father had sent it to him indirectly—by way of the armorer—to avoid the appearance of favoritism. Jefferji had been clearly fated to grow tall from an early age. Jaisal Singh had known from experience that he would need the length.

Boy was here, alongside Shikander Beg. She crouched on the ground on the far side, checking the priming of Shikander's weaponry: four loaded pistols set in array and ready to his hand. When Captain Fontenoy joined them, Jefferji would go with Fontenoy, but for now he stood with Shikander, who was eating an apple. Jefferji's own stomach was firmly clenched into a hard and painful fist, and he knew for a fact that he wouldn't be able to swallow so much as a pistachio.

"Captain Fontenoy will be all right, lord?" Nobody had asked Jefferji how he felt about the role Fontenoy had claimed—or been assigned by Shikander, Jefferji wasn't sure which. He hadn't had a single moment to spare to talk to Fontenoy, and the plain fact that he might never talk to Fontenoy again unnerved him.

"That is a question none of us may ask." Shikander's answer was no help. Why was it reassuring, regardless? Because of the thoughtful kindness in his voice: *I know how you're feeling but I decline to lie to you.* "But consider that the task is critical, and I have trusted him with it. Listen. I think I hear the wall."

The enemy had fired the great pyre they'd built outside the gates, flames reaching up and over Old Fort's walls as if starving to feed on those within. The fire was taking hold of the scaffolding that Shikander had made to be built. Nobody was eating now. Up and down the line—sepahis to the left, more sepahis to the right, Captain Katische halfway down the line, Shikander Beg standing dead center—everyone was on their feet, pistols in hand and rifles braced, waiting.

They'd have the enemy between them and the fire, while the enemy would see nothing but shadows. Jefferji's job was to shoot as many men as he could in his assigned field, or whoever was getting closest, or anybody else who caught his attention.

Jefferji heard groans that seemed to be rising from the very earth, the crackling of dried wood, snapping and spitting as it drank in oil and its own resin.

Shikander had been right. The gate was talking. There was a long scream like an actor's evocation of Arjuna in Hell, then thunder shook the ground. The gate had fallen open, back and away from the enclosure, an open road for Cassim's men but still a barricade in its own right, protecting its people to the last.

"If you like," Shikander said to him, very softly, "you can imagine that your bullets miss, that none of it is your doing. If it helps you to shoot. But don't miss."

The firewall began to burn. So Fontenoy had let down his incendiary lines. Two of Old Fort's men were running across the back of the firewall with smoking pots filled with pitch, flaming bombs to ensure the firewall burnt hot and furiously.

They were Lamish's people. They'd retreat to watch and wait for their turn to fight and defend on the village roofs. There were no firearms to be spared for Lamish's people tonight. It was all up to them, to him. Jefferji had to shoot and not miss. Shikander Beg had said so.

He saw the dark silhouette of a man come hurtling through the fire with his shoulders hunched and his head bent down and his arms outstretched as if to shield himself from the heat.

Raising his pistol, Jefferji aimed, but Shikander put his hand on Jefferji's wrist and said "Not yet." Shikander meant to wait until more of them were through. A shot too soon might discourage them, or warn them off.

How could Shikander be confident that they wouldn't be overwhelmed? Then Jefferji realized that Shikander wasn't. Shikander was gambling with his life, and not only his.

There were two, three, five more men breaking free of the rapidly growing forest of white fire in the scaffolding. Which target was Jefferji's? He had to hold his fire, no matter how nervous he was. This was a new sort of courage: not that required to keep to a formation, but the self-discipline required not to charge ahead screaming, simply in order to keep from running away.

Shikander clearly knew Jefferji's turmoil, because he leaned close and said "Wait for Katische."

Just then Captain Katische called out, sharp as the cry of a kite with a tender young kid in view. And before Jefferji had more than taken a good aim the rifles, he didn't know how many, spoke all at once, and Jefferji saw six men go down.

"It's all right now," Shikander said. "Shoot when you can. I want *that* fellow." But Jefferji stood at Shikander's side in a paralysis of confusion—wait, he was supposed to fire but there were no targets, other people were shooting all the targets—until Boy, coming out of nowhere between them, took Jefferji's arm by the sleeve and pointed him toward one dark fast-moving figure. Oh. Yes. His. Jefferji took quick aim and fired. The man went down.

For a moment, black horror descended over Jefferji and blinded him. The man twitched, but didn't rise. Had he done it? Had he dropped a man and killed him? Then he heard another shot, almost at his ear; it startled him back into alertness. Maybe he'd killed that man and maybe he hadn't, but he'd meant to. He knew his reasons and had already found them good, and he was wasting time.

His next shot hit, but didn't stop his man. Somebody else did that. The smoke from the firewall grew nearer to them as the fire burned, and their attackers were getting much closer. There was screaming, but whether it was from men trapped in the fire or men who had been shot Jefferji didn't know. Picking his targets with expeditious care he fired, and fired again, feeling strangely removed now from the burning scaffolding and the smoke and the cries of men in agony.

The invaders were firing back. Jefferji ducked down behind the wooden barricade to reload. A bullet struck the barricade, so near he felt the splintered wood against his face; it sharpened his senses and connected him with his body, again. He heard the groans of wounded men, the crackle of the fire. He smelled the smoke, wood, burning flesh, gunpowder. He smelled blood and knew it wasn't that of a wild pig brought down with lances from horseback in the jangal, but from men brought down with bullets.

The boy he'd picked up at the river, the girl who'd washed his clothes and combed his hair, the woman who'd given him a dish of rice and mutton with dates and apricots—all of those people were his to defend and protect. The sacred text of history, an entirely new window on the bhakti of Arjuna and his brothers, all of that was in his care.

His pistols had grown too hot to reload. He smelled an entirely new fragrance of singed leather as he holstered them, but he could spare no time to wrap them any better. Beside him, Shikander Beg kicked over the section of barricade that had sheltered them and leapt forward with a throaty snarl, sword in hand. Jefferji drew steel and followed.

There were still people coming. He had to dance as he ran forward, to avoid tripping over bodies whose identities—friend or foe—he had no time to ascertain. The men emerging from the burning scaffolding held pistols, and he had none left, so it was important to lay them out before they could take aim. Perhaps the fire had already cooked their powder and drawn their shot, but there was no sense in making assumptions.

Here was a man, tall and broad-shouldered, leveling his rifle in Jefferji's face. Jefferji cut the man's arm to force him to drop his rifle, but the man drew a pistol with his other hand. They were so close to each other that if the man fired at all he couldn't miss. Jefferji couldn't allow it.

Raising the pistol had left the man's neck unprotected. Both hands on his sword's hilt, Jefferji cut down across the man's throat as hard as he could, striking with his whole body, hearing the remembered voice of the arms-master. *Every muscle in your opponent's body is against you and the resistance that even an old shirt can offer will astonish you.* Recoiling in shock Jefferji stood stunned, blinded by an explosion of hot thick blood as the sword's edge cut deep and found an artery.

Someone took him by the shoulder, speaking into his ear. "Baptismal blood." Shikander had to shout to make himself heard. Jefferji wiped his eyes; Shikander half-turned Jefferji to face him, and kissed him full on the bloodied mouth with sudden savage gusto. "Come on. Time for us to fall back. Mind the wall."

White-hot and raging, the fire ate away at the wall's foundation. It had been built to admit air, to admit men. Now as its support bars and beams were eaten up in flames it started to collapse, trapping the attackers in a fierce Hell. Taking a fistful of Jefferji's jacket in his hand, Shikander ran him back to the barricades.

Jefferji couldn't see any more men coming out of the fire. There were men on the ground, and sepahis stooping over them, but it was only to take their pistols and powder, so that was all right. Shikander gave him a push toward the village walls where the ladders waited, and Jefferji in a sort of fog ran after the sepahis, who were already on their way to gain the safety of their second line. Far above the billowing smoke, the fog of airborne ash, the sky was turning blue. Dawn was coming.

As Jefferji climbed the ladder, friendly hands reached out to pull him up, past the barricades, down into the house. Simon looked him over, thumped him once or twice with his expression changing from alarm to relief, and sent him on down the connecting ladder to the lower floor. There someone sat him down on a stone bench and gave him a drink of water. After that, there seemed to be nothing else for him to do but go to sleep.

His last thought before he surrendered to the friendly dark was hope that nothing he had done had reduced him in Shikander's estimation, and an intent to seek reassurance on that score from Captain Fontenoy when Jefferji saw him next.

Fontenoy had thrown his torches into the building flames. Dropping to the ground, he'd scuttled away from the scaffolding on all fours to climb the rope, ready and waiting for him, up onto the parapet. The bandits who charged the firewall headlong were drunk with their momentum, blind to the soot-smeared figure of one man.

Below in the yard, Fontenoy had seen the scaffolding filling up with their enemies, fighting their way through. He'd seen the fires taking hold, their prey—the attackers— trapped and entangled, desperate to escape the flames, pushing forward through the lattice-structure to the other side where Shikander was waiting for them. He'd seen others turn away in terror and flee back the way they'd come, where the fallen gates had opened a road for them.

What he could see when he gained the parapet filled him with despair. There were too many men, more than they'd anticipated. That meant too many men would survive this attack, and that too many more were almost certainly still in reserve.

A last-minute, desperate change in plans was required. Fontenoy tested the rope's anchor on the wall. It reached from the ground to the parapet on the inside; it would reach most of the way down on the outside.

No. Too risky. If someone outside found the rope, they could use it to climb up and then back down into the yard where the scaffolding met Old Fort's wall and might have burned through, behind the defenders. He'd have to climb down hand over hand, and he was not fond of heights.

"If it were done when 'tis done, then 'twere well it were done quickly," Fontenoy quoted to himself with determination. Hoisting himself over the wall he reached for a foothold, found one, found a handhold, found another. When would he run out of chinks in the wall, like a scaffolding of its own? There was only one way to tell; he had to continue. To be caught and killed on the wrong side of the wall would be unbearable shame. Grimly he fought on.

Something struck at his foot with a jolting shock that staggered him and almost knocked him off the wall. Body flattened against the cold stone he rested for one determined moment. Strengthening his grasp as best he could he lowered his foot again, seeking the next hold, and found something as solid as a stair-step underneath him. He'd found earth. He'd made it.

He didn't have a second to spare for a feeling of relief. Skirting the main gate he worked his way to the road, and looked around. The blazing fires cast long shadows in which a man could hide; there was a chance. He could see men fleeing the burning gate, some staggering, some running, some whose clothing seemed to smoke from the fire. Such men did not like to look at one another.

Snatching up somebody's fallen cap to help disguise himself as one of the attackers, Fontenoy hurried down the road as quickly as he dared. He needed a horse. There should be horses. He'd seen them when Holyoke had come to the gate with Mirza Cassim.

Even in flight there were too many of Mirza Cassim's men, and he was leaving Shikander Beg short two of their few pistols. The loss of one fighting man was only going to make things even worse; that sure knowledge pricked him like a goad.

The first horse he came to at the foot of the ramp road was a shaggy little yabu hill pony, with a shabby saddle and a rope around his nose cord as a bridle. It was a lucky find. Fontenoy had a lump of date sugar well compounded with fine Patna opium in his bosom, Farouk's favorite treat. Breaking off a substantial corner, Fontenoy offered the bribe; the yabu accepted it, and they were on.

Leading the pony away into the darkness, they forded what was left of the flooded stream. There, once he'd gained the other side, he looked to the full moon with a prayer for swift passage and mounted. He would have to ride harder than he had ever in his life if he was to hope to bring help back before it was too late.

The day that had dawned in fire and smoke had cleared, with the help of a pleasant breeze flowing up into Old Fort from the valley bottom. It carried the bulk of the smoke from the still-burning gate fires with it, though a white haze lay over the village, like a bright fog. It was warm, but whether from the sun or from the fires, Shashka couldn't say.

He wasn't in the habit of bathing in public. A man with any self-respect kept himself covered in open air, and the pale complexion of his skin once uncovered took the heat of the sun too quickly, leaving him in danger of a painful scorching.

But today he had good and particular reasons for standing in the middle of the village square in his bare feet, with a linen towel knotted around his hips for decency's sake. The people of Old Fort needed reassurance. If a man bathed naked in the open air, he had no hurt to hide from those who needed him to be strong in their defense.

Peri held the basin. Shashka washed his face, his arms, his chest where the splashed blood of dead enemies had soaked through to the skin. He'd been very close to Tamisen when Tamisen had cut that fellow's neck, and Tamisen had done a good job of it, too. If Tamisen had had a better angle he'd have taken that man's head halfway off. It was an impressive show of strength, especially for a young and untried man. Someone had trained him well, and had Tamisen practice on dead pigs and goats, perhaps. That was what Shashka's teachers had done.

Bending at the waist, Shashka suffered Peri to pour the

rest of the water in the basin over his head, splashing across his neck and shoulders. It wasn't a proper bath, but it was a shame to waste hot water. She had a fresh dry towel for him ready to hand. She dried his back while he scrubbed at his damp hair, and now he could get a shirt and put his slippers on while he waited for the sun to dry the rest of his clothing.

He'd given up the outermost walls. There'd been too many of them, and he didn't like his chances of holding them with as few as he had. The village roofs could be seen from the walls, but the range was by no means certain, and he was pleased with the barricades. They were safe enough for now to let some of the villagers and caravan men stand the watch while his sepahis slept and ate and looked to their kits, and sorted through the pistols they'd taken from the dead this morning.

That left Tamisen and Fontenoy. Or Tamisen, because there was no Fontenoy. Tamisen had been blood from his dust-darkened turban to his trousers; and was sitting on the same box Fontenoy had been using two days ago, waiting even as Shikander was while his clothing—freshly washed for him, by Berni's parents, Shashka thought—dried over a little fire. Somebody's girl had been washing Tamisen's shirt just the other day. If this kept up, he'd be the cleanest man in Old Fort.

They might want that fuel for cooking fires in a day or so, but there'd be time enough to worry about that later. In the meantime there was Tamisen with bare shoulders slumped over his knees staring at his feet, and Shashka didn't think that was a good thing. Shashka went over. To comfort, of course; not because the contours of Tamisen's body with its sinuous muscle and the flat black hairs of his chest put pleas-antly distracting thoughts in Shikander's brain. Now was not the time. That would come later, if it was to be.

"You did good work last night," he said, to Tamisen's lowered head. "Indeed, as Captain Fontenoy suggested you were trained well, in Jaisal Singh's house." He hoped he remembered the name. Tamisen flinched when Shashka said Fontenoy's name; Shashka's heart fell for him.

"Thank you, lord. I can return with honor to Tengarpore, with your praise in my ears. But not with Captain Fontenoy."

There was in Tamisen's voice the bewilderment of the newly bereft. Shashka knew Tamisen's look too well, the face of a man overtaken by a catastrophic shock.

"You think him dead?"

Of course Tamisen did. Shashka wasn't so sure; in fact he had good hope. Tamisen's head snapped up, and he glared at Shashka with a face that had gone dead clay white with fury: *What other explanation could there be?* Something on the wall caught Tamisen's eye before he could spit out his furious reproach, however.

Shading his eyes with his hand, Shashka turned around and squinted. One of the sentries was waving energetically, and Shashka could see Captain Katische there as well. After a moment Captain Katische climbed down, coming out into the square through the interior of the house whose roof it was.

"A man, alone," she said. "He comes without state, carrying a white scrap for a flag. He asks for Tamisen 'sahib.' Or Hakim Jericho."

Tamisen was watching them, following the conversation despite his state of shock. "Your pardon," Tamisen said. His fury had gone out of him, Shashka was glad to see. Such passion was corrosive, and he didn't want Tamisen to be angry with him over things that could not be helped. "There was a man from Peshawar who came to the gates with Mirza Cassim. His name's Rashid. He'd know to call Simon a doctor."

Captain Katische heard Tamisen out with a sort of indulgent interest. The sepahis had one-eighth taken Tamisen as a mascot. They were women, Tamisen was young, and Shashka approved of it because anything that reminded the Hell-riders they'd been women once—before the Cossacks had turned them into wolves—was a good thing.

"If we bring him in, he won't be going out again," Shikander said. "Let's see what he has to say."

Boy brought Shashka his drawers, his trousers, his outer shirt, his coat and turban. Tamisen's clothing might not be dry, but he put it on. And as they climbed up the ladder and back down again into the outer battleground under the watchful eyes of the sepahis on the roof looking for snipers, Tamisen asked suddenly "Why didn't he ask for Captain Fontenoy?"

The irregularity of movement inherent in going down a ladder covered for the pause the question gave Shashka. There were two possible reasons why a man might have not asked for Fontenoy. He would hazard a guess on neither until he had more information, and Tamisen didn't ask again.

The man who waited for them outside the village walls was much the worse for wear, his beard untidy, his face unwashed. "Tamisen sahib." His voice was resigned, but not hopeless. "I'm sorry. I've made a terrible mistake, and helped to bring this trouble on you all. I was greedy."

Tamisen, frowning where he stood at Shikander's side, responded without seeming to realize that it might not—strictly speaking—be his place. But Tamisen knew the man; Shashka didn't.

"Why did you come? Carrying messages from Holyoke?"

To Shashka, Rashid looked genuinely sick at heart. "He stays with Mirza Cassim. I have leave to go. I came to take responsibility for at least a portion of my part in this, if you will allow me."

Shashka knew better than to trust this story. Nor did Tamisen seem much more persuaded.

"You're a liar, and were sent to infiltrate in order to betray the garrison. Why ask for me or Jericho? Why not for Captain Fontenoy, who you betrayed worst of all? Afraid he'd shoot you on sight?"

It was Tamisen who was afraid. It put a dangerous edge to his anger; Shashka appreciated that in a man.

Rashid looked confused. He tried to lean forward to speak to Tamisen alone, but Tamisen stepped back and wouldn't let him near. Whatever Rashid had to say he was going to have to say in front of the sepahis and Shashka, no matter how reluctant he might be.

"Captain Fontenoy went north," Rashid said. "I saw him, just after the gate fell, from the bottom of the hill. He took a pony. He didn't see me."

Shashka felt Tamisen's anguish in his own gut. If Fontenoy had stolen a horse and ridden away toward the northern pass into the valley, he was obviously alive. Why— Tamisen would wonder—had Fontenoy gone?

For all Tamisen's learned dancer's poise Shashka could

sense Tamisen's core instinct, explicit in his body, scant hair's-breadths of time before he struck. Before Tamisen leapt for Rashid's throat, just to silence the smallest hint of a suspicion that he dared not acknowledge in his mind. Had Fontenoy run away?

Shashka knew he'd better intervene. "To seek Deravass Khan," Shikander said, moving just enough, as casually as possible, to turn his shoulder up close against Tamisen's chest, imposing his body between Rashid and Tamisen. "At my request. As he and I discussed." Shashka couldn't be completely sure. So many of the men he would have trusted with his life had betrayed him, and he'd known them better and longer than he'd known Fontenoy. "I think he saw the numbers that came in, last night, and decided on a desperate course of action."

If that monumental betrayal had taught Shashka how deeply treachery could hide, didn't that mean his judgment was better for the bitter lesson? He'd trusted Fontenoy with a critical role in Old Fort's defense last night, and not been disappointed.

Of course it was possible that Fontenoy, having played true with the fire and the wall, decided that he'd done enough and made his escape, and had gone north only to avoid Mirza Cassim's men, knowing that if he met with Deravass Khan he could contrive some story, and return to Old Fort to make what terms he could with whomever was left. He could probably find the cave, collapsed as it was. He was one of the few men who'd seen it after the earthquake.

"He didn't tell me." Tamisen's face was drawn and creased with the powerful complexity of the emotions he was so clearly struggling with. "He gave me no indication. He didn't say anything to me."

Two days ago, Fontenoy had said that he expected Deravass Khan in six days. So now the man was four days from here. In four days they'd know why Fontenoy had gone, wouldn't they? Or they might never know. So many mishaps could befall a man riding by night over an unfamiliar road, no matter how full the moon or clear the track.

"What do you know?" Shashka asked Rashid, to give Tamisen a little time to master his emotion.

"I can tell you what I saw. Mirza Cassim did not prevent me from looking and watching. I think he hopes it will persuade you to make terms, if I report the numbers of his men. Fifty-seven that I could count, I'm sorry, Shikander lord."

There could be a difference between what Rashid thought he knew and what he'd actually seen, and Rashid seemed to be sensitive to that important distinction. So far, so good.

"Is that all?"

"I could help the doctor. Or I could leave, and find my way back to Fayzabad, maybe back to Peshawar. I have money. See?" Rashid reached into his bosom and pulled out a purse, opening it to reveal several very handsome coins of bright gold. Not a treasure by any estimation, but adequate traveling money. What was the point? That he was a genuine volunteer with his way home paid, not a man grasping at straws for survival.

Shashka looked to Tamisen, curious as to what he would do next.

"Did anybody else see Captain Fontenoy?" There was so much deadly venom in Tamisen's voice that Shashka understood why Rashid took two steps back on pure instinct.

"No one else was there, Tamisen sahib. Only me." It was an honest answer by every test Shashka could put it to of tone and pitch, expression, eye contact. He wasn't ready to extend a hand in trust, but it was a point of information.

"And are there truly other men, not Cassim's men, come here on a rumor of treasure, joining him?" Shashka asked.

Frowning a little in apparent confusion, Rashid nodded. *Yes.*

Tamisen turned the full force of his emotional intensity on Shashka, who almost wanted to take two steps backwards himself. "If Rashid leaves, he may be stopped by latecomers and robbed. And they may torture him for information about the supposed treasure, if he's coming from this direction. In that case he might let slip about Captain Fontenoy, and they might give chase in case Fontenoy took the treasure with him, and he might not reach Deravass Khan. Let Rashid help Simon. Shoot him the moment he steps out of doors."

Could he take that chance on Rashid? Shashka tested all the links in his mind while Tamisen and Rashid waited.

Tamisen was right about the fate of single travelers discovered on the road by adventurers, men of highly variable integrity. Was it worth the risk?

This wasn't the man both Fontenoy and Tamisen felt so strongly about. This was apparently a hapless accomplice, one who'd had second thoughts and was willing to hazard the peril he himself had helped create, in atonement. One man. With some nursing skills to recommend himself, apparently. What could he do to them?

He could report on Shashka's exact strength and his dispositions, that was what. Valuable information for anybody planning a raid. But not if he couldn't get out of Old Fort once he'd gotten in, and Shashka could have him locked up in someone's cellar if he got the faintest sniff of a suspicion, if he didn't shoot Rashid outright. He decided.

"I only almost trust you," Shashka said. "You're with the doctor, every moment. If you are seen anywhere with the wounded, you forfeit your freedom on the spot, your life perhaps with it. When Captain Fontenoy gets back, he'll decide what your ultimate punishment shall be."

"I accept, lord," Rashid said. "Thank you."

The sepahis took Rashid in custody, climbing up the ladder into the village roofs with him. Reaching out, Tamisen took hold of Shashka's arm with a desperate grip. "He didn't say," Tamisen said, in a voice like a man abandoned by his brother or his father or his son. "He didn't say a word to me. Shikander, lord. He didn't say goodbye."

Tamisen was on the edge, and didn't know it. Shashka had the power to teach Tamisen an important, valuable lesson, by leaving him to agonize in doubt over whether Fontenoy had simply and unthinkably run away or ridden in forlorn hope of rescue. But how would Tamisen be better for it, in the long run?

If Tamisen, by the will of God, did not live to see Fontenoy again, should he be left uncertain of his friend Fontenoy at the point of his death?

Should Tamisen be robbed of God's gift of love and trust in his friend, and did not Fontenoy as a brave man deserve the final honor of Tamisen's love? Shashka's own faith and trust and hope was in Fontenoy to have gone for Deravass

Khan. Was it for Shashka to poison Tamisen's last breaths with doubt?

Shashka took Tamisen by the shoulders, embracing him fiercely. "He had no time," he said. "He saw how many they were. He knew I would remember our discussion, and explain it to you. He didn't say goodbye because he had no good time to say it, and he means to come back."

Tamisen put his forehead to Shashka's, and drew a long breath. In that instant Shashka could feel the pulse of Tamisen's heart, close to breaking, and held on. The moment passed. Tamisen's heart beat strong and sure.

"Yes." Straightening up from Shashka's embrace, Tamisen stepped back quite easily and naturally, without the slightest hint of embarrassment to create an awkwardness. "Of course. Thank you, lord. We should go up."

Nodding, Shashka turned to climb the ladder. Rashid's news was good news for them all. Captain Fontenoy had been seen alive last night, riding north for reinforcements. Where life was, was hope.

And now it was time to get back to the war.

Full daylight. Fontenoy had been grimly determined not to stop, nor to shift in the saddle more than it took to follow the motion of the yabu. The pony itself—a mare, he'd been glad to see, with the superior stamina of her sex—had slowed its pace to a relentless trot at dawn, and seemed quite confident of its path. He and Farouk had walked most of the way back to gain familiarity with the route. Farouk was so much taller than a pony that it was hard to tell how the distance covered might compare.

Fontenoy recognized an outcropping of anomalously red rock across their line of travel where the path split—one side coming up; the other going down. He was almost certain he'd seen it recently, but where had it lain on the reconnaissance route he'd taken with Deravass's messenger, during the ride out, or on the way back, the day the river had flooded? Two hours? Six hours? He tried to think, because he needed to know, and it helped distract him.

The pony didn't need his help. Why not? How could the pony know the way? It didn't. The pony only took the path of least resistance, and that path was the one that he'd been on, the same path by which Deravass Khan had come and gone. An animal migration path, a merchant traveler's path, perhaps even a smuggler's route, a thin brown line through scrub firs in the rocky terrain but clear enough to a pony with minimizing effort on its mind. It was a hopeful sign.

By sundown tomorrow, he'd have reached the farthest extent of his travel with Deravass's scout Runji, and have no guidance but to trust in Fate and the innate conservativism of a yabu. When Fontenoy had returned to Old Fort four days ago, Deravass Khan had been eight days out; that left four days yet to go. Old Fort would not stand so long against such numbers as greed had collected. Fontenoy had to shorten it somehow. He'd ride as long as the yabu would go, and let the pony decide when it had to stop.

It was dangerous to think such a thing. If the pony got any hint of his intent, it would reasonably stop going right now and claim exhaustion. *The work I've done. The loads I had to carry. You have no idea.* Maybe it would anyway, but not until they got to some fresh water, and if there wasn't any water this wouldn't have remained an established route.

He had no crop or quirt to urge the yabu on. If it came to cutting a supple branch he would, just this one time—if it wouldn't just stubborn up the beast, and he wouldn't blame the pony if it did: *if you're going to be that way about it you can walk. You can't make me do something I don't want to do by hitting me.* But if the beast kept on, he wouldn't need to beat it, and he had the lump of dates and opium for use as a bribe, the wages of carriage. Farouk could go for hours on end with cake opium to inspire him.

If the yabu played out, Fontenoy would have to walk. It was no use thinking about what might happen without Deravass to ride to the rescue. Heavy thoughts would only add to the weight the yabu had to carry forward. So Fontenoy fixed his mind firmly on what he meant to do to Broderick Holyoke instead. Angry thoughts were hot, heat rose, and that would lighten the load for the yabu. Fontenoy set his eyes on the road ahead and traveled on.

In the deepening twilight, Shashka paced his battlements restlessly, stepping from roof to roof behind the wooden walls. They'd spent every moment they had reinforcing the barricades today, piling up earth dug out of peoples' cellars to strengthen the wooden shield-walls that would make their final defense against the shock of the next attack. Too little time. Not enough fighters. All the sepahis were still on watch; Captain Katische; some men from the caravan; Tamisen. Shashka needed Fontenoy—no, three dozen Fontenoys. With reinforcements—with another twenty, twenty-five men—Shashka knew that he could hold this village, with the defensive position on his side.

Nine bodies in the enclosure yard this morning. Three wounded enemies had crept away during the night, by best guess. There was no way to tell how many men had been burned to death in the fire, because it was still smouldering.

Rashid had counted fifty-seven men in Cassim's camp before the fire attack. If Rashid was right, Cassim could have as many as forty-five left; and although some men might have left after the fire, some more might have arrived on the scene this morning to make up the balance.

If Shashka were Cassim, he'd have climbed up the outer walls and had a look around. He would have seen the tower, where Shashka had two of his camel-men on watch. Cassim would have seen the village walls, twenty houses to a side, but would not have been able to see inside the communal square to tell how many people might be sheltered there.

Cassim would know that the southeast corner of the ring-wall was least visible from the tower, and he'd guess that Shashka had taken steps to address that problem. He might judge the southwest corner second weakest, the northwest corner closest to the tower and therefore strongest, the northeast corner most strongly defended by terrain. Where would he strike?

About to find out, Shashka told himself. He heard gunfire from the scrub woods downslope from the foot of his south wall, and two alarms went up almost at once. Yes, the northeast corner had the best defense from its natural position, the ground falling away steeply toward the precipice. Cassim's men would have brought ladders. With the fast-deepening dark to cover-and some diversionary gunfire-Shashka would have been able to get some men up the outer walls.

That was what Shashka would have done, and nothing he'd seen so far from Mirza Cassim had been anything but well planned, which was unfortunate. Except to the extent that Shashka could extrapolate, to a degree, from his own instincts about what would happen next.

Mirza Cassim wouldn't have reckoned with the Hell-riders, though. He didn't know their strengths. It had taken Shashka months to begin to understand their aptitude for war, though he'd seen their capabilities much earlier than that.

He started for the shooting. Kula and Satsi couldn't go, because they had to hold their post. Had they been horses, they would have been champing at their bits to join their sisters, but Shashka knew their discipline would not fail.

Hurrying toward the south wall, Shashka drew his pistols. If Mirza Cassim did get a man up onto the walls before full night to have a look around, Shashka wanted to be very sure that no information got back to Mirza Cassim. The sepahis knew he meant to take no prisoners. He hadn't told Tamisen; the sepahis would take care of that for him, if the occasion arose. Maybe Tamisen would figure it out on his own.

Poised on the tall curb that marked the roof of one house from that of the next, Shashka aimed and fired at an unfamiliar head, and was gratified when it disappeared from sight consequent to his bullet's flight and lodging. One of the things that was handy about sepahis was that they were relatively short, and could be safely fired over, on occasion.

Tamisen was tall. Shashka saw Tamisen, and went to join him, reaching around to the small of his back where he had another pistol. Four in all. If Peri found him she'd be taking them off his body as he went and returning them reloaded, but he didn't know precisely where she was. It would be exactly where he most needed her to be, but she was the only one who knew the spot.

Five men were up, with more coming fast. Two sepahis

and Tamisen stood against them. Two of the sepahis pressed one of the attackers, two more had an assailant each, and Tamisen fired at the fifth enemy at such close range that the blood spray drenched him all over again. War was proving hard on Tamisen's clothing. It was lucky that the women indulged him on the point of clean laundry.

One man came at Tamisen from the right with a long knife, and Tamisen turned to defend himself. That seemed to be going well, so Shashka drew his own knife and stabbed the man who was giving his two sepahis so much trouble from behind, pushing the body over the now-exposed edge of the wall and to the ground below. They'd gotten some of the wooden barricade torn down, he saw. Their mistake. They'd be easier to knock off that way.

Babira shot something very close behind Shashka, so close Shashka felt it when the something fell over. Thanking her with a grin, Shashka went on. One attacker was down on the roof but still moving, until Linye slashed his throat with her sword. Two over the edge, Tamisen in pursuit of an assailant, Nagua shooting someone in the neck to separate his head from his body as he climbed. That was three bodies over the edge. Any more coming? Not at this instant. How were things going elsewhere on the wall?

They were losing the light. Cassim's people weren't going to be able to see much of anything, soon. Cassim would be calling off his attack. Away to Shashka's left he saw Setanay leaning over the wall, firing at someone climbing up the village wall near where Shashka had tipped the stabbed man over. Anything more going on here, before he went to check on his others?

Yes, there was. A man was rushing up from behind Tamisen while the sepahis were addressing other problems. Too far for Shashka to reach with a sword, and the sepahi's struggles denied him a clear shot, but Tamisen turned quickly, dropping down on one knee to open the man's stomach with an impressive, very effective, slice up into his gut from his groin to mid-chest. A dance step of some kind, Shashka supposed. He admired the effect.

The dead man fell heavily down and across Tamisen where he knelt even as Tamisen struggled to pull his sword away.

The impact knocked Tamisen off balance, setting him sprawling backwards to crack his head against the sharp edge of the masonry wall. Shashka didn't like the angle of the blow, but he couldn't take a moment to check on Tamisen for himself. He had work to do.

They pulled the ladders Cassim's men had used up and over the walls to deny the enemy their future use. Cassim would have to get new ladders, and that might take him an hour or two. Shikander checked the rest of the perimeter. Captain Katische gave the all clear, but quietly, passing the word from sepahi to sepahi as she went.

Peri came with the report: five injuries that were not serious, three that would cost him. Babira had taken a bullet in her lower leg and wouldn't be able to stand or walk.

Hetsatsa was stabbed in the back of her shoulder and was still bleeding. If she died there'd be another spear standing broken and aslant in the forecourt of his house in the valley to the east in which he'd taken sanctuary.

Wila had been slashed hard against her ribs, and the extent of her injury as yet unknown, while Tamisen had yet to regain consciousness. They'd taken him downstairs, and that was all the information there was to be had for now.

Another circuit around, for lordship's sake, showing his face, spreading calm resolution by being calmly resolute. Facial cuts. Sprained, possibly broken arm, already tied up, and one good arm was better than none. Stab wound, fairly shallow, not so much blood loss as would endanger Kusha's ability, although the wound would hurt very badly once the initial shock wore off around morning.

Lamish had donated all of his impressive store of narcotics to the doctor, so there was at least that much to the good. All relatively well as far as that went, but Shashka was down three fighters for the defense—no, four. That meant the equivalent of nine, of twelve, effectively unopposed, in open battle.

The fighting had come too close. Shashka decided to move his wounded sepahis to the tower. His sepahis deserved the best he had to offer, and for women with the history he shared with them that was the knowledge that he placed his uttermost faith in them to protect his wife and his infant child.

The moon was rising. The defense had the advantage of

the light. Any shadowy heads rising from the outer walls would be clear sharp targets, and no reasonable man would do that to himself, especially if he was fighting only for treasure that he had to be alive to use and enjoy.

Shashka was satisfied that the excitement was for the moment passed. Now he could afford to go check on his casualties, and see if Tamisen still lay unconscious from that blow to the head.

Boy shadowed her lord down the ladder to the hospital house. They'd knocked a low passage in the interior walls on either side, so people could go quickly from house to house. The walls were good ones, very thick. Now more than ever, she thought the lord should have this place: well built, good water, hard-working people who were grateful for his protection and direction, and even Lamish was gradually awakening to his responsibilities.

"Can she be carried?" the lord asked Hakim Jericho, at Wila's side. The bleeding from her wound had been staunched, and at the sound of the lord's voice she pulled in her knees, trying to sit up. The lord put his hand on her arm to stop her. He only had to touch her once, tenderly, because she knew who was lord, and lay back down.

The hakim was frowning. "Where did you have in mind? We do need to clear the surgery. But I want her moved only the once. Not again after for at least three days, if it can be done."

The lord nodded, turning his head to find one of the women from New Wife's house who stood there near Boy. "Get some of Lamish's people. Carry my sepahis into the tower, put them where your lady and yourselves can tend to them."

Hakim Jericho seemed to be startled—but why not? It was dark and quiet in the tower. New Wife's women had shown themselves adept at field medicine. New Wife herself showed good courage and was not proud, putting herself beneath her women to be taught and directed, bloodying her hands without reluctance.

The lord spoke to Wila. "I set you and your comrades as the final guard over my best treasures. Conserve your strength and rest until called upon for your last efforts. You will have Babira with you, and Hetsatsa. Hearten each other. I know you long to be with the others, but I need you there, for their sakes." In case the worse happened.

It was hard that he was here with his family. Had Ismara and her women been safely removed he would have fought a very different kind of war. His son? Yes, but Boy knew that the lord could get other sons far more easily than he could replace the women Ismara's father had so foolishly discarded.

When the lord turned to Babira, she was staring at him with desperate pleading in her face. "I can defend the walls," she said. Boy knew Babira was in pain, because she spoke first, out of turn. The lord let them take liberties, but he was lord, and it was his to permit or deny. "There are children here. Please, lord. Let me at least stand watch."

The lord looked to the hakim; the hakim shook his head, but reluctantly, in Boy's estimation. Sensitive to Babira's desperation. That could be. "If she weights her leg she'll start bleeding again, and do herself grave harm," the doctor said. "But I can't tell you to make her lie down and be still."

No indeed. "Pact," the lord said. "You are my squad leader, Babira, until further notice. Your orders are to keep the watch and guard the stairs to the second floor, where I entrust your sisters to my wife, my wife to you and your sisters. Do you accept this charge?"

Babira smiled. Her leg was broken, Hetsatsa was stabbed, Wila was cut in her belly, and still Babira was grateful for his good lordship. Boy approved. "Yes. Thank you, lord."

He smiled back. "My thanks to you all. Peri, you'll talk to Katische."

It made her nervous when he called her that in front of other people. That name was private; no one was supposed to know.

"Next on your list is Jefferji," the hakim said. "Tamisen. Head injury. His eyes are open but I don't think he's with us. He should be watched. Can Jefferji go too?"

"Put him to bed with us, you and I," the lord told Boy. "Babira can see to it that he doesn't try to leave."

Yes. The lord knew a little medicine, and of course he was an angel. He needed to take a few hours' sleep, and with Tamisen in his bed the lord would be more likely to remember where it was and go there, because he was concerned for Tamisen whom he liked. He would want Boy, too. She knew what was required to calm his mind so that he could find sleep in between wars.

Boy beckoned for an orderly. Tamisen lay against the wall with his feet propped up, in an apparent daze. "You come with me," Boy said to him, firmly and slowly, because since his mind was away somewhere it might be some time before her words reached him. "This man will help you. Stand up now."

The lord would go and see the rest of them, the villagers who had taken injury. Some of those injuries had been accidental, but some of them had been on the walls, and honor was rightly due. Boy made herself overseer of the expedition, three sepahis and a dancing stork—Tamisen— for the tower where the lord slept and kept his treasured things. She had water to heat for the lord's hands and face, and they would sleep for a few hours before their enemies would try again.

⛰

Something was worrying at Fontenoy's jacket, hot and wet and urgent. His head ached. What was it? Why was he lying here on the flinty ground, in broad daylight?

The hot wet something breathed a humid gale into his ear, then sneezed. Fontenoy was awake at once, rolling over onto his stomach with a pistol in his hand. There was a large black eye inches from his face holding him in its steady regard: the pony. The yabu pony. What was going on?

It wasn't broad day after all. It was midnight by the moon, which shone so full and bright that it had beguiled him. His head ached. He'd fallen from the saddle, that would explain it. He hadn't dared sleep when they'd stopped for the yabu to grab a mouthful of forage, drink a little water, take half an hour's stand time.

The pony had been willing to go on, with a bit of date cake for a bribe. The pony was in better shape than he was, and that was a sad verdict on him because the pony had been doing all the work. All Fontenoy had to do was keep his seat and worry.

There was no telling how far they'd gotten. The landscape looked no different in any salient detail than it had for the entire day past. Under the strange light of the moon he'd completely lost his bearings. He could see the road, though, a dark thread across the hill ahead where the moon cast it into relief. So that was all right.

"Sorry," he told the pony. "Just a reflex. Dates? Of course." He was grateful to the pony for staying near, for rousing him. He couldn't reward it as lavishly as he would have liked, though, because the bit of date cake grew smaller hour by hour, and they had yet to reach Deravass Khan. It was night, which meant they'd only been traveling one day. He had a day and a half yet to travel before he could begin to hope to reach his goal. Could the yabu keep it up for that long?

He hadn't seen Deravass Khan in twenty years. He hadn't thought to meet with him again like this, unkempt, unshaven, ill mounted, and in a desperate hurry. Would Deravass recognize him on sight? Would he recognize Deravass?

Wearily Fontenoy mounted and took up the reins. The yabu bobbed its head—*About time, you old turnip, and pay better attention*—tasted the breeze for a moment, and started off for the hill that came after the last hill and before the hill beyond. All he could do was keep going, as fast and hard as possible, and hope he could somehow be in time to save Old Fort and Ganders Tamisen's son Geoffrey.

After a long program of heroic adventure—from the Ramayana perhaps—some several of the god's handmaidens would take a tired young dancer deep into the temple, shampoo his body from head to foot with thick white creamy suds of sandalwood-scented soap, and put him to bed in a sanctuary space where a goddess—or her temple-proxy, or a devotee—would join him in the incense-perfumed dark, and sing him to sleep with the lullaby of her body. And all the while Jefferji would still be in the dance, in the presence of his Beloved, unable to see where the liminal space of trance-like abstraction yielded to material reality.

Jefferji remembered how it felt to be so tired he had no will to open his eyes, so relaxed there was no muscle that retained the least bit of even resting tension. How it felt to be so exalted in spirit that there seemed no separation between what he knew and what he just imagined, what he'd just danced and what he'd just experienced. He felt like that now.

On the fourth day of the great battle Jefferji Tamisen, he who was the son of the famous warrior Ganders and the foster son of the renowned Jaisal Singh of Tengarpore, was wounded in the head with a celestial weapon launched by an enemy whose mantra was stronger than the hero's armor. His charioteer, seeing he was dazed and unable to defend himself, carried him away from the battle and laid him down in the tent of Arjuna to do him honor and so that he could recover from his bewilderment and return to the affray.

Jefferji could hear voices.

"You asked to be awakened, lord."

Who was that? Jefferji didn't know. One of the men in Arjuna's camp, perhaps. They'd put him on the same couch with Arjuna, which seemed strange; Arjuna was purest kshatriya, of divine parentage, and Jefferji was only a very low impoverished Rajput of the third age and Englishmen had no caste anyway. It could be that Arjuna was willing to grant him indulgence for love of Jaisal Singh, whose dharma was clear and pure and true.

"Report. Are there any signs?"

That would be Arjuna, because Jefferji was in Arjuna's tent. Therefore, necessarily, it was the son of Indra. The sound of Arjuna's voice was strangely garbled, though; it was as if he spoke through the music of the waters of a stream cascading quickly down a bed of rounded stones.

"There may be some activity along the west wall. But we're not sure."

Jefferji heard small sounds: a man putting on his boots, taking a drink of water. Then there was a woman's voice.

"This one—does he go with you?"

"Better left where he is for now, it could be dangerous to try to wake him. I'm going to the west wall. Find Captain Katische for me. Nothing from the south?"

"No, lord. It's been very quiet."

It *was* very quiet. Jefferji was alone now in Arjuna's tent. He could see rich walls of red silk heavy with embroidery in pure gold depicting the heroic exploits of Arjuna's friend and brother-in-law, Krsna Vasudeva. The beams were fragrant sandalwood, the incense of the rarest and purest sort, Arjuna's armor carefully arranged on its tree. How could Arjuna's armor still be here? How could Arjuna go into battle without his armor, no matter how powerful his weapons?

He doesn't need his armor, someone said. The voice was as deep as the stillness in the forest at noon during the great heat, kindly and amused, with a faint sound of thunder lying far and far away beneath the words. *The shankha is his armor. He only wears the golden breastplate to warn men who have no eyes that his dharma protects him like a brilliant shield of priceless diamonds.*

Jefferji frowned, his eyes still closed. He heard noises from outside Arjuna's tent. Was this the night when the enemy crept into the camp while the victors slept, and slaughtered sons and brothers in their beds? No. That couldn't be. That didn't happen until much later on in the story.

But Shikander didn't have the shankha trumpet. Jefferji did. He'd been carrying it with him, tied in a soft leather bag across his back like the hand of a friend, like a shield. It had saved lives when the flood had come.

The shankha is his best shield. It can protect all who fight in his train. You need not fear for him.

But Shikander didn't know that he was Arjuna. The shankha had been venerated here in disguise as a votive offering, but it was the celestial trumpet. Jefferji knew it by its deeds, though it hadn't revealed itself in its true character until now.

It had spoken once, and piled earth upon the cave temple to protect it until Fontenoy's men arrived. It had spoken the second time to warn the people about the river. Devadatta could summon up Deravass Khan, whom Captain Fontenoy had gone to hurry to their rescue. If Shikander blew the conch trumpet, Deravass Khan would be there, and not unless. Jefferji had to get the conch to Shikander Beg.

Through the windows in the tower room he could hear a jumbled noise of shouts, screams, fighting. If he didn't hurry, he would be too late. His boots were here, at the side of the bed—Shikander's bed of silk rugs, soft and lustrous—but Jefferji pushed the silken coverlets aside with no thought for their value. The sound of an explosion, then another, hurried him on. Where were his things?

There, on the chest that stood against the felt wall of the tent. His sharp curved sword, his pistols, powder and shot, the shankha. Devadatta. He'd had it all this time, but it wasn't his. It was Shikander's. Shikander was Arjuna in this war, the dharma prince, the son of a prince, a peerless warrior. If Jefferji didn't get Devadatta to Shikander in time, Jefferji would be to blame for the disaster that crouched in ambush for Old Fort and everybody in it.

Cassim's people were taking no chances with him, which was only a minor annoyance to Broderick Holyoke. He hadn't been the only man who'd elected not to charge the fire through the gates to almost-certain death so early yesterday morning. What good did it do anybody to get themselves killed just so someone else could enjoy riches and luxury?

It *was* the strategy he would have recommended—that they should all get themselves killed, since his exact purpose would have been to get rid of as many men who were in competition with him for the treasure as he could. Even then it wouldn't have worked as well as he might have liked, because too many of Cassim's adventurers had shown their independence of spirit by declining to submit themselves to slaughter.

It was an object lesson for men with eyes to see, how Captain Fontenoy could deploy his limited resources to prevail against a more numerous force. Had Cassim taken a lesson? Was he regretting having deprived himself of Broderick's superior military expertise, imaginary though it was, by letting his interpreter run away? If so, it was too bad. For Cassim. Because it was too late.

Still and all, it all worked out to Broderick's advantage. Cassim's attack would keep both his own and Fontenoy's men occupied, and the field clear for Broderick. Not only Fontenoy's men, but Fontenoy himself, and that meant Broderick knew just where to look. Fontenoy had lied in front of his whole garrison. So the men whom Fontenoy had recruited with whatever insane tale of chivalry or promise of pay he'd employed didn't know about the treasure. So Fontenoy hadn't told them. So Fontenoy had concealed it.

So it was a treasure of diamonds, emeralds, pearls, things that were light and small and easily carried, just as the man in Zebak had suggested when he'd spoken of rubies the size of an egg yolk that had been seen in the bazaar at Fayzabad. And it was hidden in Fontenoy's effects. Fontenoy would naturally want to carry them on his person, but that was too great a risk. Money carried on the person could be discovered and taken, no matter how cunningly concealed—as Broderick had learned, to his cost.

Last night as the sun had set, Cassim had sent another round of probing attacks and scouts. Some of the casualties had managed to crawl away from the walls to safety. Broderick himself had rescued a fallen comrade, and if anybody had remarked that dragging a man's bleeding body away from the fighting was an effective form of self-preservational withdrawal Broderick had heard nothing of it. Sometimes an inability to understand what people were saying was of particular benefit to a man.

Cassim had divided his remaining troops into three parties. The one in which Broderick was included would logically be the one in which the most casualties were to be expected, because they'd pushed Broderick to the forefront.

After a night of lying facedown in the dirt, silent and motionless, Broderick was happy when his fellow prodded him with the point of a knife. *We're about to go.* They thought he would run away if he had the chance. They didn't know he meant to have the treasure all to himself. Maybe they did know that. Maybe he was here because they trusted him to follow his own self-interest into the fort, and meant to follow *him.*

He'd crept along with fourteen other men carrying soot-blackened ladders through the ruined gate to get here, keeping low to the ground, hugging the shadows all the way around the base of the outer wall, faces to the earth. He'd crawled carefully with the others into position within sprinting range of the village's wall, still far enough away—he hoped—to escape observation from the tower. He'd waited. The sky began to lighten. They wouldn't be able to lurk waiting in the darkness undiscovered for much longer.

The man next to Broderick in the dust spoke softly, low-voiced, one word, two words, three words—a countdown—but Broderick couldn't count in foreign languages, so he waited. Four words, and fourteen men rose with a shout and started running, two men to a ladder, five ladders in all. Broderick got up and ran with them, because if he held back, he would be all that much more obvious a target.

Looking left and right as he ran, Broderick saw men crowding at the base of the wall, throwing the ladders up and scrambling to climb them while the defenders—more likely to be conserving ammunition than taken completely by surprise, Broderick thought—didn't start firing until the first man was almost to the top. He hadn't seen very many defenders on the walls last night, once the barricade had been breached—a few of Fontenoy's Amazons, and the man in the blue wool coat. Broderick assumed the man's coat was still blue.

Broderick's party ran directly for the arched gate into the village itself, one not so venerable and solid by its looks as that in the outer wall, and lower—only camel-high. Sheltering as best they could behind the shallow lip of the gateway, one of the men pulled objects from his bosom, round and heavy. Grenades. Where had they gotten grenades? Broderick took the hatchet pressed into his hand and chopped at the center of the door, his exertion impelled to remarkable heights by the fact that people would be shooting at them the moment they were noticed.

The gates were too thick to challenge with a hatchet, but that didn't seem to be the point. The grenades had spikes. Broderick's chopping exposed the raw wood of the gate, and the grenades stuck there. The grenadier touched a slow match to the fuses. One of the men pulled Broderick to one side, where he and they alike would be shielded from the blast. The grenades took a wide slice of the wall away with them along with the gate.

Oh, good, Broderick thought with disgust. *We have their attention now.*

Speed alone could save them. The other men of Broderick's party would keep Fontenoy's men pinned down at the wall. The defenders couldn't afford to shift their attention to the gate without running the risk that the entire place would be overrun. Broderick began to like Cassim's strategy.

If Broderick had been Fontenoy, he'd have built two gates into the village, one on the outside, at the village wall, and one inside. So Fontenoy had, but Cassim had planned for that, and sent more grenades. This time they could work unthreatened from above, with the overhang of the bombed-out gate to shield them, but they worked as desperately as before.

The village gate was narrow. Four or five men on the other side could hold it forever, so they needed to get through before Fontenoy could get four or five men there. The blast from the grenades would injure, perhaps kill, whomever was too close on either side. That was good for Cassim's men, but only if they could avoid being killed themselves.

Broderick had barely enough time to make it past the lip of the shallow bowl of the crater that the first round of grenades had blasted into packed earth before the second round of grenades blew an even deeper hole out of the second gate. Broderick seized his moment and ran, seeing—he could hear nothing yet, after the blast—that the two men alongside him had the same idea. They could get in. There wasn't any time to spare.

He was through the gate. The village was full of smoke; dust from the explosion—but wasn't there something else, as well? Had Cassim launched another fire attack? That would further distract the defenders, draw off resources, and there was no danger of burning any treasure. And the time to find it was now, before Fontenoy—where was Captain Fontenoy?—had a chance to react.

There were bodies, and men and women struggling to free themselves from the piles of rubble and debris. Villagers?

Civilians? There were no civilians in a siege. Here was a grim-faced man who'd clearly lost his wits, coming after Broderick with an antique sword so rusty Broderick could tell it would snap at the first impact. The silly old fool fought as if he'd never picked up a sword before in his entire life.

It was unsporting to kill the ineffectual madman, but Broderick had things to do. The fellow wouldn't get out of the way, and the edge of his rusty sword cut very annoyingly across Broderick's shoulder, making him angry. Stepping inside the man's sword-arc while he fought to raise the sword and miss again, Broderick struck him in the neck with the hatchet. He knew how to keep his weapon under control, if the other fellow didn't.

The blood spray when he pulled the hatchet back was not the yard-long jet of bright red blood that would signal an immediately lethal blow, but it would do to slow the man down. There were people coming, their attention focused on the casualties and another—fiercer, more well-matched— fight between Cassim's other men and villagers. Broderick had the advantage of smoke and dust. It was a good opportunity to get away.

Backing away from the engagement, Broderick ran along the wall at the base of the tower. The tower would logically be where the fellow in the blue coat kept his rooms; Broderick decided to look there first. Fontenoy would be guesting there, in the best rooms.

He heard horses screaming in terror. Turning his head on instinct for the source of the sound he saw Tamisen's animal across the square, and a tall chestnut that looked like Gunnery. How could it be Gunnery? He'd left the nag in Attok, played out, ridden out, ruined and worthless. But if it was, that would be convenient for Broderick's escape, since Gunnery already knew Broderick as his master. The stables were on fire, too; that was also convenient. He'd be able to find a saddle, he was sure, unless the tack room was on fire as well.

First the treasure. There was no one in the tower on the ground floor. There were signs that people had been here on watch, though the guard had rushed outside when Broderick and Cassim's men had blown up the gate. Those men had all been villagers. Villagers, defending Fontenoy's treasure?

Pathetic. Or brilliant. No one would expect Fontenoy to entrust valuables to a band of rabble. It was an obvious part of Fontenoy's campaign to conceal any hint of the existence of the treasures from his credulous pawns.

Up the stairs, then, where the finest accommodations would logically be found. There was a camp of sorts set up on the second level, but Broderick didn't do more than glance through the clearly makeshift door for a quick glance at windows, camel packs, someone's trestle desk, a whimsical felt enclosure like a tent pitched indoors at one side.

There was a guard sitting three steps up the stairs curving up to the second level, which was as good as a printed announcement—"*Seek ye your treasure here.*" It was one of those Amazons. Broderick was almost glad to see her, because he cherished a resentment of their cavalier treatment on the night the river had flooded. This one had a splint well knotted around her leg, so she'd been hurt; that would reduce her capacity. She had a pistol as well, though. He'd have to deal with that.

Broderick had a pistol too, the shabbiest pistol he'd ever seen—a flintlock—and two rounds. A chance glimpse of the glow of a matchlock might have queered their overnight concealment, he guessed. It seemed to take the Amazon a moment to realize Broderick wasn't one of the villagers. It was a very short moment, but she was evidently slowed by her injury.

Rushing forward, he kicked her splinted leg, hard, and scrambled over her crumpling body as her sword clattered to the rough-hewn steps of the staircase at Broderick's feet. He meant to save his ammunition—how much of a threat could a woman incapacitated by pain really be? —and he only had two rounds.

In four more steps he was at the turn of the staircase, facing another Amazon. This one leaned heavily against the wall, also clearly impaired, and fired at him as soon as he cleared the inside curve of the stairwell. She missed. She should have waited for a more certain target. Unlike Broderick, however, she had another pistol, held ready in her other hand—apparently injured, to go by the bandage and the blood.

Broderick retreated behind the turn of the staircase as she started to reach across her body to steady her second pistol for what would be a much more considered shot. Every moment he made her wait would be a further drain her limited physical resources. He could make that work in his favor. He had a good chance here, even though she'd be prepared for him.

Ducking back down the several steps between him and where the first Amazon had fallen, Broderick took a moment for a swift check. She was still breathing, but she made no sound, so he felt secure that she was unconscious—and no threat to him now, in any case.

Pulling off his filthy turban, Broderick stuck it on the sword's point. Quickly he thrust the decoy up and toward the head of the stairs, hoping to draw the woman's fire by pure reflex, while at the same time he jumped to the far side of the stairwell to rush the guard.

It didn't exactly work. The woman fired at him, not at the sword—a miscalculation on his part, the ruse not so uncommon that it hadn't been anticipated, perhaps. But the sudden shift in focus that his feint had forced betrayed her to her own compromised balance, and she fell back against the staircase as she fired, missing him again.

She screamed in pure rage but Broderick didn't care. Pulling her down the stairs behind him, brandishing the hatchet he still carried to warn her off, Broderick went on. He'd have to get past her again on his way out but he wasn't concerned about that right now. He had a pistol, two rounds, and an uncompromised arm. He would have no difficulty with her later.

And here he was. A fabric frame, a flimsy curtained door that didn't slow him down for an instant. Inside there were three old women holding what appeared to be broomsticks at the ready, along with a girl who was holding a baby and standing by a woman on a sickbed—another Amazon. No shortage of hostages for leverage if he needed it. Raising his pistol, Broderick took aim at the baby on the sickbed and shouted. "Where is it?"

Chapter Thirteen
Devadatta

Jefferji struggled into his boots. He was unaccountably dizzy, and his fingers were maddeningly clumsy. He heard something snap, clear and cold, but he couldn't make sense of the sound. What was it? It was something he had to take care of. There was another. Finally, he got his boots on, and his hearing came back into focus. Pistol-shot from nearby, within the tower; the sound made Jefferji desperate.

His pistols and his sword were to hand, and the shankha in its soft leather sack; he grabbed them by their carry-straps, rushing out of the room with a pistol in his hand. He'd been in the tent Shikander Beg had pitched on the second level of the tower. Of course he had. Where had he thought he was?

Outside the room on the landing, Jefferji found Babira on her side with the bandages on her splinted leg bright red with fresh blood, reaching for something that wasn't there and moaning. He stooped swiftly to help her to turn over, but he heard sounds from up above, a man's voice on the upper floor where no man had any business being. He had to hurry on.

Shikander's wife and child were up there, and her women as well. The man's voice rose again, threatening, though Jefferji couldn't make out the words. Were those women armed? If they were, could they defend themselves? They weren't Rajputs; they weren't Hell-riders. They had not been trained for war. Jefferji started up the stairs. There was a second sepahi lying there, Hetsatsa, working to get her back against the wall. That was proof. Whoever was up there was an enemy, and needed to be stopped.

Passing Hetsatsa with a quick nod of apology—answered by a glare that would have shattered steel, *hurry, you idiot*—Jefferji took the stairs two at a time to reach the landing, fighting dizziness all the way. He heard shouted words, but they were in a foreign language. English. Then Jefferji knew who it was, in the women's quarters, threatening unarmed women and a babe in arms. And hated him all over again with savage fury.

Bursting through the fabric-draped entryway, he took in the stage-setting at a glance, making sure he knew where all the players were. There was Shikander's wife Ismara. A sickbed, and Wila lying on her side in too-evident agony, Shikander's child in her arms, cradling the child's head against her chest. The other women, moving too slowly toward Holyoke with whatever they'd been able to find at hand for weapons.

Holyoke had a pistol, aimed at Shikander's child. A child! What if Holyoke fired in anger, when he heard Jefferji's voice? No, Holyoke was ruled by reflex. Jefferji knew that from the temple on the road to Rawal Pindi. He'd turn toward Jefferji.

"Everybody down!" Jefferji shouted, dropping sword and shankha. A sword would be no good in such close quarters. Shikander's wife stooped over Wila and the baby on the bed as if she thought she could stop a pistol ball with her body; it was an instinctive gesture of hopeless gallantry that inflamed Jefferji to the point of near-madness.

"Holyoke, you coward!"

Flinging himself headlong at Holyoke, Jefferji knocked him hard, flat on the floor. But a rug cushioned the blow, and what Jefferji had meant to render Holyoke unconscious only stunned him. Jefferji went for the pistol Holyoke had in his hand. Holyoke had a hatchet, as well; the hatchet would do Jefferji no harm if he could avoid a wide-swung blow, but a pistol shot could hit any of the people in the room, women, wife, baby, sepahis.

He wrestled ferociously with Holyoke for the pistol. Holyoke fought him with matching savagery. It was all Jefferji could do to hold his own. The moment Holyoke got the better of him, Holyoke would be free to shoot the women. If Jefferji didn't get the shankha to Arjuna, Shikander Beg would die, but Jefferji couldn't leave the women undefended. That would be murder, and betrayal. Shikander had told Jefferji about betrayal. Jefferji was not going to be the man who added to Shikander's store of history.

Holyoke got his arm free, the one with the pistol. Jefferji wanted Holyoke to fire it, as long as it was aimed right. He got an elbow underneath Holyoke's armpit and pushed, wrenching Holyoke's arm to straighten it toward the doorway through which he'd come. Jefferji heard the shot, but there were no screams of fear, no screams of rage. There had been no ricochet.

Holyoke rammed the sharp point of his elbow into Jefferji's stomach, and Jefferji curled into an involuntary spasm with a shout. He hadn't realized he was so vulnerable there. Broken rib? Holyoke rolled him over onto his back and knelt on his arms, pinning them to the ground as he smashed the back of Jefferji's head against bare stone paving—not a cushioning rug, this time—once, twice, three times.

The impact knocked Jefferji's mind to one side of his body. For an instant he could see nothing at all past the white haze filling his field of vision. When the fog lifted everything was indistinct in outline, doubled, blurred. He was pinned to the floor by one and a half Holyokes with one and a half black blades coming for his throat.

Probably not a good idea to wait for that, Jefferji thought, twisting his legs behind Holyoke's back to unseat him, leading with his left knee to send Holyoke head over heels and the knife flying. Holyoke knew nothing of Rajput kathak dance, but his body went where it was told regardless.

Before Jefferji could breathe his way past the agony in his ribs, Holyoke was back at him, knife in hand. Jefferji parried, but not quickly enough to avert the blow Holyoke struck at his right arm. Holyoke connected, bringing blood and white agony that weakened Jefferji's grip.

There was something Holyoke might not know about Arjuna, beloved of Krsna. The hero fought as well with either hand, and had to show it on stage, passing his weapons effortlessly from right to left and back again, deploying them from either side convincingly. Jefferji had enough strength in his fingers to make the toss, he had the knife in his left hand now, and almost succeeded in stabbing Holyoke in the throat. But only almost.

Jefferji was getting desperate. He had to get to Shikander with the shankha, the weapon of Arjuna, before it was too late. Holyoke had broken away; Jefferji couldn't allow that. Fighting his way to his knees Jefferji lunged, his arms around Holyoke's legs. Holyoke twisted as he went down, landing on his side, rolling over with a kick that connected with Jefferji's head.

He couldn't think. He blinked; the next Jefferji knew he was flat on his back on the floor again with his knife hand pinned to the floor at his side and Holyoke's knife in his face. Holyoke laughed, working the knife in his fist, and at that moment something came spinning across the floor and touched Jefferji's free hand. It was the hatchet that Holyoke had dropped. One of the women had kicked it over to him.

The pain in his arm was of no consequence so long as he could take a firm enough grip on the hatchet, because this was absolutely his last chance. Grasping the hatchet handle Jefferji swung for Holyoke's head with all his strength. The back of the blade hit hard against the side of Holyoke's head; Jefferji had struck out with the dull side.

One of the women screamed. Holyoke himself made no sound, staring out into some distant place with a confused look on his face and black blood streaming down the side of his head and into his eyes, blinding him. He crumpled and fell.

The old women pulled Holyoke's unconscious body away, onto its belly, while Wila shouted her instructions—*Stand by with the pestle! Find rope! Sisters come to me if you can!* Holyoke lay still. What now?

Jefferji crawled across the floor to where he'd dropped the shankha, pulling it out of its leather bag in a frenzy to make sure it was safe. Its cool weight in his hands restored some of his strength.

He stood up. "Must go. Weapon. For the lord." If Holyoke wasn't dead, he was at least in no condition to threaten anyone. "Thanks for the hatchet." Someone had saved his life; he'd thank them later. There was still time to reunite Devadatta with its master, and save the village from destruction.

Now, at long last, Broderick had his enemy. There could be no escape for Tamisen now. Shifting his grip on the knife, Broderick stared into Tamisen's face, trying to fix every detail of Tamisen's expression in his mind. Broderick wanted each second to drag into eons as Tamisen watched the knife descend inexorably, irreversibly, to cut and tear his throat and let hot blood spurt out. He wanted Tamisen to know that he was going to die, dying, dying, dead.

Holyoke had never hated a man so much in his life as he hated Geoffrey Tamisen now, at this moment. Could Tamisen realize what an honor that was, how many people Broderick had had good reason to hate, how fiercely, and for how long? But Holyoke had gotten them back, each and every one of them, one way or another.

Broderick tightened his grip, he tensed his shoulders, he lifted the knife. But then Tamisen swung at him from the wrong side. He had no business using that hand, Broderick had cut his arm too badly, and yet there was something in Tamisen's hand that struck him with astonishing impact. He was falling, unable to reach out and stop himself, and when he hit the ground a clear calm silence filled Broderick's mind.

Tamisen wasn't on him anymore. That meant Tamisen had taken the treasure and run, taking everything Broderick had ever wanted, ever dreamed of, with him. Broderick remembered how that had felt, standing on the banks of the Nerbudda river, staring at the unlit pyre and the bodies he'd piled up so awkwardly and gracelessly on top of it any way he could.

He had no evidence, no proof. He couldn't report it. All anyone would see was an ugly drummer boy, eighteen years old but would never be a man in their eyes if he lived to be a hundred, and twenty men dead—of the fever, but he'd be blamed somehow, he was always blamed—one of them an officer. A beautiful officer. The most beautiful man Broderick had ever seen and the only one who'd ever shown him so much as a scrap of human kindness.

Broderick Holyoke had only arrived from England eight months before then, twenty-two years old. He hadn't been in Madras Presidency long enough to hear the things the men said about filthy little Bung-hole Boy, who had always ever done only what he had to do in order to survive. It was catch as catch can and the devil take the hindmost. *The divvil.* His mother. She'd been dead by then, but not soon enough.

Holyoke had been different. He'd spoken kindly. He'd taken an interest. He'd shown Bung-hole Boy how to write his name, with his own name written out as a model. And in return Bung-hole Boy had adored him, with every scrap of undeveloped religious passion in his being, watched him and studied him and learnt everything about the way he walked and talked and laughed and dressed and breathed.

Now Broderick Holyoke was dead. He could remember Bung-hole Boy weeping in despair, setting torch to the pyre on which the body of Broderick Holyoke lay with the rest of the detachment that had set out from one obscure cantonment to another two weeks ago. The fire had burned and burned, fed by fat rendered from human flesh, the smoke with the stink of Hell from roasting meat. He'd watched it. He'd sat and hugged his knees and rocked back and forth on the ground and wept for Broderick Holyoke while the heat from the fire had scorched his face.

Then he'd gathered up his things—Broderick Holyoke's things laid aside at the onset of the fever, change of linen, discarded uniform—and left Bung-hole Boy to burn on the fire with the rest of them. It didn't hurt to burn, because Broderick Holyoke—at least—had been truly dead before Bung-hole Boy had lit the fire, not like some of the others.

Bung-hole Boy was sure that he was dying now, on the floor of a tower somewhere along the Wakhan north of Kabul and Chitral, and he didn't care, because it seemed to be the first moment of true peace he'd had in his entire life. He could dimly sense hands and ropes binding him, but what did he care? The final escape was there for him to grasp, and he followed that blessed promise down into the welcoming darkness.

Fontenoy and the yabu had stopped before dawn to drink some water. The yabu had offered to share its scrub grass with him in exchange for some of his date cake, but Fontenoy didn't eat scrub grass. The offer had been made in good faith, though, so it had been common politeness to share what was left of the date cake laced with opium. It had seemed to cheer the yabu, perk it up a bit; they'd been back on the trail for hours.

He was desperately drained. The early morning sun, not more than half an hour clear of the mountains, made his head throb even more fiercely than it had last night, after his fall from the pony's back. If he'd had any opium left, he would have been sorely tempted to eat it up himself. His old bones ached, the knowledge that he hadn't unsaddled the pony for a day and a half filled him with shame, and his heart pounded in his ears with a staggered beat like that of a horse's gallop.

The pony's pace had quickened, and while Fontenoy welcomed that—whatever the reason why—the physical demands it made on him were suddenly much more pressing. The sound of his heartbeat grew louder, and he realized with dread that his vision was deteriorating. The near horizon was clouded as though with mist, although the air was still. There was no dust to the left, none to the right. Only on the road in front of them.

The cloudiness in the air dead straight ahead could only be the blindness of old men, the fog that came into a man's eyes and blurred the clear crystalline windows of the eye into milky opacity. Cataracts. It didn't matter. The yabu would follow the road. When at last the yabu found Deravass, the presence of a derelict on its back would be enough to hurry Deravass back to Old Fort, if only the yabu could be somehow persuaded to keep going. Fontenoy had no more date cake to offer.

There was a shadow beat in his heart, now, a second beat lagging behind the first, irregular and varying in intensity— now louder, now almost inaudible. He didn't feel any more light-headed than the lack of sleep and food, and his hurry, and his headache, would make him. He felt steady in the saddle, as far as it went, but there was an increased indistinctness on the road ahead, rising from the depression of a saddle-pass between two hills and coming toward him.

The yabu lengthened its stride, for all the world as though it saw a giant cake of dates and opium just beyond that dust-colored haze, waiting for it with pure sweet water, oats and hay, and seven vestal virgins in white silk to stroke its neck and call it nobly born and valiant. But the pony couldn't see the murky obscurity in the road, because it was Fontenoy's eyesight that was failing, not the yabu's. If it had been the yabu's eyesight, Fontenoy's vision would be unclouded.

If Fontenoy and the pony both saw it, it was because it was not the fading clarity of cataract, but a cloud of dust in grim reality. Coming closer, with a sound like that of horses coming at him as fast as they could run. That made no sense. Who would be riding hard down this road? There was no one on the road but Deravass Khan. Deravass's scout had said so.

Something black and indistinct in outline resolved itself gradually out of the dust cloud on the road. Out of the past. There was a man on horseback, and it seemed to Fontenoy that he recognized him, even through the tarnished glass of memory. No one put his head down over his horse's neck quite like that, his shoulders hunched like those of a water buffalo, coming down the road like the first thunderhead of the spring monsoon.

It was a wonder he could still ride so hard. He was as old as Fontenoy, and Fontenoy knew in his bones that he, for one, was nothing like the man he'd been when they'd last met.

They were going to collide head-on. Fontenoy pulled the yabu's head to one side, sharply; the yabu was much more agile than Fontenoy, and kept her feet as sure-footed as a mountain goat while Fontenoy stood in grave danger of falling off again.

Deravass Khan. His age lay on his face like dust from old roads traveled, dust that blew away and left the face of Fontenoy's old friend there before him.

His moustache was still black, though his trimmed beard was white. The lines of his face were deeper by eighteen years of sun and squinting. There was more flesh to him, the bone and mass of a grown man, where once upon a time they'd been yearling colts together—only beginning to learn how well they could run and how well fight, and how much joy there was in comradeship and adventure.

Dismounting, Fontenoy embraced his friend, standing in the dusty road, filled with wonder at how little Deravass had changed.

"The scout said there was a man who rode as though he was asleep." Deravass's voice had changed. But it was as if the strings were altered in pitch, or the instrument retuned; cadence and inflection, they were the same. "I told him that the only man I'd ever known who could sleep on a trotting horse was Fontenoy. So I came on ahead."

"Good thing you did," Fontenoy replied, his voice rusty and weak in his own ears. He'd done it. He'd found Deravass Khan. That was the first great requirement accomplished. He wasn't going to sit down for a talk. Deravass could doubtless tell that there was trouble, and there'd be time to fill him in while they were *en route*. "Be a shame to waste a good head of steam. Let's hang on to that. Forward all camels for Old Fort. Can you spare a horse? I stole the pony, and there'll be dilapidations to pay, I'm afraid."

A much dustier cloud was coming up from behind Deravass. Deravass took a flask off of his saddle furniture and gave it to Fontenoy, who drank, warned by the luscious apple perfume that rose from its lip to do so sparingly. Excellent brandy. Sharpened a man's wits remarkably.

The road was full of men now, and Deravass was giving directions. "Talib," Deravass said. "Let my friend Fontenoy take your second horse. Beshar, take charge of the pony, and bring it on with the pack mules. It's close to run out. We're going to hurry on."

Talib's second horse was a handsome dun, a tall elegant animal so out of place that Fontenoy knew at first glance not to ask how it had gotten here. It took a moment or two to fit its stirrups to Fontenoy, who was a taller man than Talib. During that time one of Deravass's men pressed a packet of bread and cold mutton into Fontenoy's hands and Deravass stood, content to say nothing in the interests of not slowing things down.

"I'm indebted to the pony beyond telling," Fontenoy said to the man who took its reins, once Fontenoy was mounted and ready to turn back to the road. "I'm significantly obliged to it, and in awe of its powers of endurance. I owe it a life of green pastures and sweet forage. Please, tell it so for me." And opium cake. Dried date cake with opium. But they were already moving, and starting to pick up speed.

"I was getting anxious for the meeting," Deravass said, as the horses moved into a trot. "We hurried. Is it Shikander Beg's doing?"

Fontenoy was much farther off the ground now than he'd been on the yabu; he hoped he wouldn't fall off this one. Deravass had apparently talked him up, and he had a reputation to maintain.

"Not even a little, from what I've seen of him. Shikander Beg I like, Deravass. It was Lamish who started the trouble, though in all innocence."

How long had it been since he'd left Old Fort? A day and a half? Longer? But now they had fresh horses and good light. With luck they could be back in Old Fort valley by sundown tomorrow, if they rode all night. With luck they'd be in time to ensure the garrison's survival.

The bread and meat someone had given him was one of the most delicious sandwiches Fontenoy had ever eaten. What made it disgusting under normal circumstances—the congealed fatty part of the mutton—was comfort and energy in these.

"Shikander will hold them off if anybody can. He's good. But seriously shorthanded for the situation. And I thought, there's my friend Deravass, he'll have reinforcements."

Together Deravass Khan and Shikander Beg could dispel the threat that Broderick Holyoke had brought down upon them. If only they could get back to Old Fort in time.

The sun was two fingers above the horizon, the air so clear in the morning breeze that Shashka could see the struggles of the fallen and the faces of his enemies as he killed them.

He'd killed Russians. He'd killed Cossacks. He'd killed the noblemen and common soldiers of his enemies, allies of his foster-father. He'd killed his foster-father, and he'd killed his foster-brothers, because once he'd killed their father he'd had no choice. That he'd loved them made no difference.

He'd killed bandits and he'd killed men with his fists when they'd challenged his authority in the ranks or in caravan or camp, even though it was a waste of a strong back to kill a man. He'd killed women when he'd found them tortured and dying, their blood on his hands one last reproach for his failure to have protected them. He'd killed traitors when he was through with them and needed their heart's blood to cleanse his knife.

But never in all that time had anybody been as close to killing him as these rough stinking bandits from Fayzabad, here, now, on the roofs of the village of Old Fort, in final desperate defense of the sanctuary where he kept his caravan and his caravan people, Old Fort's people, Ismara and her women and his infant son.

He'd failed them. He should have ridden out in force against Cassim and his men on the first day. It was a mistake, he'd made it, but everybody here was going to pay the price for that mistake, because he'd failed to protect field and flock and forest and all the people in them. Again.

He'd given up the edge of his best weapon, the deployment of his sepahi cavalry, when he'd made the choice to stand and defend in place. He could have drawn off and waited while the enemy sacked Old Fort, looking for the rumored treasure.

Mirza Cassim's men—or the other bandits on the road—would have tortured the men for information. They would have killed the men and raped the women and taken the children as slaves. He would have been waiting in the woods to take revenge, but he couldn't have protected them, not from the woods. He would only have avenged their deaths, having let them die while he waited for his moment.

Sheer despair gave Shashka strength. Rising to his feet, he staggered to the wall and dragged the body of a now-dead man over the shallow parapet to fall in a misshapen heap at the foot of the village's perimeter walls. The body hardly looked recognizably human any more, and that at least was something.

He had only three things working in his favor. One of them

was Peri. The other was that so far they'd kept most of the fighting isolated on the rooftops, out of the village square. That forced the enemy to fight in twos and threes for sheer lack of space, and gave his twos and threes the advantage. It evened up the odds a little bit, but they were not going to be able to hold the rooftops forever.

And for the third thing, he was Shikander Beg Kavkazki, with everything to fight for.

He struck another of his enemies down. Old Fort's people fought bravely but it would all be over soon. Dacha had fallen; her sisters would fall, he'd fall, and then the raiders would team up on Old Fort's struggling people and take them one by one. Peri handed him one of his pistols and he shot a man. It didn't do him any good. He could only shoot one man at a time, and there were so many of them, and not enough of him.

Two paces to his left a hand reached up to grasp the low rim of the flat mud roof that made his battleground, a man whose headgear of whatever sort had been lost at some point. Down on one knee, reaching out, making a fist in the collar of the man's shirt and coat at once, Shaskha pulled the startled man toward him, and beat the man's head against the hard pounded surface of the rooftop again and again and again until he stopped twitching, while Peri stood at Shashka's side and shot anybody who might have taken advantage of Shashka's frustrated distraction.

He would not surrender to despair. He would not spend his last moments crying out against himself for failure. God who knew all things knew that Shashka had failed. He was going to take as much pre-emptive revenge for what would inevitably follow as he could, before he died.

Hand-to-hand with one loutish brute, Shashka struggled until Peri cocked his pistol underneath his arm and fired. The man went down. Taking one step forward, Shashka stabbed the man deep into the heart with his sword, just to be sure. The trap door on which he stood began to lift against his weight; Shashka staggered off, keeping his balance with an effort.

Sometime during the battle he'd been stabbed in the leg, just above his knee. He hated that. It had happened to him before, and a man had to ride, whether it hurt or not. He didn't have to worry about that this time. He wasn't going to be riding away. He'd lost his final battle, and it was the only one that counted from now until forever.

The trap door pushed out and away onto the roof and fell back with a crash, and up came Tamisen, pulling himself up through the trap door with an agile spring, a pistol in one hand and something folded close to his chest in the other. None of this was Tamisen's fault. Tamisen hadn't failed anybody. Maybe that would take away some of the bitterness of dying.

Peri swung the trap door closed and turned Tamisen with her hands so that he stood back-to-back with Shashka, so that the two of them were covering the wall in both directions. There was nobody on the ladders at this instant; all the ladders were down. For now.

"You shouldn't have come," Shikander called to Tamisen, over his shoulder. "I should have managed better. I'm sorry."

A man had climbed up the wall from the village square. Shashka could see by the man's clothes that he wasn't one of Old Fort's, but Tamisen just watched him, as if he was waiting for the man to move. The man clung there, apparently exhausted, hugging the wall with both arms. Why didn't Tamisen shoot?

"I've brought your weapon, lord," Tamisen called back, holding up his hand. What was it?

The shankha, the conch trumpet from the cave. That wasn't a weapon. Shashka wondered if Tamisen was hallucinating. He'd taken a hard blow to the head last night, on top of the knocks he'd sustained in the earthquake.

"Take it, Shikander lord. It's Devadatta. Your war conch. Sound the voice of transcendence. Tell them who you are."

The man hanging off the wall dropped one arm and came up with a pistol. Tamisen shot him—finally—but with what seemed to be reluctance. He did the job, right enough; neatly through the forehead. The man's body dropped back down into the village square once more.

It wasn't a good sign for them to be coming up from the village side of the rooftops.

"It's no use," Shikander said. If he'd had more rifles—if he'd had more time—if he'd been able to teach farmers to shoot in two days—"Look to your sword, Tamisen. It's the one with the sharp edge."

Peri reloaded and pushed Tamisen's pistol back into his belt. Shashka looked around him, left, right, down, searching for a target.

"Blow the war conch, lord," Tamisen insisted. "Raise your shield over Old Fort. Please. Hurry."

There would be no shield, and no salvation. Tamisen had to see that. Or maybe it was just as well if Tamisen died in expectation of winning out against all odds. Shashka couldn't wish a better death on this beguiling young man, with his peculiar habits and his open heart and his long braid and his heathen theology.

And in return for Tamisen's freely offered friendship, Shashka had condemned Tamisen to death out of Tamisen's own best instincts. That was what came of wanting to have friends. Tamisen had been ill served for his good intentions. No matter who killed Tamisen, Shashka was the one who had murdered him.

Someone came up the other side of the wall and Tamisen deflected the sword-cut that had been meant to kill him with a telling riposte from his own sword. Tamisen didn't seem to remember his reloaded pistol. Whether or not he was still in a daze from the blow to his head, he apparently had the idea so firmly fixed in his mind that he would hazard his life holding the conch, intent on Shashka's taking it.

The sooner Shashka bent to Tamisen's appeal the longer Tamisen would live, then, because a man was better able to protect himself and fight with both of his hands.

Two seconds, and no attack to be answered then and there. Shashka took the conch from Tamisen and set his lips to one end as Tamisen had shown him once before, in the valley after the earthquake; and blew. Nothing happened. Oh, yes, there was a sound, but it was nothing like the noise it made when Tamisen gave it voice.

"It's not mine," he said, tossing it back to Tamisen. Why did Tamisen look so stunned? "It's yours. You make it call." *And guard yourself.*

Three men, two coming for Shashka, one for Tamisen. Pushing off against Tamisen's back Shashka surged forward with a pistol in one hand and a sword in the other, cursing as his knee buckled beneath him, mollified only slightly by the blood of the man he killed despite his pain.

The second man backed away from Shashka's pistol. Was he planning on getting out of range in three paces? Shashka fired, but something was wrong. The man he shot fell bleeding; that wasn't it.

Tamisen was standing, just standing, there on the roof, no cover, no defense, raising the conch in both hands with his face uplifted to the heavens. He'd dropped his sword.

There was a man on the other side of Tamisen, taking aim with two pistols in hand. Shashka knew he wasn't going to be able to stop the man before he fired. Pulling out one of his reloaded pistols, Shashka pointed it anyway. He couldn't save Tamisen, but he could send Tamisen's murderer to Hell before Tamisen's body hit the ground.

Tamisen took a deep, deep breath, pursing his lips, raising the shankha to his lips. There was a sound.

The man who'd had his pistols aimed at Tamisen let them drop from suddenly palsied hands, falling to his knees, covering his head with his arms, groveling in the sandy layer of bloodied dust that lay on the flat roof with an expression of pure terror on his face. What was that sound?

The shankha. Only the shankha. Shikander had heard Tamisen's conch before. But now it resonated ancient and deep from the shell, its voice rolling across the rooftops, filling the village square, reverberating across to the walls beyond the village and echoing back again to the walls behind it, building in volume and authority as it resounded, echo after echo. Tamisen stood with his eyes closed and the conch raised to his lips, an expression of near-angelic serenity and joy on his face as the shankha sang.

Shaking himself from the paralysis of astonishment, Shashka looked to see who needed killing next, who needed to be driven off and pitched over the roof onto hard ground, who meant to attack the clearly insane Tamisen, how quickly he could fight through to the tower for one last desperate defense of Ismara and his son.

No attackers. No marauders. Only men cowering on the flat rooftops, sobbing aloud in fear.

Dacha stood up from where she'd fallen slowly, looking around her in disbelief. Shashka heard screaming; looking down into the village square he saw men in blind panic rushing toward the gate to escape, to get away. Running from the shankha as if from an entire Russian army.

Tamisen's conch had done all this? Was that what Tamisen had meant, when he'd said it was a weapon?

With a wild whoop of bloodthirsty triumph, Shashka slid down the ladder into the village square to hunt down those fleeing men and kill them while the conch had them on the run.

You take it, Shikander had said. All right. Jefferji let his sword drop. This would work or it wouldn't, and if it didn't, it was the end for all of them. *You are Devadatta*, he whispered to it in his mind. *You must have come into my hand for a good reason. May it be the one I hope for, Beloved.* Taking a deep breath, raising his face to the sky, Jefferji surrendered himself to hope and faith, and blew the war conch trumpet of Arjuna.

Like the spark of a flint, like the opening of the sluice gate of a dam, like the sinking of a spear point deep into its target the sound surged through Jefferji, emptying his body and mind alike of fear and doubt.

The voice of the conch roared out across the cosmos, and inside its massive golden bell Jefferji stood alone with the eternal sacred reverberation. *I am. Know me.* It was the voice of God, and it was neither terrible nor angry but full of love. *Let me back into your heart. Come home to me.*

What was that? Jefferji tried to catch the meaning of words he could grasp only imperfectly. *Come home?*

Because Krsna was lord, and not Shikander Beg. Krsna was lord, Jefferji was his servant, and Krsna had come home to Jefferji's heart to hold him there, close and beloved once more.

Not once more. Jefferji had heard that voice four times now since he'd left Tengarpore. He hadn't been listening. *I never left you. You went away from me, for a short while. Now you've come back, and we're together.*

What of the silence that had been in his heart, the pain of Krsna's absence, the anguish of exile from the divine Presence?

The door between us has been closed, but it was barred on your side, Jefferji. Not mine.

Jefferji blew the trumpet out of sheer joy, the tears streaming down his cheeks warm and welcome against his skin. It was all right for Shikander Beg and his people, the people of Old Fort. The bandits were defeated. The village was saved. That was the story of Arjuna's Devadatta, the celestial weapon that had scattered the enemy armies from the field of Kurukshetra, in the Kaurava wars. It was an important story, the most important story: lives protected, families saved.

But there was another story, personal and private, between Jefferji and the conch, just the two of them. A shankha had sounded outside the gates of Rama's city to tell his people that their prince was coming home, at last, after his years of exile. That was the conch that resounded in the streets of Ayodhya as the people, frenzied with joy, went out to welcome Rama.

Jefferji felt none of the pain from his wounds that he'd carried earlier. There was no doubt, no fear, no self-questioning. He knew his Beloved again, and this time he understood what it all meant. He'd heard his dear Friend's voice. Alone on the rooftops, with the trumpets of the defenders and the defeat of the attackers all around him, Jefferji held the shankha trumpet in his hands and danced the jubilation that possessed the city of Ayodhya when its Prince returned to its aching heart to be its King forever.

⛰

Shashka rode the hastily saddled Cherkess stallion through the gaping breach where the great gate had been, bits of burned wood and charcoal scattering beneath Cherkess's hoofs. Rounding the southwest corner of the village wall he kicked his heels against Cherkess's flanks out of sheer exuberance and joy in the sprint, and Cherkess flew over the debris, past the bodies in pursuit of the fleeing attackers.

Shashka wanted Mirza Cassim. He wanted the English Holyoke. They couldn't run very far. There was only one way out of Old Fort. He was going to find them, and when he found them he was going to kill them, one by one, until they were all dead. That would be good. It would be very, very good.

And there they were, just outside the gate, gathered in the road: fifteen, twenty men. One at least for each of his sepahis, two for him, because he was lord. He'd share the rest among them. Also because he was lord.

They'd piled their weapons in the road—pistols, rifles, swords. It was one of the oldest messages in all the world: *We surrender. Kill us if you like. We can't stop you because we have disarmed. Now make your move.* Shashka reined in and turned Cherkess's flank to the road, taking it in. He should be desolated. He should be disappointed. But not even this setback could destroy the strange exhilaration that had possessed him since he'd heard the conch sing. He was still drunk on it.

It shouldn't matter to him that they had surrendered. But it did. He knew that they were beaten, broken, put to flight; they did too.

He walked the Cherkess stallion forward. "Mirza Cassim?" At least him. Shashka was entirely within his rights to execute Cassim as a criminal, whether or not he had surrendered, because he'd lost. Shikander didn't know yet whether he'd kill Cassim or not. He'd decide later. "Where is the English Holyoke?"

Shashka had only seen Cassim the once, but the dirty and exhausted man who stood out in front of the assembled enemy would logically be him. Stepping forward, Cassim bowed as deeply as befit a man of war fairly bested in a bitterly contested battle. Still alive? Shashka could change that.

"I am Mirza Cassim. Your defeated enemy," the man said, in public acknowledgement of his position. "We've spoken once before, before your gates. We ask to surrender to Captain Fontenoy. The English Holyoke is not here."

Of course they'd prefer to surrender to an English Captain. Such men had generous natures. Not like Shashka. "When you say 'not here,' what do you mean? Dead? Deserted? Run away?"

"I sent Holyoke to help blow up the village gate, lord." Cassim's voice was steady, but underneath its surface calm Shashka could hear a sort of panic terror, fiercely reined in. "I haven't seen him since then. Have any of you?"

Shashka knew that sound in a man's voice. He liked to hear it from his enemies. Was Cassim his enemy? Yes; but also no.

Once a man had owned himself defeated he was a sort of commodity, not an enemy. Unless he was a Cossack.

In either case, neither Cassim nor any of his men could do anyone harm, anymore. Shashka could see it in their white faces, the way they stood, their worried frowns. Something had destroyed these men. It could only be Tamisen's shankha trumpet.

No one came forward with information, and Shashka knew for a resounding truth that if anyone could have, they would gladly have done so.

"Very well. Here it is, Cassim. You declared war on *me*, not Captain Fontenoy." He'd have to pursue the question of the English Holyoke's whereabouts separately. "It is of me you ask permission to surrender."

According to the rules of war as Shashka had learnt them there were two parts to a proper surrender: petition, and acceptance. They were not English rules. He was under no absolute obligation to accept Cassim's surrender, and the men were all at hazard of their lives until Shashka made up his mind.

Shashka had not accepted the surrendered weapons, either. He could as easily back up twenty paces, advise the men to defend themselves, and slaughter them outright whether they rushed for their weapons or not. Shashka struggled with himself, bloodlust against the peculiar drunken benevolence that resonated through his entire being like the voice of the conch. Finally he didn't decide so much as yield to the singing in his heart, the voice of God.

"Then I ask *you*, lord." Cassim was clearly determined, despite the fact that he was afraid. "Take what forfeits of us you will, it is your right. I brought some of these men here, and I led them all against you. You can be lenient, and let them go away."

It was honestly offered, and deserved an honest response.

"I will accept." Shashka turned to Captain Katische, who had come up beside him. "Destroy their weapons. Set them to work clearing away their dead and wounded."

She took the news more calmly than he had expected, merely nodding, and took a cigar out of her breast pocket, biting off one end and lighting it. The shankha had clearly affected her as well.

They'd need graves dug. The morning was still young, not

yet noon; fortunate, because there was much to be done. Casualty list. Survey of damages. Finding Holyoke. *He* wasn't covered in Cassim's surrender. He wasn't here. Holyoke was still fair game.

Shashka had to send someone to his wife to tell her of a successful and victorious resolution, and to see how his injured sepahis were. They would resent that they hadn't been in on the end.

"It shall be so, lord," Captain Katische said, as though she was talking about drill. She was as tranquil and serene as he had ever seen her. Where was Peri? Shashka wondered. Was Peri different too?

Hard by the thought, Peri came trotting up with prisoners in train, herded by villagers with long sharp sticks. "Here are these men. Some bodies are coming on a cart. We have put the English Holyoke in the cellar, so that the lord may consult with his women and Tamisen about his fate."

What did Tamisen have to do with it? Shashka had had sepahis in the tower. "I saw Tamisen dancing," Shashka said. Peri would know what answers he needed, here and now. "On the rooftops." Silhouetted against the sky, as though the thought that someone might shoot at so provocative a target had never crossed his mind.

"It was before, lord," Peri said, patiently, as though she believed he already knew. "When he woke up out of bed. The English Holyoke threatened Babira and Hetsatsa, then Wila and the women. Tamisen fought with him. New Wife fought as well. She provided the weapon."

Shashka noticed that for the first time Peri called Tamisen by name. That settled the question: they were all in one way or another under the same spell.

"Well, move these men down into the valley bottom. Let none remain inside the walls." The skies were clear, the day warm. No one needed a roof for protection this time of year. They could have small warming fires built from scrap half-burned wood from their fire-drake if a chill fell on toward morning, there was no need to torment them. Beaten men were—beaten.

What had happened? Tamisen had blown the trumpet, the enemy had lost all heart and fled in panic, Shashka himself was filled first with the sweet ecstatic certainty of victory and triumph and then a strange, unaccustomed forbearing sort of benevolence. His triumph was sudden and complete. He should feel drained and exhausted after the challenge of the battle; he did not, he felt refreshed, optimistic. His leg hurt, but in a sort of offhand, absentminded way.

There could be no harm in enjoying the experience. Shashka rode slowly back around the village walls and into the square, cheerful of mind and grateful in his heart to God for the deliverance of Old Fort from destruction.

Jefferji was the city of Ayodhya.

Wearing his finest clothes, his hair dressed with flowers, his arms heavy with bracelets of gold and jewels, he ran from room to room in the palace carrying enameled lamps with silken wicks filled with fragrant oils, lining the balustrade railings with lamps to light Rama home. Rama was already home. Krsna was in Jefferji's heart, and Jefferji's heart was full to bursting with the divine Beloved.

Old Fort's inhabitants were also people of Ayodhya, and simply didn't know it. That was all right. They didn't need to know why they were rejoicing, to rejoice.

Come down from the roof, Tamisen. You're wounded. The doctor wants you.

He didn't need a doctor. The supreme Doctor was within him. Jefferji danced at the lotus feet of the Dark One, full of praise and gratitude.

He was a peasant of Ayodhya. His wife drew patterns of joy in the street with their best wheat flour. Dripping from a bath at the town pump, Jefferji lined the top of the low wall outside his little house with shallow lamps of sun-dried clay whose roughly twisted cotton wicks burned clean and clear in the lightest sweetest rapeseed oil he had, to light the way through the dark December night and welcome Rama home.

Rashid was here. Jefferji knew Rashid. Rashid had been friendly and kind to him in Peshawar.

Come down from the roof, Tamisen sahib. You need to be examined. Your arm is injured. You must rest.

He could have kissed Rashid for the pure joy of being friends again, but he didn't want to stop dancing.

There was no more war in Ayodhya. Old Fort was safe. The crops would yield plentifully and all the female animals would bear sturdy, handsome young. Sri Krsna had spoken his name. He was reunited with his divine Beloved. Jefferji's happiness was too great to be spoken and too large to be contained within his body. Without the release of dancing, he would burst with it.

Some of the other nurses were from Shikander's women's quarters, and at least one of them had saved Jefferji's life. He saluted them respectfully within the dance as they came up onto the roof. Sita had come with queens and empresses in her train, all of them eager to serve her, all of them accepted and blessed with exquisite humility by Sita to show her husband increased honor.

Tamisen, come down. You'll fall off. You have a head injury. Everyone is worrying about you.

The soul was Sita, was Radha, eternally yearning for union with the Divine, and the Divine yearning in equal part for union with the soul. The soul was lover and beloved of Krsna.

The place in Jefferji's heart where he'd thought there was no longer any Krsna had hurt so much that he'd only survived by pretending that it wasn't there. Now his heart lay open, its aching wound soothed with balms of Paradisiacal sweetness. The prince was coming back to Ayodhya to be king. Sri Krsna reigned in Jefferji's rejoicing heart.

Shikander lord's wife was different from the other women of Ayodhya. She was a warrior woman of virtue and fire, the fierce defender of her son, her hearth, her husband, even without weapons or training. Hadn't she been the one who'd sent the hatchet spinning across the floor to Jefferji, and saved his life?

He greeted her with reverence. "I worship the god in you, wife of Shikander Beg," he said, and touched the ground at her feet. He didn't know her name. "May I benefit from your example in dharma. May I marry a woman with whom it would not insult you to be compared."

But she didn't speak Urdu. She wouldn't know what he was saying. "Hakim Jericho can't come up to see you," she said. "You must go down to him. Your lord would will it. Captain Fontenoy would will it."

She could say *I will it*, and he would go. Who did she mean when she said "your lord?" But she was right, which didn't surprise him. Sri Krsna was tender of his bhaktis. Jefferji was as drunk on Krsna as a Mira Bai; Shikander's wife had come to sober him up, just a little.

He put aside the music in his mind for later, and followed her down the ladder from the roof-top to the ground floor. She led him across the rubble-strewn inner court to the tower, and carefully he climbed one-handed up the ladder to the first floor, the one where Shikander Beg had pitched his tent.

Simon was there, with the women who served Shikander Beg's wife. Simon sat him down on a box outside the tent, cutting open his sleeve to wash the wound in his arm and bind it up. Jefferji didn't mind what Simon did with his arm so long as nobody tried to take the shankha away.

"It's deep enough," Simon said, maybe to Jefferji, maybe to Shikander's wife. "Wounded men can sometimes go for hours without noticing, or so I've been told. It's a sort of euphoria. It won't last, I'm afraid."

But Jefferji knew the source of his euphoria, the joy that came from knowledge of the presence of Sri Krsna in his heart. He wished he could explain. They seemed worried about him. They didn't need to be. He of all men in Creation was most was in perfect health, in perfect happiness, in the perfect presence of the divine Beloved.

"Drink this," the wife of Shikander Beg said. Something bitter; also, there was opium. They thought he was in pain. Should he be? It didn't matter. "Now lie down and rest, yes, here in the bed, just as before. The lord wills it. Close your eyes. Sleep."

Wasn't there still work to do? Shouldn't he be out with the sepahis, with Shikander Beg, with the people of Old Fort, helping Simon treat the wounded and the sick? Apparently not. Simon had washed and wrapped a wound, Shikander's wife had told Jefferji to lie down. A woman of her caliber wouldn't do that if there was anything else she needed him to do.

Someone laid a fine silk quilt over him, tucking it up under his chin. This was good. It smelled like woodsmoke and resin incense, green herbs and tobacco. Smiling, Jefferji commended up his soul to Krsna's lotus feet and went to sleep.

Chapter Fourteen
Liminal Space

Boy had made the bath for her lord herself, though she was tired. Everybody was tired. There were people in this place to make baths, but they as much as the lord's women and his sepahis deserved rest, because it was not their place in the world to fight and kill, and yet they had been warriors.

Nor had Lamish's people waited for Boy's word to fetch hot water for her into the tower bucket by bucket. She herself carried them up to the second floor.

There was a leather tub that the lord used for bathing. Ismara and her women had used it to bathe too-tall Tamisen who was as skinny as a stork before they had put him to bed. In the lord's bed, as it had been before, because Boy thought it made good sense do that and New Wife clearly agreed and had directed it already for convenience.

It was the best bed in all of Old Fort, after all. Tamisen Stork-Dancer had earned the privilege of sharing it with the lord who was an angel, because with the magic in the conch trumpet Stork Tamisen had served the lord well. And served equally all other souls abiding in Old Fort, men and women and children and chickens and oxen alike. Also horses and ponies. Everybody. Even—an odd thought, outside of Boy's understanding—the lord's Peri. That was a sort of serving the lord, as well.

She bathed her lord with a rich soap she carried hidden from him for such a time as this, its scent of frankincense and roses like the prayer offered up to angels. She knew the weariness in his body from his patient silence, letting himself be bathed. The towels were warmed over the hearth fire opposite his tent on the bare stone floor. She didn't bother with his shirt. He would be warm enough; she would see to it.

Nor did he give any sign of awareness that he had Tamisen in his bed, not even though it had been by his direction. She had good reasons to observe her lord's orders, when they corresponded with her sense of the fitness of things. When her lord was settled with his head on the pillow, Boy went to wash herself in turn.

There was one last bucketful of hot water. She saved it for the rinse. It was a blessing and a grace from God to have hot water. She would be sure to thank the women who had boiled it. More than ever, she was sure that Old Fort deserved the lord's protection.

Toweling her short hair dry, putting on a fresh clean shirt, she stopped at the top of the ladder down to the first floor, calling down quietly and calmly so that she wouldn't wake the lord. "Is all well? We sleep."

In the days that they'd first come to Old Fort, she would not have let Lamish guard an egg, but now she would grant him the honor he had earned.

He answered, "We clean up, Miss Boy. The doctor works. Four men stand with weapons so the lord may sleep."

The lord's enemies were outside the walls, in the valley. Their weapons were all gone; the lord had them. Let Lamish think that his people on watch were the reason the lord could sleep. It did no harm, and made part of the lord's thanks to Lamish.

"Thank you," Boy said, sounding the words carefully in her mind so that she was sure of the pronunciation, because it was not a thing she could remember saying before. "We rejoice in your care. We all sleep now within, secure in your protection. It will be hours."

That was a hint for Lamish to go away. Boy didn't wait. She went into the lord's tent instead, and took off her shirt. She wouldn't be needing it either. She got into the bed on the other side of Tamisen; that was how it had been when the brother of Princess Bride had wished to share her body.

That one had been surprised to find two rather than just one other in the bed, and to realize that the lord might share Boy, but did not loan her out. Here and now for all his warrior passion the lord was tired, the fury of his rage did not sustain him, and he might not wish to mount. She made no assumptions.

Before she lay down, she took Stork Tamisen's measure. Tall. Bony. His right arm injured, but he would roll to his left with her behind him and toward the lord, so that was as it should be. Angular and skinny to her taste, but she had an angel as the model of perfect masculinity, so it was no shame to Stork Tamisen to be called less. Gently she touched his mouth, parting his lips with the tips of her fingers. Gently she stroked his chest.

Gently she caressed his privities, and set the play in motion in that manner, urging him to roll toward her lord with judicious petting and pats where they would be best sensed and sought after. She sensed the stirring of Jefferji's body. She heard his breath begin to come more quickly. Reaching beneath his right arm she shifted him, carefully, so that his hand lay upon her lord's body near the hip.

She could feel muscle move as Stork Tamisen shifted his hand, in his sleep, as though his fingers sought the warmth of her lord's body there beside him. Now she had done what she could, and it was up to them. She lay down close behind him to wrap her arms around him and amuse herself, but she had serious intent in mind all the same: because now she would find out whether Tamisen was a fit companion to her lord in all things.

Jefferji lay in blissful reverie, his body resonating still with the touch of the Dark One. He knew this feeling. It was safe, familiar, comforting; it was the memory of the caress of Sri Krsna in his mind, after Jefferji had danced to delight his lord. It was a place outside of time. He didn't try to call to mind the exact details, the where, the when, or the with whom.

Sometimes the beloved of Sri Krsna came to him in the

quiet dark, embarrassed by their desire for the Beloved, unwilling to face the risk of recognition when the day came new and Jefferji was simply a dancer, Hari-Prasad, again, and not the spirit-filled surrogate of God or the divine Consort.

Sometimes it was dark because it was the night of the Vrindavana forest. Jefferji didn't know whose hand caressed him sweetly, but integral to the love play of the Beloved and his consort in the scented paradise of the night and the forest were the gopis who held the candle, and who for their reward stood in joyful witness of the eternal play between the soul and its Lover.

It was a woman at his back, he could tell that by the touch of her sweet soft breasts. The other who lay in the bed with him had brought a perfume of green herbs and tobacco—so Jefferji knew that he was being approached with reverent desire in the person of the god himself, as one of the milk-maids of the forest.

He knew this dance. It was one he'd rejoiced in practicing since he had been judged fit by wise old priests to go sport in widely various ways in all of the fields of the Lord. He was happy, he was relaxed, he was filled with the love of the Dark One. He reached out, and touched the strong supple muscled thigh of a warrior, and sighed with pleasure.

He was a milkmaid on a bed of flowers, marveling at the beauty of Sri Krsna's body in the blue moonlight. It was permitted. It was encouraged. The gopi at Jefferji's back reached around his chest, and scratched him with specific intent with her fingernail. She, too, had read of Sri Rama's sport with Sita in the garden, and joined them in love play.

But where was the divine Beloved? Had Jefferji misread the situation? Had he been too drunk on the reverberation of Arjuna's Devadatta to understand what the drumbeat was, and what the dance? Jefferji frowned in his half-sleep, in confusion.

Then the warrior put his hand around the back of Jefferji's head and kissed him. Jefferji opened to the kiss, welcomed, reassuring, promising. He knew the taste of that mouth. It was of recent acquaintance, one he was anxious to cultivate, and at its touch he thought he heard a rumbling in the background of his arousal, a muted sound as if of thunder or a lion snarling in the woods.

Did lions snarl in woods? The thought passed across the threshold of his consciousness, like a warning note from the strings of a rubab lute. *Or did they rather snarl in a wide grassy basin of green wheat blowing in a cold wind, with black clouds full of thunder all around?*

Jefferji thirsted for that kiss, asking for another, and then another. The lion-warrior traded with him, kiss for kiss, tenderly, until in his eagerness Jefferji reached forward to explore his lover's body more intimately and expand the range of his caresses.

The lion turned toward him as if by predatory instinct, seeking contact skin-to-skin, marking a shift in the tempo of the drums from pleasurable dalliance to more passionate urgency. Jefferji shifted, so that he could press into that intimate arousal more closely, eager for the touch.

The lion slipped his arm beneath Jefferji's hand where it lay against his flank to reach toward the back of Jefferji's thigh, as if to hold him in place while the lion sought the perfect fit. The unexpected gesture seemed to touch something in Jefferji's arm, something painful, making him cry out softly in surprise. *Oh, yes*, Jefferji thought, fuzzy and unfocused, as his physical senses sharpened instant by instant with increasingly intense focus. *Wounded, somewhat. Right arm. Doesn't hurt, exactly.*

The thought was overwhelmed. The overriding message of Jefferji's body was unambiguous, clarion-voiced, convincing. *Again.* He sought the right place to fit himself against his lover—did he have more practice than a lion did?—and knew that he had found it when the lion gasped in delight, and began to move with deliberation, searching for a rhythm that would please them both. The joy of the communion filled Jefferji's heart with grateful prayer, and yet somehow he could still hear a whisper in his mind. *Again?*

The woman behind him, the gopi with the candle to watch their love play, pressed herself hard close against his back to bolster him against the lion's strength. The lion held to a walking pace, as if he was looking for something. What could it be? And still the voice in Jefferji's mind—*again.*

The lion lifted his hand away from Jefferji's hip, laid it over Jefferji's arm at the elbow, slid his hand up toward Jefferji's shoulder—as though looking for something—found what he sought, and pressed down gently where it hurt. Firmly, but with the diffuse pressure of the heel of his hand, and not hard.

Oh, yes, Jefferji's body said to him, distress displaced by amorous alchemy into a pleasurable sort of sharpness.

The night sky above the Vrindavana forest was full of stars, each one of them brilliant bursts of blue-white joy. Jefferji danced himself into dissolution in the arms of a lion whose breath tasted of tobacco and green herbs, and went to sleep.

It was quiet, the sunlight muted, in Shashka's tent in Old Fort's tower, in his bed made up on its stack of carpets, silk and wool overlaid with linen sheets that smelled of sun and well-packed pillows. New Wife had worked the embroidery in silk on the pillow covers, the same blue as the sapphire he wore for a turban jewel, the sapphire of their young son's eyes. He would call her Battle Wife. She'd proved herself a warrior as much as any sepahi Hell-rider.

That thought came across his mind from left to right and vanished from his consciousness. He was exhausted, afloat in bliss. The dancer Tamisen lay sleeping beside him, for all the world as though his whole body had melted into the sleeping-carpets, as if Shashka's entire bed was Tamisen's embrace and Shashka in it. It was hard to keep his thoughts together, in such a state, nor had he any anxiety on the subject.

Shashka knew the pleasure that came after ecstasy, yet this was different. He was Shikander Beg Kavkazki. He'd never lain with a partner but that always in the back of his mind was caution, warning, a state of alertness however attenuated, because it was when a man was most at rest that he was most in danger.

Tamisen had sounded the conch. Shashka felt no fear.

The war-trumpet, Tamisen had called it, the conch of his heathen hero Arjuna, peerless in battle, beloved of the God to whose service Tamisen had devoted his life from childhood, even as a Circassian noble might devote himself to war.

Shashka had felt its reverberations, in his heart. He felt them still. He lay with Tamisen in his bed as though at the center of the universe, secure, fortunate, protected and protector.

His eyes were closed, and yet he saw right through his lowered lids. But it wasn't the wall hangings of his tent he saw before him, pitched within the tower. It was the sun-dappled forest girdling the slopes of his home mountains, as if his eyes themselves were remembering, as if he were not Shashka at all. As if he saw visions from his childhood.

He knew this forest, its great towering oaks and elms and evergreens, its torrents of sweet cold pure white water, the great snow-covered mountains he'd once believed were the tallest in the world, with power to protect them from any invader.

That forest wasn't even still there, any longer. The Russians had come, and taken fruit and grain and horses for themselves. Shashka had gathered who he could and fled to higher mountains, but he no longer believed they had a power to shelter and protect him.

It was a land out of time, a longed-for unreality, in which the horse of his will and of his wishing rode through a fairy-land without grief or blood or sorrow. By that fact alone it was proved unreal. He cherished its visitations even so, but this time it was different. There was somebody there. A shadow of a man seemed to ride beside him—to one side, and nose-to-neck with the Cherkess stallion—someone who should by rights of expectation be "Jefferji" Tamisen, yet who was not.

Whoever it was, was Tamisen-sized. And somewhat Tamisen-shaped. He rode peculiarly attired, his shoulders wreathed in garlands made out of marigolds. There was the shankh trumpet, the conch with its gleaming pearlescent lip and its mouthpiece of gold, hanging on a sash of rich brocade around the man's neck.

It felt good to be riding with that man. It felt right, fitting, appropriate, as if with a reflection in some sense of Shashka himself. And yet, and yet, and yet.

Shashka couldn't see the man's face.

Shashka knew the man was riding beside him. Yet he couldn't turn his head to look the man in the eye. The man rode bare-chested, but there was something draped over his back: a deer-skin, with its hooves intact and hanging down across the man's arms. A headdress. He wanted so much to see the face of his companion—

With an effort Shashka seized control of his own vision, stopped the Cherkess stallion, let the man who rode beside him walk on ahead.

It was the deerskin entire that the man wore, head and horns as well as hooves, the antlers of a giant stag rising from its skull that was fitted on the man's head like a helmet. Or a crown.

Shashka had seen antlers and skull alike only once, a cherished exhibit and a wonder mounted on the hall of the greatest lord in all the land of Shashka's birth. The skeletal skull and antlers of an extinct breed that had gone away from the world too many centuries ago to be counted up and numbered.

They were no longer on the slopes of a high meadow in the Caucasian mountains. It was an immense grassy plain, the air pregnant with rain and perfumed with a coming storm.

The man who wore the shankh trumpet turned his horse to face Shashka, but Shashka still couldn't see the man's face. There was a full blue-white moon caught within the points of that great antlered headdress, like a gemstone in a setting of silver prongs. The light was too bright for Shashka to see the man's face.

Shashka raised his hands toward the antlers of that ancient, extinct stag, and thought: *If I can but take the moon between my hands I will perish, and not regret the cost.*

Not yet. It wasn't time. Not yet.

Shashka longed for the moment. The man with the full moon in his antlers seemed to long for it as well. But it was not for him to demand the moment of transcendence. Shashka dropped his arms.

Dismounting, the man who wore the great stag paced a few steps in front of where Shashka sat astride the Cherkess stallion, and began to dance in the green grass that blew in the wet wind of the advancing storm.

Shashka felt himself dissolve into the universe: and slept.

Chapter Fifteen
For Love and Friendship

Deravass's scout rode up quickly, pulling to a halt at the last minute to bring his horse alongside Fontenoy's. "All quiet. There's nothing to be seen. No fires. No sounds of fighting."

Fontenoy's heart sank. Had the conflict been so soon concluded, after all? But if it was, wouldn't there be a noise of looting and debauchery, and enslaved men at work to unearth the treasure cave?

"Temporary lull," Deravass said, so swiftly that Fontenoy knew exactly what was in his mind. "They may be waiting for us. Or they may have run away. Let's go find out."

If there was a trap, the less time they gave their ambushers to prepare for them the better. If there was no trap because the issue was decided, it was best to grapple with the truth head-on, immediately, and spare themselves the agony of hope. Fontenoy pushed forward into the lead; Deravass permitted it.

Here it was, the place where the road crossed the crest of the hill and started down into the valley following the stream. Dismounting, Fontenoy led his borrowed horse through the low scrub well off to one side of the beaten path. There was no point in recklessness or stupidity. He had to see the valley for himself, but without being seen. At least until he knew the shape of things, and what might have become of Old Fort.

It was as the scout had said. There was nothing. Anxiously Fontenoy scanned the valley bottom for any sign, any clue. Some horses were at graze at the streamside, down at the foot of Old Fort; they were too far away for him to tell whether they were the sepahis's steppe ponies or enemy horse. There were goats in the valley below his vantage point. No fire, no smoke rising into the air from Old Fort, no sounds of fighting. Everything was calm—the calm of conquest. They were too late.

Oh, Tamisen. Fontenoy closed his eyes in bleak despair. They'd done their best. It hadn't been enough. He should have gone in search of Deravass much sooner, even before they knew Cassim's numbers.

Deravass came up and crouched down in the brush at Fontenoy's side. "Come on. We'll ride down into the valley and have a look. All need not be lost."

Yet from the grim note in Deravass's voice, Fontenoy knew that his old friend saw the same signs as he did. "Right you are." *Never jump to conclusions.* Making a snap judgment when it was required was one thing. Defeating oneself in advance was quite another.

Well spread out across the line of advance, keeping clear of the road, Deravass's men led their horses over and across the crest of the hill that formed the northern extent of the valley. Fontenoy traveled down the road alone; as a single man and on foot he would not seem to be a threat, and if the worst had come to pass—as it seemed it had—Mirza Cassim's men would want Tamisen alive, because Tamisen knew where the supposed treasure lay.

They would be searching for gold and jewels. Had they already found the cave, and its contents? What would become of the inscriptions, the statuary? What had become of Tamisen, and Simon Jericho?

As the road descended, more of the valley came into view. There was the little lake at Old Fort's feet. The floodwaters had receded; there was a marsh between the lake and the mouth of the valley, but no longer one undivided body of water. There were the walls of Old Fort, standing serene and silent beneath the afternoon sun. There was the little grove of trees in which Fontenoy had found Tamisen that evening a scant six days ago.

Fontenoy turned away into the roadside undergrowth like a man in search of a dry spot that needed watering, and joined Deravass Khan, who had been shadowing him, so he could point out the grove to him. It would make a good command post. Holyoke had been there, but he'd been brought there on foot, and it had been nighttime. Holyoke probably had other things on his mind right now: treasure, gold, jewels. How did Holyoke mean to take those things for his, when it was Mirza Cassim who had stood all the risk?

The question gave Fontenoy a moment's worth of bleak satisfaction followed by bitter regret. Holyoke. If he hadn't asked Holyoke to escort Tamisen to Peshawar in the first place, none of this need ever to have happened. There might well have been some miscellaneous treasure seekers to be discouraged, but Holyoke's intervention had shifted things onto a much larger scale. Because Holyoke had thought he'd take a share. Because Holyoke had planned to create the threat, and then offer to rescue them.

A sudden flash of white light caught Fontenoy's eye. A leaf could catch the sun, when the breeze turned it, but this was a much stronger spark, like the sunlight reflected in a running stream or a wind-raised wave. A good time to step back into the road, Fontenoy decided. With a nod to Deravass, Fontenoy walked back into the road, making a show of adjusting his trousers, to see if he could locate the source of that signal, for signal it was.

There it came again, a sun flash from a reflective surface of some sort. Someone had been waiting for them? Fontenoy felt a savage satisfaction in his heart. Holyoke knew nothing of Deravass Khan, because Fontenoy hadn't said anything about him to Tamisen before Tamisen got to Peshawar, and very little even there. Nor had Fontenoy spoken more than a few words about his old friend while he was in Peshawar where Rashid might have overheard him.

Holyoke would not know Deravass's history. He might well try to use Deravass against Fontenoy. They could get into the fort, they could infiltrate, they would be revenged.

After a moment Deravass joined him, as close as he could get and still hope for concealment among the scrub bushes at the roadside.

"Sloppy work," Deravass said softly. "We shouldn't have seen that. What kind of amateurs does your Holyoke have in his employ?"

Someone burst from the bushes the signal had come from, someone very small. A boy. A boy, breaking from cover and running right for them up the middle of the road, waving his arms wildly over his head and yelling at the top of his lungs.

"Aye-yay-yay! Fontenoy sahib! Fontenoy sahib!"

Fontenoy traded glances with Deravass, perplexed. He knew that little boy. That was Berni, Tamisen's companion the last time Fontenoy had come down by this path. Berni didn't sound frightened; he sounded excited, and happy.

If Berni was Holyoke's sentry, he had no idea Holyoke meant Fontenoy any harm. Berni didn't sound like a boy whose parents were being held hostage to guarantee good behavior and advance warning of Fontenoy's return. With a quick nod to Deravass—*I know this child*—Fontenoy put took two steps forward and put his hands on his hips.

"See here, what is the meaning of this, young man?"

He hadn't meant that to come out as sternly as it had. Berni didn't speak Fontenoy's dialect of stern, however, coming to a standstill just short of flinging himself bodily on Fontenoy for an exuberant hug. Unabashed, Berni smiled and waved his arms again, for the benefit of someone watching from Old Fort's walls, perhaps.

"They're going to kill some sheep and have a feast. Where are your men? Tamisen sahib said you'd have some."

Fontenoy simply couldn't reconcile Berni's good cheer with the catastrophic destruction of the garrison. "Who are 'they,' Berni?" Despite himself, despite his certainty of the dangers of wishful thinking that had betrayed him more than once in the past, Berni's reference to "Tamisen sahib" engendered hopeful feelings in Fontenoy. "And where are the sheep?"

There hadn't been sheep to spare in Old Fort when he'd left. Berni wouldn't call a lamb a sheep. It was too late. Fontenoy was already hoping.

"Those sheep, Fontenoy sahib," Berni said, pointing out across the valley at a slope-side field littered with grey rocks. Fontenoy squinted; some of the grey rocks were moving. "Come, Fontenoy sahib, the lord is waiting for you."

And what is his name? Fontenoy couldn't decide if he had the courage to ask that question or not. What if the answer was Shikander Beg? But what if it was Mirza Cassim?

Deravass came up out of the grass and stood in the middle of the road, looking through a monocular field glass. "I see a skewbald horse. Tall rider. Coming this way."

Tamisen was the tallest man in Old Fort. Deravass didn't know that. There was only one skewbald horse that Fontenoy had seen there, and he hadn't mentioned Tamisen's mare to Deravass either, as far as he could remember.

Deravass was still watching, carefully. All Fontenoy could see was a smallish speck of some sort coming up the road past the still-swollen pond, and he wasn't sure he saw even that much. He could be imagining it.

"Something to catch the eye about his pagri," Deravass said. "Wears his hair in a braid, maybe. Do you know him, Fontenoy?"

Running past Fontenoy to Deravass's side, now—clearly confident that Deravass was a friend, and why wouldn't he be? He'd come with Fontenoy, after all—Berni pointed. "Tamisen sahib," Berni exclaimed, and took the burden off Fontenoy's shoulders. "The doctor said not to tell him until we saw you."

Deravass whistled sharply two times, a signal for his men to stop where they were and wait for developments.

Fontenoy couldn't wait. At his horse's side in seven long strides, he mounted, setting off down the road at as fast a pace as the borrowed horse could manage. It had to be Tamisen. But Fontenoy couldn't be sure until he saw for himself, until he could put his arms around the boy. The man. No one who had survived the battle Fontenoy had left could be less than that.

The dun horse didn't know why Fontenoy was in such a hurry, but exerted itself to the utmost regardless. Luckily, it was a sure-footed beast.

Fontenoy got as far as the foot of the slope when he could see, could *see*, that the man on the skewbald horse still minutes away but closing fast was Tamisen. It couldn't be anybody else.

Fontenoy stopped his horse and wept, to get it out of the

way. He didn't want Tamisen to know how close he'd come to believing Tamisen was dead.

Tamisen came pelting up at top speed. The flying dismount he executed was not among the finer examples of Rajput horsemanship but would do in a pinch. He was bandaged around his shoulder and at his right arm, his braid hung free at the back of his neck beneath his pagri turban, and he hadn't shaved for several days by the look of his face. But for all the outward signs of his almost twenty years, when he took Fontenoy in his arms it was with the artlessness of an eight-year-old. Now Tamisen was the one who wept.

"Thought you might be dead, sir," Tamisen said, half-choked, and cleared his throat. "Simon promised he'd examined all the bodies, and Rashid said he'd seen you. But still. Night rides, confusion. I'm so glad to see you. Sorry."

"Don't be sorry," Fontenoy said, and kissed the boy on both of his stubbly cheeks. How proud Ganders would have been. "You're safe? The village is safe? Jericho? The women? Shikander Beg? What happened? Tell me all about it—no, tell me later. See here. This man is Deravass Khan."

Deravass, with Berni riding pillion, had come on rather more slowly, and his men with him. "Someone manured that plot better than his father's," Deravass said, dismounting, looking up into Tamisen's face. "This is he? My name is Deravass Khan. Your father was a friend."

"I'm very pleased to meet you, sir."

Fontenoy saw the smile in Deravass's eyes, passing so quickly that it could easily be missed entirely. Ganders had been a faultlessly polite man, for all his piratical appetite for mayhem.

Tamisen continued. "You're expected, Captain Fontenoy, Deravass Khan, all. It's my pleasure to invite you and your men on behalf of Shikander Beg to Old Fort to share our party. Shikander won't allow it to be called a victory party, but 'survival' seems less festive to me somehow."

Tamisen wasn't dead. Neither was Shikander Beg. There were enough people to eat at least eight sheep. Something had averted a tragedy in the making, and Fontenoy was willing to wait to find out what it was for the gratification the bald fact provided to his heart.

"Let's say gratitude, then, perhaps," Deravass suggested, without shifting his gaze away from Tamisen.

Fontenoy wondered what Deravass saw. Fontenoy himself had known Tamisen for so long, and watched him grow; maybe he wasn't the man to judge whether and how much Geoffrey looked like his father.

"For myself I will be sincerely grateful for hot water and roast mutton. Bring me before Shikander Beg, Geoffrey Tamisen. I've been curious to meet him, and now more than ever."

"And tell us everything that's happened since I left," Fontenoy added, watching Deravass watch Tamisen mount his mare with an artless grace that would be perhaps wrenchingly familiar. Old times. He hadn't been able to afford thinking about it in the past few days, but now that it seemed things were going to be all right, it was safe for him once more to look forward to Deravass getting to know Tamisen. "Start out with how things are in the village, right now."

Now, very soon, the secret treasure of Deravass Khan that Fontenoy had brought Tamisen all of this way to discover would be revealed.

The rooftops of Old Fort village had been all cleaned and cleared, bloodstains washed away, the surfaces freshly smoothed with white clay. If he looked over the low parapets into the village square below Jefferji could see that there were feasting platforms covering half the area, just a foot or so off the ground, but high enough to provide the dogs with many opportunities for their own feast on scraps and the bits and pieces of things that invariably found their way to the ground when so many people were eating at one time.

The sepahis were there; Deravass Khan's men; Shikander Beg's party; the villagers. Four sheep, and Shashka had a lamb prepared for Ismara and her ladies. Shikander's wife and child feasted alone in the tower with her women, but she'd sent out sweets prepared by her own hands, pastry and crushed nuts drenched in honey and rose water. Fontenoy had brought Jefferji something like that pastry from time to time, when he'd been a little boy, to share with his mother. Jefferji still treasured the memory.

He and Simon got to sit with lordly men on the roof with the best view of the festivities, sharing the lowermost corners of a rug with the entire leadership—Mekmout the headman, representing the village in the convalescent Lamish's absence; Shikander Beg, Fontenoy, Deravass Khan, and Captain Katische counted all together. It was a privileged company.

The sun was shining. It was warm. The mutton had been rubbed with garlic, roasted with onions and potatoes, and was served with hot flat bread and sweet relishes of apricots and raisins. There was tea and milk-thinned yoghurt sweetened with honey and wine to drink, and all in all life was very good, even if Captain Fontenoy had suffered a disappointment with respect to maps.

"So the fires didn't do much damage, Fontenoy sahib," Mekmout was saying. "There were none until the last day, and then mostly in the stables. We think somebody tried to steal a horse to run away with his loot, or claim one as a prize. The lord's Cherkess stallion would have made any man's fortune."

And whatever "somebody" it might have been had struck a flint, perhaps to light a spill and see what was what in the windowless stable.

"All of the horses came out safely. But your saddle furniture suffered, and that of Tamisen sahib."

Saddles and tack gone, charred and flame-eaten and simply burned. Fontenoy shook his head. "My map was with my saddle," he said to Deravass sadly. "And I hoped to sell it for good money to the Bengal British. And some other people with an interest, perhaps, as well."

From the way Deravass laughed, Jefferji guessed this was an inside joke of some sort. He liked Deravass Khan, and not just because he told stories about Jefferji's father that Jefferji had never heard from Fontenoy. Fontenoy had known Jefferji from childhood, and still sometimes seemed to slip back into a semi-parental role. Some of the stories Deravass was willing to tell were not suitable for children.

"My notes are safe," Simon said. "But they were supplemental, not primary. I'm sorry, Captain Fontenoy."

But Fontenoy waved the apology off. "No, no, you did just as I asked you, and I'll see you well requited. It's the least I can do."

What was so good about this was that it gave Jefferji the opportunity to spring his surprise on Fontenoy at exactly the right moment, for maximum effect. Well. Whether it was the *very* best moment he had no way to know, but it was unquestionably a good one. Jefferji stood up and backed away off of the sitting rug, looking for a little room.

Fontenoy was looking at him with curiosity, as were they all. Jefferji hummed a little to himself, and knew by the quick flash of irritation that raced across Fontenoy's face that he recognized it. Nodding to himself—yes, that was where he'd started—Jefferji started to dance.

"Leaving Chitral," Jefferji said, and put a few steps down. "Twelve miles to cross the river, open country, some eggs from a farmer's house at six and a half miles. Three miles up a defile to a watercourse still running but probably dry later in the season. We camped early, though we had started a little late."

Fontenoy was staring, now. Jefferji continued to dance, delighting in the success of his surprise.

"Eight miles to the next water. The road climbs three times up and two times down, two and a half miles, north by northwest but only seven seconds by your compass 'reckoning', if I have the word right. Another climb at six and one-third miles, for two hundred feet. The saddle is very stony, and there was no water for the horses, but after eleven miles from our camp there was a spring and good forage. We found lucerne and grass. I'll stop there for now, because it was a long way here."

Because the point was made, and he knew how to yield the floor before the audience was sated.

Fontenoy burst into applause. "That was your damned tune all along! Geoffrey. My boy. This is wonderful."

"And I have your compass readings in my notes, sir." Jefferji sat back down on the rug, immensely pleased with how it had gone over. "From Peshawar to Old Fort. We can check them, on the way back."

Deravass shook his head. "Your father..." Stopping for a moment; what? Caught up in nostalgic emotion? "Your father had the devil's ear for music, Tamisen. Mostly love songs of, ah, all kinds. It made him good at carrying dispatches when we couldn't afford to have them written down. I remember once—"

"Dar Hadji," Fontenoy suggested.

"Yes, Dar Hadji. General Annet sent very detailed orders to Colonel Clark. Your father carried them in his head for fear of interception, and Colonel Clark's orderly wrote them out from Tamisen's recitation. We compared them later, Colonel Clark's copy, the ones General Annet's clerk had recorded. One word different, because, Tamisen said, the general had made a grammatical error in the heat of the moment; but otherwise a good man's career was saved, on that evidence."

"All because of Tamisen's report," Fontenoy said to Jefferji.

Nobody had told Jefferji this about his father before. Nobody. All of his life he'd thought that he was good at picking up dance steps and patterns because his grandfather Daoji, his mother's father, had passed the talent on to him. Maybe it was both. Or maybe it had been his father all along. That was an interesting thought. Maybe he liked it.

"So you and Deravass both knew Tamisen's father." Shikander's voice carried a little note of polite reservation, as if to see whether he was to be welcomed into this conversation or not. "But Tamisen did not. The world is cold. It seems he was a father well worth knowing."

Jefferji had told Shashka about that, yes. After the earthquake. Fontenoy and Deravass exchanged glances, smiling, and suddenly Jefferji smelled a secret, one even greater than the one he'd just sprung on Fontenoy.

"It is a very great shame. We loved each other very much," Deravass said to the table. To the dish of dried figs stewed in honey-water, in particular. "He went north across the Hindu Kush on some errand, and never came back. For nearly twenty years we've searched for any information about who sent him, or where he'd gone, and why. Fontenoy with his friends among the Bombay British, and the Mahrattas. Jaisal Singh amongst the Rajput princes. Me, in the mountains and villages."

Fontenoy glanced from Deravass's face to the sky with what looked to Jefferji to be a somber expression on his face, as though the face of his friend was too full of shared bereavement for Fontenoy to be able to bear it. "Nothing," Fontenoy said. "No trace. A note in the commissary records in Bombay about kit and money drawn on hand receipt. Ready cash to keep a man six months, perhaps. No word of explanation."

"Until eighteen months ago." Deravass Khan seemed to have made up his mind about something, squinting up into the sun—much as Fontenoy had done—as he spoke. "I wrote to Fontenoy, of course, but such things are too precious to be entrusted to any courier." Reaching into his bosom he drew out a flattened packet, and held it out across the rug-table for Jefferji to take. "That's why I couldn't risk sending these. That's why you had to come."

Taking the packet Jefferji turned it over in his hands. It was wrapped in leather, and had been for so long that the ragged edges of what had once been a scrap piece of some animal's skin had been compressed into a solid mass. The packet had been pried open, recently; Jefferji raised his eyebrows.

"I had to make sure there was still something there," Deravass said. "It would have been no good if the ink had gone, or paper had just rotted away. If there even were any papers."

Jefferji opened the packet very carefully. There was a button, a plain gold ring, a tarnish-blackened silver case—and in it, revealed slowly by the reluctant yielding of old hinges, two portraits in miniature. Jefferji's mother, with some young man. Ganders Tamisen. He'd never seen a picture of his father.

"He left them with a woman in a village on the mountainside." Deravass spoke quietly and slowly as Jefferji tried to focus on the face, and not let tears fall on its twenty-year-old surface. "In a wooden box. Her husband was jealous, so she hid the box where he wouldn't find it. Tamisen—your father—promised her that he'd come back for it. He never did. She kept it safe for him all of this time."

Papers, showing wear but not much age. Some folded sheets. The stub of a pencil, some scribbled notes. A diary. Jefferji opened up the diary; he couldn't help it, even though the chance he took, opening it out here in the open air, terrified him. What if there was a breeze? A thunderstorm? A fall of hail, out of the clear blue sky?

"We believe he died somewhere in the mountains," Fontenoy said, to Shikander. "Because that's the only thing that would have kept him from coming back. He was that kind of man."

There were letters, tucked between leaves of the diary. Could that be his mother's handwriting?

There was a note in the margin of the uppermost letter, on its outside fold; a different hand, but one that was startlingly like Jefferji's own when he was writing in English. *Don't give a damn whether it's a boy or a girl, no, well, of course I give a thousand damns, but oh I love you.*

His mother had tried to teach him how to write a formal hand. His had always come out differently from hers, and his teachers had fared no better. It was a shock to recognize it now. His father's. He'd been dead before Jefferji was born, but he and Jefferji had the same handwriting.

Carefully Jefferji folded the package back up together, close. Carefully he put it away into his bosom. "I'm overwhelmed." What else could he say? "If I may be excused, lord, Captain Fontenoy, Deravass Khan. Doctor Jericho."

Yes, he could call Simon "doctor." Simon Jericho had been that to Old Fort, to them all. No one would gainsay it. And Captain Fontenoy had brought Jefferji all this way, through all of these adventures, to bring him what Deravass Khan had found of his late father.

"Of course," Shikander said. "Use my tent if you want to be alone. We'll be carousing here for some time yet." Shikander nodded to Jefferji with an expression full of profound affection. And yet Shikander had no way to know what treasure lay in the packet Deravass Khan had brought.

It was his father's voice, that Jefferji had never heard. The last thing his father had ever written. He'd known there was going to be a child. It was probably the last he'd ever heard from his new bride, but he'd known he was going to be a father.

Standing up from the rug table, Jefferji bowed, and turned away. When he'd been a boy, too young to understand, he used to ask his mother. *Where is my father?* He'd asked his nurse Myamah. He'd asked Daoji. He'd even asked Captain Fontenoy. *Where is my father?*

Here. Here in these papers.

But also here in Captain Fontenoy and Deravass Khan, twenty years searching for a man disappeared and presumed dead. Captain Fontenoy, who had stood uncle to him. Deravass Khan, who'd never met him before, but who was clearly prepared to love him for his father's sake. Jaisal Singh, who had sheltered him and his mother and half-mad Daoji for his father's sake, and raised him equally with his own sons.

There were no dances in all the repertoire, for this, no story from the Mahabharata. He was going to have to focus everything he had on creating one, if he was to hope to contain the emotion in his heart.

Jefferji felt the music forming in his mind as he hurried down the ladder to seek the sanctuary of Shikander's tent, where he could light the lamp and look these treasures over one by one and meet his father face to face at last.

He'd thought that all of his troubles were finally over. He'd had promises extended by smiling Fortune: first by Fontenoy in a garden in Bharaj, next in the courtyard of a heathen Hindu temple at Hirpa, finally as he sat on the rug of a jeweler's in Churu. Any of those promises realized would have put him beyond the reach of discovery; he could have changed his name, again, and disappeared. He would have been safe. Instead?

Those promises had been ripped out of his very grasp one by one: first in the courtyard of a ruined temple on the road to Rawal Pindi, then mockingly snatched away in the Resident's compound in Peshawar, next stripped away from him beside a fire somewhere along a road north of the Wakhan River — finally and absolutely denied on the third floor of a shabby old tower in a shabby old fort that should have fallen to rape and ruin, if Broderick had had anything to say about it.

That was only the most recent of the shameful crimes he'd

committed in the name of Broderick Holyoke. It joined a full
roster: embezzling from the mess accounts, and letting an
innocent man take the blame—and the shame. Bespoiling a
girl scarcely nubile to secure a loan, and then abandoning her
after robbing her of her virtue. Attempted theft. Attempted
murder. Theft of a good horse, and—not a crime in black
letters so much as a shameful act of vandalism—ruin of
another, running Gunnery far past what should have been
demanded of him.

Threatening unarmed women, one with a babe in arms.
Betraying a blameless community to rapine and murder, and
on false report as well, with only luck—and Fontenoy, and
Shikander Beg, Tamisen's panic-inducing shell trumpet, and
Tamisen himself—preventing it. Lying to so many people, to
Fontenoy and Rashid and Mirza Cassim, within the past few
weeks alone.

He could have acquitted himself of an excess of cowardice,
because what he had done had taken nerve and daring; if not
for the fact that he'd done all of those things in the name of
a good officer and a better man, and dragged the name of
Broderick Holyoke through mud and filth in the public street.

Outside the walls of the Old Fort Mirza Cassim's men—the
ones who'd survived, all prisoners now—had built up a great
fire. Deravass Khan had sent them a bullock's hide. Propped
up on tripods at both ends, sticks stuck through the stitch-
sealed leather where the beast's legs had been, it made a sort
of a basin. They'd filled it with water, and cast heated rocks
into the water until the water was hot. A bath, of sorts, not
for sitting in, but to stand beside and rinse oneself by
dippersful.

Broderick's turn came last, of course, but the water that
was removed by the serial rinsing of each bather in turn was
cast aside rather than being returned to the bullock-hide
tub—fresh water added to top it up, fresh heated stones to
warm it—so the water itself remained as clear as water from
a muddy river still draining from its flood, sloshed into the
hide of a bullock and heated with fried stones, could be. They
wanted him to strip, fine, he'd strip, so long as he got his
chance at the hot water.

In Bombay water was cursed for being hot, when all a man

wanted was cold. Cool water in a tub to soak when the humidity of the bath and the air were equivalent. Iced, cold beer in a glass, the height of luxury. Cool breezes from the draft of ceiling fans evaporating the sweat from a man's body as he lay panting at two o'clock in the morning, stark naked, desperate to escape the heat. Standing beside the bullock skin, feeling the cool breeze around him, Broderick took off his clothes piece by piece, thinking about Bombay.

They carried away his clothes. They had no business being there at all to look at him when he was naked, whether or not they'd all seen him stripped naked already. There was a work crew from the prisoners washing clothes, busy over other fires. The garments were stretched out across whatever bush and brush pile could be found, to dry at the same time.

There wasn't anything like a pair of poles to stretch a drying line between, and horses couldn't be relied upon to stand still for any decent period of time, so people put their clothing back on half-dry and dried the clothes and their bodies at one and the same time in front of whichever fire was least crowded at the moment.

How did they know whose clothes belonged to whom? Broderick wondered. What was to stop him from just picking out the pieces that looked least contemptible and claiming them for his own? That was what *he* would have done, but Broderick Holyoke, Lieutenant Broderick Holyoke, he would never have stooped to such dishonesty. He would have given all of his clothing away before he would have taken anything that was not his.

As he stood and brooded, one half of his body warmed by its proximity to the hot water in the skin bath and the other half cooling as the fires burned low, Broderick realized that the men who'd been tending rocks at the bonfire had all moved away to do other things. So there'd be no more heated rocks, the water was as hot as it was going to get, and it would cool rapidly in the cool air as it tended on toward sundown. He needed to hurry.

And he had company: one of the men on laundry detail with something held hidden in his hand. He seemed to be still deciding what he was going to do with it. When he made his choice he seemed to surprise himself, as well as Broderick.

"Take it," the washer-man said, reaching out his hand. "Sahib says. English soap."

And it was, by God. It was a cake of creamy soap, buttery in his fingers, fine European cake soap with the fragrance of almonds. He'd been forced to leave his kit behind when he'd escaped from Fontenoy in Peshawar. He hadn't seen a sliver of soap since. He'd gotten as dirty as ever Bung-hole Boy had been, and this chunk of English soap smelled like—it smelled like—

It was the last straw, the one that broke the camel's back and destroyed what Broderick had left of fortitude in the face of his challenges. His failures.

The washer-man went away and left Broderick standing naked in front of the bullock-hide bath holding a cake of soap, turning it over in his hands. Broderick wet his hands in the hot water and rubbed; the lather that came up was like silk or sea-foam, turning dirt-colored and brown in his hands. Slowly he worked the lather up his arms, scrubbing himself until the suds stayed creamy white. His face next. He couldn't see his face, but he could see the color of the suds in his hands. His face was filthy.

He was naked beside a bullock skin surrounded by people whose language he could understand only imperfectly. His arms and legs were bruised and galled and his hands were blistered from piling wood and burned from pulling still-smoldering logs away from the gate. He had nothing. He was nothing. He knew it. Why had he ever believed that he could change that?

He remembered what it felt like, to be universally despised, universally contemned. He'd thought he'd escaped from that forever, because he had rank and rank brought money. But he hadn't gotten away from it at all. And this time there wasn't so much as a single friendly face, a single voice of compassion, a single sympathetic word. Broderick Holyoke was dead. He'd been the closest thing to a friend that Bung-hole Boy had ever had, but he was dead.

Broderick began to cry. He couldn't help it. It could only have been Fontenoy or Tamisen who'd sent him a cake of soap, and Broderick didn't know which one of them it was but he hated them both and himself worse than either. Scrubbing his face, his dirty greasy unkempt hair as hard as he could he tried his best to disguise his sobs, because he couldn't stop them.

There'd always been the chance that someday someone would find him out, but he'd found himself out, and that was worse. He hadn't left Bung-hole Boy to burn on the pyre after all. Bung-hole Boy was here with him right now, weeping uncontrollably, inconsolably—because someone he hated and despised had given him a cake of good English soap to wash with, after everything that had gone before.

Was there nothing he could do, to wash away his shame?

The soap was gone and the water was cold, but he kept scrubbing himself. If he washed from now until Doomsday he'd never get clean of who he was.

When they brought him back his clothing he dressed himself numbly beside the fire beneath a fading sky and waited in hopeless silence for what new humiliation the next day would bring.

The sun shone full on the paving stones in front of Old Fort's tower, now newly chinked, with freshly rebuilt stairs all the way up—only one of the repairs and refurbishments made possible by a captive labor force with reliable supervision. It was warm.

Fontenoy sat with Deravass Khan and Shikander Beg. Away at a little distance Lamish stood waiting, leaning on a stick, with two of his children to tend to him. Fontenoy hadn't seen him addled even once, since the trouble had begun. Maybe he'd stay sober; now that he had seen what trouble spending too much money could cause, he might decide to cut expensive intoxicants out of the community's budget. And beside Lamish, Mirza Cassim, waiting to hear his fate.

"I was asked to keep an eye out for Russians, Shikander lord." Fontenoy had been unprepared for the savagery of Shikander Beg's expression when he'd mentioned the mission to him before. Now that he knew why Shikander hated Russians, he was all the more glad to have the ambiguity resolved. "I will clarify *your* status with my contacts in various bureaus, when I return south."

Circassian, not Russian. A refugee Circassian warlord with a savage red-haired concubine, a troop of all-female sepahi cavalry—culled from the survivors of the destruction that the Cossacks had wrought among them—commanded by a green-eyed Hungarian noblewoman who smoked cigars, all of them mounted on ugly vicious steppe ponies fully as tough as the yabus of the mountains... not Russian. No. Not by a country mile.

This time Shikander only nodded, with a smile. "Thank you, Captain Fontenoy." Shikander's English was improving. Fontenoy understood that he spent the odd moment with Tamisen, so perhaps it was the company that was improving him. Shikander actually seemed to spend quite as many odd moments with Tamisen as they were able to manage, together.

Fontenoy didn't know how serious things were between the two of them. He could only hope that Tamisen wasn't going to pine all the way back to Tengarpore. But Tamisen was a good deal older than he'd been when Fontenoy had first proposed this expedition, and there was good hope. Or Simon Jericho could prepare a philter of forgetfulness, perhaps.

"These then are our undertakings," Deravass Khan said. "On your part, Shikander lord, you leave Old Fort under my protection While I in turn establish this as a safe haven of operations and accept new settlers as I see fit, using the money we've accepted from you for stewardship. You'll tell Lamish?"

"And Deravass Khan, to be a good lord, as I doubt not you will be. To provide shelter, forage, and space for goods and cattle should my caravans need it, in the future," Shikander replied, with a nod. Shikander Beg was a generous man. Fontenoy thought Shikander and Deravass Khan would sort well together. "And I will give advance warning should I need to make use of Old Fort as a caravanserai, as much as I can."

Summarizing. Not because they were all leaving tomorrow, but because the time had come to decide what to do with Mirza Cassim, and their other prisoners.

For himself Fontenoy was finding that he loved Deravass Khan as much as he remembered ever having done, even after all these years. It wasn't going to be easy to say good bye to him all over again.

You promise not to lure Tamisen into China, or wherever you're going, Fontenoy thought idly. But it wasn't up to him to say. He'd tell Tamisen what he thought, but only if Tamisen asked him.

"Now there are just Mirza Cassim, and the prisoners, and Holyoke," Fontenoy reminded them all. They'd been interviewing prisoners for three days. Lamish had provided translators to assist. "We're agreed on Mirza Cassim?"

"Easiest," Shikander Beg agreed. "He seems an honest man, and Deravass has had good report of him, yes? I am willing to take his word about the rest of them, who may stay *or* go, and who *must* go."

Deravass Khan had indeed heard of Mirza Cassim, but, more to the point, Deravass Khan had contacts in Fayzabad and Zebak. He'd sent to them. Nothing not in Cassim's favor had come back. Notwithstanding Shikander Beg's personal feelings, a man not averse to a bit of slaving now and then was not, apparently, in violation of social norms in Badakhshan. Mirza Cassim had agreed with Shikander Beg that he would engage in no such activity or lose his parole, so Fontenoy was willing to call it good, and let it go.

"We are really just down to Holyoke," Fontenoy said. "I have a grievance. Tamisen has a bigger grievance. You and Old Fort have the largest grievances of all, lord, so we must know your thoughts, before I try to put the man to use."

The wounded sepahis would recover, even still-bedridden Wila, but they'd be some time at it, and men like Shikander Beg quite naturally resented being deprived of their fighting strength.

"I have taken thought," Shikander said. "With Deravass Khan to protect Old Fort, I can believe it safe. And that no new effort to recruit would succeed. So for Old Fort I can allow it. For my family, and my sepahis, I will have them away from here and safe. If I see Holyoke again I will kill him."

Not presuming to say what Tamisen had decided, no. Very diplomatic, Fontenoy felt.

"I've spoken to Tamisen." Not as much as Shikander had been doing, but who knew what the two of them talked about together? None of Fontenoy's business, he was sure. "He'll agree so long as he can kill Holyoke if *he* ever sees him again, and still feels like it. Otherwise he yields."

Leaving only Holyoke. And Fontenoy's plans for him.

"Let's have him, then," Fontenoy told Deravass, standing beside him. He wasn't looking forward to this.

When they brought Holyoke he was a little cleaner, yes, but as slovenly and sloppily dressed. It was hard to tell whether the soap Fontenoy had sent had made any difference. The expression on Holyoke's face was one Fontenoy didn't think he'd seen before. He couldn't quite put his finger on it.

"Broderick Holyoke," Fontenoy said. "You've built up quite a record for yourself, haven't you?" He'd written up notes. The only actual documentation he had was the brief Bombay had prepared to forward with him to Peshawar, where Holyoke was to have been sent out toward Herat and given the opportunity to show himself a changed man. If he'd changed at all since they'd left the Bharaj fair, it had only been for the worse. "We've been trying to decide how we can neutralize your bad influence, the three of us. What do you think we should do with you?"

"I'll tell you something you don't know about me," Holyoke said, sounding stubborn and resentful and defiant. "I will. In return, I'll write you a confession. And it will be as complete as I can make it, it will be that. And I'll sign it, and you'll witness it, and you'll take a copy to circulate in Bombay and Calcutta just as you please, so long as you send the original to Madras."

His voice was changed in some way. Fontenoy's conviction that there was a difference was as strong as his perplexity as to what it was, exactly. Fontenoy took his time, putting his thoughts in order. Leaning back in his chair, he looked at Deravass, he looked at Shikander Beg, he looked over at Lamish and Mirza Cassim.

"And, ah, what do *you* get out of all of this, Lieutenant Holyoke?"

Holyoke's recoil was almost physical. "No, you say first," he insisted. "You promise me."

"I am losing this," Shikander murmured to Deravass, in the variety of caravan language that they most nearly shared.

"I'm not understanding very well myself," Deravass said back.

Fontenoy made up his mind. He didn't want to spend any more time with Broderick Holyoke than he had to.

"All right," Fontenoy said, slapping the table with the

palms of both hands decisively. "I promise. You tell me something I don't know about you, but it had better be enough to cover your demands. You write up a confession, a complete confession, and we make a copy. You sign them, we witness them, we send them to Bombay and Calcutta and especially Madras for their use as... whatever. Done." Anything to be rid of the man.

"You're a man of your word," Holyoke said, in a tone of voice that seemed somehow between sorrow and a sneer. "A man of honor. And so was Broderick Holyoke. But he didn't do any of the things laid against his name on your list, or anybody else's. I did."

This was making less and less sense. "You're either Broderick Holyoke or you're not," Fontenoy said, but all the while some peculiar stories were coming to mind. Charles Masson, had that been the name? A deserter twice over, but a man remade as an archeologist in Kabul? "Which is it?"

"Not." At first it seemed that Holyoke had just decided to shut up. Then Fontenoy realized that he was struggling to maintain his composure. "I'm not Holyoke. I'm the drummer boy. Holyoke died on the banks of the Nerbudda. They all died. I burned them. Became Holyoke."

And Fontenoy could see, now, that Holyoke—the man they'd all known as Holyoke—was trembling. What were they to make of this outrageous claim?

"I have to admit you've told us something we didn't know about you." And maybe why Holyoke had refused to say what he expected to gain: the least he could expect was a lengthy jail sentence; the more probable outcome was flogging beforehand and then prison, a death sentence, in fact. "I'll have paper sent to you. You'll be under guard."

Beckoning, Fontenoy called for the guards, while Shikander—leaning back in his chair comfortably, his hands folded across his lap, his knees crossed in a relaxed manner—canted his head back to talk past Fontenoy's back to Deravass Khan. "Anything?"

"Take this man to the first empty room you find," Fontenoy told the guards. "And watch him. Do not leave his side. I'll send supplies. Take a third one of you, to be sure of him."

"He says he's not Holyoke at all," Deravass Khan was telling Shikander Beg. Fontenoy reminded himself that Deravass had more English than Fontenoy had of Fayzabad caravan dialect. "This changes things."

So much so that Fontenoy's head was spinning.

"He—" Fontenoy gestured after the man he'd thought to be Broderick Holyoke, all of this time. He couldn't bring himself to call the man "Holyoke" any longer. "If he wishes to make amends, and if he can learn a new language as well as he learned to impersonate an officer, we might find a useful place for him, in which to do penance. North of Kabul, perhaps."

One thing was for sure: it was going to be another day, at least, before they would be able to dispose of not-Holyoke, regardless of what they decided upon between them. Shikander Beg's people would be starting to get anxious to be away, and they all needed to leave Deravass Khan with Mirza Cassim and his men to start building new and lasting relationships.

And Fontenoy, he was getting anxious to get back to Tengarpore, in hopes that Jaisal Singh was somehow still alive—and anxious to hear all the gossip from Deravass Khan.

Chapter Sixteen
After the Rains

Scanning the blue sky, the white clouds, the hills all around the valley and the mountain-tops beyond, Shashka sighed deeply in the late summer air. This was the second time he'd moved his caravan out from the valley where Old Fort stood, and there was more of it this time. He was hopeful that it would be the last time for, for this year at least.

"You have much to be satisfied with, lord," Jefferji Tamisen said, as the laden camels moved through the open gates in stately procession down the long ramp, onto the path that led back out of the valley and to the river road. "Old Fort is the better for your being here."

"Some might question that." Yes, there'd been improvements, but there'd also been repairs that would not have been required had Mirza Cassim's men not tried to take the village. If Cassim had burned the village, however, the entire place would have had to be rebuilt, so they were ahead by that much. "But yes. I like the new gate."

It had taken them weeks of effort to replace that, especially since the villagers had had to restore the flooded fields and the herdsmen had to collect the animals and Deravass Khan's men had to excavate the treasure cave all at the same time. They'd found lumber on the river, old hardwood trunks ripped out of banks upstream and scattered all down the river's course as the floodwaters had passed; that had been the saving of the project. Old Fort had a gate again. And three dozen fine old tree trunks lay in the enclosure, seasoning for next year's repairs.

Half a dozen of the camels were new, their harnesses and trappings still bright from the market. Not every animal that that fled when the river had come had been recovered, but the bazaar in Fayzabad had made up the deficiencies. More sheep; some to replace those of Old Fort that Shikander's people had eaten up.

"Fat goats," Peri said, with satisfaction. "There is good grass here. For wives and babies, too." She sat on Birkit a little behind him as she always did, and on his right because Tamisen was on his left. She had abandoned most of her resentment of Tamisen. Shashka didn't think she'd mind Tamisen not being there, but for now she tolerated him very well.

"Oh," Tamisen said, as if reminded by Peri's remark. "Look what I have. Slippers." Tamisen pulled them out of his jacket and showed them, proudly, to Shashka and Peri alike. Ismara's work. Ismara had adopted Tamisen in a strange sense, and Tamisen, Ismara, as a sister. Shashka smiled to see her present. Tamisen had long feet.

It had been eight weeks, now, since the war and Deravass's arrival. Shashka had had a messenger just ten days ago, news of the road at Tilted Slope, letters from home. And a few extra hands as well, so that he could pack up and set out.

He had men and women well rested, a thriving son, a closer friendship with his wife, an understanding with Deravass Khan—whose contacts in the caravan escort business ran deeper than his own—and money in his pocket, because Captain Fontenoy had been anxious that he not suffer for his stewardship of Old Fort. Shashka had no objection to a generous reimbursement of expenses when he knew it had been fairly earned. He'd had wounded.

There was only one thing that Shashka found lacking. "You should come with me, Tamisen," he said. "I'm going into China, in the spring." For medicine against goiter. His people had not been long in Sanctuary, but it was a valley far from the sea, and a prudent man planned for the long term. "You could watch the people dance in Kashgar. In Tashkurgan. In Yark-hand." *And I've grown fond of you. As well as the other thing.*

"I'd like to go to China," Tamisen said thoughtfully. "But not this time. Thank you. I'm sorry. We aren't done here, and I'm needed. Hakim Jericho still needs an assistant, truly, lord. I wish."

Tamisen had responsibilities to Captain Fontenoy and the enterprise of the antiquities trade. Tamisen knew the stories on the walls that the doctor wrote down as they came up from their pit, and could provide technical guidance as to which inscriptions were so important that rubbings had to be made in triplicate for sale in Varanasi and Mysore. He had an old woman, his nurse, to look after at home where he had come from.

Shashka had already known these things, and yet he'd wanted to be sure he asked.

Tamisen couldn't take the shankha to China, either. He had other plans, to take the relic to the temple at his home in Tengarpore, or else rebury it in Old Fort Valley. Shashka hadn't inquired too deeply. He coveted the power of the conch trumpet, but only Tamisen could use it.

"The lord might send a message, in the spring." Shashka was surprised to hear Peri speak, and so, apparently, was Tamisen. "Someone will know. If you returned here in the next season, maybe someone would bring you to the lord's place."

Tamisen smiled at Shashka and Peri alike, an open-hearted smile that showed all his teeth. "Thank you," he said. "Maybe next year. I'll write. They can hold a letter here."

And trade it for one that I might write in turn, perhaps, to fix a rendezvous, Shashka thought hopefully.

"You should get out in front of the camels," Peri reminded Shashka. "Cherkess doesn't like them." Peri was much more confident of Ismara's ability to manage on her own, these days. Old Fort had been good for them all.

"Well, kiss me, Jefferji," Shikander said, turning Cherkess nose-to-tail with Tamisen's mare so that they could embrace each other. Tamisen's mare had gotten to tolerating the Cherkess stallion very well, although he had at one point taken an unseemly interest in her. There had been rumors of an affair, but Tamisen had assured Shashka that the mare had said nothing to him about it. "We'll be off. Good digging to you. I hope to see you again."

"Perhaps next year," Tamisen agreed. How long had it been—Shashka wondered—since he'd embraced a fellow man as a friend, still less a lover, and of so strange a sort? "Meantime, Godspeed, Sri Krsna holds you in his heart."

If Tamisen's heathen god did any such thing it was for Tamisen's sake alone, Shashka was sure. "And you."

Turning away, Shashka set the Cherkess stallion on his course down to the river road, waving a final good bye as he went. It was more dangerous a thing than he'd done for a very long time, opening his heart to another human soul on so dangerously equal a basis as he had with Tamisen. But the world was warmer for Tamisen's presence in it.

Now he had work to do. Setting his thoughts on home, his families, and how Ismara would take to his other wives—and they to Ismara—Shashka rode out to complete his interrupted journey back home to Sanctuary at last.

In Peshawar, the Residency was opened to Captain Fontenoy once more, though there was less room than there had been earlier in the year. Ranjit Singh was still dead, Kharak Singh's tenure unconsolidated. The Dogra rajas were widely viewed with suspicion, and instability in the Punjab put multiple pressures on the British occupation in Kabul.

Captain Fontenoy had claimed aloud that he was, on balance, well clear of it, though Jefferji wasn't sure anybody truly believed that. Fontenoy had fought his wars amongst the Pindaris and the Marathas, after all, and Fontenoy's last one—the defense of Old Fort north of the Wakhan Valley, in the approaches to the high Pamir—had surely demonstrated to the exclusion of any further doubt the fact that Fontenoy had fight left enough in him, and more to spare.

They'd had a week to stop, and rest, and have all of their clothing refurbished, before the administration had started in on them. The horses and Marigold were on light duty, in charge of eating better food and checking pasturage for any faults or flaws, so that they could both recuperate and not be surprised when the time came for them to work again.

As it was they'd all been put to work, Fontenoy most of all, because he had fewer defenses against their British hosts Jefferji supposed. But they were all put to harness—him, Simon Jericho, Captain Fontenoy: writing and narrating reports; sitting for interviews; reviewing transcripts retranslated back to be sure nothing had gotten out of true in the process.

And, along with everything else, they'd had the opportunity to make themselves very clear about whether or not an otherwise unnamed warlord called "Kavkazki" had anything to do with Cossacks. Jefferji had more details than either of the others, so he was in a position to be especially emphatic, with Fontenoy doing nothing but endorsing him all the way.

A team of scribes from Patiala had been installed in one of the Residency's old guesthouses, working to consolidate and reconcile the maps, between Simon Jericho's few surviving notes and Tamisen's personal and—in his modest, self-effacing opinion frankly brilliant—presentation. Since interest in their travels was sharpened in light of the uncertainties in Kashmir as well as the Punjab and Kabul, since the information in their combined map was so detailed and cross-referenced, there was apparently a significant premium that would be credited to them all.

Jefferji had found his danced map to be a wonder and a perplexity to the British intelligence community of Peshawar, a source of admiration and amusement—just as he'd hoped it might be when he'd hit on the stratagem of making it. It made him proud to reflect well on Captain Fontenoy.

There was a search on throughout Rajputana and Delhi for a team of knowledgeable teachers who could evaluate and cross-reference the route Tamisen danced, but they'd have to assemble in Tengarpore, Fontenoy had warned the authorities. Jefferji wanted to go home. Neither Fontenoy nor all the British in Bombay could justly prevent him.

Tamisen's foster-father, his adoptive father, Jaisal Singh was dead. That wasn't unexpected, though Jefferji was sorry he hadn't had a chance to tell Jaisal Singh all about their adventure—Deravass Khan's significant role—the things Jefferji had to show, his father's relics. It couldn't be said that he'd been unprepared for the disappointment.

Jefferji had little by way of very definite thoughts about

the afterlife, with so many propositions—Christian, Rajput, Hindu, Moslem—to choose from. But Fontenoy, for one, had stated strongly that Jaisal Singh would be hearing all about it from Jefferji's father, Ganders Tamisen himself, in whatever afterlife they shared. That they *would* be sharing an afterlife, in some pleasant form, was something Fontenoy appeared to be firmly resolved was absolute and undeniable.

There was one positive outcome to be found in the sad inevitability: Madhu Singh had been formally recognized by the Bombay British as the master of Tengarpore. There was no longer any reason that Jefferji should not return to Tengarpore, and there was a letter from Jaisal Begum herself to say so.

So here they all were, Jefferji told himself happily, in the room Captain Fontenoy was still using for an office at the Residency in Peshawar. Him, Captain Fontenoy, Hakim Jericho, and Colonel Talifer, recruiter in chief, who apparently had his eye on at least two out of the three of them. Lunch had been cleared away, so the only food and drink left to them was beer and whiskey, soda water, lemonade, tea and sandwiches, cold roast mutton and a roasted chicken or two, fruit and rich cakes with their sugary frosting slowly disintegrating in the heat—and that luxury of luxuries: ice. Plenty of it.

Captain Fontenoy had described the room as built by Scotsmen homesick for a library, with a broad hearth and heavy black tables, solid carved-back baronial chairs like those from one of Jefferji's mother's few picture-books, with red velvet cushions that were totally unsuited to the heat and the damp of a Peshawar summer. Only two of the tables were not covered in refreshments, and those were loaded with trays of shawls and silk, instead.

There were khilat, dresses of honor, laying over all, in unspoken respect for the journey they'd completed and the treasure they'd brought back, as Jefferji understood it. They were of traditional pattern, with a bodice or blouse that fastened in the back. And because they were so heavy with gold brocade and wire-thread embroideries, Jefferji shared Simon's skepticism over the inadvisability of trying to wear one. None of them would begin to fit him anyway.

"They'll be passed on, Hakim Jericho," Colonel Talifer said, reassuringly. As unofficial persons they probably wouldn't have been presented to Kharak Singh under any circumstances, still less during these unsettled times. But rumors of gold and rubies generated celebrity, and Talifer—as one of the Envoy's liaison officers—had formally escorted the khilats to the Residency this morning.

"Surely good manners alone require thanks to be rendered," Simon protested. Jefferji imagined himself in the khilat bowing to a fierce Sikh monarch, and thought it would have been a very great shame to cut so splendid a garment down its back in order to fit it to his body. The whole thing would have to be sliced open; not even the arms would be spared.

Talifer laughed, and shook his head. "We've already made suitable presents in return, Hakim. The regulations require it. All of this has to go to auction anyway. I'm sorry, but rules are rules. I'll make sure they set the lowest possible price for anything you'd like to ransom."

So Jefferji had heard. It was a shame, though. All of these presents, sweets, jewels, silks, swords and daggers, fine Kashmiri shawls, cloth-of-gold, ornaments of gold filigree wire. It was all the property of the Crown.

"Not *these*, no." Fontenoy had sat quietly at the table surveying the booty and smoking his pipe—an English pipe, not a hubble-bubble—with quiet satisfaction. "Those presents sent with my name, yes. These others, however"—Fontenoy pointed with the stem of his pipe—"these were expressions of admiration for Tamisen and Hakim Jericho. Not in the employ of the Crown, or Company. Those go with their rightful owners back to India."

Talifer looked surprised.

Jefferji scanned the presents with new and sharper interest. There were three sets of seven trays each, with equivalent goods—one for him, one for Simon, one for Fontenoy. There were extra trays of sweets and delicacies as well, presented by the British themselves as theirs to enjoy.

Jefferji hadn't really thought of the Kashmiri shawls as his. They were of exceptional quality. Even he could tell. And of course he had prior acquaintance with the very best by way of clothing presented to Sri Krsna and the divine Consort to clothe them with honor.

An eighth tray with jewelry and shawls had been sent for Simon to distribute in Varanasi. Varanasi had sent a messenger to Peshawar with emphatic words about how lucky the British were to have an association with so promising and brilliant a student as Simon Jericho with nothing paid to the university in consideration of their role in the creation of such a paragon of learning. And the British could take a hint.

"Of course you're right." Talifer didn't sound the least bit put out about it, just surprised. "Sorry, Tamisen, Jericho. Not thinking. Of course the gifts are yours to keep. But you, you're on your own, Fontenoy." Was that a hint of abiding affection, there, Jefferji wondered, in Talifer's teasing phrase? Remarkable.

"And as to that," Fontenoy continued, "Free to Varanasi, yes, but they're independent agents. As we've just discussed. I've promised them both pay and expenses commensurate with their contributions."

No he hadn't, Jefferji thought, making the face of a statue in stone to cover his mild surprise. Fontenoy had proposed a share in the proceeds for the maps, and a part of his share in return for their help with his originally proposed expedition in search of antiquities. He was making this part up.

Talifer took a moment to light a cheroot, apparently to give himself a moment to think. For himself, Jefferji was just as glad of a small pause in the conversation. If Fontenoy was taking things in the direction Jefferji thought, he'd been waiting for the subject to come up, and wasn't sure how it was going to work out.

"Well, as to that. As you say, Fontenoy. Quite so," Talifer said, looking from Fontenoy to Jefferji. "With reference to Tamisen, if Hakim Jericho will excuse the shift in subjects. One rather expected. Family tradition, service with honor, grateful nation, et cetera. There's a place for you with the Bombay Presidency at least, Tamisen, you've just to ask. Usual assistant undersecretary sort of a thing, but no one doubts your mettle. You're a proven man with very valuable linguistic skills. Not enough of you."

The awkwardness lay in the fact that surely Fontenoy had gone to great lengths to make Jefferji just that, a proven man, in the clear expectation that there was nothing Jefferji would like better than a career in government. Fontenoy had had other motives as well, yes—Jefferji's help to map and translate, the pure adventure of it all, and above all the things Deravass Khan had brought to Old Fort, relics of his father.

"My father's sworn duty was to the English crown," Jefferji replied. "I've always known that." Crown and country. But what country? "And Captain Fontenoy, who's been my English uncle, in a way. To follow the path of two such men would be a very great honor."

Talifer heard the "would." So did Fontenoy, as Jefferji had known he would.

So Jefferji took a deep breath and went on. "Also I was raised by a foster father whose whole life has been spent in executing his duty, as the protector of his people. There can be no higher calling than that."

"Then it's agreed," Colonel Talifer said, in a tone of voice that sounded like *Tell me what's on your mind.* "You're in a position to be a credit to your father and Captain Fontenoy alike. As well as your foster-father, a Rajput prince, I understand. No finer fighting men in all of India."

"And I earnestly hope to become so." If Jefferji could figure out a way. "But as I left, sir, I was asked to take a widowed kinswoman of Jaisal Begum under my protection. Beset by people who wish to force her to remarry, in order to obtain her property." This was only a very modest embroidery—nothing like that which adorned the dress of honor. Jefferji hoped it would ring sufficiently true because the widow herself had said almost as much, to the god—or in the god's presence, which was just as good. "I couldn't say no."

And well done to you, Simon's approving nod seemed to say. Talifer was looking to Fontenoy for his lead.

"Jaisal Singh was on his deathbed," Fontenoy said. "Not a time to raise objections. You needn't have been embarrassed to tell me, Tamisen. It's to your credit. There's no shame in protecting a woman from predation."

Jefferji *was* embarrassed, and he *was* a little ashamed. He could easily have brought it up, explained, asked for Fontenoy's advice. Up until quite recently he hadn't thought much about it, though—Jaisal Begum had meant for him to leave, he'd left, and that was where it ended. No. That wasn't where it ended.

Talifer seemed to choose his next words with great precision. "Ah. You have responsibilities. I respect that." *Maybe you're not ready to commit yourself. You've been raised native. You need a little time.* "We need your languages, and you've proven your worth under dangerous conditions. Go home and do what you need to do—but I hope you come back."

Jefferji didn't know if he could honestly agree. Fontenoy spoke before Jefferji's silence could become too awkward, though, for which Jefferji was grateful.

"Might the Envoy possibly provide a letter?" Fontenoy asked Talifer. "As a reference. I'm an old man, and face it, my name's not well known outside—er, rapidly aging circles."

It seemed to be a lot to ask, but after a very brief moment's consideration Talifer nodded. "I think he will."

Fontenoy stood up, so Jefferji stood up as well. Simon Jericho was as clearly encouraged to stay seated by a courteous gesture on Talifer's part. Jericho was his own man, and an acknowledged medical professional could not be expected to observe rank protocols specific to British officers, beyond self-respecting courtesy.

"I'll have a letter for you before you go. Tamisen." Talifer extended his hand, so Jefferji shook it, politely. "The sooner we see you again, the better. Fontenoy."

"Talifer," Fontenoy said, shaking hands in turn.

It occurred to Jefferji that neither man used the other's rank. That seemed a little odd.

When Talifer was gone Fontenoy turned to Jefferji, who stood there waiting and apprehensive. "Widow?"

"Jaisal Begum offered me money to marry her." That sounded so mercenary Jefferji wished he'd phrased it better, but it was out now. "And with the greatest respect and heartfelt gratitude, sir, I'm not sure I'm ready to be British."

"Well, Tamisen. If it was Jaisal Begum I'm surprised you weren't married on the spot. She's a force of nature, and I've lived in terror of her for years." Fontenoy clasped him by the shoulders as he spoke, stood there for a moment looking at him, then clapped him genially and continued, in a changed tone of voice. "Now. The thing is to make sure the best things go on *your* trays, you two, so let's be sorting before anybody comes for the Fontenoy share. Are there almonds there? Just nudge the tray in my direction, yes, thank you."

Jefferji was relieved, but not deceived. Fontenoy was disappointed. Fontenoy was also willing to leave the decision with Jefferji, however—and the meeting with Deravass Khan had been the important thing, the offered place in the service of the Crown only an added benefit. Maybe.

He made an artistic arrangement of snacks on three trays, one for each of them, distributed them appropriately, and set to work to apply what he knew of costuming to the evaluation of the relative worth of fabrics, shawls, jewelry, loot.

Back in Sanctuary at last, Shashka concentrated on everything that was going well—his caravans both home without further casualties among his sepahis or civilians, goods in store, supplies for the health and comfort of his people, adequate food, sufficient warmth, dry shelter. He'd done the rounds protocol demanded with Second Wife—his First Lady—with Princess Wife, and with Wheat Wife.

"First Wife" was an inauspicious title under the circumstances of his personal history, and they didn't use it. Peri was technically speaking Fifth Wife, but the title was an embarrassment to her, and she was different. Peri, it was, who kept track of his domestic duties, reminding him when it was time he visited one wife versus another, and of any immediate concerns that required his attention.

Peri it was who'd informed him, somewhat to his surprise, that Wheat Wife had yielded precedence over the next few days—her turn—to Battle Wife, Ismara, and hoped that he would go and enjoy her hospitality one night at least, although it was still Wheat Wife's time. Shashka stayed out of the politics of wives. It was none of his business. He went where he was told, he concerned himself when concerns had been identified to him, and for the rest of it?

He'd worried about how Battle Wife was going to be received, how accepted, even coming as she did with a son on her hip. He'd seen her in the houses of his other wives on miscellaneous occasions as he'd settled back into Sanctuary. He'd stopped for tea, from time to time, but protocol would only allow that on an occasional and relatively brief basis. Was it a good sign, if Wheat yielded to Battle?

He'd had no indications of unhappiness from Wheat Wife, who read poetry to him, and massaged his back. That didn't have to mean anything. He couldn't always tell, and Peri wouldn't say unless she found fault with his behavior in some sense.

If Wheat Wife thought Shashka, as their mutual husband, should go spend his evening hours with Ismara on a particular day and Peri said nothing, apart from a vague endorsement of the idea, it meant that Shashka should properly listen to things unsaid and do as he was told.

So it was that on an evening a full month after they had all gained Sanctuary, when the sun was setting noticeably sooner and the nights grew cold and colder and the work parties went farther afield to collect enough fuel for a long winter, Shashka called a boy to carry the packages Peri had set out for him. There were sweetmeats for Ismara's women, a bolt of silk from Kashgar, dried fruit, and spices for her kitchen from beyond the desert to the east to serve as presents, and also as the announcement of his impending arrival.

Then once a decent twilight hour had arrived, Shashka crossed the courtyard of the extended compound where he kept all of his wives and children and coughed loudly at the threshold of Ismara's house. Ismara had been strangely secretive of late. It worried him. Was she suffering more than the others did, she and her women? It didn't get this cold in Persia.

"Your lord, my lady, your lord!" one of her women—it was Sarika—cried, opening the door, pulling back the curtains that they'd hung all around the walls to contain the warmth inside. "Welcome, lord, you honor us with your presence."

No, something was going on. He heard it in her voice. There was some mystery afoot, but so long as it didn't seem to be that something had gone wrong he supposed he didn't mind.

"Welcome, my lord!" Ismara said, taking him by the hand to draw him to an arranged set of already-plumped cushions ready and waiting. She'd been warned to expect him, clearly enough, and not just because he'd sent her presents. He'd brought a pot of cherries in syrup from Boy's secret hoard with him as well as a personal gift, because a man could not visit his wife empty-handed. "Sit down here, my lord, beside your handmaiden, I beg you. Gladden me."

She was in a cheerful mood, and it was catching. There was little left in her of the child suffering a conviction of unworthiness. She had been the senior lady of Old Fort, and it had suited her. He'd worried how she would fit in amongst his other wives. He'd come to feel that she would hold her own, and was grateful to her for it.

He let one of the women take the jar of cherries and his long coat, and sat down. Ismara gave him a thimbleful of strong coffee steeped with cardamom in an enameled cup that he supped gratefully. She made the best coffee in Sanctuary, or maybe it was one of her women, but it was in her gift one way or the other.

"How is your health?" There was an object at one end of the room, something like a chest covered with fabric. "And that of your child?"

Ismara smiled at him. "I'm well, and the son of my lord also." The boy was growing at an astounding rate. Shashka almost expected his youngest to have started his beard by the time the summer came again. "Do you remember when the English came to Old Fort, lord, with the Hakim Jericho, and the person called Tamisen with him?"

Of course he did. Shashka was sure she had very good reason for the question, and nodded. "Yes, and am still sorry we didn't get more chances to see him dance."

One afternoon, only, Tamisen had danced for Old Fort, with Ismara and her women watching. There'd been a warrior doing valiant battle with an ogre. There'd been a man trying to get to sleep and tormented by the stinging of an obnoxious black fly, as well. Shashka remembered that that one had made him laugh out loud.

There were other things he'd seen Tamisen dance: on the rooftops of Old Fort, with the trumpet Devadatta; the map from Peshawar to Chitral to Old Fort; the stag pursued by divine vengeance. Some of the things he'd seen Tamisen dance were his and his alone. The night after Old Fort was saved, when he'd had Tamisen in his bed. Other times. Those were his. Shashka had no intention of sharing. He tried not to think of Tamisen too often, so that the memories would not get worn and frayed.

Now with a joyful gesture Ismara beckoned to her women, both hands at once. The box against the wall was clearly very light; Fatima and Tamar managed it between them, one to a side, setting it down carefully a little space removed from where Ismara sat with Shashka on the cushions beside her.

"My lord had wondered aloud in the presence of this unworthy person whether Tamisen would come with us, and help to while away the winter months. But he had to go home to India and mind his household. Is it not so? My lord's people would have enjoyed his artistry."

Shashka nodded. "It is so," he said. "Should I have put him into a small box for transport to Sanctuary, and told Captain Fontenoy that he'd left on his own the night before? I've failed you, my wife."

She gestured to her women once more, her hand rotating at the wrist, in a universal signal for *come on, come on.* "Surely that would have been ill-advised, my lord. Your servant hopes to give her lord distraction. Here, just look. Your wood-shop made this, and we've decorated."

The women uncovered the box, and underneath its drapes there was—a box. Open at the front, painted in bright colors all around; the open front was framed with fine decorative edging, and curtains in miniature across the front concealed what lay within.

Shashka looked at Ismara, who gazed with such utter delight at the black faceless box that he smiled too. "What is this, my wife?"

"Not what." When she settled herself more comfortably on her cushion she came to rest side touching side, and sat close next to him, quite easily and confidentially. Trustingly. "Who. Who, not what. Watch, listen."

Tamar had gone back to the corner to fetch something— her lute, Shashka decided. Fatima had crouched down behind the box and was all but invisible. Striking a chord Tamar began to sing.

"Only a poor beggar in the bazaar, oh, a hard life had our hero to feed his old blind grandfather. No, Ali wasn't a thief, but who could blame him if on some days God put bread in his way with a hand not visible to mortal men?"

The curtains drew back in perfect imitation of those in great theaters in Europe. Shashka had described them to Ismara himself, without a clue as to why she'd led the conversation in that particular direction.

"Hard-worked and humble, Ali did whatever he was asked if it was honest. Oh, he worked as hard as would make his mother proud, to feed his grandfather, but his mother—alas! had gone before."

The inside of the box was hung in black, but at the back there was a painted scene within a black wooden frame. Shashka could recognize the place, or thought he could. A bazaar in the city near the house of Ismara's father. Then suddenly, from one side a stick appeared, a stick with a face painted on its flat side, wearing clothing. Rags. Tatters. A beggar, in an old worn headdress.

"Very many times he was disappointed by the cruelty of men who took his labor, and paid him nothing. Yet still he worked willingly and well, trusting in God to help him feed his grandfather, asking only for a bit of bread left over for himself. Listen to the work that Ali did: he carried water. Carried stones. Carried fodder. He knotted fringes. He carded wool. He dyed yarn. He cured hides. He sold melons."

The stick figure crossed from side to side, carrying burdens and boxes, going out one way with a barrow, coming back across the stage with a bucket.

Puppets. She'd made a puppet show. And there wasn't just young honest Ali; there were other people in the market as well. A baker went by with a great tray of loaves on his head. A woman had a bolt of cloth. A goat ran across the front of the box, being chased by a little boy with a stick.

Shashka stared, fascinated. Paint, fabric, embroidery, woodcraft—it was a marvel. How did it happen that the simple stick figure could so clearly communicate his feelings? Magic. Sorcery. But it was benign.

"Then one day the street sweeper found an old oil lamp in the dust of the gutter, and gave it to Ali. He pretended it was payment for the work Ali had done. But the street sweeper thought it was trash, of no worth to anybody."

Shashka was almost certain it wasn't trash. Hadn't he heard this story before?

"Ali was disappointed. He'd worked all day, and had no money to buy food for his grandfather. His grandfather was a man of wisdom, though, with second sight to replace the sight of his eyes that he'd lost. His grandfather always said 'Do your best, and work without resentment. Trust in God. God looks after those whose hearts are pure.'"

Shashka's grandfathers had both died before he'd been born, and his father's mother was a dim memory. The pain that went with the memory of her dying came and went through his heart, vanishing into the air; he hardly noticed. He was increasingly sure he'd heard this tale before, though he wasn't certain he remembered how it went.

"So Ali took the tail of his turban and wet it with a little water." Spat on it, really—the little stick figure made that clear enough. "'If I clean this lamp, perhaps I can sell it, and buy Grandfather bread,' Ali said to himself. He rubbed and rubbed and rubbed the dirt away. He worked late into the night by the light of the moon." Nightfall was a bit of black gauze, coming down between the puppet Ali and the bazaar. "And just as he made the final speck of dirt disappear—"

Poof! A sudden chord, a little ball of fluffed-up cotton for a cloud of smoke. On a thread, suspended in the air. A bouquet of flowers sprang up suddenly as if by magic from the spout of the lamp, startling Ali considerably, by the looks of it.

"There was a great explosion, and the smell of strong gunpowder. Then in a cloud of attar of roses, there appeared—"

Maybe not this version of the story, but Shashka recognized the bones of the story now. It didn't have to be a magic lamp. How much work had she put into this? He'd given her the wrong impression, in all inadvertence. She thought he'd been regretful because he'd halfway hoped for Tamisen's help to entertain them all during the wintertime.

His feelings had been so much more selfish than that, but she'd taken action to address what she'd believed was the cause of the trouble. To offer him amusement, with the dancer gone. All this, from a woman who'd been treated so shamefully by her own father, who'd been taken away in caravan by some moody brute of a husband all alone, with only her women and her child to comfort her and remind her of her home.

Ismara had made a puppet theater with care and artistry, and was giving him a story. It was comforting to him on more than one level of his being. With a feeling like that left in the body after a deep sigh has relieved distress, Shashka sat with Ismara on the cushions in her room and watched the tale about puppet-Ali and the djinn of the magic lamp.

He stayed with Ismara for dinner, ordering up a small feast to praise her women for the impressive achievement of the puppet theater, knowing that making a fuss over the women pleased Ismara more than praising her. Sitting with his young son on his knee, Shashka joked politely with his wife's ladies until the child grew restless with an excess of excitement. The retirement of the baby made a good breaking point.

"Thank you again, Ismara."

She gathered her skirts to stand up with him, so he gave her his hand to help her up. The women were occupied with the child. He put his arms around her, and she delighted him by embracing him in turn, laying her head against his breast with absolute confidence and familial tenderness. It made him feel once more, as he'd felt these months past in her company, that it must be a wonderful thing to have a sister, and it seemed that she'd consented so to be to him. That should have worried him. Where there was attachment there was pain.

The attachment was worth the pain. At least he was beginning to think so. "You are as ingenious as you are wise. I don't know how you made the monster fly into so many bits and pieces at one stroke—no, don't tell me, I cherish its magic."

The little kiss she gave his mouth was as innocent as a dove's. "We're all delighted to have pleased you. And so proud of ourselves that we needn't eat for a week." Puffed up, he supposed she meant. "Now send us someone with Kabardian stories, that we may do one for you. You promise?"

"That I do." He kissed her back, and let her go. "Excuse me that I leave you. There's business."

Peri was waiting for him outside Ismara's house, respectfully halfway to the gate of Ismara's courtyard so as not to present the odious appearance of taking precedence over Ismara with her lord. Ismara knew that Peri was waiting. Ismara and Peri had become friends, for which Shashka was almost as grateful as he was for his new son.

Ismara dropped the curtain, Shashka closed the door. "You had how large a part in this?" he asked Peri, passing her a piece of honey-soaked bread wrapped up in a napkin. Ismara had had the pastry set aside especially for her.

Unfolding the napkin Peri took the sweet up in her fingers to munch it greedily, following him and talking as she went. "Very small. All her doing. But she had to show Second Wife and the others before she dared show you, for their approval."

Why would that be? Surprising him with her achievement with permission, in a way. Making the surprise a common property that they could all share in. She'd been raised in a large household, Ismara had. There was a sense in which she might actually know more about negotiating complicated political relationships than Princess Wife, for example, who'd been the eldest daughter of a principle wife.

"Such a fine thing should be shared," Shashka said. "Let us think on how it should best be done."

They had all winter.

He couldn't spend *all* of it wondering if he would ever see Jefferji Tamisen again.

Jefferji sat in the howdah of the lead elephant, feeling a little insecure at being so far off the ground. The elephants—there were five—were splendid with tinsel, pink chalk, and rows upon rows of tiny silver bells that jingled and chattered at every step. They could be heard a mile or more before they came into sight, especially from a temple that was on a hilltop and whose lines of sight were obscured by forest. Jefferji had drummers and trumpets to go before him, with men on horseback riding alongside the elephants throwing handfuls of candy and small coins to the children as they passed.

He'd been looking forward to this for weeks.

It had been very good to return to Peshawar with Captain Fontenoy, to be praised in few but meaningful words by men twice and three times his age, to be gravely listened to by men whose names were legend and by powerful people in government. Better even than that, Colonel Talifer had told some interesting lies about Jefferji and the role that he'd played in their adventures that Simon had insisted Jefferji accept as poetic exaggerations merely.

Fontenoy had stayed behind in Patiala. Simon's presence had been very pointedly requested at the medical college at Varanasi; Simon had taken Gunnery with him. This home-coming was Jefferji's alone.

Coriander was led on before Jefferji's elephant in a costume dripping with wreaths of marigolds. She had clusters of silver bells at each ear, her mane braided with flowers, the horse-furniture all velvet and gold wire. She felt herself beautiful in her fancy dress, and he thought her so too. If he could've ridden her and an elephant at the same time he would gladly have done it, because her adventures were as dashing and songworthy as his, or more so. He had two legs. She had four. It followed logically that she'd gone twice as far as he had, and come back from twice as far away.

He had a dress of honor, gauze-of-gold, a gift from the government in the Punjab. He meant to drape it around Myamah's shoulders. The English in Peshawar had given him a great deal of money, a sum Fontenoy claimed with a straight face was due Jefferji as payment for services received from a gentleman adventurer not yet a member of her Majesty's civil service. That had been very good as well.

His procession climbed the road onto the hill where the temple was. The outriders stopped throwing candy and coins. They were approaching the temple, now, and people from miles around were crowding into its outer precincts.

He'd sent a messenger on ahead. *Be sure that Myamah comes out to see the spectacle.* He was as gorgeous as a bridegroom in silver tinsel, and the runners proclaimed him as if he were. *The prince, the warrior, the beloved of Radha, like Krsna he comes.*

There were so many people there as the procession neared the gates that Jefferji was almost afraid someone would fall beneath the feet of one of the elephants. The riders, though, had closed up to make a moving wall of sorts, the horses dancing a fancy step to keep pace with the elephants. And these were professional elephants, hired from a business in Safdarpore that provided parades for weddings and festivals. The elephants watched their step very carefully. Jefferji could hear their wide feet in the juicy grass that grew up everywhere when the monsoon had passed.

He saw the temple as he'd never seen it before, over the top of the compound wall. His outriders rode ahead to open the gates—unnecessary, because they were already open, but Jefferji appreciated the gesture. The drummers and trumpeters ran ahead as well, to clear the avenue of approach. The lead elephant strode majestically into the temple compound after Coriander, put up its trunk, and cried out to announce the return of the hero.

Myamah was there with the priests at the top of the stairway, a tiny little woman in a clean white salwar-kemiss with a look of utter astonishment on her face. The elephant knelt down; the mahout released the rolled-up ladder that clattered into place from howdah to the ground for Jefferji's descent. It wasn't very dignified. But a man did have to come down off an elephant.

Jefferji went up the temple stairs and stopped halfway to the top, turning around with his back to Myamah, waiting. The other elephants arrived, and knelt in turn; mahouts handed down boxes, chests that had ridden in howdah all the way from Safdarpore. That was only four miles, but it was the spirit of the thing. And four miles was a good length for a procession of elephants.

When his chests had been brought, Jefferji nodded. His hired men set them on the steps between Jefferji and the top of the stairs, opening them in series from topmost to bottom and then standing at attention, one man to a chest. Presents for the temple: a box of shawls of pashm wool from Kashmir for the priests; beads of turquoise and red coral to adorn the statues of the god and his divine Consort; fine enamelware pots and platters; boxes of sweets and fresh fruit for the feast they'd have. Amber. Incense. Tea in bricks from China. Fine woolen rugs from Bokhara and Persia.

When all of the men had opened their boxes for display

and admiration—pulling out the top layer of each one, showing it to the assembled crowd for their applause—Jefferji turned around to ascend the stairs to the top. One chest hadn't been opened. The chest that rested on the topmost step was still closed. Three steps from the top Jefferji stopped and made his namaste, humbly and also proud, to each of the temple's senior priests.

Myamah looked like she would lose her composure at any moment. But she was Rajput. Jefferji knew that she was more than a match for anything he could put before her. He opened up the last box; he lifted out the dress of honor, burning with its brilliant light where the sun struck its thick encrustation of gold thread. It was heavy, with all that gold.

He showed it to the crowd. He climbed the final steps. He draped the dress of honor over the front of Myamah's salwar-kemiss like an apron, circling around to stand behind her, holding the khilat up in front of her in his hands to help support its weight. She was trembling with emotion, but she stood as straight as any cedar tree.

"I have been to Peshawar," he said, pitching his voice as far as he could. This was a temple. It had good acoustics. Sound carried. "I have seen the great men in government, who placed this dress of honor in my hands. And they said—"

No. None of them had *said*, not in so many words. But it was the sort of thing any one of the officers he'd met could have said, if called upon to say something of the sort. Jefferji had discussed it with Captain Fontenoy and Simon Jericho. Both Simon Jericho and Captain Fontenoy agreed.

"They said that for a man to win renown and undergo such adventures, a man had to have been taught to be a hero by a woman of nobility and strength. To this woman they presented this dress of honor. To this woman." This was getting harder. He had to struggle to keep his voice clear and coherent. "To this woman I present this dress of honor, which is given to her by grave-faced British with fierce moustaches. To Myamah of Tengarpore, who taught me how to be a hero."

That was it. He'd only just got through it. The trumpeters blew their trumpets with passionate fervor, and the drums all but shook the compound walls. The mahouts, now, from the backs of elephants, threw candy and gifts in frantic profusion into the crowd.

Jefferji turned Myamah around. "Have you been well?" he asked her, anxiously, because she was weeping, even though he was very sure she knew that he'd been embroidering on his story. "Has your room been dry? Have you been warm? Have they taken very good care of you? And all in all have you been well?"

He was babbling. He knew he was. And repeating himself. He felt such overwhelming tenderness in his heart for her that he could hardly stand it.

"Elephants," she said, and put her arms around him as she'd done when he'd been ten years old. "Oh, Jefferji. You've grown. You're very brown. You're lean. They're beautiful."

Smiling temple servants carried the boxes and chests up the steps up to the sanctuary to present them to the god, so that the feast could be distributed. The elephants knelt two by two in the courtyard to have themselves admired in their tinsel-gilt finery, and Coriander tossed her head happily in the sunlight so that the garlands around her marigold-bedecked ears flew like birds startled into flight before coming to rest again.

The trumpeters played triumphal music with far more enthusiasm than precision, which was precisely the way it was supposed to be. Jefferji stood and wept with Myamah, holding her as she held him. It was true. Myamah was the one who'd taught him how to be a hero.

A procession of elephants was the least that she deserved.

A man had to get up early in the morning to evade the ever-vigilant eye of Myamah. Jefferji woke up before dawn. He'd been shown to a guest room on the other side of the temple complex from that in which Myamah had waited here for him to come back, so he had good hope of accomplishing his goal. He thought that maybe his being away for months might have lulled Myamah into an alteration of her habit of very early rising, but it wasn't the least bit safe to make assumptions where Myamah was concerned.

Hurrying out to wash his face at the great tank behind the

temple, Jefferji dressed in garments one of the temple servants had readied for him: respectable salwar-kemiss with a shawl cummerbund, new slippers. The grooms had Coriander saddled and waiting. She grumbled at him a little bit, but resigned herself to the exercise nonetheless on receipt of a suitable bribe of lump sugar.

Birds were singing in the trees, the earth breathing out in slow respiration. Jefferji had taken instruction on where to find the farm of Jaisal Begum's kinswoman, the widow Minrami, even before he'd come to the Hirpa temple, sending a letter on ahead in good time, with several chests of presents as well. She would doubtless have heard of his return soon enough, but it was only good manners to send her official and advance notification. He had to be on his best behavior with her.

The farm was a few hours' ride to the east from the Hirpa temple while Tengarpore lay south-southwest. As Jefferji neared the whitewashed wall of the farmhouse compound he drew Coriander to a walk, so that he could take it all in. The fields to either side for five miles were Minrami's, and extended back from the road several miles deep as well.

There was the vaguest look of wilderness about the place, as though it hadn't been quite kept up, as if the upkeep was just barely beyond the ability of its people to maintain it. The compound was well lined with trees within its walls, and the birds assured him that it was a good house, good trees, a very good farm indeed with plenty of gleanings to be had for birds.

There was a fountain in the front court and a tidy little house, five or six rooms wide on either side of the gated entrance into its inner garden. Two stories, well-arched verandas in good repair, a sweet fragrance of morning jasmine in the air. Some men armed with stout batons lined up in front of the house, blocking the way into the private courtyard. Well. A reception committee. They didn't look particularly friendly to Jefferji.

If he'd come as a bridegroom, he might have had a fight on his hands, but he'd carefully avoided suggesting any such thing in his letter. On the other hand maybe his letter hadn't arrived. There was sometimes a problem with letters.

"Is this the house of the respected Minrami Begum, noble

and honorable widow, kinswoman of Jaisal Begum?" Jefferji asked the man in the middle of the defensive line, the one with the biggest stick. "If it is, I who am called Jefferji Tamisen from Tengarpore have come to ask whether she might consent to let me shelter under her roof, and consider myself in the position of a brother."

He wasn't going to marry her. He didn't think he could in honor and respect do that, not without a much better idea about whether she wanted to be married, among other things. There was the issue of Englishness to consider, that would call him away from this farm if he decided to give being English a go. As a brother by adoption or proxy, he'd be in a position to defend her honor, respect the proprieties, and assist her in the management of the farm. She would tell him what needed to be done. He would learn how to direct a farm by doing it.

The men seemed to be relaxing, a little. "Our noble lady has been affronted by the insolence of suitors on several occasions," the foreman said. "And Jefferji Tamisen sends rich presents without permission, as one who assumes the answer he wants is his to take or set aside. As a husband, I tell you, you aren't welcome. Take back your gifts and go away."

No. He wasn't going to go away. He dismounted from Coriander to make that clear. He didn't have a baton. He hoped that fact would discourage them from using theirs.

"A brother may not send gifts to his sister, to make her house and his place in it comfortable? I've been away, and owe her an apology. Also I mean to beg a corner of her house. I have an old woman and her girl to be kept safe, if I go away again. If I am accepted as a brother I hope we may be friends, and that you'll put your sticks away. I slept on the floor of the Krsna temple last night. I already ache as though I'd been beaten. There's really no need for you to put yourselves to any trouble on my account."

Minrami herself came out of her garden court to stand with her arms folded, looking at him. Her face gave nothing away, but her hair was dressed with flowers; her salwar-kemiss was done up in some silk that he had sent her, and draped with one of the Kashmiri shawls. It was an encouraging sign.

"Jaisal Begum said husband," Minrami said. "I was grateful enough for that." Jefferji knew; she'd told him when she'd told the god months ago. "A brother would be better still. I could keep all these luxuries. And truly I'm in need of a dear brother."

"Indeed, I brought them from Peshawar for a sister of noble blood and of a royal house begotten." He thought he'd better stick close to the facts. A falsehood—no matter how well intentioned or excused as a bit of poetic exaggeration—would almost certainly be ferreted out by a sister. He'd heard stories. "Grant me a place in your house as a guest for a few days, and consider whether I might do good service to you in your brother's place."

She had no brother. No family. Her only relatives were on her dead husband's side, and they were eager to force her into purdah or some other equally extreme step that would place her lands in the hands of her husband's family. The farm was hers, not theirs.

"Let him pass, Jhalkot," she said to the foreman. "It may be that he is a long-lost brother hitherto unknown. Come into my house, my may-be brother, and have something to eat."

Jefferji wasn't going to marry her without better reason than Jaisal Begum's matchmaking, especially not knowing whether that had been more aimed at ensuring he ran away from Tengarpore than anything else. But he'd been offered the role of her protector, whether or not she needed any. It lay in his power to be a friend, a brother, and carry her will and her instructions into places only a man could go without dishonor.

He would join with her in battle against forces that would reduce her to the tyranny of a mother-in-law and the usurpation of her land. In return she'd give him breakfast. It sounded a fair exchange to Jefferji.

"You'll have my husband's rooms," Minrami said, leading him toward a pavilion tent that stood in the garden. The cloth was purple, striped with a golden brown. Beneath its high roof were a rug, cushions. Breakfast. He could smell food. He was famished. "Myamah and her Cowrie can stay there as well, if they like." So Minrami already knew all about them. Jefferji was happy to hear it.

She'd laid a sumptuous feast on a low table in her pavilion, and showed him where she meant him to sit—beside her.

"Here is what a brother of mine would have to make his morning meal," she explained. "The produce of this farm. You'll find it good, I hope. And you'll understand why I will fight to my last breath to preserve it."

Fruit. Grain. Milk. Yoghurt. Curds. Chutney. Onions, mutton, duck, eggs. It was a rich feast of a breakfast. She sat beside him like a queen on a musnud throne of pillows, watching him eat.

After some time had passed she spoke again. "Why would you come here as a brother?" Her voice was softer than it had been before, and carried genuine curiosity. "Surely I'm not so old and faded as that. And lightly used. Almost as good as new."

If she'd known how her perfume had beguiled him when they'd first met, she wouldn't have wondered, not about the "old and faded" part.

"Jaisal Begum said you were alone." Jaisal Begum had only halfway wanted him to leave. She'd halfway wanted him to stay. "So am I. Maybe we can be not so much alone, together, though I won't be fit to husband anybody for a few years yet, I'm afraid. Again I may have need to come and go, and to have a place of refuge would mean much to me."

"More than those trunks of riches from the north?" Minrami watched him sop up gravy from one of the dishes with a torn piece of bread. "Well then. Brother Jefferji. We'll see how it works out."

As fair an offer as could be ever made. Tearing off another piece of bread, Jefferji caught up a bit of meat, some rich white sauce, some peas, and offered it to her. With her slender fingers she accepted it, and ate; and so the bargain was concluded between them.

Epilogue

Dismounting from Coriander in the courtyard of the Hirpa temple, Jefferji lifted Myamah down from the mule—Marigold—he had on loan from Captain Fontenoy. Myamah pled humility and would not ride a horse, though even her girl Cowrie had a pony for her own; but Jefferji wasn't going to tolerate any attempt on her part to walk beside Coriander all the way to Varanasi. For one thing, it would take too long to get there.

"Has Captain Fontenoy arrived?" he asked one of the temple boys, surrendering the reins and some coins for their use in buying themselves some snacks while they attended to the comfort of mare and mule. Fontenoy had asked very specifically to meet them at the Hirpa temple on their way north.

Jefferji felt he could just as easily have joined them at Tengarpore, or come to visit at Minrami's farm—where Fontenoy had indeed visited and toured and praised, and been kissed on the cheek by Minrami as a visiting uncle—but Fontenoy's schedule had apparently had no room for that, this time.

"No, sahib," the boy said cheerfully, with his hand frozen in mid-space and his expression one of happy expectation.

Jefferji swore at himself for ever having made a generous gesture in his life and added a few more coins. They were very small coins, after all, and he was widely reputed to be a rich man. "Please tell him we'll be inside."

Although it would be just as pleasant to wait out here, in the forecourt, under the clear blue morning sky. The weather was crisp, clean, and blessed with the welcome warmth of the sun in mid-winter. It was cold at night, but Myamah would not feel it, on that Jefferji was determined.

Even now she wore two of the warmest, largest shawls he had been able to find wrapped around her. She could insist on keeping to her plain cotton sari, and she did. But not even his iron-willed Myamah had been able to resist the creamy richness of the pashm wool shawls that Jefferji had brought from Peshawar.

The Bengal British had apparently been very happy with Fontenoy's map, and Jefferji had had the proud pleasure of dressing Myamah in princely gifts. It was not the last privilege he'd discovered accruing to his account since his return from Old Fort Valley with Captain Fontenoy, and Simon Jericho, and a string of mules and camels carrying what fragmented statuary had escaped damage beyond repair in the earthquake.

Simon Jericho had been received back to university at Varanasi on the strength of his documented survey of the medicinal plants of Badakhshan, rather than anything so crass as the set of inscriptions he brought back with him. Captain Fontenoy had spoken with one of the deans of medicine in private, at length, about Simon's role in providing medical services during and after the siege of Old Fort, which had also smoothed Simon's return to a degree.

Jefferji went up the steps to the temple, but paused. "Would you rather sit out here?" he asked Myamah. "Warmer."

"More beggars," she replied. "Yes, I'll sit. You go say hello. I'll have some nuts." And some hot tea, doubtless.

Kissing her on the cheek, Jefferji turned back up the wide stone steps to go inside and greet the god and the divine Consort. It was dark inside; it was always dark. It was warm from the ghee lamps and the braziers set at intervals, fragrant with the perfume of resin and incense.

Putting his hands together palm-to-palm, Jefferji bowed low before the little images in their shrine, his heart full of love. They were still little plaster dolls dressed in tinsel finery, and they were still chipped in places and they still needed to be repainted, but he could speak to Krsna within them again, and be answered. Radha had a new pashm wool drape, so fine it could be rolled up cord-thin and passed through a stone ring the thickness of the end of a man's little finger. Krsna had a new silk garment.

He could have buried them in gold leaf out of his gratitude for their love, but it wasn't his place to overwhelm the god with gifts as if Jefferji's love was better than anybody else's simply because he had more money now.

Good morning, my lord, my Beloved. We're leaving for Varanasi today. When we get there we'll see my friend Simon Jericho. Myamah will bathe in the waters. I think they're probably too cold. But Jefferji had his path, and Myamah had hers. She didn't scold him about dancing; she never had. He had no business telling her she should not bathe in the holy confluence.

The voice in Jefferji's heart was deep and full of peace. *It's good of you to cherish her. I love her as I do you. You act my part in this.*

Ever since that bright morning on the walls of Old Fort, Jefferji had Sri Krsna back, but he was not the playful village boy of Jefferji's childhood. The Krsna in Jefferji's heart was still Krsna, and still full of joy and humor, but different. Jefferji had noted the change, and it didn't matter, because compared to the great wonder of being reunited with his lord nothing was of significance. But now, waiting for Captain Fontenoy, it occurred to Jefferji to ask why.

Child for child, Jefferji. Man for man. You are no longer at play in the forest, herding cows.

Wasn't he? He didn't feel he'd changed in any particularly decisive way. He was far from being the man that Jaisal Singh was, or Captain Fontenoy, or Shikander Beg. Nothing like that.

But you did not know either Jaisal Singh or your friend Fontenoy when they were your age. Remember that. They remember who they were—and do they find you wanting?

No. Captain Fontenoy had treated him and Simon alike as equal partners, with an allowance made for his own responsibility towards interests of his syndicate. Now when Jefferji went to Tengarpore Jaisal Begum had him lodged in a room suitable for a junior retainer, rather than in bachelors' quarters. He hadn't come back the same man that he'd left, and it was more than simply that he'd killed a man, though that was part of it.

"Yes." The sound of Old Fanum's voice called Jefferji from prayer back into the outer world, where a temple was a building in time and space as well as an audience chamber. "The girl may rest here, against the wall, if she can lie still. The father? Yes, yes, beside her. Jefferji. Here is Captain Fontenoy."

What was that about "the father," then? Some people who'd come in with Fontenoy. That was what.

"Tamisen," Fontenoy said warmly, shaking his hand, suffering Jefferji to kiss his cheek. "My boy. You look well."

The expedition had done Captain Fontenoy a world of good. He'd lost ten years of age and care since their return, even though there was trouble in Kabul.

"Thank you, sir. I'm well, and I hope I find you also in very good health." His relationship with Captain Fontenoy had changed even more than his relationship with Tengarpore, and Madhu Singh. He'd never understood how much he loved Fontenoy until the moment at which he had first thought him dead.

Nor, in the thoughtlessness of childhood, had he realized how much Captain Fontenoy loved him, and not only for his father's sake or out of gallantry to the widowed wife of a fallen comrade. He'd taken Captain Fontenoy for granted, and then been granted the boon of time in which to learn how to appreciate and reciprocate that love.

"Looking forward to the journey," Captain Fontenoy said. "I may take the water myself. But see here, Tamisen, before we leave. I'd like to ask a favor of you." And it was something to do with Old Fanum, too, Jefferji smelt it suddenly in the air that wreathed Old Fanum's bland benign bald head like an aura.

"Name it, sir, it is already yours." Jefferji was suspicious.

The long scar on his right arm did nothing, nothing whatever, to call attention to itself, and still he was aware of it. It had been deep, Simon had said. They were very lucky it had healed as quickly as it had, as well as the other wounds suffered by men and women who'd been within earshot when Jefferji had sounded the war trumpet.

The medicine is very fresh and of high quality and very efficacious but I don't see that as being the whole of the explanation, Simon had said.

"That conch you brought back as a present," Fontenoy said. "I only got to hear it once, just after you'd found it. But I heard something about a young madman dancing on the rooftops of Old Fort with a shankha trumpet as his weapon; people said things to me about that. May I hear it now? We do have to leave before too much longer. Myamah will have all the boys of the temple scrubbing the bricks with toothbrushes."

They hadn't said much about the conch to anybody. It was a rare and valuable one, a worthy gift to any temple, and Jefferji had the trick of playing it. That was all anybody needed to know. For all Jefferji knew neither Captain Fontenoy nor Simon believed that it was actually Devadatta, and that was all right too. It was his secret, shared with Sri Krsna alone. He was the only one who understood what they had found.

Except that a father with a child had come surely not coincidentally with Captain Fontenoy, and something wrong with the child. Hurt, crippled, injured, Jefferji didn't know, but Captain Fontenoy had an interest of some sort and Captain Fontenoy was an honest and honorable man. If he'd brought father and child here on the slim chance that there was an occult healing power in the conch, could Jefferji deny him?

May I? It wasn't his to decide. It hadn't been his doing. Devadatta was a celestial intelligence and could only be approached with the correct mantras. It had spoken for him three times out of its own grace and generosity, but he had no standing to call on it again.

He'd brought it away from Old Fort partly because he wanted it for Tengarpore, its beneficent presence alone conferring benefit on believers. He'd partly brought it here out of pure selfishness and desire to have it and his heart in the same place, at the Hirpa temple, once it was no longer needed at Old Fort for protection. Deravass Khan sat at Old Fort now. The village would prosper without the conch's intervention.

The trumpet hungers to confer peaceful blessings, and share in life again. It will sing for you as it has before. I also like to hear its music.

Very well. It could be used at festivals, after all, and be part of the general blessing conferred by the benevolence of the god on his birthday and on other special occasions. Its identity need not be noised about. It was enough in this debased age for it to be a Dakshinavarti shankha, and of such size and beauty, to explain the value Hirpa temple put on it.

Who had been gossiping with Old Fanum, to put such a smile on his face?

"I'm not ritually pure," Jefferji said.

He hadn't been ritually pure at Old Fort, either. Blood was polluting, and he'd been covered in it, fresh from a violent killing. Nobody at Old Fort had had time to change or wash for more than a day. He'd eaten meat. He'd been unshorn. And, of course, he was not a Brahman, he was not even twice-born, he was an outcaste Englishman for all his Rajput upbringing.

And still Devadatta spoke for you. The voice of God in Jefferji's heart was deeply loving, and amused. *Perhaps it will condescend so far again, who knows?*

Jefferji nodded. "But if Old Fanum is willing to overlook the sacrilege I will gladly oblige. Only, Captain Fontenoy, please, could someone go for Myamah? I'd like for her to hear it, too."

The prayer was for a little girl whose father held her as if his life was in her hands, rather than the other way around; who sat there with his back to the wall staring straight through Jefferji and Old Fanum at the statues in the shrine with eyes that burned with anguish from the shadows, illuminated from within by inexpressible pain.

May the Beloved grant the prayer, and all the prayer be for the girl, Jefferji prayed in his private thoughts, and fiercely. *But if there is anything left over, may it benefit Old Fanum, and Myamah, and Captain Fontenoy and Cowrie, and everyone within the walls of Hirpa temple, everyone who hears it far and wide.*

The conch had its own place at the shrine, a subsidiary altar with a blue cloth and a wreath of marigolds. Old Fanum called for a basin, soap, a towel.

Jefferji washed his hands. Sitting down on the ground with one foot tucked under his rump and one flat to the floor, his knee bent for balance, Jefferji took as deep a breath as he could—filling his lungs from the bottom of his belly to his collarbones—and blew the trumpet.

Softly, at first, and its ancient wise reverberation rippled out softly on all sides, filling the sacred space from the ground up so that it would not splash upon the ear and startle anyone. Then its voice deepened as Jefferji concentrated on maintaining a steady flow of air, on metering the flow of his breath so that it would last as long as he could possibly extend it. It deepened and grew stronger, moment by moment, as it became acquainted with its space, and the temple atmosphere pulsed with its power.

Jefferji felt the profound joy in his heart deepen and swell as well, his mind emptied of everything, conscious only of the voice of the shankha and its persuasive language and its celebration of Krsna's creation and all the good things that there were in it. The great voice of Devadatta rose to the roof, spilled out of the doors, snaked up through the ventilator louvers into the heavens to spread its message out from the Hirpa temple to all of Tengarpore.

Krsna is Lord. He is your invincible defender, your eternal protection. Listen to the voice of Devadatta and know what it is to be cherished in the tender heart of the lord of all that is and was and will ever be.

Then, as gently as the perfume of jasmine flowers breathing in the night, Devadatta hushed its tone. As softly as the cool fine mist of morning dew on the tenderest of green leaves and pale young shoots, the trumpet muted the intensity of its power. As tenderly as a new father kissing his infant's forehead, the voice of Devadatta smoothed out the air into serene silence.

Jefferji sat for a moment of absolute peace, his lungs empty of air and his mind at rest. Then he drew breath and opened his eyes.

Old Fanum was staring at him—no, at the shankha—with

an expression of vindicated reverence that could have been funny had it not been so sincere. Captain Fontenoy had gone to speak to the man who was sitting against the wall with the child. The father had started to weep, rocking his child in his arms. It wasn't grief. It was devout thanksgiving as deep and clear as the voice of Devadatta itself.

Fontenoy stood up and turned around, pinching the bridge of his nose between his eyes as though something hurt intensely but only for a moment or two. "Thank you, Tamisen." His voice was almost very steady. "Wonderful instrument. I hope to hear that again someday. Maybe when we get back from Varanasi. Hadn't we best get started? Thank you, Old Fanum, I'm obliged."

Rising to his feet Jefferji kissed the conch, and gave it back to Old Fanum. "Coming directly, sir."

Myamah stood near the door in what seemed to be a bit of a daze, but it was apparently a good one, because she was smiling. Maybe she wouldn't feel the fatigue of riding quite so much.

Maybe it would be a good time to suggest to her, meekly and absentmindedly, that there might be a letter waiting for him in Badakhshan, and that he would quite like to go see how people danced before their gods in Turkestanian Kashgar, if perhaps she would consent to be adopted by Simon or Captain Fontenoy while he was away.

He collected Coriander and the mule Marigold. He settled Myamah in Marigold's saddle and mounted Coriander. Captain Fontenoy patted his good Farouk on his gray neck, and together they set off on the road to Varanasi to see Simon Jericho and talk about art, poetry, medicine, and Captain Fontenoy's latest thoughts about antiquities markets.

Afterword

In the novel you've just finished, The Wild High Places, you met Jefferji Tamisen, foster-son of the Rajput Jaisal Singh, cherished courtesy-nephew of Captain Fontenoy, son of a man whom warriors of courage and cunning loved so much that they never stopped searching for answers to the mystery of what had become of him. You met Deravass Khan. You haven't met Jaisal Singh himself—not yet—but I have thoughts on how to make that happen.

You've met the villainous Broderick Holyoke, and Hakim (or Doctor) Simon Jericho, whose willingness to put himself at risk has given him new depths of wisdom and understanding. You've made the acquaintance of a young woman— scarcely more than a girl—who has matured from the casually discarded daughter of a foolish and thoughtless man into Battle Wife, a warrior in her own right, a woman with an honored place by acclamation as well as marriage among the wives of Shikander Beg "Shashka" Kavkazki.

And you've met Shikander Beg himself, a man intent on keeping safe the people he has left to him, a man of passionate character—fierce in temperament—the lion wearing boots about whom Jefferji's teacher Guru-Ji had warned him. You'll have sensed, I hope, even beneath what started out at first as a surface relationship, that I have a future in mind for Shashka and Jefferji. A partnership. Comfort and strength to one another.

The next novel, The Ley Lines of Kashgar, is the second of the three in the trilogy The High Pamir. Kashgar is around about the north-northwest of the great Taklamakan desert in China, an old old city with old old bones. Here you'll find Shashka and Jefferji traveling in caravan together—Shashka has promised to take Jefferji dancing, well, in a manner of speaking, at least.

Jefferji has been accompanying Shashka on caravan escort duty from Kashmir to Kashgar by way of the Karakoram Pass and Yarkand. The caravan they've been escorting is dispersing, the terms of the contract complete. Shashka's caravan-master has been awaiting Shashka's arrival. There are final accounts to settle up, final purchases to make, extra beasts of burden to purchase to carry extra burdens, final repairs and refurbishments to be made.

For now Shashka's job is to stay out of his caravan-master's way. There was an elderly Chinese gentleman-doctor with the caravan they've been escorting; the doctor left the caravan—without advance notice given—to hurry ahead to Kashgar for reasons of his own, a minor breach in caravan etiquette. The doctor's invited Shashka and Jefferji to a small drinking party, by way of apologizing for his abrupt departure.

In this scene, you'll find out that the elderly Chinese gentleman-doctor (Doctor Lo-ang) has apparently left on an emergency errand, leaving his son (also called Doctor Lo-Ang) to do the honors. He, Shashka, and Jefferji are all sitting at their ease in the relatively intimate banqueting hall of his modest mansion, nested in comfort on soft rugs with many cushions and bolsters.

There's rice wine in small cups and seventeen different kinds of soup and a dizzying array of tidbits and treats liberally distributed amongst the drinks, along with efficient servants sufficient to ensure that cups don't run dry and snacks are replenished. Jefferji is particularly interested in the musicians and their instruments, of course.

Their host says that his father sent a letter commending Jefferji's dancing and suggesting that his son, their host, perform a traditional gentlemanly dance of the sort appropriate for a drinking party, by way of demonstrating his interest

in Jefferji's dancing by sharing a Chinese dance. It's both
familiar in some of its technical aspects and unlike anything
Jefferji's seen before, at one and the same time, so Jefferji is
fascinated.

Before the scene is over, however, Jefferji is going to see
something that amazes him, and if you care to read on he'll
tell you all about it.

Turn the page for a preview of the next

HIGH PAMIR novel from

of Zarabeth Abbey

THE LEY LINES OF KASHGAR

THE HIGH PAMIR
Book Two

Once the Yarkand caravan arrived in Kashgar, things got busy.

Shikander Beg had business to transact with the man who'd contracted with him to escort the caravan from Yarkand to Kashgar, and negotiations to work through with respect to the bonus Shashka meant to claim for transit time. The full allowance agreed to for timely arrival, with additional consideration for each day that improved on the standard estimate.

The dust storm that had delayed the caravan was by way of an act of God, rather than anything to be set against the escort party. There were testimonials from the caravan's constituent members and a measured endorsement from the caravan-master himself. Taking the innate conservatism of caravan-masters into account, that amounted to a glowing recommendation, and—Jefferji was happy to see—things had been settled to Shashka's satisfaction.

Now Shashka's own beasts in caravan were settled into their own caravanserai. The sepahis were about the bazaars of Kashgar with lists of provisions required to keep the settlement of Sanctuary, in the valley where Shashka kept his people, running smoothly.

Shashka's people had done business in Kashgar before; the merchants were familiar with them, and sending woman warriors with the in-some-cases dramatic evidence of their battles was apparently a solid piece of silent negotiation in its own right. Shashka's chief of sepahis, the green-eyed Hungarian Captain Katische with her cigars and her astrakhan hat, had subtlety and craft in the war between buyers and sellers, on top of her other areas of expertise.

Shashka and Jefferji had been invited to a party.

It was the elderly Chinese doctor who had invited them, the request presented shortly after their arrival. Jefferji knew that Shashka was anxious to speak to Dr. Lo-ang, so that Shashka could assure himself that the doctor and his small group hadn't had some kind of misadventure on their way from the caravan to Kashgar. For himself Jefferji felt that the invitation itself went far to resolving that question. Had there been trouble, would Shikander Beg Kavkazki been invited to come have music and wine and a feast hosted by the client himself?

It was a beautiful evening. A little breeze from the river to the land had taken the edge off the enervating heat of mid-afternoon, the sky was a delicate shade of pale crystalline blue, and the waxing moon stood near mid-heaven shining like silver in the twilight. Even Jefferji's mare Coriander, his darling girl, seemed to be enjoying the atmosphere.

She and Shashka's Cherkess stallion walked side by side in perfect amity, putting aside for once their constant if not completely serious bickering about who was the more noble and admirable horse between them.

Was a Kabardian mountain horse of finer quality, because he was the war-horse of a refugee Circassian warlord? Or, given that she'd shown she could match him in endurance and sure-footedness and stamina, was Coriander the one who should be granted pride of place by virtue of being a Marwari, the breed of Rajput princes to be ridden by none other, and mother of a young colt as well?

Jefferji had his own convictions as to the father of Coriander's colt, though he had yet to challenge her on her oft-repeated story that she had been impregnated by a god: one of the divine Asvins, maybe, the twin gods of horses and of medicine, that had engendered the youngest two of the Pandava brothers.

It was perhaps a little unusual for a mare to drop her first foal at Coriander's advanced age. Still, it was an age of miracles, and she was not yet twenty. Jefferji had been there in the valley of Old Fort when Coriander and the Cherkess stallion had met, so he knew quite well that they'd struck up a relationship, though the precise degree of their intimacy remained unclear to him.

Their host, Dr. Lo-ang, had sent two men to run to either side of each horse's head and guide them. The road they took led them away from the manor-house that Shashka was using as his Kashgar base of operations; five full miles, Jefferji estimated. They were well clear of the mud-brick buildings of caravanserai and bazaar, now, passing the walls of the house-compounds of the residential quarter that lined the road on the other side of the river.

Slowly but surely the houses spaced out, their walls white-washed and in better repair. There were trees whose topmost branches could be seen, green and refreshing to the eye after the long journey from the vale of Kashmir into the foothills of the Himalayan mountains. There'd been its own kind of desert, cold and stony, most of the way from the famous Karakoram pass toward Yarkand, that sat with the hems of its skirts brushing up against the arid borderlands that led north to Kashgar.

One of the runners picked up his pace, getting out ahead of Shashka and Jefferji as well as his partner. Turning around he ran backward at a respectable rate of speed; Jefferji knew how much practice that took, what kind of effort was required, and adjusted his thinking on how large a tip the man should receive when they arrived.

"I go ahead to bring the word of your approach, Shikander lord, Jefferji-the-dancer," the man said. "We are near. My master will be waiting, with a suitable greeting party fit to his appreciation of your abilities."

Face-forward now, the runner was away up the road and around a turning into a side-road at a rate Jefferji judged to be that of a scout bringing news of an unexpected troop movement to the advance forces of a besieging army. Cherkess cocked an ear back toward his rider, Shikander Beg; so Cherkess was having a thought about a turnip in his near future, possibly, or at least some snacks.

They'd reached the place where the road branched off. As the remaining runner led them forward, Jefferji could see a strange sort of a mansion, not very far ahead. The walls appeared to be the mud brick of Kashgar, but the wooden doors at the tall arched gate were painted red—red! In this climate, with this sun!—and as the servants of the house pushed the gate open to welcome them Jefferji could see brilliant blue roofs half-screened by a line of tall and very green trees.

Surely red paint and blue-painted roofs would fade out within a few months in the summer, and have to be repainted every year? That decided it, for Jefferji. Doctors were very rich men in Kashgar. At least Doctor Lo-ang was.

"A very Chinese house," Shashka murmured softly, for Jefferji only to hear him. "I haven't seen its like since I left Chang'an, and it is almost as far from here to there as it is from here to the place where I was born. Two weeks's travel longer, I think, scarcely more than that."

They had passed through the tall red-painted gates into the outermost court. Jefferji thought they'd dismount, but two new grooms had come forward, one for each horse as before, to lead them forward. Their costume was perhaps not so different as that Jefferji had seen in bazaars all over the country north of the Panj River—trousers wrapped close to the lower leg with something like puttees, a long-sleeved tunic with skirts just above the knee—but their shoes were distinctive, the uppermost parts sewn to the sides with a long seam.

"Chinese costume," Shikander said, in the same low tone of voice as before. "These people are far from home, it would seem. One wonders where exactly they come from."

The second gate was well off-set from the first, and once they were in the second courtyard they were led around to one side and through a narrow passageway between two blind walls to a third gate yet. It seemed to Jefferji as though some surely buried memory of architecture remained careful to slow down and entrap an invader.

The gateway at the final end of the forecourts was sized for men on foot, though. There were mounting-blocks set at the ready, and Jefferji was amused to see that they were subtly different in height as he was taller than Shikander Beg but Cherkess taller than Coriander.

Through this gate they walked. There was a set of low steps

that rose to a veranda of the sort the English built for their cottages, its soft cedar-yellow wood gleaming in the beneath newly-lit torches like a full moon when the air tasted a bit of wood-smoke. Four women each stood on either side of that wide veranda to greet them, carrying trays and pitchers, dressed in light silk flower-patterned garments and beautiful ornaments in their hair; and in the middle, their host? Not Dr. Lo-ang.

Two of the maidens came forward with full beakers. Jefferji took his in both hands for politeness' sake; wine, cool, sweet, and not too strong. That was good. He didn't want to get tipsy too soon, even though it was a party. He was not particular friends with quantities of alcohol.

Now the gentleman himself descended to the courtyard level and advanced five steps toward Jefferji and Shikander. This much closer it was even more obvious that he wasn't Dr. Lo-ang, but was there a family resemblance, or—Jefferji wondered—was he simply distracted by a trick of the light?

"Welcome, honored guests," the man called out, though they were not far from each other. "Your presence is a gift. Condescend to enter, we have prepared food and drink and music to refresh you, here, this way."

Turning, he led them up the shallow steps onto the veranda, through a sweet-smelling corridor of fragrant green hedging that arched overhead, and finally three steps down into a spacious room walled and roofed with wooden lattices to admit the air. There were musicians to Jefferji's left, seated all together on a large honey-colored carpet.

They struck up a tune as Shashka came through into the hall. Jefferji wished he could stop then and fix the music in his mind. But there were places set on separate mildly-raised little platforms to either side of what would logically be the master's place, to which they would logically be expected to go. So Jefferji went.

He could listen from a seat on a carpet, cross-legged amongst cushions and bolsters, as well as on his feet. And he had more freedom than Shashka, more latitude in his movements, because he was after all the subsidiary or second guest, he sensed that clearly enough. It was no sign of disrespect. Shashka was the escort commander, after all, and Jefferji was the escort commander's especial friend: as well as a dancer.

What did he hear? These Chinese instruments were strange to him, unusual and beguiling in their tone and tuning. He didn't like to stare because he should rightly be giving at least most of his attention to their host. Long before he'd met Shikander Beg Kavkazki, however, he'd been a dancer in the service of his own sweet Beloved, Sri Krsna, the divine Bridegroom.

As a dancer, since he'd been eight years old Jefferji had been sharpening his senses to separate out the threads of everything that he heard around him. He had to know where any other dancers were on the stage, and to take advance warning when a minute hesitation in the beating of the tabla drums meant the drummer was going to change cadence on him, a time-honored a practical joke as much as part of the service of the god as any other of its ritual elements.

Along with that came learning to expand his peripheral vision to its natural limits as well, in service of the dance. Which meant that Jefferji could see the musicians's place out of the corner of his eye, and almost-recognize some of their instruments. There was something that was like a rubab with its persimmon belly, its neck gleaming beneath its frets; the Afghan instrument of poetry, its national treasure.

"Please, be seated, honored guests, and partake of some poor refreshment," their host said. There were serving-men almost surrounding Jefferji as soon as he sat down, clustering little dishes all around. "I am Doctor Lo-ang. Perhaps not the one you were expecting, however, shall I explain?"

Jefferji could smell meat, garlic, peppers, sweet melon, so many delicious things that his head was swimming. All of them came portioned out in two bites's worth each: to keep their variety from cloying, Jefferji thought.

He put his palms together in a namaste, something that he had found communicated its core meaning of respect even where there were no Hindus familiar with the prayerful gesture. Yes, please, by all means explain.

But Shashka was the one who answered. Jefferji was happy to exploit the fact that being a dancer rather than a man in a position of more material authority could be used to gain a degree of freedom for someone who would sometimes just as soon avoid too heavy a burden of social conventions.

"Please, Doctor Lo-ang. The acquaintance we had with—your father?— was too short, and I in particular could not sit in his presence as much as I would have liked. We wait, eager to listen and to hear."

Dr. Lo-ang nodded, with a small smile. "I am of my father's sons the youngest and most unworthy of such a sire. I have arrived from Samarkand only two days ago, and found a letter. My father had been sent for by a man who has been a generous patron of our family for many years."

The little dishes were replaced as soon as Jefferji emptied them, almost as though they were raining down from heaven in the hands of invisible maidens. Not only dishes but bowls filled up with drink.

There was something that smelled a little like the sweet syrupy apricot brandy that an admirer had offered one time to the god in Jefferji's person, and that the priests had especially enjoyed after Sri Krsna had tasted of it.

Several sorts of wine as well, fragrant with a gentle perfume of grass and sunlight. Rice wine, at a guess, and Jefferji was wary of it. He had no chance of drinking as much as he was served, not and maintain his composure—let alone his balance. But there was soup as well, in its own array of little dishes. He could drink soup, and live.

Jefferji rebalanced his ears to give the musicians the most part of his focus while keeping enough of his attention on the conversation between their host and Shikander Beg to guard against the potential embarrassment of being startled if called upon. Where was he in his catalog of these instruments?

He'd already made note of the rubab. There was another instrument placed at a slight remove in front of all the others on its own elevated stand, a stringed instrument as long as Jefferji was tall, a peculiar sort of a horizontal harp. Then a small round drum.

And finally, the furthest away from Jefferji, one that reminded him of a santur, something like the English "dulcimer" he'd first seen and heard at the Bombay Residency. The hammered kind, struck with light wooden hammers. This one had lovely delicate tiny basin-shaped mallets of inlaid wood, almost like wooden spoons. It had the voice of an angel.

Shashka's peculiar red-haired concubine "Miss Boy" was firmly convinced, apparently, that Shashka himself was an angel. She'd said so, in confidence, seeming to caution against a too-open mention of that fact, lest it be overheard by unfriendly spirits. She'd apparently wanted Jefferji to understand the importance of protecting Shashka from malevolent creatures of the air, so Jefferji had taken her sharing of confidential knowledge as an act of considerable intimacy, and been honored.

Yet if Shikander Beg was an angel, and the instrument had the voice of an angel, they were clearly two separate species of angel entirely. The santur was tuned to a pleasing tenor range. Shashka's voice was as deep as black chocolate.

"We're very glad that no harm came to your respected father and his people on the road to Kashgar, as I hope to be the case," Shashka was saying, his sincerity evident in his voice. "A caravan guard would rather keep all of the people under his care together, both for their own security and for that of the rest of the caravan as well. And yet it's no business of mine to try to enforce unwelcome constraint, so I could only hope for the best."

Doctor Lo-ang's father had been very firm about it. Jefferji had been there, and could bear witness. Shashka was right: he'd been given no choice but to let Doctor Lo-ang's father go on ahead of the caravan. The dust storm that had come up so suddenly had been providential, in the sense that it might be its own kind of protection against brigands for the party of Doctor Lo-ang's father.

"Indeed the letter I received was very clear on that," Doctor Lo-ang said. "He was particularly firm that no blame could possibly be laid. But there was something else of great interest in his letter. It was about you, Mr. Tamisen, I think? The phrase he used to name you was Hari-Prasad. The letter claims it means "dancer-before-God.""

Jefferji was beginning to think that he would like to see the letter of the father of Doctor Lo-ang, to find out what exactly it said. If it was in the beautiful but perfectly unintelligible Chinese writing, however, to see the letter would tell Jefferji nothing at all.

"I rejoice in that appellation, yes, Doctor," Jefferji replied.

"My given names are Jefferji and Tamisen. More meaningful is the name I lay at your feet in tribute. I am more a dancer than I am anything else."

Was that true? It had been, once, Jefferji had no question. But that had been before he'd gone on an adventure with Captain Fontenoy. And walked in mountains with snow upon the ground, learning of many kinds of snow, so many kinds. And met Shikander Beg Kavkazki, and learned another thing: how to want Shashka's company more than he had wanted anybody else's in the entire world, Sri Krsna excepted because Sri Krsna was the divine Beloved and not in the world at all, not in the way Shashka was.

"In my homeland when honored guests gather together they sing and dance for each other's entertainment," Doctor Lo-ang said—with what Jefferji felt to be a transparently obvious motive. Doctor Lo-ang drank off a dish of the pale golden wine at one draught, a sight Jefferji found a little alarming. Still, if it was Doctor Lo-ang's habitual tipple he would reasonably be well able to handle it; better than Jefferji could, at any rate.

Doctor Lo-ang gestured toward Jefferji with his newly emptied cup. "Of you, my respected guests, no such indulgence can be hoped for, let alone expected," he said. "I am enough in your debt already. My father speaks of his particular pleasure in watching one of your dances, Mister Tamisen, and instructs me to return a token of his gratitude—oh. Here are snacks."

No, Jefferji thought, making a heart-felt prayer to the beautiful god, his Beloved, Sri Krsna. Not more snacks. Platters and trays with delicate dishes full of all the sorts of food there were in the world, meat, soup, sweets, sauced vegetables both hot and cold, bitter and mild, fiery with peppers or creamy with milk of coconut or the pressed meat of almonds or of the tofu Jefferji had once been served in Calcutta.

Jefferji didn't think he'd ever seen so sumptuous a banquet, and he'd been feasted at the table of Krsna temples from Dhaulpur to Jaisalmer, Banswara to Srinagar. By the English in Peshawar. He was on the edge of being horrified.

"If you will allow so impertinent a performance, Doctor Lo-ang—" Jefferji began. If he got up and danced for a few minutes maybe he would survive this feast without bursting, though if he shook all of the liquid in his body down to its natural outlet he could have another sort of problem entirely. "I would ask to present an insignificant scene, even as coarse and unpracticed as I am—"

But Doctor Lo-ang had picked up a fan that he'd laid down beside him, resting on the carpet at his side. It seemed to be unnaturally like the one Jefferji had seen in the hands of Doctor Lo-ang's father. The plumage had been unfamiliar but very handsome, so Jefferji had paid special attention to it.

It was hard for him to imagine how such an apparently perfect match could be effected, feathers being as individual as they were, even on a single bird. Perhaps both fans had been painted to be alike, and that was all there was to it.

One way or another Dr. Lo-ang's fan was a sufficiently dramatic accessory to serve as an emphatic interruption when Doctor Lo-ang drew it across his face with a brisk gesture.

"Forgive me if I hasten to demur, Mr. Tamisen," Doctor Lo-ang said. "I fear you are about to expose me to the uttermost embarrassment. It would indeed be a privilege beyond my merits to see such a man as you dance, Jefferji Tamisen, but you are my honored guest, and I won't have it. No, I must insist."

Jefferji was a little startled, Shashka apparently no less. "I dare not oppose the will of my deeply respected host," Jefferji said politely. "Indeed if it is your will, Doctor Lo-ang, I can think of no higher privilege than to witness such a thing. The wine is very good. I surely would risk toppling amongst your musicians and suffering discredit."

Doctor Lo-ang nodded once, briskly. "I am no dancer," Doctor Lo-ang said, rising to his feet with seemingly effortless grace. "What poor dances I once learned can hardly compare with those my father has described in his letter. I was taught correct forms, however, according to tradition, and as it is said 'It is right and proper to greet friends from distant places, who come to your door. Hasten to admit them.'"

Jefferji's courtesy-uncle Captain Fontenoy, the man

who'd brought Jefferji into this business of secret agency, was a no-longer-young man, though by no means as old as the father of their host by decades. But Jefferji had seen Fontenoy get up from rugs and cushions on the floor with more stiffness and slowness than their host-doctor showed.

Jefferji wondered if there was Chinese medicine for the pain in the joints of the aging that would help to restore Captain Fontenoy's ease of movement: because Doctor Lo-ang moved like the slowly billowing sweep of a fog coming off a river in the morning, with the slow deliberation of clouds traveling across a blue sky on whatever business they might be pursuing.

The musicians started to play a slow dawning-morning sort of a tune. Stepping down from the low dais on which he'd been seated Doctor Lo-ang moved with deliberation toward the great blue-and-green carpet in the middle of the room, falling as naturally from a simple walking pace into a rhythmic ebb and flow that Jefferji could not have identified a transition.

Slowly and apparently effortlessly, Dr. Lo-ang moved with a sort of energy in constant flux as natural, and as irresistibly powerful, as the tides pushing in from the ocean to ruffle the salty waters of the Rann of Kutch. And there was no doubt but that Dr. Lo-ang was dancing, with his whole body, a flowing sort of step that followed the music perfectly—unless it was the music that followed him; and why, Jefferji asked himself, should it be the one rather than the other?

The all-but-visible patterns that Dr. Lo-ang was describing with his body was a new dancing. Jefferji surrendered his whole being to the beauty of it, the sense of the shifting and balance, slow in tempo as a light snow falling lazily from the sky. As smoothly as water flowed from one rock to the next in a forest stream amongst the trees offering its refreshment to animals and hermits, carrying bright red golden-throated blossoms into a tranquil gem-like pool of living water.

Like the best of dancers Doctor Lo-ang's physical phrasing was utterly seamless, almost invisible. He danced as though the long full-sleeved embroidered coat he wore in honor of the occasion, his sleeves, the skirts of his coat, were dancers in their own right with him upon the silken carpet, his bird-feather fan his partner.

Something swirled past the furthest edges of Jefferji's peripheral vision, like a visual shadow of gold and vermillion. Jefferji blinked. Had the doctor called in a partner, one in a brocade coat?

No one had come into the room. None of the musicians had set an instrument aside to join Doctor Lo-ang on the carpet. Jefferji looked to the dishes full of wine resting like altar-offerings at his knee, but for now nothing was refilled, and he wasn't feeling the effects of alcohol.

And yet he saw it again, something that moved coyly and almost completely concealed behind the dignified movement of Dr. Lo-ang's body. There was another dancer, not even human, sketched in a sense by Doctor Lo-ang's fluid gestures in ever-shifting figures of abstract art in his body. Something was there.

It formed and faded with every move Doctor Lo-ang made, a shadow behind him. A great—serpent?—with gorgeous scales of iridescent gold and green, and no, not a serpent, it seemed to have its own short claw-footed legs, and Jefferji had never seen a salamander of that size. With a beard. Three times the size of Doctor Lo-ang himself.

Nobody else appeared to be seeing a thing. Jefferji tried as hard as he could to grasp the outline of the creature, following dynamic patterns of energy flowing like water from one side of Dr. Lo-ang's body to the other. The doctor's movements were hypnotic. It was hard for Jefferji to keep his attention focused.

The strange shadow had gained solidity, now, as it seemed, as if foregrounding past Dr. Lo-ang's body to show itself. Seeming to laugh out loud, tossing its head in pure joy.

But now, from what Jefferji could make out of the internal logic of the music, the music had moved into the conclusion of the dance. The creature that danced with Doctor Lo-ang seemed to coil up, to condense itself, as Doctor Lo-ang softened his body's song, settling his life-force within himself, collecting his perfectly self-disciplined energies back into the reservoir of his body once again.

Where had that miraculous vision gone?

Jefferji searched the outlines of Doctor Lo-ang's body, trying to see behind. There. Just the end of the flamboyantly fan-tipped tail, holding a fast-fading clutch of bells that it seemed to shake at Jefferji as if wishing him good-bye before it disappeared behind Doctor Lo-ang entirely.

No, Jefferji realized. Not behind Doctor Lo-ang.

Into Doctor Lo-ang.

That creature was within Doctor Lo-ang? Doctor Lo-ang was that creature?

Jefferji had creatures in his heart and mind, storms, wars, battles, miracles of Sri Krsna. He held them close and did them honor, because a dancer was a custodian of the divine. He could make the devotees of Sri Krsna see the stories of the Mahabharata, the adventures of Rama. This was different.

What Jefferji had just seen in Doctor Lo-ang's dancing was not an invocation in any sense that Jefferji had ever experienced. Not the evocative representation of a well-known and cherished story, shared in common between the dancer and his audience.

As well as Jefferji knew those things he knew one thing more, also. He knew that what he'd seen had been different in essence, different in its fundamental reality, from anything that Jefferji had ever danced to express his love for Sri Krsna.

Applauding the musicians for their artistry—he dared not applaud Doctor Lo-ang himself, who was settling into his comfortable seat once more—Jefferji determined to do whatever it took to find out more about the creature he'd just seen dancing out of, dancing with, dancing back into the peculiar Chinese Doctor Lo-ang.

Coming in 2021 from

FOREST PATH BOOKS

Zarabeth Abbey

is a pen name of Susan R. Matthews, Nebula-nominated author of the science fiction series *Under Jurisdiction*.

Her interest in the history and religion of the high Pamir, Central Asia, and westernmost China date from living in India when she was a girl. Zarabeth has been reading widely in the ethnography of some of the religious systems of the world for a long long time, starting with her first exposure to Frazer's *The Golden Bough* when she was in high school (a long, long time ago). Her interest in the history and religion the high Pamir, Central Asia, and westernmost China date from living in India when she was a girl (even longer ago than reference paragraph one, above).

Her mother, a scholar of the Old and New Testaments, provided Zarabeth with her first framework for the varieties of religious experience, and in her family a streak of mystical communion with the Divine ("plugging directly into the power source") was a respected, if not universal, experience.

The Wild High Places is her first historical adventure novel.

https://www.susanrmatthews.com/book_series/the-high-pamir/

www.ingramcontent.com/pod-product-compliance
Lightning Source LLC
Chambersburg PA
CBHW031607180726
48284CB00005B/1438